AWEN TIDE

ALSO BY O. J. BARRÉ:

Awen Rising: Book One of the Awen Trilogy
Awen Storm: Book Two of the Awen Trilogy
The Druids of Marduk, Part I: An Awen Prequel
The Druids of Marduk, Part II: UnderEarth

AWEN TIDE

O. J. Barré

PeaceMakers Publishing

PEACEMAKERS PUBLISHING, JULY 2024

PeaceMakers Publishing
9169 W State St #3332
Garden City, ID 83714
olivia@ojbarre.com

For information about special discounts and orders for trade bookstores, wholesalers, book clubs; or for film options, translation rights, etc, please contact the publisher.

PeaceMakers Publishing Paperback ISBN: 978-1-7332736-6-4
Cover Design © 2024 by 100Covers

First Printing, 2024
Printed in the United States of America

TO MY WONDERFUL READERS:

Especially those of you who have waited (whether patiently or
impatiently) for this book to be out in the world!

ACKNOWLEDGMENTS

First of all, I'd like to thank my mama and daddy, Jean and Yank, for doing the deed that brought me into this world. Daddy, thank you for instilling your love for the earth and its glorious creatures; Mama for passing on your love of the written word, and for always being there when I needed you. To my brothers, Bill and Jon, you have left this planet to join our parents, but you will ever live inside my heart.

To my sister, Cheryl (whom I call Cherry), thank you for being my childhood reading buddy, my lifelong friend and sounding board, and a shining example for all of us. Your and Don's undying love and support kept me going through good times and bad.

Grandmother Willoughby Herrell, you always knew that I was special. Thank you for encouraging my curiosity, answering my endless questions, and for teaching me the names of every plant, flower, and growing thing in your vast yard. But more, thank you for being a veritable force at a time when women weren't allowed.

To my ninth grade English teacher Mrs. Lucy Harris, thank you for recognizing my gift with words. I wish I had understood the import of your revelation, rather than waiting so long to start writing. To the West Georgia English Comp teacher whose name I don't remember, thank you. You raised my hackles *and* my awareness, and taught me to write an essay or argument that can stand the test of time. I only hope that holds true for novels.

To Andrew Post, Roland Yeomans, the late Eric Trant, Elliot Grace, and all the other authors and kind souls who read *That Rebel with a Blog*, thank you. Your feedback helped me find my voice, that elusive quality every writer must have. To you, I owe my writing life. Without you, this book might not exist.

Also, a special thanks to Liv Rancourt and Janine Willey for helping shape the original story; to my friend and therapist, Brian Keith, for helping me stay sane; and to my beta readers, Debra Holm, Margaret Both, and Janine Willey for generously providing excellent editing skills, guidance, and feedback on Awen Tide.

Lastly, thank you to Philip and Stephanie Carr-Gomm for providing the inspiration for the Awen Trilogy's animal characters via your book *The Druid Animal Oracle* and its related card deck.

TABLE OF CONTENTS

AWEN:

*Life Essence, Inspiration,
Divine Creative Energy*

"He who talks, does not know.
He who knows, does not talk."

~ The Emerald Tablets of Thoth

TURBULENT TIMES

Lugh MacBrayer surveyed the animals in the compartment tucked behind first class in the PetJet. Designed for travelers with large pets, the last-minute fares had cost the Order a pretty penny.

"I have a bad feeling."

Hope shifted in her cage.

"Me, too. Between that and this infernal airplane, I have not slept a wink."

"I did, but not well." He glanced at Cu, the Irish wolfhound, snoring upside down in the next cage. "I fear Emily is in trouble again."

After being sucked into an earthquake, Emily Hester, the love of Lugh's life and the head of his Order, had disappeared for weeks, finally resurfacing on an obscure island in the Bahamas. Lugh was optimistic his nephew would turn up next.

Heaving a heavy sigh, Lugh scratched the underside of Hope's chin.

"You may be right." The Scottish wildcat licked her lips, a nervous oddity for Hope. "But we're seven miles high, and there's nothing we can do. Did I tell you flying is my least favorite thing?"

"You did. Several times. But this was your idea. Go to Wales, you said. Find the dragons, you said." Lugh ran his hand across his sandpaper chin. Last night's shadow had become the beginning of a thick beard.

"We do what we must for the Order. And the Awen."

How well the druid priest knew. He wouldn't be here if not bound by duty. But Emily needed him. And in the process of searching for her in Europe, he hoped to stumble across a clue about Jake.

"At least you didn't have to ride in the cargo—"

The plane dropped unexpectedly, throwing Lugh against Hope's cage.

The wildcat yowled her displeasure as the overhead bell dinged. The jet bucked and pitched, and Lugh clung to the cage. The cabin lights flicked on, and the captain's voice crackled across the intercom, cautioning passengers to return to their seats.

Jarred awake, Cu howled. The other animals joined in.

Wild-eyed flight attendants emerged from their pods. One staggered to the mic and instructed sleep-soaked passengers to lock seatbelts and stow electronics and tray tables.

A first-class attendant appeared at Lugh's elbow. "Sir, you have to return to your seat." He pressed a button that unfurled padded ticking insides the cages, and the animal Elders disappeared from view.

Lugh gripped the steel mesh and slowly moved toward his seat.

The loudspeaker hummed, the pilot taking them higher to get above the storm system. The plane shuddered, and the bucking grew worse.

Bracing his thighs against the armrests, Lugh clung to the seatbacks and pulled himself forward row by row until he reached his pod. He buckled in, then recoiled when an overhead bin sprang open.

The attendant tried to close it, but the plane lurched, throwing him into the aisle. Carry-ons, briefcases, and a diaper bag rained down, assaulting the attendant and an adjacent passenger who cried out. The baby belonging to the diaper bag squalled.

The juddering plane climbed, bucking the turbulence. Then it leveled off, and Lugh peeled his fingers from the armrest and breathed a sigh of relief. The seat-back monitor showed they were now cruising at forty thousand feet.

The attendant hoisted himself up, checked on the passenger, then wrangled the cases back into the bin. The seatbelt sign remained lit.

Lugh eyed it and debated whether to obey or chance a visit to the bathroom. He'd been bound there earlier before stopping to talk to Hope.

His aching bladder won. Unbuckling the belt, he hurried to the head, peed, and splashed cold water on his face. He blotted it with a thin paper towel and studied his drawn features in the mirror.

Purple splotches pooled in the hollows beneath his eyes. He had a whopping headache, courtesy of the head injury he had sustained in the earthquake the day Brian and Emily disappeared.

He raked his fingers through ebony hair in perpetual need of a trim, and a pocket of nothingness opened beneath the plane. Lugh's stomach lurched as they dropped toward Earth. Grateful to be wedged between the sink and wall, he held his breath for several seconds until the trough bottomed.

The captain's voice echoed inside the tiny stall.

"Ladies and gentlemen, please remain in your seats. We have received word that this storm extends across the entire Atlantic seaboard. We are currently over the Azore Islands and have received clearance to land in Caen, France, the nearest airport with favorable ground conditions. Please hang tight and fasten your seatbelts. The ride promises to be—" he went silent for a long moment while the plane tossed from side-to-side. "—bumpy," he finished.

That was an understatement, to say the least.

Lugh opened the door cautiously and clung to it as the plane lurched and shuddered. Then he pulled himself along the seatbacks avoiding the contents of another spilled overhead bin.

Distressed passengers peered up at him with terror in their eyes—terror that matched Lugh's own. He hated flying, hated it with a passion. Now his loathing had ramped up exponentially.

Reaching his seat, he collapsed into his pod, but the plane seesawed. He overshot, landing on the woman in the next seat. She screamed bloody murder and shoved him away.

Apologizing profusely, Lugh dragged himself into his seat and buckled the belt, then craned his neck. Hope and Cu were hidden behind the padding. He prayed that and their restraints would keep them safe.

The plane tilted and descended at a steep angle, coaxing sweat from Lugh's pores. What in Brigid's name was happening? Why wasn't the pilot pulling up?

Twisting in his seat, he realized the flight attendants were no longer standing. His ears popped, and the plane continued diving. Lugh's knuckles whitened on the armrests.

A screech, like metal ripping from the hull, was followed by a loud bang. Lugh's heart thudded. He'd heard a similar sound not long ago when a tornado wrenched the roof from his restaurant. Was the plane shearing in two?

It shuddered and tilted to one side, then righted again.

But they were still descending. Lugh asked his pod mate to open the shade.

It was barely daylight. Rain streamed against the pane, making visibility next to nothing. Stalks of lightning streaked across the sky, backlighting the clouds as the plane sliced through them. The woman yanked the shade down.

Rigid in his seat, heart thumping wildly, Lugh MacBrayer prayed. He had never been so afraid of dying, even when the tornadoes threatened Jocko's. He thought of Emily and how she had given him courage by helping herd the patrons into the basement. He prayed he lived to see her again.

Then Lugh began running spells through his mind. The Hester family could affect the weather. The MacBrayers? Not so much. Lugh had never created nor stopped a storm. But he had watched Emily calm that volcano and earthquake. It couldn't be that different. Could it?

But the whistling roar of the laboring engines made it difficult to concentrate in the pitching, bucking, nose-diving plane. Lugh plugged his ears with his fingers and tried again, sending an etheric cord down to Earth to anchor into her stable nature. Another he sent heavenward, calling on Father God.

Then connecting with the remaining elements, Lugh mouthed the calming spell and projected it outward into the storm.

The plane continued shimmying for a long moment, then the whining ceased. Jubilation buoyed Lugh. Had his spell worked?

Then the plane hit another air pocket and jerked up short at the bottom of the trough, metal screeching. An ominous rumble rose from the engine, and the aircraft tilted to Lugh's side. Carry-on luggage and other personal belongings bombarded passengers who screamed for dear life as bin doors banged against overhead compartments.

Calming his breath, Lugh focused on the storm and repeated his spell.

The plane shuddered mightily, and the dive continued.

Lugh checked the monitor. They were approaching the ground much too fast. If they hit at this speed, they would die instantly.

He hurriedly wove a spell of protection around the plane and its occupants. He poured all his power into the incantation, then cast it wide, and sealed it with another, equally potent one.

Then, removing his fingers from his ears, Lugh eyed the monitor. Only a half-mile to go. A third. One-quarter. Then the shudder ceased abruptly, and the plane righted.

Lugh's pod-mate cheered and slid the shade open.

Below them, lights blinked. They had cleared the ocean and were over land. At least if they crashed, it wouldn't be in Davy Jones' locker.

Then the damaged engine sputtered and died, and the plane tilted to his side. Lugh flung up his arm to shield himself, but a hard-sided briefcase struck him in the head.

The world went dark.

CHATEAU FALAISE

Emily Hester crouched, ready to run. Eyes as large as traffic beacons ogled her in the lamplight. Why did the firedrake bring her to this cave? Did he plan to kill her? "Of course not. I mean you no harm."

The gentleness of Tienu's scoff belied the fierceness of his demeanor. And like the other dragon Keepers, he'd read her mind without qualm.

"I have been less than honorable, aye," the dragon continued. "And for that, I beg your pardon. But I would never, *ever*, mistreat you mi' lady. You know as well as I that I am unable to harm my master." Tienu bowed so low his horns swept the ground.

Relieved, Emily returned the gesture, then peered at the dim surroundings.

"Where are we?"

The dragon's great eyes blinked.

"Your cave, of course. Do you not recall your home beneath Château de Falaise?"

A frisson of déjà vu tickled Emily's spine, but she wagged her head.

"Where you lived? Bore your heiress?" Smoke curled from one nostril.

"I have no recollection of this place."

The dragon snorted. "Lady Awen, how can you not remember?" Anger sharpened his tongue. "Has that accursed sickness stolen your memory, too?"

"If by sickness you mean the mind veil, then yes. I have dreams and visions of Awen's glade, but my only memories are of my current lifetime. And those are blurred." But excitement buoyed her. "Is the glade nearby?"

"Aye." The dragon sighed, and a resigned cloud of smoke surrounded them. But they were finally getting somewhere.

Emily fanned the smoke and inched closer to the scarlet drake.

"Can you take me there? I long to walk barefoot in Awen's glade. To bathe in the healing waters of Luftshorne."

Tienu cast a consoling glance in her direction.

"On the morrow, mi' lady. For now, you must rest. Your spirit is thin. When did you last take food?"

It seemed like ages, and Emily said so.

The light from the nearby lantern intensified, glowing brighter and brighter until its gentle energy surrounded and enveloped Emily. Softly, lovingly, it filled her being, displacing a heaviness she had not known she was carrying.

Then the brilliance ebbed, and a cozy, simply-furnished living space appeared. On a low table snugged against the wall, a tray of fruit and nuts enticed. The aroma of rich cheese and warm, buttery croissants wafted to Emily. Her mouth watered, and she was suddenly famished.

She fell on the food as if Khenko Blitherstone, her Bahamian caregiver, had been starving her, shoving a grape in her mouth. She followed that with a bite of a steaming, flaky croissant dripping with salted butter.

Moaning with delight, Emily sipped what tasted like freshly squeezed pomegranate juice mixed with a splash of orange. Or was that… Bergamot? She shoved another bite in her mouth and studied the firedrake while she chewed.

Its spikes and horns were longer and more pronounced than those of the other dragons, and its teeth were even more frightful. Gemmed scales in hues ranging from a brilliant scarlet to a muted pinkish-orange ended in spikes much like those of a pine cone or a pineapple. His belly plates shone a rosy beige.

The dragon returned her scrutiny. Not in a threatening way, but like a scientist might examine the unexpected results of an important experiment.

When she could stand it no longer, Emily protested.

"What? Don't like what you see?"

The dragon yawned, and a puff of smoke eked out.

"I see an Awen who is yet untested," he rumbled. "Though you do seem further along than at the animal prison."

Emily's head whipped up. "You mean the zoo? You could have saved me that day. Me *and* my friends. Why didn't you?"

Tienu's head dipped sheepishly.

"I had no time mi' lady. I barely managed to cast a protective spell. Then the earth caved in and you were gone. I dove into the lava to rescue you, but Talav was closer and able to reach you first. So, I went with the magma until it ejected me in UnderEarth. After that, I flew north to Beli, hoping to rendezvous with the other dragons. Only…" Tienu hung his head.

"There were no dragons," Emily finished.

Surprise widened Tienu's eyes.

"Aye. But how did you know?"

"The air dragon, a-Ur, told us. He flew to Beli for the same reason. When the dragons weren't there, he sought the other Keepers and found them in Zephyr Cay with me. He told us the city and your meeting place lie in ruin. But he believes that together we can restore both. We were on our way there when you waylaid me."

Tienu's thick, mahogany tongue flicked over garnet lips.

"That was for your own good. The Cailleach has seized control of Yr Wyddfa and nearly captured me." A faraway look clouded the ancient eyes. "I do not know for certain, but I believe she may be responsible for scattering the dragons. The winter hag is evil."

"The winter hag? Is that the Cailleach?"

"Aye, the old witch of the mountain. Long ago, she was a beautiful goddess. But her heart was black and twisted even then. Now her outsides have become like her insides—withered and bitter and filled with rage. But her magic is no less potent."

A premonition stirred within Emily.

She shivered and wrapped her arms around her shoulders, wondering if this was the same Cailleach Lugh had mentioned. If so, they had hoped she could help them translate Awen's diary, a handwritten tome of magical spells. It was the only known compilation of its sort.

"Aye, she is one and the same. But you will find no help from that quarter. Besides, all that is in the book is also within your memory."

"Stop reading my mind," Emily snapped. The practice irked her to no end, though she had come to understand it when she, too, began hearing thoughts with no effort on her part. "I told you, I have no access to Awen's memories."

A woeful expression befell the dragon.

"But, tell me," Emily changed the subject. "What did you see in UnderEarth? My father and friend are there. I'm worried about them."

"As you should be, mi' lady. The earthquake released tons of magma below the surface, enough to destroy at least one of the Reptilian cities. I dared not linger."

"There are cities down there?" Emily's curiosity was piqued.

"Aye, mi' lady. You don't remember that either?"

"No, Tienu."

The fire dragon wagged its head sadly. "There are cities and military bases—a whole civilization that predates any to be found on Earth's surface. Until a few thousand years ago, the interior was the only livable space."

Chill bumps danced along Emily's limbs. The revelation explained a lot.

"So, why is UnderEarth's hidden civilizations not common knowledge?"

"The information is available," the dragon rumbled, "but the memory veil keeps most humans from accessing it."

"That figures. Did you happen to see my friend Brian down there?"

"No, I saw no humans, only Reptilians and a few less-hostile species. I left quickly and flew straight to Yr Wyddfa. It was there I encountered the crone."

A shudder through Emily at his reference to the Reptilians.

"And this Yr Wyddfa is in Wales?"

"Aye. You may know it by another name—Snowdonia." An odd light entered Tienu's eyes. "Did you say the Keepers were on their way to Beli?" An edge of desperation colored his tone, chilling Emily. "I hope they steer clear of the Cailleach."

"They should be there now. Assuming they had better luck than I." She rubbed her face in her hands. How would she get to Beli now? Talav and the others would be worried about her.

"*Here* is where you are supposed to be." Tienu rose on powerful front legs, and Emily leapt backward to avoid the flames of annoyance that flickered from his snout.

"But why here?"

The dragon calmed and settled on its haunches.

"The Beltane moon will shine soon. Only then can a vital component of your preparation be completed. Without it, Beli is a death trap."

The dragon yawned as if bored with the conversation. She wanted to ask him what he meant, but he turned a tight circle and settled on the ground much as Emily's cat Ralph might. Then his great eyes rolled back and closed.

The thought of Ralph had homesick tears threatening to break through Emily's carefully constructed defenses. Would this nightmare never end? Then shock rippled through her as the dragon's thoughts rang in her head.

"*This* is our Awen? She who would save the world?" Disapproval and fear oozed from the firedrake. "Brigid? Are you there? Druantia? Please hear and help, else all will be lost. Bé Chuille, our old enemy, has entered the fight. If you do not help, the Humans will not survive. Then our long history of vigilance will have been for naught." The dragon's troubled eyes opened to contemplate Emily.

Unaware that she could hear his thoughts, Tienu continued his silent, one-sided conversation.

"No, it is too late. This one is hardly Awen material. Humanity is doomed."

"Your haste blinds you, Great One." The husky feminine voice echoed from the dark recesses of the cave.

Emily leapt from the chair she had settled in and peered frantically into the shadows.

"Who's there?"

Tienu, too, reacted quickly, knocking table and chairs over as he whipped around to face the voice. Then he laughed, a long, rolling rumble that lifted Emily's spirits as it filled the cave.

"Queen Druantia? Is that you?"

The voice spoke again, nearer this time.

"Yes, Tienu. It is I." Then it addressed Emily. "Little Wren, I am Druantia, Awen's mother. Your grandmother many generations removed."

Goosebumps waltzed across Emily's shoulders. "I know that name. The dolphins and whales spoke it in the vortex." She went down on one knee and bent forward until her chest rested on her thigh.

"Hail Druantia, Goddess of the Lost, the Broken, and the Free." Heat rushed to Emily's bowed face. She had no idea why she'd said that or from where it had come.

"Rise, my darling," the voice commanded, and Emily did.

The pale silhouette of a woman appeared on the wall beside her.

Tienu's red eyes flicked between Emily and the silhouette, and the light of hope dawned.

"We meet at last," Druantia crooned. "Long has it been since I gazed upon the fair face of my daughter."

Startled, Emily almost corrected the silhouette, then realized there was no need. Druantia knew precisely who Emily was—the one through whom Awen was to have incarnated.

"Yes."

The affirmation was a caress, but even her dead ancestor could read her mind. That irked Emily.

"Awen would have done so had my mother not kidnapped me as a child."

"There is still time."

"How?" Emily leaned closer, hoping for an answer to that which had eluded her thus far.

"Just let it be so. Stop fighting. Relax into your body. Step back mentally. Then let Awen take over."

Emily snorted. The elders, the dragons, and now her ghostly grandmother—could they offer anything but platitudes? They made it sound so simple. Just let it be, they said. Let go, they said. Give up control, they said.

Uh-huh. Sure. Easy to say. But impossible, so far, for Emily to do.

Hopelessness settled in. Emily sank to her knees beneath the crushing weight of all that had happened over the last many hours and everything else she feared was to come. Falling forward on hands that had suddenly gone numb, she planted her face against the cold floor.

Breathing in and out slowly and purposefully, Emily fought the panic. But the waves were too steep and the troughs too low. It overpowered her, and she collapsed to her belly. Then the nausea hit as the room spun round and round.

A ping, like a drop of chilled oil, landed in the center of Emily's crown. It spread across her scalp and down her spine, then out through her palms and the bottoms of her feet. A sense of calm followed in its wake. The panic was gone.

Grateful, she rose on all fours.

"Thank you."

"It wasn't me." Tienu's plate-sized eyes cut to the silhouette.

"Thank you," she repeated to Druantia. "Can you teach me to do that? It would come in handy."

A rich, throaty laugh filled the cave.

"I can. But you already know how. Just ask Awen."

This time, the panic remained at bay, but the outline of the silhouette began fading. Desperate for more, Emily stood.

"Any other words of wisdom?"

"Call the dragons. Then go to the sacred place known as Stonehenge."

"And do what?" Emily hiccupped.

"You will know when you get there. Ask Awen."

Frustrated, Emily glared at the wavering silhouette.

It moved closer to Tienu. "Thank you, old friend. Between your plea and Thoth's merkaba tinkering, a weak portal opened, and I was able to cross over for the first time in millennia. My spirit, at least."

Tienu's horny brow creased. "Do you speak of Earth's merkaba? It malfunctions again?"

"It never stopped. But the gravity wells are taking longer and longer to dissipate." Druantia sounded worried. "We seek a solution, but do not know how long Earth has left. If her merkaba fails, a pole shift is imminent."

The revelation struck terror in Emily's heart.

"If the poles reverse, catastrophic global events will wipe out all life on Earth. We can't let that happen."

"No, dear. We cannot. We are doing everything we know to do, and then some," Druantia said, then addressed the fire dragon.

"Dear Tienu, as always, I am in your debt for counseling and protecting my daughter's daughters." She reached a shadowy arm toward the grisly dragon. "I have missed you, old friend. I long to wrap my legs around your saddle and fly off into the wild blue yonder." She paused as if remembering a long-ago pleasure.

"But, I must go. The portal is collapsing." The silhouette faded more. "Take care of this one. She is our only hope. And, Tienu, she is bullheaded for good reason."

No doubt thinking Emily could no longer hear, Tienu lowered his voice to a whisper. "You think that stubborn streak is an asset?"

Emily grinned. The hearing thoughts thing was coming in handy, but Tienu's speculative glint gave her the tingles.

"You believe Emily's upbringing made her strong enough to end the fighting, don't you?" Tienu sounded doubtful.

"We hope that to be the case. We will know soon enough."

Then Druantia's silhouette was gone, and Tienu eyed Emily askance.

"Well?"

"Well, what?"

"Will you accept your ancestor's advice? She *is* a goddess, after all."

But that ancestor had piled another impossible task on Emily's overburdened shoulders. A thread of anxiety stole back to taunt her. Hadn't she endured enough for one lifetime?

A giggle escaped—proof that she had far exceeded her limits. It bubbled over in hysterical waves, and Emily collapsed to the floor again, convulsing in laughter until the last helpless titter faded. Finally, she picked herself up, dusted herself off, and rounded on the staring dragon.

"Do you even have a clue what I've been through in the last hours? On top of little to no sleep, I've been drunk and stoned, had a major panic attack, nearly drowned in my own vomit, and was captured and bound by a witch who tossed me in the bottom of a heaving boat like a sack of potatoes. Then I was mauled by a well-meaning dragon, learned to heal my wounds and create a protective spell, then stopped a raging storm in its tracks." She paused to suck in a deep breath.

"After that, I said goodbye to a friend I may never see again, survived a watery whirlpool, a vortex, and a wobbly wormhole, was waylaid by an unfriendly dragon, then chastised by the spirit of a grandmother I have never met. Now, I have one thing to say and one thing only: BACK. OFF. JACK!"

By the time she spat out the last word, Emily was trembling like an aspen leaf.

The dragon guffawed, but a light of grudging respect had snuck into its crimson eyes. Feeling slightly vindicated, Emily slumped into the chair, beyond exhausted.

"Child, you are right," the dragon allowed. "Anyone would be spent after what you have been through. Tomorrow, I will take you to Awen's glade. But tonight, you shall sleep."

That wasn't exactly what Emily wanted to hear, but it was enough for now. With a yawn, she curled in the oversized armchair and immediately sank into a deep slumber. She didn't see the concern that darkened Tienu's eyes as he watched over her, or the ethereal creatures that silently gathered to gaze upon the returned Awen.

YR WYDDFA

Tienu burst from the wormhole with a roar, fire pouring from his snout. Below him on the rocky shore, two of the Keepers roared back.

"About time you showed up," Talav bellowed.

"Where is Awen, you conniving traitor?" Ooschu thundered.

Tienu swept past, wishing he could ignore them, but time was running out. He circled twice before landing at the edge of the rock-strewn beach. Talav charged immediately, knocking him backward. Tienu righted himself slowly and faced two angry Keepers poised to pounce.

"Truce!" he roared, front claws in the air.

But the Keepers advanced.

"The Awen is safe," he assured. "I'm not looking for a fight. She is secreted in her caves beneath William's castle."

But Talav shrieked and attacked. She slashed at Tienu's face with long, sharp claws, then her tail came around, knocking him sideways. Tienu scrambled up, and Ooschu lumbered between them.

"Where have you been? And why did you hijack the Awen? We were bringing her here to call the dragon-meet."

Ooschu's fury surprised Tienu. The water dragon was usually level-headed.

"Awen is not yet powerful enough to call the dragons. You forgot a crucial step."

Talav muscled forward to glare beside Ooschu.

"What step?"

"The Healing Waters of Luftshorne. Awen and William must come together for her to access her full powers."

Talav's jaw fell open. Ooschu's head drooped in shame. Then an angry screech had all heads snapping up.

"That's a-Ur," Talav rumbled.

Tienu surveyed the upper peaks of Yr Wyddfa where the cry had originated.

"The Cailleach is here. I sense her presence. Have you seen her?"

The Keepers' heads wagged.

"Stay here. I'll be back."

Lifting mighty wings, Tienu scaled the peaks of Yr Wyddfa, and his heart expanded. Oh, how he had missed his homeland. He soared higher until he reach the top, then circled to scan for a-Ur and the Cailleach. Thick, snow-laden clouds veiled his sight.

Catching a rising draft, Tienu opened his wings and rode it until the wind petered out and dropped him back toward the cloud-covered summit. There was an anxious roar, and Tienu honed in on a-Ur's location.

As he dove, the wind whistled through his horns. Then, lightning split the sky. Tienu feinted, and it streaked past him. Near where it struck, he spied the witch and the dragon.

Thunder boomed and rolled across the rugged terrain, masking Tienu's angry roar. He had barely escaped the winter hag's clutches. He would not let her take the air Keeper.

Scaling a peak, he reversed direction and landed with a ground-shaking thud between the hag and a-Ur. Then, wings lifted and ready to do battle, Tienu lumbered toward the witch. She eyed him with interest.

Draig a-Ur bellowed and charged. Tienu stepped aside, but the air dragon turned and spewed fire, strafing Tienu up and down.

He reveled in the heat. "Bwaaahahahaa, you can do better than that, old boy. You know fire makes me stronger."

"Have you no shame, Tienu?" The air drake panted like a dragon ready for the boneyard. "The Awen is missing. What have you done with our master?"

His question brought Tienu back to the matter at hand. Stifling his anger, he drew to full height and forced a stiff bow.

"You forgot, my airy-fairy friend—an important event must occur before the prophecy can be fulfilled." The fire dragon's chest expanded with pride. "Luckily, I remembered and detoured Awen to Falaise. You can thank me later."

Behind him, the Cailleach cackled.

Horrified, Tienu faltered. Arrogance had made him forget the hag's presence. Now he had done the unthinkable. He had revealed his master's location to her mortal enemy. Lifting his formidable wings, Tienu lunged for the winter hag.

She skittered sideways and hooted amicably as if they were friends, "Draig Tienu, you old rascal! How good of you to return."

Thrown off guard, he hesitated. Why would the Cailleach be happy to see him? Surely she had not forgotten their last encounter?

In answer, her smile twisted into a leer. She snarled and struck the tip of her staff against the rocky terrain, and a sheet of ice raced toward Tienu.

Not afraid of frozen water, Tienu released an intense burst of flame and then followed it with a long, scorching, fiery breath. The ice slowed, wavering like a living thing before advancing toward him and a-Ur. Refilling his furnace, Tienu blew another long, focused stream of fire.

This time, the ice was impervious. It surrounded Tienu's front claws, searing the bottoms of his feet, then traveled up, consuming his forelegs and racing up his chest. Tienu roared in agony as millions of tiny ice needles pierced armor that was supposed to be impenetrable.

The Cailleach cackled triumphantly.

"Welcome back, fire dragon. You are mine now."

Struggling against the ice that burned like fire never could, Tienu tried desperately to access his flames. Behind him, a-Ur let out an unearthly screech. The hag-ice was taking the air dragon, too.

NEXT IN COMMAND

Shibboleth paced Irkalla's control room, wings fluttering in agitation. Another of his regiments was gone—his oldest and finest warriors burnt to a crisp by the raging magma. Worse, Maw, his first-in-command and favorite spawn, was among the fallen.

The Reptilian leader gripped the console, careful to maintain a composed appearance before his subjects. He stared at the monitor until the sight of the burning complex etched itself into his retina.

When he could bear it no longer, Shibboleth averted his gaze to assess the damage. Agartha's control room had endured, but the magma and its fires had annihilated the rest of the base. It still flowed, burning through the chutes and chambers beneath and around the city.

Agartha's support staff perished. Luckily, the Drac guards and personnel had been more fortunate. Most had escaped, but between Ishkur's rampage and Maw's demise, there were precious few left. The hybrid ranks were also severely depleted.

On top of that, all four of the human Connectors recruited by Azi had perished in the first round of trials. The initial Connector and its intermediary survived but could not be roused.

Dejected, Shibboleth lowered his frame into the chair. Why had he thought Nergal's project might work? Of all the Dracs he had encountered, Nergal was his most hated adversary.

He had tried more than once to end the worm's life, yet Nergal continued to survive, a testament to Draconian resiliency. Unfortunately, it had earned the Drac respect among his peers and followers, as evidenced by the Ishkur, the brilliant scientist who had sided with Nergal. Shibboleth slumped deeper into the chair.

The search for access points to AboveEarth was also going badly. Every team they sent to investigate potential portals returned none the wiser—or not at all. But if Shibboleth and his Dracs were to exterminate the humans to seize control of Earth, they must first breach the infernal barriers.

And if they couldn't? Shibboleth slammed his fist into the console, drawing the startled gaze of several techs. The Reptilians would continue to be stuck in UnderEarth as they had since landing millennia ago.

What good was technology if they couldn't climb out of Earth's belly, much less get off the forsaken planet?

And that was Shibboleth's deepest desire.

He stayed that way for a long time, staring at the screen and feeling sorry for himself. He hated Earth. Hated it with a passion. He would give anything to be back in space. Or anywhere besides this starless, airless wasteland inside planetship Earth.

But there were matters to attend to. His Drac troops were scattered and in disarray. Shibboleth would order them to regroup and reconnoiter, then recall Mot to Irkalla. Then, he would assign a small company to Azi to help with the human domination program and to breach the barriers to the surface world.

Feeling better now that he had a semblance of a plan, Shibboleth sat up to access Mot's feed. After slaying Ishkur, Mot imprisoned Nergal and his accomplices and then returned to Naraka beneath the District of Columbia.

Now that Maw was dead, Mot would be second-in-command. Mot was more intelligent than Maw, and his cerebral capacity exceeded even Shibboleth's. But Mot was sneaky, and his reticence concerning.

When he appeared on the overhead screen, Shibboleth ignored his nagging concerns and recalled Mot and his trainees to Irkalla. He would keep his fledgling warriors close until they were ready to attack AboveEarth.

Striding out of the control center, he nearly collided with a Draca returning to her duty station. Shibboleth snarled, and she gave him a wide berth. He stalked through the compound to his quarters and gazed down at the city. The Irkallans went about their day-to-day business unaware of Shibboleth's dilemma or the forces at play.

Then his old ally, the witch, came to mind. Shibboleth tore through his quarters, looking for the black stone she had entrusted to him. He had not used it in many millennia, but Bé Chuille could help get a handle on matters.

Assuming he could find the stone. It was the only means he had to contact the witch.

THE ROAD HOME

Brian MacBrayer showered and dressed in new clothes, courtesy Morgan Foster. He almost felt like his old self, but now he was getting nervous. Morgan had promised to get in touch with his mom, but so far, she had not called him.

Tears welled up. He really, really needed to talk to his mother. She might not be able to help, but just hearing her voice would be a comfort. Punching her number into the throwaway phone, he calculated the time in Bali. They were fifteen hours ahead, making it ten-thirtyish in the morning—tomorrow. He pressed send and prayed she would answer.

"Cybele MacBrayer."

"Mom! It's me. Brian," he sobbed. Then all the tears he'd been swallowing since the earthquake rushed out.

"Hold on, baby. Are you okay? Don't go anywhere."

Feeling better already, Brian blew his nose and wiped away the tears. He could hear his mother in the background, speaking in muffled tones, like she'd put her hand over the microphone. Then she was back.

"Oh, Brian, I'm so happy to hear your voice. I've been—" she paused and he could hear her sniffle. "Thank God! I've been so worried. Are you okay, sweetie? Are you hurt?"

Brian assured her he was fine. He'd gotten a hot shower and a good meal, now all he needed was to sleep for a week. Once convinced of Brian's safety, his mom sighed.

"Sweetie, I've been so worried. Your Uncle Lugh called after the earthquake. We've both been frantic. Where are you now? The whole Order is searching."

"North Carolina."

"North Carolina? Holy crap! How did you get from Atlanta to North Carolina? That's hundreds of miles."

Brian thought of what he and Ethnui had gone through to get to Blowing Rock, and couldn't help but glow with pride. The prepaid phone beeped. It needed a charge.

"It's a long story, Mom. I can't wait to tell you, but this battery is nearly dead. I had enough juice to call Uncle Lugh and leave a voicemail, then I called Morgan Foster because his recording said I should. She paid for the hotel rooms and is supposed to be sending us tickets to Atlanta."

There was a sharp intake of breath on his mother's end.

"Us? Is there someone with you?"

Brian chuckled. "Yes, a girl named Ethnui rescued me after the earthquake. The Reptilians had enslaved her whole family, and she came home with me. We're hoping the druids can free them."

"Reptilians?" Cybele Cray MacBrayer gasped. "Jesus H. Christ! Where in Brigid's name were you? What happened down there?"

The beep came again.

"Ma, this phone is dying. Did you talk to Uncle Lugh?"

"Yes, he's on his way to Wales. Did you leave him a message?"

"Just a quick one to let him know we made it out." Brian hesitated. Hamilton Hester, the 'deceased' Druid leader whose spirit had taken up residence inside Brian, clamored in the back of his head.

"Umm, Mom? When you talk to Uncle Lugh again, would you please remind him that he tried to make me and Cu stay home from the zoo that day? He tried, Mama. He tried." The tears flowed in earnest again.

Brian dashed them away and cleared his throat. He had walked through hell. Literally. He would not fall apart on the phone with his mother.

"I'll tell him, Love. But you know your uncle. He'll blame himself until the swallows fly home. He still feels responsible for not talking your daddy out of leaving us." A knife-like pain twisted in Brian's chest. He had not known that.

"Now give me the number of your hotel. And don't worry about a thing. I will talk to Morgan about your transportation. Then I'll find a way to get to Atlanta myself."

"Morgan didn't call you?" Brian's heart beat faster.

"No, sweetie. Was she supposed to?"

He plopped on the bed and noticed his messy hair in the dresser mirror as the phone beeped.

"She said she would. Maybe she got sidetracked." But Ham insisted it was more than that.

When they said goodbye, Brian felt a lot better. He plugged the protesting phone into the charger and nearly launched it across the room when it rang in his hand. Thinking it was his mom or Uncle Lugh, he answered on the second ring.

"Brian MacBrayer?" The man's unfamiliar voice was stern and official.

Brian's blood chilled. He'd bought the phone this morning, and only three people had the number. The hairs on the back of his neck bristled.

"Who's asking," he said cautiously.

"My name is Becket Warren. Morgan Foster called me and asked if I could give you and your friend a ride to Atlanta."

In the back of his mind, Hamilton Hester hissed, "I don't know that name. Ask how he knows Morgan."

"Who is this again?" Brian stood to pace, only to be jerked backward when the wire reached its limit.

"A friend of Morgan Foster's. My name is Becket Warren, and I am leaving Washington, D.C. to drive to Atlanta. Since Blowing Rock is on my way, Morgan asked if I would pick you up and bring you to her place in Atlanta. Assuming, of course, that works for you."

Brian wrinkled his nose, and Hamilton growled, "Why didn't Morgan tell you that?" Brian repeated the question.

"I do not know. She said she would. Maybe she got distracted. If you'd like, call her then ring me back."

"Yes, I think I will. But your number didn't come through. Can you give it to me?" Brian scribbled it on the pad beside the bed as the man rattled it off.

"I'll call you back."

He laid the phone by the outlet, and paced the room. Then, Brian paused at the window and stared at the steady stream of cars. Across the street, a sign pointed to the entrance to Blowing Rock Park. He and Ethnui had escaped UnderEarth there, somehow ending up on a boulder high above the canyon floor.

A flood of gratitude coursed through Brian. They had been lost in the bowels of Earth for what felt like years, but he had no idea how they had gotten out. Making a decision, he crossed and tapped lightly on the door to the adjoining room.

"Ethnui?"

"Yes?" The lock snicked, and his door knob rattled.

He told Ethnui about the strange phone call. If his news concerned her, it didn't show in the pretty Fomorian's expression.

"So, what do you think?"

Her nose scrunched the way it did when she was deep in thought.

"We need a ride. If your friend Morgan trusts this man, we should be safe, don't you think? I was looking forward to flying, though. It sounded like we would get to your home sooner. Plus, I've never been on a plane." Ethnui settled on the edge of a chair. Brian plopped on the bed to face her.

"It *could* be faster. I thought that was what Morgan was working on. But maybe the flight's not until tomorrow. It might be quicker to hitch a ride with this man."

But his gut wrenched on the last words, bringing him up short. The last time Brian had ignored his instincts, he had ended up in a dungeon in UnderEarth. If not for Ethnui, he would still be there— or, more likely, dead, a Reptilian's dinner.

"Let's see what Morgan says."

Leaving the phone plugged in, he punched the saved number, and studied Ethnui from the corner of his eye. She had showered and dressed in her new outfit from the boutique downstairs. The American clothes changed her looks considerably over the jumpsuit she'd worn since the day of his rescue.

"Morgan Foster."

"Morgan, this is Brian MacBrayer." He activated the speaker so that Ethnui could listen.

"Did my friend Becket call? He's driving to Atlanta and said he can detour through Blowing Rock to pick you up. The next flight to Atlanta doesn't leave until tomorrow."

The Fomorian's eyes grew wider.

"Hold on. I need to check with Ethnui."

"Brian, I'm in a meeting," Morgan countered. "Decide and call me back." Then, the line went dead.

"So, what do you think?"

"What does the Master Druid think?"

"Ham?" Brian called, but the erstwhile Grand Druid of the Awen Order didn't answer. "Ham, are you there?"

"Shhh!" The druid hissed out loud. "I'm checking the dude out."

Ethnui adjusted her jaunty new cap to hide her pointy ears. It matched the hot-pink top she'd found, and the sequined letters spelled 'Sassy.' It was a brand name, not a comment on the wearer, but Ethnui was that and so much more. Brian had been drawn to her from the get-go, and the better he knew the Fomorian, the more tempting he found her. Even better, Brian was sure she had feelings for him too.

Hamilton spoke. "So, this Warren dude is FBI and a friend of my sister Morgan. She worked with him at the bureau before leaving to be the Awen Order's Head of Security. I think we will be okay hitching a ride. Just be careful what you say."

"What do you mean?" Ethnui asked.

"For one, don't tell him you're Fomorian. In fact, don't mention UnderEarth or anything about it. If we're lucky, Morgan kept that part to herself. If she didn't, you'll have to improvise. But don't tell him anything. If something should happen and we need to ditch him, we will cross that bridge when we get there."

"Works for me." Brian called Morgan, but it went to voicemail.

"Hi, it's Brian. I'm calling your friend for a ride. With luck, we'll see you in Atlanta tonight."

ZEPHYR CAY

Mitchell Wainwright caught a whiff of his underarm and wrinkled his nose. He hadn't brought a change of clothes, and it was sweltering here in the Bahamas.

Mopping his face with his shirtsleeve, he paid the motorboat captain. Then, draping his suit jacket over one arm, Mitch hefted his briefcase and strolled to the front desk of the brightly-painted inn.

"BE BACK SHORTLY," the sign on the counter of the tiny lobby declared.

It was past noon for chrissakes. Mitch was starving.

He stepped outside and wandered past the guest rooms. Spying a cleaning cart in front of a propped-open door, he stuck his head inside, startling the woman changing the bed linens. She laughed nervously and said something Mitch didn't understand.

"There's no one at the front desk. Can you help me?"

She blinked as if not comprehending. Mitch's frustration mounted.

"Check in? Can you help?"

The diminutive local eyed Mitch up and down, then went back to tucking in sheets.

Did she not understand English?

"Cuándo volverá a abrir la recepción?" But there was still no recognition in the dark eyes.

The maid placed a mint on the pillow with a flourish, then bustled to where Mitch waited by the door.

"We open now, sir."

She brushed by Mitch, and he followed her to the office, where she lifted the bar and slid behind the desk. The phone rang, but she let it jangle.

"Only one? You like single?"

"Yes, I'd like a room for two nights with a king-sized bed."

The woman looked blankly at Mitch.

"Single only."

Sighing, he gave her his credit card. She ran it and handed it back, along with a large, brass key on a ring stamped with the inn's name, Seaside Villas.

"Room Three for you. That way." She motioned toward where he had found her. "Check out eleven." She nodded toward one corner of the lobby. "Ice and vending machine there. Anything else you need?"

"A store to buy clothes?"

She beamed and turned to a small display case. Producing a map of the island, she pointed out two shops, then took a pen from the cup on the counter and circled their icons.

"How about food? And a liquor store?" After all he'd gone through getting to Zephyr Cay, Mitch could use a stiff drink.

The woman drew circles around the icons and looked up. "More?"

"Not at the moment." He thanked her and hurried to Room Three.

The air conditioner hummed, but the room was only slightly cooler than outdoors. Bumping the thermostat down several notches, Mitch slid his money clip in his pants pocket, his briefcase under the bed, and hung his suit jacket on the lone hanger in the tiny closet.

The furniture was dated, and the island decor a bit ramshackle. But at least the room appeared to be clean. No roaches or lizards that he could see. He eyed the bed dubiously. It was small and looked uncomfortable, but it would have to do.

Mitch had noticed a large building on a promontory on the way in to Zephyr Cay. Apparently, the Atlantean Center did take guests on occasion. But the man who'd ferried him from Nassau said this was the only inn. Still, Mitch would see if the center had availability. It certainly looked nicer.

Removing his tie, he opened the top buttons of his shirt, rolled up his sleeves, and splashed water on his heat-reddened cheeks before patting them dry. Then, sliding the brass key and the map in his pocket, Mitch exited the room in search of food and a cold drink. Once he'd eaten, he would begin the search for Emily Hester.

He had yet to come to terms with the revelation that she was his sister and possibly twin. His mother had confirmed a few days ago that Hamilton Hester had sired them both. But, Ham had chosen

Emily to be the Order's Grand Druid while refusing to acknowledge Mitch at all.

And not just Mitch. Hamilton Hester had fathered a myriad of unclaimed children. All in the name of finding the next "Awen"—that one girl child who would inherit the original Awen's power and lead the Order against some nebulous threat.

Angry now, as well as hungry, Mitch gritted his teeth and hurried along the narrow path that paralleled the muddy road. As he approached a group of brightly painted shops, a delicious aroma wafted to him, making his mouth water. But before Mitch could duck into the courtyard, a rickety bus rumbled past, splashing him with water.

DESK DUTY

Determined to drown out the annoying Sergeant's tirade, Elise Hester Johnson turned up the volume on her headphones. But even glass walls and an unreliable witness couldn't compete with Banner's abusive rant. Tapping on the glass, Elise glared and pointed at her sensitive ears.

When Banner flicked an offensive finger and turned his back, Elise's internal pressure inched up to DEFCON One. She pressed the headphones against her ears.

When that failed to blot out Banner and the other quieter but ever-present voices, she ripped them off and let go of a long, silent screech, followed by a string of swear words that propelled her from her chair.

She'd been confined in this loony bin too long.

Sliding her headphones into a case and the case into a large, pleather purse, Elise paused to inhale and exhale deeply, then did it two more times. Feeling a tad more relaxed, she plastered on a smile and checked it in the mirrored doorframe before shoving through the door.

Heads snapped up, eyeing Elise as if she were a poisonous toad. She threw the bullpen a sullen glare and stalked away, snorting at the irony of being assigned the coveted corner office. Like that could make up for being benched.

The Alien Intelligence Agency was Elise's life—had been for the last forty years. Recruited straight out of druid school, they had whisked her to Europe at seventeen. Now, Elise was more agent than druid. But she would soon go bonkers if not allowed back in the field. Or at least stateside. And, according to HQ, that would not be happening.

Shocked to see a tall Fomorian barreling toward her, Elise juked to avoid it, then realized it was a wraith when it disappeared. She should've known. Aliens weren't allowed in the bullpen or on AIA's upper floors. But, though their voices constantly vied for her attention, she hadn't seen a ghost in a long time.

Elise had almost made it to the elevator when the door from the stairwell creaked open. Not wanting to speak to anyone, she ducked into the lady's room before Cybele MacBrayer's profile appeared.

She skulked behind the door, willing Cybele to pass, as anxiety clawed at her insides. Elise had managed to avoid her goddaughter for the last many days and would rather not break her streak—especially in her heightened state of agitation.

Ever since her ex disappeared, gloom had enveloped Cybele. Like a black hole, it sucked the life out of everyone and everything. For the empathic Elise, being in her presence took a herculean effort. Now Cybele's son had gone missing, and the weight of her darkness was even more unbearable.

A pressure change signaled the door was being opened. Elise hurriedly hid in a stall, secured the lock, and slid her slacks down. She might as well pee while she was in here.

"Aunt Elise, I know I'm a lot right now," Cybele said softly. "I get that. But I need you."

So much for what Elise needed. She sighed, knowing she was being an awful godmother. *This* is why she didn't have kids. Well, this, plus she had never met the right man. Then, she'd gotten too old to put up with one.

"Can you need me after I pee, please?"

"Oh. Yeah. Sorry."

Groaning inwardly, Elise finished her business. Then, as ready as she could be, she exited the stall.

Cybele's gray eyes glittered with hope. Her long, dark hair was pulled back in a ponytail, away from a gamine face she had inherited from her mother. Their gazes locked, and Cybele's thoughts tumbled out silently.

Brian had resurfaced with a companion—a tall alien girl with pointed ears and kind eyes. But he was in trouble again. *They* were in trouble. And Cybele wanted Elise to help.

Breaking eye contact, Elise moved to the sink and hiked her purse higher on her shoulder. She scrubbed her hands vigorously for twenty-two seconds. Twenty was enough, but twenty-two held the magic of repeating numbers.

Rinsing, she studied Cybele in the mirror. The younger druid waited, respecting her need for silence. But her thoughts were noisy and not very kind. Swinging around, Elise frowned at her goddaughter.

"Seriously, Cybele? You think I view my purse as a surrogate baby? Where'd you come up with that psychobabble bullshite?"

Cybele blushed deeply. For an AIA operative, she had a flagrant "tell."

Elise sniffed, "If you want my help, walk with me." She pushed the door open and glanced back at Cybele. "I need air."

AGENTS WARREN AND JETER

Special Agent Becket Warren hung up the phone and glanced at his partner in the passenger seat.

"The boy agreed. We'll pick them up at the Green Park Inn in Blowing Rock. Punch in the address for directions, will you? Then text him with our estimated time of arrival." He handed his cell to the junior agent and watched him out of the corner of his eye while keeping the other on the road.

Derek Jeter was an enigma, one Becket would rather not have along—especially on this trip. The son of an acquaintance from Becket's academy days, Agent Jeter seldom spoke and rarely participated in small talk. And though Becket had worked with the field agent on several occasions, he could never get a read on the man. For Becket, that made Jeter untrustworthy whether he was or not.

"Why are we acting as chauffeur for these kids?" Jeter handed the phone back. "Isn't that against Bureau policy?"

Becket cast the rookie a side-eye. "Yes, normally. But these are no ordinary kids. Remember that girl in Los Angeles who claimed to be able to see into the mind of the Reptilian alien?"

"Yeeessss," Jeter said suspiciously. "What about her?"

"These kids have made a similar claim."

Jeter's head jerked up. "Seriously? The aliens have contacted more kids?"

Seeing his quizzical expression, Becket laughed.

"No. This boy and girl claim to have escaped from UnderEarth." He chuckled again.

"That's where Patrika Tolbert said the Reptilians live."

"Exactly." Agent Jeter did remember. Becket had purposefully not shared any details on the flight from L.A., preferring to see how things unfolded. "These kids may be able to corroborate Tolbert's story." Becket hoped like hell that wasn't the case.

If the girl was telling the truth, the Reptilians were mounting an attack. The last thing they needed was an intraterrestrial invasion from underground. The United States was not ready for such an assault. Neither, he suspected, was the world at large, though the U.S. had sunk trillions into space defense through NASA and the Space Force.

In the early twentieth century, the Department of Defense had secretly partnered with a private contractor in the Pacific Northwest to weaponize the moon. Toward that end, a massive particle beam accelerator remained poised to bounce lasers off the mirrors placed during the first moonwalk.

Such measures had given Earth a semblance of security from space invaders. But, they were not designed for an attack from the interior, despite the fact that Becket and other experts had warned the powers on countless occasions.

Becket glanced at his silent partner. He had paled beneath his dark coloring.

"You okay there, Jeter?"

The man shook his head. "Not even. I haven't slept well since we interviewed the girl. If she is right and the Reptilians are mounting an attack, can we stop them?" He sipped from the metal canister he carried everywhere. "I mean, an alien invasion would go a long way toward unifying the world against a common enemy. But I can't see it going well for Earth or us."

"My thoughts exactly. Which means time's a wasting."

Becket repositioned his side mirror, flicked the warning lights on, engaged the siren, and floored the sedan.

THE CAILLEACH

Bé Chuille trudged to her simple hut. She had captured two of the Dragon Keepers. Now, two more remained. Once she rounded them up, Druantia's mighty dragons would be no more.

Awen was another matter, but Tienu had revealed his master's location. Bé thought fondly of Falaise's rolling green hills. Long ago, after they migrated from UnderEarth, Bé had dwelt there. But Awen's mother, Queen Druantia, had exiled Bé to the frigid northlands.

A roar split the silence, and Bé hurried to the window. Had one of her captives escaped?

But it was neither Tienu nor a-Ur. Instead, it was the earth dragon, Talav. Bé gleefully rubbed her hands together. The unsuspecting Keepers had converged on Yr Wyddfa. After years of tracking the dragons, she had captured two Keepers and was about to bag a third.

But Talav had changed. She had wings and horns. Bé stared at the colorful dragon, queen of her kind. Talav sniffed around the ruins, then moved to the ice cages encasing her fellow Keepers.

Drawing the robe tighter around her frail form, Bé moved to the door to confront the dragon. A velvety roar behind the hut stayed her hand. She peered out and gasped aloud.

It was Draig Ooschu. What in Brigid's name? A water dragon on dry land? This was another new development. Long ago, all dragons had roamed land, water, and air. But that was on their home planet of Marduk. After they evacuated to Earth's inner realm, they continued to do so.

But once the Mardukans migrated to AboveEarth, bringing the dragons and humans, the four dragon species gravitated to their own terrain and rarely mingled. Much less did they leave their usual habitat to venture into others. What had happened to make these dragons do so?

The water dragon ambled to the front of the cabin and joined Talav beside their frozen brethren. Bé whispered a spell to amplify their conversation.

"Nothing over there, either," Ooschu rumbled. "The witch must have left."

"Are you sure?" Talav looked uneasy. "I have a bad feeling about this. I don't fancy becoming a block of ice, and we still have to find Awen and get her here. How do you suppose we unthaw these two?" Talav's tone was rather whiny for a dragon.

Ooschu circled their frozen companions. "Draig Tienu could unthaw them." She whirled to contemplate Talav. "And so can you. My fire-bellows doesn't work or I would give it a go." Then she was off on another tangent. "Or the Awen can do it. Let's go fetch her first."

"I think we should try defrosting them," Talav growled. "You keep an eye out for the winter hag while I work on it."

"Be careful," Ooschu warned. "That witch is wily and I don't want to end up like these two."

Bé Chuille chuckled. That was precisely what was about happen. Then once the Keepers were out of the way, Bé could travel to Falaise and send Awen to join them on the Stygian Plains. Then Druantia's line would be silenced forever.

Brigid, her old friend, invaded Bé's subconscious, inducing a moment of guilt. But Druantia's mother was long gone and could do Bé no harm. She ignored her and returned to the task at hand.

UNSCHEDULED LAYOVER

"Sir, wake up. Are you okay?"

Lugh came to with a groan. The attendant's eyes flashed relief as she leaned closer.

"Your head is bleeding. Are you okay?"

Touching his throbbing skull, Lugh groaned again when his hand came away with blood. Luckily, it was on the side opposite the still-healing gash he'd sustained in the earthquake at Zoo Atlanta. Now he'd have matching scars.

Remembering Cu and Hope, he twisted in his seat. The protective padding had been raised and he could see Cu standing at attention in his cage. The hound's worried eyes were fixed on Lugh, and he yipped twice when he saw Lugh's face.

Reassured, Lugh peered up gingerly at the attendant. "I think so. It sounds like we've landed."

"Yes, in France. We're at the Carpiquet Airport near Caen." Sirens wailed in the distance. "The first class door was disabled in the turbulence, so we're unloading passengers through the midsection. That cut doesn't look deep, but you might have a concussion. I suggest you get it checked by one of the medics inside."

"But my animals. I need to claim them."

"Well, it's up to you. I can bandage it for you. But if I were you, I'd have this seen about."

While she cleaned the wound and dressed it, Lugh surveyed the scene. His pod mate and the other first class passengers appeared to be unharmed. Most stared blankly, clutching bags and coats to their chests while they waited to debark. Others spoke quietly into cellphones.

Thanking the attendant, Lugh sat back in his seat and held his throbbing head in his hands until she returned with a small bottle of water and a package of aspirin. He ripped the pack open, emptied it in his mouth, and twisted the cap off the bottle to wash it down. A wave of nausea threatened to heave it back up.

At an announcement from the captain, the first-class passengers cheered and stood to deplane. Lugh tried, but his legs were wobbly. So, clinging to the seat, he hauled himself up and held on to step into the aisle. This time, his legs held.

Flattening against the seat so others could pass, Lugh reached into the overhead bin to retrieve his suitcase, wincing when the weight and motion made his head throb harder.

Willing the aspirin to hurry and take effect, Lugh reassured the two Druid elders, then hurried down the Jetway and into the terminal to watch them unload.

Heavy rain from a sky bruised black lashed the workers and the tarmac. A forked streak of lightning shot from the sky, and Lugh jerked back from the window when it struck the runway with a clapping boom. Thunder reverberated through the small terminal.

Lugh eyed the overhead monitor, waiting for it to change from French to English. Then, locating his baggage turnstile, he joined the crowd heading toward customs.

Once that was accomplished, Lugh ducked into a bathroom where he inspected the bandage over the new cut. The flight attendant had done a good job of dressing the wound. Lugh washed his hands and face, careful not to get the gauze wet, and thought of his cell phone. In the chaos, he had forgotten to turn it on.

He moved toward the turnstile as it powered up. There was a message from an unknown number, one from Morgan, and another from Cybele. Then a loud yip demanded his attention.

Waiting impatiently in their cages, were Cu and Hope. The wolfhound danced and yipped with excitement, while Hope ignored Lugh to lick her already-clean fur.

Lugh listened to the voice mail from Cybele with glee. Brian was alive. And in North Carolina.

Eager now, Lugh listened to the message from the unknown number and laughed at Brian's short, but disturbing, message. His nephew was safe in Blowing Rock, North Carolina, with the girl who had rescued him, a Fomorian from UnderEarth named Ethnui. Morgan was paying for their hotel rooms and transportation to Atlanta.

The last part was garbled, but it sounded like the lizard men were plotting to take over Earth and eat all the humans.

Lugh shuddered and checked the time. It was just after seven in the morning—nighttime on the East Coast. But Brian's mom, Cybele, was on this side of the Atlantic. Still, his call to her rolled to voice mail.

AT WIT'S END

Patrika Tolbert slammed the receiver onto its base. Latoya had installed the land line because Patty kept getting prank calls on her cell. They had replaced it twice, opting for new numbers both times. But the loonies somehow kept finding Patty.

Of course, it was her own fault. She shouldn't have shared the dreams she'd begun having while living with Shalane Carpenter with a reporter. But they were so real, people needed to know. Didn't they?

Unfortunately, it had backfired. Rather than doing something about the upcoming attack, the Federal Bureau of Investigations had hauled Patty in and interrogated her like a common criminal.

Now she couldn't get the vision of last night's dream out of her mind. The Draco, Ishkur, had been killed right in front of her.

Well, not *her*, exactly. In her dreams, she was the one named Nergal, and both he and his companions had been ambushed by their own kind. Then, Ishkur was skewered by an instrument used for jousting in medieval times, and there had been so much blood.

Patty shivered and buried her head in her hands. She could still see Ishkur's blood spurt and feel her own agony as a blade slashed across her, or Nergal's, face.

She flipped on the television and ran through the channels, searching for something to take her mind off the nightmare. They always felt so real. She paused on a local station where the news anchors swapped good-natured barbs. Then the perky blond read the teaser.

"Next up, we'll go to Sunrise Hospital in Las Vegas, Nevada, where Reverend Shalane Carpenter is in critical condition following her collapse onstage at the MGM Grand."

Shocked, Patty sagged into a chair and stared blankly at the television where two doughnuts danced and sang.

Shalane was in the hospital. Patty should have stayed.

It had to be those awful headaches. Had they returned like Patty's dreams? She stared at the screen. Should she go to Shalane? Try to make things right?

Latoya would be happy about that. Since Patty's interview, the singer turned actress had been increasingly withdrawn. They didn't have a sexual relationship. Latoya treated Patty like a friend. Or a younger sister. During Patty's first week in Los Angeles, Latoya had taken her everywhere, even to the studio to watch Latoya shoot her latest film.

But when the crew and actors recognized Patty from the L.A. Times article or the ancillary pieces it spawned, Latoya stopped bringing her to the studio. And when it happened in public, she stopped taking Patty anywhere. Since then, life had pretty much sucked.

The only place Patty went was the restaurant. There, she dressed up as Marilyn Monroe, a femme fatale from long ago. Yes, it was a high-end establishment frequented by actors and the rest of Hollywood's beautiful people. And the tips were great. But it was a far cry from the scene she'd experienced before the interview.

The commercial ended. While the newscasters discussed the weather, Patty's thoughts wandered. Shalane had rescued Patty from that bar in San Diego. Then, after a night of eye-opening sex, she offered to take Patty on tour with her.

That had been the beginning of a magical few weeks. For the first time in Patty's life, she was spoiled and pampered.

The phone rang, and she nearly jumped from her skin. She eyed it warily. After the last prank call, she had decided she wouldn't answer it again. But her mother and Latoya were the only ones who should have the number. Patty lifted the receiver.

"Hello?"

"Patrika!" a male voice bellowed.

It was definitely not her mother. Or Latoya. The FBI, maybe?

"Yeeesss?"

"This is Commander Shibboleth, calling to let you know that the mothership is arriving this afternoon. I wanted to give you the coordinates to leave Earth with us." The jerk snickered, and in the background, someone laughed hilariously.

"NOT funny!" Patty shouted and slammed the phone in the cradle as the announcer mentioned Shalane's name.

Wheeling, she cranked up the volume and slumped into the chair. Shalane had collapsed a few minutes into her first night's performance in Las Vegas. She was in the hospital in a coma, and her condition was critical.

When they cycled to the next story, Patty stared at the screen, thinking. She still had the cash and credits she nicked from Shalane, plus her tips and earnings from the restaurant.

Hurrying to the closet, she reached for the black thigh-high boots Shalane had bought. Extracting the yellow bandana, she opened the small box, removed its contents, and laid the money out to count.

Sure enough, it was all there, all two thousand, one hundred and forty-nine dollars. Enough to buy a ticket to Las Vegas with plenty left over for when she returned to L.A.

Assuming she decided to come back.

Accessing the travel app, she found the bullet train that departed LAX for Vegas every two hours. There were also hourly flights. Either way, she would have to pay in person, so fly it was.

Patty contacted Latoya's limo service, hastily throwing clothes, shoes, toiletries, and her makeup bag into a suitcase. Then, she texted Latoya to let her know she would be in Las Vegas for a few days.

She thought of texting Shalane, but the woman was in a coma. She called instead, hoping Cecil or one of Shalane's employees would answer.

When it rolled to voice mail, Patty left a message, then followed up with a text for good measure before calling in sick to the restaurant.

DEATH SENTENCE

Emily woke, senses acutely sharpened. She was in a hard bed rather than the chair in which she had fallen asleep. Tienu's magic, she assumed. The quiet was filled with barely perceptible sighs and mutters that she'd figured were the fire dragon. But when she finally sat up, he was gone.

Fear nibbled at Emily. The dragon had said he would take her to Awen's glade. He would have to come back for her do that.

At least the room felt cozy. A fire glowed in a fireplace, supplying a bit of light and knocking the worst of the chill from the room. But where was the dragon? And odder, how had the enormous thing fit into what she could now see was a small room?

Puzzled, Emily drew the blanket to her chin and studied her surroundings. There were other differences as well. Tienu had apparently made some changes after she had fallen asleep. Either that, or he'd whisked her to a different room.

The chairs were gone, replaced by the bed and fireplace, and the room was enclosed rather than cave-like. But the remains of the meal Tienu had provided were still there on the wooden table.

On a nearby peg, hung a heavy robe. She slipped from the bed, shivering, and pulled it over her head, hugging the warm fabric to her. Thus enveloped, she turned her backside to the fire. That quieted her shivers, but Emily's stomach growled. She popped a strawberry in her mouth and nibbled a cold croissant.

Something about the place seemed familiar.

Noticing a narrow door, she peered into a tiny closet filled with women's things, mostly dresses. All were of a similar cut and style, loose and flowing, in soft, natural fibers.

She withdrew a long gown of supple, forest-green material that felt like velvet. The bodice was hand-embroidered with the tree of life, its roots reaching into flowing waters. Emily fingered the rich material and had an overwhelming urge to try it on.

Shrugging out of the robe and her clothes, she shivered and slipped the dress over her head then smoothed it into place. It struck her at the ankles, and was a perfect fit. Emily added a pair of brown suede, moccasin-style boots that enveloped her feet and hugged her calves. Again, a perfect fit.

On the other side of the closet was an opening to an even smaller room. This one held a free-standing tub, a dressing table with a bowl and pitcher of water, and a short stool. Candles blazed in an overhead candelabra. Odd. Had Tienu provided the light, too?

Pouring water into the bowl, Emily brushed her teeth and took a mini bath, grateful she'd brought toiletries. Then, gazing at her reflection in an ornate, wavy mirror, she did a double-take. Her hair was longer—at least two inches more than yesterday when she had left Zephyr Cay.

She stared, astounded. What the heck? She studied scarlet ringlets that now swept below her shoulders. Not the strangest thing that had happened to her lately, but still.

Fastening the wool cloak, Emily slung her backpack over her shoulder and searched for a passage to the castle. She might as well investigate while she waited for Tienu.

Fishing the flashlight from her bag, she passed from one dank room to another. Emily didn't expect much. She had learned from the research she had done at Wren's Roost that Chateau Falaise was a tourist attraction, but had fallen into ruin centuries ago.

Emily shuddered. So, who had lit the sconces that blazed every hundred yards? Surely not the fire dragon. He wouldn't know that Emily would wake early and explore.

She passed through a wide entryway into a dimly lit dirt corridor, rejoicing when she spied a flight of stairs leading upward. She shouldered the backpack and climbed.

At the top, was a heavy wooden door. The iron latch squeaked when Emily lifted it, but the door creaked open despite its considerable weight.

Cautious, she peered up and down a long hallway. Doors lined both sides. She slipped through the opening to stand in the hall, wondering which way to go. Voices decided for her.

Her heart thumped wildly as she hurried in the opposite direction to duck inside one of the doors. A pungent odor accosted her, and she pinched her nose to block the smell.

The voices grew louder, then passed her by. Two males, one younger, one older, both speaking French. Emily's heart pounded. The castle should be abandoned.

When the voices subsided, she stole down the corridor, coming upon an ancient kitchen. A large fire blazed in one corner. Laughter burst from the rear, and Emily gasped and scampered up a nearby staircase to find herself in another part of the chateau. Up here, it was warmer and the air was fresher.

A pimply boy in knee britches dashed from a doorway, nearly knocking Emily over. He stopped short, mouth gaping, then turned and ran back into the room.

"I found her, I found her. The witch is here."

Utensils and plates clattered, and chairs scraped across stone. That must be the dining room.

Emily ran down a long flight of steps into the dark. But this wasn't the kitchen. She huffed, pausing to catch her breath. But a hand crept from behind and covered her mouth.

Squeaking, Emily tried to jerk away, but her attacker yanked her close, hissing, "Shhh. It is you for whom they search. Don't make a sound unless you wish to be caught." The man's accent was thick and familiar, sounding much like Hope, the Druid elder.

Stifling the urge to drop and punch her captor in the nuts, she nodded. He loosened his grip, but didn't let go.

Then heavy boots clomped down the staircase, and the mysterious man pressed Emily to the shadowy floor.

He crouched above her and yelled up the stairs, "I searched the caves and lower floor. The witch is not here." Wiry and lean, the man was little more than a boy. Maybe nineteen, if that.

The boots stopped above them.

"Suits me. This place gives me the creeps." Reversing direction, the guard stomped up as loudly as he had descended.

"Who are you?" Emily whispered.

The boy put a finger to her lips. When the sounds of pursuit faded, he leaned closer.

"You are in danger, mi' lady."

"In danger? Why? Who are you? And, who do you think I am?"

The boy blushed in the low light and looked at her sideways.

"I am Jehan, vassal of Duke William. And everyone knows you are his mistress, Awen."

Eyeing him with interest, Emily played along.

"Why are Duke William's guards searching for me?"

"The master is in England, and the Duchess has issued a warrant for your arrest. You're to be hanged, mi' lady." The boy stared unhappily at his boots. "As a Druid witch."

The breath left Emily with a whoosh. This couldn't be happening. Had that tricksy dragon sent her back to Awen's time? Was she in the eleventh century? Emily shivered and wrapped her arms around her shoulders.

In the early days of her druid training, she had had frequent brownouts, periods when Awen would take over her thoughts, and sometimes even her body. Her nights had been punctuated by Awen's dreams. Could that be happening again? Had she dream-walked into another millennium?

Pinching her arm, Emily winced. She would not be waking from this nightmare.

More frightened than ever, she pressed Jehan. "And what would His Grace have you do? Throw me in the dungeon to await death?"

"No, mi' lady. I am one of many sworn to protect you, even from the Duchess, though that be under the penalty of death. Now, I must return to my post before I am missed. Come. Follow me. You should be safe down here."

On high alert, Emily descended two flights of stone stairs, staying in the light emanating from his torch. She was doing okay until they reached the end of a dark, dingy passageway that stank of sickness and death. Jehan lit a wall torch and motioned to a door.

Emily planted her feet, cocking an eyebrow. She was not going in there, nor would she stay down here in the dark. She was about to say so when a gruff voice yelled something from the top of the staircase.

Yanking the door open, the boy hustled Emily inside as the clatter of boots approached.

"Hide here," Jehan hissed. "Stay quiet and someone will come for you soon."

He shut the door and a key turned in the lock. Emily's heart leapt into her throat. Would the boy betray her? But after a muffled exchange in French, two sets of boots retreated up the stairs.

Heart pounding and anxiety attack threatening, Emily fumbled for the latch and pushed. The door did not budge. She shoved again with all her might, but the door held tight. Her heart sank all the way to her toes. What had the fire drake gotten her into?

She peered at her surroundings in the tiny bit of light that leaked through the slats. With terror gnawing at her frayed nerves, she circled the tiny space. It was definitely a cell. In one corner, sagged a steel cot with no mattress. In another, a hole was dug into the floor. She gagged when the stench of human waste wafted from below.

Returning to the door, Emily tried pushing, then pulling, then prying it open—all to no avail. Despairing, she sank to the floor, back against the slats, and closed her eyes to think. Drawing her knees to her chin, she hugged them close and dashed away an errant tear.

For the moment, she was safe. Awen's boots and robe should keep her warm enough to avoid hypothermia. For a few hours, anyway. A tiny hint of light bled through the cracks, and she had her flashlight and a couple of emergency candles should the need arise. But what would happen to her if the guards returned?

As her concern grew stronger, Emily let the tears flow. What if they marched her to the gallows? Or worse, what if Emily escaped but couldn't get back to her own time like that woman in the old Outlander shows?

Wiping her tears with the hem of Awen's dress, Emily pondered her alternatives. She could use magic to get out of the cell. But then what? She thought of Lugh MacBrayer and wished he was here with her. He had become her rock during druid training, Emily's go-to for anything she couldn't do or comprehend. And, yes, he had even stolen her heart.

Now, she was imprisoned in the eleventh century beneath William the Conqueror's chateau and had a sneaking suspicion she would soon be hanging from Matilda's gallows if she didn't find a way out.

A warmth drew Emily's attention. She touched her thigh and felt two hard lumps. The otter stone nestled in the pocket of the woolen robe. Beside it was the talisman Losgann had given her. Remembering that day on Zephyr Cay lifted Emily's spirits.

She extracted the stones and cradled them between her palms. Warmth spread through her. Then, Losgann's words came to her. His stone was imbued with powerful magic and provided protection. But the Frog Elder had also said Emily could use it to call him in times of need.

Dragging herself to a standing position, Emily clutched the stone to her chest, emptied her mind, and then called out to the frog elder.

"Losgann, Oh Great One, I need your help. I am a captive in Awen's caves below Chateau Falaise, but worse, I am in another century. I fear for my life and the world's fate should I die or remain outcast."

A quiet 'thwap' startled Emily. Just outside the circle of light seeping from the door came three short croaks, a pause, and three more. Then, Losgann, the frog Elder, hopped into sight.

He croaked and bowed. "I am here, Master Druid."

Hope surged inside her. Even across time, the Elder had heard and responded. Could she reach the Dragon Keepers the same way?

"Of course, mi' lady," the elder croaked, having read her mind. "Each of us is attuned to you. We are bound to serve you in whatever manner you desire or need."

Emily squatted. "Can you get me out of this prison? Maybe transport me to Beli?"

"No, but you can."

The frog's yellow eyes peered at Emily, flicked to the door, then back at her. There was a sudden scrape of boots, and the latch snicked.

Gulping, she slipped behind the door as it creaked open, and Losgann spoke in her mind.

"No need to hide. Help has arrived."

A flaming torch appeared, then a grizzled head came into view.

"Henry is Duke William's most faithful servant," the frog pronounced out loud. "He will lead you to safety."

An older man dressed in a gray and blue uniform entered. Spying Emily, he closed the door quietly and bowed. Then, he stood at attention, though slightly bent.

"Be stealthy," Losgann croaked. "The guards have been doubled, and they would like nothing more than to offer you up as a prize to Duchess Matilda. You have the benefit of the dark, but first light is not far away. Make haste."

The man bowed. "Follow me, mi' lady,"

"Gladly," she murmured. "But, I need to retrieve my belongings."

His bushy gray eyebrows lifted, etching the wrinkles deeper into Henry's forehead.

"If you must," he grumbled. "Where did you leave them?"

"In the small bedroom in Awen's suite."

Eyeing her oddly, Henry shuffled from the cell. Emily thanked Losgann, and followed Henry down the corridor and up a flight of stairs. At the landing, he paused.

Emily glanced both ways, then pointed to the left. "I think it's that way, but I'm not positive."

The servant hobbled in that direction, and Emily followed closely. Above and below them, sounds of the search rang out.

Soon they reached the archway leading to Awen's suite. Emily slipped inside and availed herself of the privy, then stuffed her clothes in her pack. She hung the woolen robe on its hook and rifled in the closet for the heavy cloak she'd seen earlier.

Wrapping it around her, she fastened it at the throat, draped her backpack on one arm, and slipped into the corridor to join the old man.

As they hurried through the dusty passageways, Emily heard a loud crash from somewhere below and could just make out the cries of the soldiers.

With a fresh burst of energy, Emily scrambled up a flight of stairs behind her rescuer, then another and another. By the time they arrived at a skinny door, Emily was out of breath. She passed through the narrow archway behind Henry, and a blast of frigid air struck her face, drying her flop sweat instantly and giving her a bad case of the shivers.

Crouching low to the flagstone, Emily wrapped her arms around her shoulders, rocking back and forth until the chills let go. Then she followed Henry, quietly slipping from one shadow to another as they made their way around the castle.

Until a guard materialized from the shadows.

With a sharp intake of breath, Emily flattened against the wall, adjusting her hood to better hide her face.

"Halt!" the sturdy guard commanded.

Henry kept shuffling toward him.

"Halt or I shall run you through!" The guard raised his sword.

Emily held her breath and pressed against the cold, rough stone, grateful for the moonless night.

"Hold up, sonny boy. It's Henry, William's valet, out for my early morning stroll."

The guard lowered his blade and lifted his visor.

"Take care, old man. I almost ran you through with my sword. You know none are allowed out at this hour, especially when a prisoner is on the loose."

Henry hesitated. Emily wondered if he would argue, but he turned and slowly plodded back in her direction holding his torch low to the ground.

Before the light could strike her, Emily separated from the wall and slipped around a corner out of the guard's sight. Then hounds bayed, and soldiers poured from a nearby gate, trapping them in between.

Henry rushed past her and slipped through the door they had exited earlier. She was shaking when she paused inside to catch her breath.

Then voices sounded above them.

Terrified, Emily padded quietly back down the staircases behind Henry. At the bottom, the servant clutched her elbow. He leaned close to whisper something in French, and she felt better. The effect reminded her of Aóme and the necklace the crone had given her in Zephyr Cay.

Emily reached for the ruby nestling beneath her bodice, and twisted Aóme on her finger, chuckling. She had amulets at her disposal yet had forgotten the most powerful ones. She shouldered the backpack and gripped her cloak together.

"I'm ready," she murmured, and was shocked when it came out as, "Je suis prête."

The valet nodded approval and led the way. She gritted her teeth, shutting down the fear, as they descended deeper and deeper into the bowels of the castle.

Finally they reached a narrow passage that stank to high heaven. Emily gagged and held her nose, fighting the urge to throw up.

Henry gestured toward a crack.

Horrified, Emily eyed the opening from whence the stench spewed. It appeared too narrow, but William's aged valet turned sideways and squeezed inside it, nonetheless.

Desperate for a different solution, Emily squinted up and down the corridor, hoping for another way out. But a hound bayed overhead, and boots sounded on the staircase.

Fearing worse, Emily tried to slip into the crevice, but her backpack got hung as the soldiers neared the bottom. Shrugging it off, she held it to her side, clapped her other hand over her mouth and nose, and crab-walked into the crack. She made it halfway on her tiptoes, then let go of her nose to breathe.

The odor of feces and urine hit full force, nearly knocking Emily down. Her throat constricted, and she retched hard. Then, trying to keep quiet and control her gag reflex while moving quickly, she pretended she was wading through sticky mud. It might've worked, too, if not for the god-awful smell.

Another spider web Henry had managed to bypass clung to Emily's face and hair. She shuddered, praying its owner stayed behind rather than hitching a ride with her.

When they finally reached the other end, she sucked in a slightly less-offensive breath and caught a glimpse of starlight. She was about to push on when Henry halted abruptly.

The tramp of booted feet sounded a few yards away. Emily closed her eyes, lowered her head, and quieted her breath until the soldiers passed. Then they slipped from the crevice into the waning night.

Below them, a nearly vertical incline dropped straight to the ground. Above them on the ramparts, guards called to one another in clipped tones. Light blazed from the chateau windows. Emily peered down. They couldn't possibly scale that slope.

But Henry turned and followed the course of the sewer. Groaning, Emily followed.

Where it dipped beneath a pomegranate bower, Henry bent back thorny branches and motioned for her to enter.

Ducking, she winced when some of the spikes pierced her garb. She rubbed the wounds and followed Henry down the steep slope through scree that filtered a steady stream of stinking, putrid human waste. Then a brainstorm hit her, and Emily whispered a simple spell.

The chilly wind shifted, lifting the stench and blowing it in the opposite direction.

Inhaling deeply of the sweeter air, Emily wished she had thought of the spell earlier. Would she ever get used to knowing magic?

When they finally reached level ground, Emily craned her neck to look up. Chateau Falaise loomed high above them. The first light of day flushed the sky behind it. She sighed and whispered a prayer of thanks. Then, Emily turned and followed Henry along a barely discernable path that led to the woods.

As the trees closed around her, a hubbub arose. Emily paused to look back at the chateau, and urgency propelled her deeper into the forest. A regiment of soldiers spilled from the gate. She hurried to warn Henry, who quickened the pace.

A MYSTERY TO SOLVE

"**K**henko Blitherstone, all you have done since coming home is sit in this den watching old reruns of Grace and Frankie."

He winced as his mother drew the drapes and stared at him in the too-bright light.

In a gentler tone, Val continued. "I've kept my silence because you seem to be in mourning."

And Khenko was. His heart ached so much he thought it might rupture. But no such luck. He was stuck in Princeton, a whale beached on a dry, lifeless shore. Weary as only the grieving can be, he eyed the TV dolefully.

"I *am*, Ma."

Sinking deeper into the timeworn sofa, he sighed. Khenko had been back in Princeton for a couple of days, but it felt like he'd been away from his beloved Atlantean Center for an eternity.

He sighed again and chugged the beer he'd just opened. Alcohol was a poor stand-in for marijuana, but Khenko needed something to dull the worm of loss that ate his insides.

His mother eyed him, as if trying to figure out how to best approach her wayward son.

"I get that."

She was up to something. Khenko set the can on the end table, folded his long, lean legs, and sat up straight.

"You get that, but?"

She cut her eyes to the television, and back at him.

Taking the hint, he paused the program and tilted his head to study his mother.

Val Blitherstone was dressed in business attire, which meant she was on her way to or from class, or maybe a meeting. Both she and his father were professors at Princeton University.

"What is it, Ma?"

A gleam appeared in Val Blitherstone's eyes. She sat sideways to face Khenko. Taking his long, thin hand, Val held it to her cheek before curling his knuckles under to kiss them lightly. Finally, she wrapped her hands around his and settled them on his knee.

"I hate seeing you like this, Bird."

The pet name was a nod to his tall, lanky form and Khenko's favorite Sesame Street character. His animal totem also happened to be a crane. A nighttime visit from Corr the Crane had set the events in motion that had propelled Khenko back to Princeton.

"I know, mom, I know." Then he mimicked her nasally tone. "Get up and *do something*."

"Exactly," she laughed. "It's good advice. And that's a pretty darn good imitation, too."

He laughed, enjoying the banter. Khenko had been gone for five years, during which he'd missed his mother and sister something fierce.

A smile played at the corners of Val's lips.

"What if I gave you a mystery to solve? Would that make you feel better?"

Khenko perked up. "Maybe. Whatcha got?"

She reached into her jacket pocket and extracted her cellphone to search for something, then handed it to Khenko.

He eyed the picture of an official-looking document and made it larger to read the accompanying memo. Surprised, he eyed his mother speculatively.

"Where'd you get this?"

There was a flicker of guilt before she scrunched her nose and brushed his cheek lightly with her fingertips.

"Does it matter, dear?"

Khenko reread the memo and the attached prophecy.

"What is this, Ma? And what does it have to do with me?"

Twirling a dark strand of hair around her finger, Val laughed nervously.

"Nothing, maybe. Or everything. It came across my desk a few years back when I first became head of the Ancient Studies Department. It is a copy of a copy of a copy, but the original document is written in Anglo-Saxon Runic. A staffer translated it after the message was delivered to the White House in 2012."

Khenko peered closer at the documents. He did not recognize the symbols or the language contained in the original, but the translation read like a prophecy. He read it aloud.

"When Armageddon threatens,

The sleeping one will wake.
Along the same meridian
The fallen steps in place.
One coast will gather light and kind
The other dark, despair,
But each will yield its suffering
To a world laid waste with fear.
The call will soon be answered
Old wounds doth fester e'er,
The battle begun before Earth was wrought
Must be won in the helm of the sufferer's heart
And from thence, She leaps forth
Once again."

Shivering, Khenko looked at his mother.

"Is this real?"

She unwound the hair from her finger and pushed the rest from her face.

"Yes, it is real. And get this. Thirty years ago, a woman of advanced years bypassed security to deliver it to the White House. That would have been a major feat, even back then. But after she delivered the prophecy, she promptly disappeared." Val's eyes narrowed.

"Disappeared? As in 'poof?'"

"Yep. Disappeared. Into thin air." Her dark eyes gleamed. "And to this day, no one knows how she pulled it off."

Khenko ogled the document on her phone again.

"So you're telling me this prophecy is authentic?"

"It is. I, umm…" She looked like she wanted to say more but shook her head and reached for the phone. Opening a different screen, she handed it back.

"Now, read this."

He read aloud, "The Azores Islands," then looked up, grinning. "I've always wanted to go there."

His mom nodded, eyebrows arched. "Read the article."

"Just west of Portugal's Azores Islands, disturbances continue in the Newfoundland Basin. On the westernmost island of Corvo, ancient underwater tunnels are becoming increasingly visible despite rising ocean levels. Could it be that that portion of the Mid-Atlanta Ridge, a series of mountains and volcanoes and clashing tectonic plates, is rising out of the sea?" Khenko eyed his mother, curiosity piqued, then continued reading.

"Only something of this magnitude could explain how the tunnels and other island treasures, under water for the last many decades, can now be seen. Or, as the local Corvinos say, 'It's a miracle, a sign end times are near.'"

Rolling his eyes, Khenko scrolled to the bottom past the ads and related article links, then back up to the "It's a miracle" line. Excitement coursed through him. He cut his eyes to his mother. Her smirk hinted at self-satisfaction.

She knew his Spidey senses were tingling. Or, in his case, crane knowledge had ruffled Khenko's feathers. Taking a screenshot of the article and the memo with the prophecy, he emailed them to himself and relinquished her phone.

Then, retrieving the emails on his iBlast, he waved it at her. "What do you know about all this?"

She smiled, and it melted some of the ice that had formed around Khenko's heart upon leaving Zephyr Cay. He hugged her close, rocking her gently on the pale grey microfiber sofa.

"God, Mom, I've missed you. I had forgotten how well you know me." He loosened his grip but kept an arm around her shoulders. "Tell me—" his voice broke. He cleared the lump and tried again. "What else do you know?"

Her eyes danced. "Only what I was shown in my dream."

"Mother!" Khenko huffed and let her go. "You do know that in layman's terms, dreams mean nothing. You *know* nothing. Was it a sleeping dream or a waking dream? Were you musing or meditating?"

"Oh, Khenko." It was Val's turn to huff "What difference does it make? Dreams reveal that which cannot be discerned in the light of day. Like the one you had of your crane totem."

Khenko nodded reluctantly. Her statement was true.

"You've been at loose ends since you arrived. Now I'm throwing you a lifeline. Grab it, Khenko. Shake off this funk and *do something*."

Khenko winced, and her reassuring hand patted his shoulder.

Her tone soothed. "You left Zephyr Cay, the place you call your heart home, on a whim. A whim is not a vision, Khenko, but it *is* the beginning of one. You told me an inner voice insisted you come back to Princeton. To your family. 'Go home,' you told us it said."

Missing her point, Khenko zoned out, gaze flicking to the mantel. 4:20 on the dot. Doobie time. If only he had one.

"Khenko?"

"Yeah, Ma?"

"Are you listening?"

"Yes, ma'am. You were talking about the voices that told me to come home."

He thought of the dawn ferry ride from the Atlantic Vortex. He had come to, ship soaked, and rocking in the swells. Spooked, Khenko had gunned it to the Atlantean Center, nursing the mother of all hangovers and bombarded by voices.

"It was weird, but there were several voices. Each telling me to go home. To prosper, be well, live long, and, oh yeah—populate the Earth with my kind, whatever that means. But the predominant theme was 'go home.' So I did."

"And my *dreams* are my voices. Have you ever known them to be wrong?"

Thinking back, Khenko shook his head and chuckled.

"Only about Brianna."

Val laugh-snorted and slapped her knee. "Thank the Maker for that!"

"Seriously," Khenko agreed. "But, yes, you usually are right. So, tell me, what did you see, Gnóha?"

His mother flushed, pleased by his use of the Iroquois endearment. She peered out the window and his gaze followed. The sun shone brightly, and a breeze rustled the fully-leafed trees.

"I need some air," she murmured, rising. "Don't go anywhere. I'll be right back."

She left the room, and returned a few minutes later with a goblet of red wine, most likely a full-bodied Cabernet. She held it aloft in one hand. In the other, she held up a small metal pipe.

"Whoa. Is that what I think it is?" His mother didn't smoke, and his father considered marijuana evil, though it was medicinal and perfectly legal.

She nodded and handed the pipe to Khenko, whose grin stretched wider.

Clutching it in his fist, he followed her to the backyard, a forested oasis abutting the back holes of Springdale Golf Club, then into the greenhouse where he ooo'd and ahh'd over her prize Dahlia blooms. Finally, she swished her wine, held it to her lips, and led him out into the heat of the day.

He waved the loaded pipe. "Got a light for this thing?"

Patting her pants pockets, Val produced a hot-pink, tiger-striped Bic lighter and wiggled her fingers in a 'gimme' gesture.

Shocked, he handed his mother the pipe. "Knock *me* over with a feather," he mumbled when she lit the pipe and inhaled.

Then Val passed it back to Khenko, eyes bulging.

He took a toke and did the same, but she waved it off. "That's enough for me."

"Lightweight." He let out a cloud of smoke, then took another toke, smiling serenely as the calm spread through his neck and arms, relaxing his shoulders and body.

"Thank you, Gnóha, I love you."

He led her to a cast-iron bench nestled against the fence. It faced a side yard littered with clover and daisies that bloomed profusely though it was not yet May. Summer seemed to come earlier every year.

The pines rustled in the wind. Khenko looked up as it reached a crescendo. Then it quieted again. Every hair on Khenko's body stood at attention. He turned to his mother, who had settled beside him.

A golden glow enveloped them both. Its shimmering evanescence framed the moment in exquisite detail—the scent of pine and old-fashioned petunias, the drone of bees, the caress of the breeze against his face, and his mother's aura glowing brightly.

"Will you tell me about your vision, Gnóha?"

Val shuddered visibly and closed her eyes. When she opened them again, they looked inward.

"In the vision, I am someone else, someone named Druantia." She let go of a long breath, and Khenko did, too.

He had heard that name before. As his subconscious searched for the memory, he urged her on.

"I am a bird."

"HUH?" Khenko snorted and slapped his knee. "Now, you're just messing with me." Then he sobered.

Not that long ago, he had literally transformed into a bird. Or had he merged with his totem, Corr the Crane?

"What kind of bird?" he asked more respectfully.

Val scrunched her nose, aware again.

"An ibis. Does it matter?"

He wagged his head, and she continued.

"An ibis, but also a goddess. It is a bit confusing, but the gist of my dream is that something is very wrong, Khenko. I cannot tell your father. He—"

She hesitated, gazing up into the swaying pines. "Your father is ill, Khenko. I'm sure you have noticed."

The uneasy snake that lived in Khenko's gut stirred. Val straightened and drew a deep breath.

"But, this is not about that."

Khenko wanted to press her, but she shook her head.

"Later, Bird. I need to get this other out first."

He leaned back against the honeysuckle-laden fence. His mother was a powerful woman in her own right.

"Tell me, then."

She closed her eyes, and the timbre of her voice deepened.

"I am Druantia. My mate is Thoth."

Val's eyes flew open, and she was herself again.

"Khenko, I looked it up. Thoth was a Sumerian. An immortal. But this is the freakiest part. He and Druantia are still alive, living inside Earth. They are desperately trying to prevent some awful event. One that will trigger a pole shift. Those inside Earth will be fine. But up here on the surface, the catastrophe will be worldwide."

His mother went silent and closed her eyes, horror contorting her face.

After another long moment, she sobbed, "Few will survive."

Khenko's blood chilled. Untwining long fingers from the metal bench, he flexed them and shuddered.

"That sounds pretty farfetched, Gnóha."

But chill bumps roved his entire body, telling him otherwise. "Is there a way to stop it from happening?"

"That's just it. If Druantia and Thoth do not succeed, there is no other solution." Val wrapped her arms around her shoulders.

Khenko felt the blood drain from his face.

"There has to be. Otherwise, why would Druantia tell you this? Do they have no answers? This ancient stranger just tapped you on the shoulder long distance from somewhere deep inside the earth to say, 'Oops, you're all about to die'?" He shook his head, angered. "That is just cruel. And it makes no sense."

"I agree." His mother studied the pea gravel path. "Except," she glanced sideways at Khenko, "they did show me an old experiment that went awry. It is beneath Earth's surface at the apex of the

Bermuda Triangle, about halfway between here and England. You'll never believe where."

"Oh, I bet I can guess. Is it beneath Corvo Island in the Azores?"

"Yes! But if Druantia and Thoth succeed, the pole shift will be delayed. Maybe for another millennia or more."

Khenko stood and stretched, mind racing. "So, there's our answer."

But her expression dashed his hopes.

She reached for his hand, and stood up, too.

"Apparently, they have been trying for centuries with no success. But I was thinking, with your help, or *our* help, they could succeed." She looked off toward the house. "I'm pretty sure you are the reason Druantia contacted me."

Chills ran up Khenko's spine. "And the prophecy? How is that connected?"

A shadow passed over, and a cawing raven settled in one of the swaying pines.

"I believe so. I had not thought of that prophecy in years. But it was in my mind when I woke from Druantia's dream. They are connected somehow, I know it."

"Works for me." Khenko sighed. It was no crazier than any of the rest.

Val cleared her throat. "There's something else about the Azores. But you're not going to like it." She scrunched her nose and looked sheepishly through splayed fingers.

"Son, you were born in Corvo."

His jaw dropped. "I was… Huh? What? I was… *what?*"

"My dear boy, I'm sorry we never told you." She cradled his face between her hands, and leaned close. "But, you were not born here, you were born on Corvo."

Staring at her blankly, Khenko plopped to the bench.

"I'm sorry to spring it on you, Khenko. But, I think your voices were referring to Corvo, not Princeton."

"Corvo?" Khenko kept his tone quiet and controlled. He felt anything but. "The site of the disturbances *and* this so-called failed experiment?"

Val's eyes widened and he could swear his mother left her body as she gazed over his shoulder. Then her attention returned.

"Yes. That is where you are needed, Khenko. Not here in Princeton. Not," she started for the house," that I don't love having you home."

"But *is* it my home?" Hurt constricted Khenko's throat.

"*Khenko!*" Val flicked his arm with her fingertips. "Of course this is your home." She leaned close. "You may have been born elsewhere, but don't think for a minute this is not your home. It has always been, and will ever be yours, my son."

"VA-AAAL!" his father yelled from the porch.

LIFELINE

I t had taken some doing, but once Cybele explained Brian's situation over dinner, Elise agreed to rescue him from the FBI's clutches. It helped that her godmother was itching to get out of the office and back into action. She'd been confined to a desk in Cheltenham after one too many clashes with their new, wet-behind-the-ears boss.

A sensitive and cantankerous odd bird, Elise Hester Johnson did not suffer fools. She was as tough as jerky, and only a few trusted friends in the agency knew she had an edge of fragility. The most decorated operative in AIA history, Elise had briefly accepted a directorship a decade ago, soon after Cybele joined the agency in Utah.

During Elise's short stint as director of the London branch, she had thoroughly and viciously cleaned house. Then, left with a skeleton crew of loyal agents, Elise had considered her job done and relinquished the promotion. *That* had earned Cybele's godmother a place in Alien Intelligence Agency history.

Elise had returned to the field by choice, and had remained there for the duration of her tenure. Until now. Her primary postings had been in Europe, but Elise had also served in Asia, India, Japan, and the U.S. Other than those, she rarely ventured stateside, except for critical Hester family meetings and the occasional orders to Washington or Utah.

Lucky for Cybele, Elise had been her mom's best friend and had a soft spot for Cybele. It was Elise who had facilitated Cybele's entry into the agency.

A lump rose in Cybele's throat. She swallowed hard, and braked for a red light. Her mom was long gone, victim of a random shooting at the local elementary school where she'd worked as a teacher. Three years later, the United States finally joined the world and outlawed private firearms.

Cybele patted the reassuring bump of her own sidearm underneath her jacket and stared out the window of the government vehicle. The law had not resurrected Cybele's mother. But, it *had* slashed the number of gunshot-related deaths in both citizens and law enforcement personnel by ninety percent.

Her cellphone vibrated and Cybele jumped. Snatching it from her pocket, she read the incoming text.

About to take off. Can't believe I let you talk me into this.

Cybele typed, *Oh, Elise, thank you for rescuing my baby boy. I owe you big time!*

When nothing else came through, Cybele dropped her phone beside her on the seat. If the flight from London to Charlotte, North Carolina, was on time, Elise would be on U.S. soil in less than nine hours.

Cybele shot a text to Brian's prepaid cell relaying the information, then floored it when the light finally changed, fishtailing through the intersection.

☼☼☼

The pilot barked instructions over the intercom. At the last minute, Elise had scored a seat on the force's newest stealth jet. The Quesst X5900 would fly them to North Carolina and back to RAF Fairford Air Base in about the same time as a standard one-way flight to the U.S.

Elise renewed her blocking spell, a simple charm Awen had taught her long ago. It filtered out extraneous thoughts and frequencies and worked well except in unusual cases—like with that asshole Banner. The jerk had no off-switch, and quite possibly, no soul.

The jet taxied to the runway, and Elise fitted a sleep mask over her eyes. Then, she began a meditation designed to empty the jumbled contents of her mind and body. When the jet purred from the runway, Elise Hester Johnson was fast asleep.

WILD RIDE

"**O**kay," Hamilton said aloud, "Our ride will be here soon. Since Morgan thought it fitting to use the FBI as a taxi service, it's crucial you have your stories straight. Do you?"

Brian and Ethnui had eaten a late lunch at the hotel restaurant. Now they waited outside for their ride.

"I think so." Brian fanned his face. It was even hotter this evening than it had been that morning. "I will tell them exactly what happened to me, except for the part about Ethnui being a Fomorian. We'll keep it simple and as close to the truth as possible."

Ethnui's head bobbed in agreement. "We will say that I am a seventeen year-old human. Not a Fomorian. That way, your government won't turn me into a lab rat."

Brian added, "Which they may try to do anyway. But we're hoping since we're children," Brian glanced at Ethnui apologetically, "they won't throw us in jail or detain us without a parent or guardian present."

"Yes, that!" Ethnui nodded emphatically, and her cap tilted to reveal the top of one pointed ear. Brian laughed.

"You can't do that in the car or we'll be busted."

Face flaming, Ethnui tugged the cap down and adjusted the pins holding it in place. "Maybe I should've gotten a different hat. This one is pretty and I really like it, but it doesn't fit well over my ears."

"Hmm, we can fix that."

Brian took her hand to lead her inside. According to the last text from Morgan, they should have enough time to buy another hat. But as the door closed behind them, a black sedan squealed into the drive and braked at the entrance.

"You'll have to make do with that one, Ethnui," Hamilton warned. "We're out of time. Be careful, though. Let's not get caught."

※—※—※

Brian had almost dozed off when the car jolted over a bump. There had been little conversation during the hour it had taken to drive from Blowing Rock to Hickory, North Carolina. When the agents did talk, it was in low tones not meant for the occupants of the back seat.

But at least there was no glass partition to make them feel like criminals—which they *weren't*. Neither had done anything wrong except escape from those awful lizard men. And what could be wrong with that?

The closer they got to Interstate 85, the heavier traffic grew. Ethnui had fallen asleep when they left Blowing Rock, but Brian kept fighting the urge. He was nodding off for the umpteenth time when a phone rang. Yawning, Brian straightened to look around. They were inching along the freeway in bumper-to-bumper traffic.

Agent Warren muttered into his phone, then to his partner. A thrill ran through Brian. Something was about to happen. Hopefully, it didn't involve him or Ethnui.

Sure enough, the flash of emergency lights bounced off the car in front of them. Brian braced for a collision, but Agent Warren whipped the sedan from the outer lane into a tiny opening in the right lane. Brian let go of his breath and glanced at the still-sleeping Ethnui.

He thought of waking her, but they'd had so little sleep in the last couple of weeks he couldn't bring himself to disturb her. Then the siren shrieked, and she bolted upright, looking about frantically. Brian grabbed her hand and squeezed reassuringly until the panic in her midnight-blue eyes quieted.

The sedan zigzagged through traffic, and Brian swayed against Ethnui. Then, they barreled down the emergency lane to the next off-ramp, lights flashing and siren blaring.

It appeared they were in for a wild ride. Ethnui scooted closer. He did the same.

Shoulders touching, he entwined his fingers with hers. She was taller than Brian and had long, slender hands, but his were wider and enveloped hers. Her lips parted in a shy smile and her eyes sparkled.

Agent Warren braked at the end of the ramp, throwing them forward. Then he gunned it and whipped through the red light, turning left under the bridge. Stomping the accelerator, he cut the

61

wheel sharply to slide sideways onto the ramp, heading back in the opposite direction as Brian and Ethnui clung to one another.

Traffic was not as heavy on this side. The agent wove from one lane to another, slipping in and out of the available gaps in the steady stream of cars. Brian strained against the seatbelt to lean forward until his chin rested between the two agents.

"What happened? Where are we going?"

Then his Adam's apple slammed into the seat when Agent Warren jammed the brakes and laid down on the horn. Goosing the sedan to swerve into the next lane, he barely avoided a collision with the tail-end of a bread truck.

Ethnui mewed, and Brian slid back in the seat to take her hand. He was thrilled, but her eyes were big O's of fright. Then, the traffic came to an abrupt standstill, and Agent Warren swung to the outside emergency lane.

He floored it again, and the vehicle fishtailed, spewing loose stones before catching and speeding past the line of stalled cars. The warning lights flashed and the siren squalled.

A squawk burst from the two-way radio. "Agents Warren and Jeter, your orders have changed. Report to the Charlotte field office immediately. What is your current location and ETA?"

Agent Jeter lifted the receiver. "We're on I-85 heading east toward Charlotte. ETA…" He glanced over at Warren, who shook his head. "We're bucking traffic. Not sure about our ETA. We'll get there as soon as we can." Warren slammed the brakes, and Jeter added, "Assuming Agent Warren doesn't kill us first." Then he holstered the radio and grabbed the chicken strap as Warren wormed into an open slot.

"What's happening?" Ethnui spoke so quietly Brian almost didn't hear her.

He shrugged his shoulders. "Dunno."

Traffic stopped, and she swayed against him as the car swerved back into the emergency lane.

The radio squawked again, then blared. "All cars report to Crowders Mountain State Park. Four subjects spotted near Kings Pinnacle Peak described as seven feet tall and wearing green, hooded jumpsuits. Approach with caution. Report when you have them in sight."

In the rearview mirror, Agent Warren eyed Brian and Ethnui. "You two sit back and hold on." Then, to Jeter, he said, "Tell dispatch we're detouring to the scene."

Jeter relayed the information, and Warren wrenched the wheel to squeal into a slot between a tractor-trailer and a cement truck. Then he cut to the next lane between a Lexus SUV and a Mini Cooper. The Lexus driver laid on his horn and shot them the finger.

Swerving into the emergency lane, Warren sped past the long line of evening commuters and barely slowed for the approaching exit. He executed a tight right at the end of the ramp, then wove in and out of two-lane traffic, siren blaring and emergency lights flashing.

Brian spotted a sign that said Highway 74. Warren hung a right on two wheels and gunned it down a side road, then turned left past a Baptist Church to cut through a golf course on a bumpy, two-lane blacktop. The road entered a forest, and Jeter killed the siren.

Soon they were winding up a mountain road in thinning traffic. They came up behind a Gastonia police cruiser and passed it in a short straightaway. Warren and Jeter threw up a hand to acknowledge the officers as they blew past.

Brian grinned, invigorated. But by the time Warren wheeled the car into a lot, Ethnui's face shone a pale shade of green, like she was ready to barf any minute.

The two-way radio squawked constantly as local law enforcement converged in the park to pursue what they jokingly referred to as 'lizard men.' Brian and Ethnui exchanged a look. Just wait until they got a load of the Dracs in person.

The agents left the car, instructing Brian and Ethnui to keep the doors locked and stay put. Five minutes later, Agent Jeter returned with a uniformed sheriff.

Jeter tapped on Brian's window, then opened the front door to lean in the car. "Son, me 'n Agent Warren are gonna be here a while. Sergeant Wallace and her partner have offered to drive you to the Charlotte field office. Would you mind going with them? We will pick you up in Charlotte when we're done here."

Not given another choice, Brian and Ethnui transferred to the back seat of the Sheriff's car.

As they threaded down the winding mountain road passing cruisers on their way to join the hunt, Brian yawned and texted his mom about the latest development. Then, weary to the bone, he fell asleep with Ethnui's head resting on his shoulder.

DEATH SLEEP

Reverend Shalane Carpenter lay very still. She had passed out on stage during a live performance; one of her worst fears realized. She tried to sit up, but couldn't. She was not in her throne chair, nor on the stage in Las Vegas. Instead, she was restrained in a glass chamber.

Why couldn't she move? Was she paralyzed? Was she in the hospital in some new-fangled MRI machine? That was the only thing that made sense.

But she'd had Magnetic Resonance Imaging before, and the machines weren't like this. Those had been long, tube-shaped contraptions in which Shalane had felt confined. But never had her arms and legs been immobilized.

Thankfully, the pain behind her eye had receded to a dull ache. But where was she? And, why was she strapped down? Had she hurt someone? Had she fought the paramedics?

Straining against the bonds, Shalane tried to turn her head, but even it was fixed in place. Fear seized her. Her heart thumped and her breathing quickened. She closed her eyes and attempted to recall the events leading up to this moment.

She remembered being late for her show in Las Vegas after finding Emily Hester for Mitchell. But Shalane had ended up losing the twit in the middle of the Caribbean. Then the flight to Las Vegas via Atlanta had been hell.

Shalane missed her connection and had to hop a flight to Dallas-Fort Worth. But heavy lightning and monsoon rains closed that airport until a window of calmer weather allowed them to land. Then, they waited for another plane to fly out.

To make matters worse, Shalane was running on no sleep, having indulged too much at Manny Chevitz's pig roast. She'd snatched a few restless hours on the plane and another in the Dallas Aero Lounge. But somewhere between DFW and McCarran International, the drilling pain behind Shalane's eye had returned with a vengeance, ending her several week reprieve.

She remembered being in the dressing room at the MGM Grand and hearing the opening strains of her signature song "Hallelujah." Shalane had stepped onto the stage amid the usual adulation—catcalls, applause, and stomping feet. She remembered singing all the verses, then speaking her opening remarks and settling onto her throne chair.

Then her eye had twitched, and an icepick-like pain had scrambled Shalane's brain. Nausea seized her, her body went stiff, and she crumpled in a heap.

But not in her chair.

Oh, no, Shalane had collapsed in the middle of the stage like an abandoned puppet.

Tears of embarrassment and shame trickled down her cheeks. What must her devotees think of her? What must the world? The performance had been being broadcast live, so everyone had seen the Reverend Shalane Carpenter collapse on stage.

She tried to wipe her rose, but her arms were tied. Literally. Which brought her back to the burning question—where in the hell was she and why the fuck was she strapped down?

She must be in a hospital. It was the only logical explanation.

But she'd been in the hospital before and never had it felt like she was lying on a cold rock.

Plus, where were the doctors and nurses? And where was all the fancy monitoring equipment? There was a noise, but she couldn't turn her head to see.

She struggled to hear a muffled conversation. Then suddenly, someone stood over her, and Shalane recoiled.

The face was not human. It was covered in greenish scales, like a snake or crocodile, and belonged to a tall, thin being with a large, round head and flashing red eyes. Fear seized Shalane again.

There was a pressure in her groin and a sharp pain. Shalane struggled to get away, but she couldn't move. The pain reverberated, radiating outward, and the stiletto-sharp agony behind her eye intensified. As it burrowed deeper into her brain, Shalane screamed. But no sound escaped her parched lips, not even a moan.

She wanted more than anything to press a hand to her groin and the other against her eye, not sure which hurt the most. But her efforts made the pain worse. She stopped struggling and gulped deep breaths, but that didn't lessen the agony either.

Finally, Shalane remembered her training. She mumbled a spell of protection, flinching when a similar being joined the first. She watched wild-eyed as they poked and prodded, speaking a guttural gibberish she couldn't understand. Who were they, and what did they want with her?

The larger-skulled being moved to stand behind Shalane. It looked down at her with kind eyes and brought his clawed hands to her head. Shalane writhed in dread, but he gently placed them against her temples, and for a moment, the pain lessened. Grateful, Shalane stared into the intelligent eyes, and a tear rolled down her cheek.

The being wiped it away gently with a clawed finger. Then it leaned closer and said something in a low voice, something calm and reassuring that Shalane could not understand. She felt a prick in her neck, and everything went black.

THE STYGIAN PLAINS

With one swift curse, the Cailleach enclosed the last two Keepers in ice, then leaned on her staff to admire her handiwork. The ruins of Beli Castle were an appropriate backdrop for Awen's four favorite dragons.

But she couldn't leave them here. Too many humans roamed Yr Wyddfa. Ancient magic hid Beli, and the memory curse was still upon the humans. But Bé couldn't be sure her prisoners would remain undetected.

Wrapping her cloak tighter, she hobbled in a circle around the dragons, then made the journey two more times. Finishing, she lifted her staff. Power surged into it, and she rammed the tip in the snow and muttered the words of an ancient spell. The frozen dragons disappeared from sight.

Bé poked her head into the Otherworld. Icy cocoons stretched across the Stygian Plains. Over centuries, she had searched them out, luring each to Beli under the pretense of a dragon meet. But of all the dragons, the four Keepers had taken the longest. Now, they, too, were trophies in Bé's dragon hoard.

She stepped her whole body into the Otherworld to stroll through her captives. The stage was set for victory for the first time since her exile thousands of years ago. Her victory. Her revenge.

But while the quest to end Druantia and her line had been Bé's driving force, each moment in AboveEarth took a significant toll. Her alliance with the Reptilians had allowed her to remain immortal. But she had not been to UnderEarth in a long time, and the years had been unkind.

One by one, death had taken her favorite consorts. Now Bé Chuille was alone. And though she prided herself on needing no mate, or anyone else, sex was her lifeblood.

To satisfy her libido, she had taken to copulating with the Dracos, and had found the creatures were even lustier than Bé. Lord Enlil's descendent, the original Nergal, had been her first. After that, she shied away from Enlil's line, preferring his brother,

Lord Enki. He and his hybrids, Shibboleth's line, made excellent mates. The only two she had not bedded were Mot and Maw.

She roamed the plain, weaving in and out of the frozen dragons. Draigs Tienu and a-Ur were the largest, but all were fierce. Most were in the throes of ice-sleep. But a few were conscious, and their eyes followed Bé as she moved through their midst. It was creepy, but knowing they were awake and watching gave Bé a massive jolt of pleasure. She despised the creatures and had bested each one.

She paused in front of Talav to study her newly sprung horns and wings. How and when had they sprouted? At the same time Ooschu developed legs?

But she was wasting time. Now that her dragon collection was complete, it was time to capture Awen. But first, she would contact Shibboleth.

Now *that* Drac was old. As the first-generation offspring of Lord Enki, Shibboleth had ruled over the Reptilians since their arrival on Earth. Like all of his kind, he despised humans and was obsessed with their extermination and claiming their world.

Twirling her staff, Bé shifted between worlds and hobbled to her hut. Soon, she would travel to UnderEarth to renew her youth. While there, she would strike a bargain with Shibboleth and his heir, Mot, and score a rowdy tumble with both. Then, she would return to the surface for Awen.

The anticipation of seducing Shibboleth's remaining spawn sent butterflies fluttering in Bé's belly. She pressed a hand against it, then let it trail between her legs where a delicious warmth bloomed.

COMBING THE CAY

Belly full and thirst slaked, Mitch pushed his plate to the center of the outdoor picnic table. Locals surrounded him, chattering gaily amongst themselves. Mitch knew a spattering of conversational Spanish—enough to get around in other countries—but it took him a few minutes to figure out they weren't speaking Spanish. It was obvious, however, they were discussing Mitch.

Leaning back on the bench, he sipped the rich Bahamian coffee and sighed. If it weren't so damned hot, this would be an ideal getaway. No tourists. No industry. No high rises. And the food had been remarkably good. Plus, the price had only been a few American dollars.

A swarthy local entered the courtyard. Behind him was a wealthy American with a gorgeous stacked blonde clinging to his arm. The other diners greeted them warmly, as did the server in the shack, reinforcing Mitch's impression that everyone here knew everyone else.

He ogled the blonde. Dressed in short cutoffs and a revealing halter, she moaned about the heat and how she needed an enormous cup of coffee after last night's roast.

Mitch's ears pricked up. Shalane found Emily at a pig roast. While the trio ordered, he tried to remember the host's name. Manfred? Manny? That was it. Manny Chevitz.

Mitch scrutinized the Bahamian man whose name conjured visions of kosher wine. He must have said something funny because the blonde threw her head back and laughed, a tinkling, merry, unpretentious sound that had the corner of Mitch's lips turning up.

But, Manny Chevitz claimed not to know Emily Hester. And while his face lit up like that of a saint's when Mitch mentioned Shalane Carpenter, he insisted Shalane had not been there either.

That was extremely odd. Shalane told Mitch she saw both Manny *and* Emily last night.

Shaking the man's hand and nodding to the couple, Mitch left the food shack and sauntered to the boutique the woman at the inn had circled on the map. A shop bell rang as he entered the store, and a male voice called from the back. Mitch fanned his collar and sighed. The air conditioner was working fine in here, making it an oasis of coolness in the Bahamian heat.

Spying the men's section, Mitch drifted to that side of the store and rifled through the racks. The clothes were quality and mostly island specific. He decided on a pair of stylish walking shorts and two brightly colored polo shirts.

Noticing a section of undergarments and footwear, he grabbed a package of men's briefs, then spotted a pair of brown leather sandals with a strap around the heel. While Mitch had been known to wear flip-flops on occasion, he preferred a shoe he wouldn't leave behind if he should need to run. You just never knew.

He combed through the sandals until he found his size, then spied a straw hat resting on the head of a nearby mannequin. Snatching it up, Mitch seated it on his pate and looked for a mirror.

In the back near the register he spied one on the dressing room door. Studying himself and the Panama in the mirror, Mitch decided it suited him. Plus, it would help with the hot Bahamian sun.

Satisfied, he laid his finds on the narrow counter and walked around the store to see if there was anything else that might come in handy over the next couple of days. When he was done, he rang the bell on the counter.

From the back came the smooth, melodious voice. "I'll be right with you." He'd said the same thing ten minutes earlier.

While he waited, Mitch drew his cell from his pocket, grateful to see bars, which was more than he'd had in the motel or restaurant.

He listened to messages from his executive assistant about legal cases. Those could wait. But why was there was no call or text from Shalane? Mitch checked the time. She had left Nassau early that morning bound for Las Vegas. Was she still on a plane?

At the end of his patience, Mitch rang the bell on the counter over and over.

"Coming!" chirped the voice.

A few seconds later, an islander ducked through the wooden beads. Spotting Mitch, his dark eyes glowed.

"Well, hello, Handsome. Where in the world did you come from? I know everyone on Zephyr Cay. You must be new."

Trying to reconcile the 'Hello, Handsome' remark with the man's rugged good looks, Mitch gaped.

"My, my, cutie. Cat got your tongue?"

Snickering self-consciously, Mitch ignored the come-on and slid his money clip from his front pocket.

"Good day to you, sir." Mitch kept his tone matter-of-fact. "You guessed right. I *am* new. Since you know everyone, maybe you could help me find a friend who was staying here."

The black eyes scrunched. "Anything, you gorgeous hunk o' man."

Mitch coughed and looked away, and the shopkeeper relented, lower lip pooching out in a pout.

"Oh, all right. Can't blame a girl for trying, can ya?"

Face flaming, Mitch shook his head and realized he was still wearing the Panama hat. He laid it on top of the pile of clothes.

The shopkeeper didn't hide his disappointment while he rang up Mitch's purchases. "Will this be all?"

"I think so, except for locating my friend. Do you know an American woman named Emily Hester?"

The man paused and looked off into the distance, then shook his head. "The name sounds familiar, but I can't say I recall knowing her. Has she been here long?"

"I don't think so."

Sandals in one hand and briefs in the other, the proprietor cocked his head. "What does she look like?"

"Short, maybe 5'3" – 5'4", with shoulder-length curly red hair." He found the picture he had saved on his phone and showed it to the man. "Ring any bells?"

"Nope. Can't say that it does. But leave me your number. I'll be happy to call if I run into her." He rang up the shoes and briefs and added them to the bag.

Reluctant to give the fresh shopkeeper his number, Mitch told him he was staying at the Seaside Villas. "I'll be there through tomorrow if you think of anything. It sure would help."

"I'll do my best, sweet cheeks." A grin wrinkled the handsome face.

Mitch glared at him good-naturedly, then paid and took his purchases to the inn.

All he needed was a quick shower and a change of clothes, then he would scour the rest of the island for clues. If Emily had been here, and Shalane had no reason to lie, someone must remember her. If not Emily, then her mop of crimson hair.

THE ELDER HOST

"This way, Awen. And hurry."

"Stop calling me that," Emily growled. "I told you, my name is Emily." But her words scattered in the swirling wind, lost on the servant that had rescued her from the bowels of Chateau Falaise.

Though old and bent, William's erstwhile valet scurried down the dark path like a cockroach, leaving Emily to stumble along in the dim light. Frustrated, and at the end of her rope, Emily planted her feet in protest.

"I'll not go a step further until you tell me where you are taking me."

She stared in disbelief when the servant hurried along the path without slowing or looking back. Apparently he was willing to leave his charge in the middle of nowhere. As the hooded figure disappeared over a rise, an animal squealed in the woods nearby. Emily bounded after Henry, heart pounding.

She was eager to reach safety—if it could be found in these foreign woods. But she was beginning to realize that security was an illusion. Jogging to catch up, she yearned for the days when she hadn't known better.

Henry was within sight when a loud snort sounded in the bushes to her right. Wheeling, Emily crouched and pried a large rock from a bed of moss. After a long silence, she parted the underbrush and peered inside. Nothing lurked there.

She backed away cautiously, clutching the rock, and ran full tilt until she spied Henry's hunched frame. Then, slowing to a more sedate pace, Emily hurried up behind him, wishing she could remember her high school French lessons.

Soon the trees thinned, and the path opened to a grassy dell. The sky was lighter here, a deep purple suffused with pale lavender, and the twinkling stars were beginning to fade. The clearing seemed eerily familiar in the predawn light.

Without warning, a deep rumble shattered the peace. For a moment, Emily thought Matilda's soldiers had caught up to them, but the silhouette of a giant bull charged out of the woods heading straight toward them.

They froze, and the bull stopped to paw the ground.

The great beast glowed a burnished beige in the twilight. Its thick horns curved menacingly toward the sky. Snorting, it grunted and lowered its head to charge.

"Run!" Henry yelled, and bolted past Emily back down the trail.

Instinct told her to do the same, but something else made her wait. The bull bellowed twice and snorted loudly. Then it moved closer, and Emily poised to leap sideways. But it stood still, stamping and huffing. When its hot breath washed over Emily, her fear faded.

She leaned forward and touched the creature's nose.

"Hello, Tarbh."

The bull Elder tossed its massive head and bellowed.

Then Henry was back, clutching at her elbow. "Come, Awen. Back away slowly, lest this bull run you through with his fearsome horns. Duke William will have my neck should harm befall you."

So, Henry did have a grasp of the English language.

"Tarbh will not hurt me, will you, fellow?" She laid a gentle hand on the angle of the bull's jaw, and he lowered his head so that she could scratch the sweet spot behind his ear.

Henry's eyes followed the beast's every movement, fearful for Emily's safety.

A haunting cry sounded overhead, followed by two more. Three pale cranes circled the dell. Dropping lower and lower, they skimmed the tree boughs and fluttered down to land on Tarbh's back.

The bull tossed its head in approval, then bent low. "Hail, Awen, Queen of the Druids."

His bugle startled a squirrel. It squawked and scampered up a stately birch, flushing a pair of waking pheasants.

The cranes tilted their heads toward Emily. "Hail, Awen, Queen of the Druids."

Not to be outdone, the pheasants and squirrel joined in, bowing low. "Hail Awen, Queen of the Druids."

Tears sprang to Emily's eyes.

Henry gasped. The deep lines in his face smoothed, and for a moment, he appeared much younger in the brightening dusk.

Wagging his grizzled head in wonder, the valet gawked at the bull and other creatures, then fell to his knees in supplication. "Hail, Awen, Queen of the Druids."

Overcome, Emily swept forward to return the salutations. "Hail Tarbh, King of the Bulls." She then turned slightly to face the cranes. "Hail cranes, ye who impart the gift of long life and secret knowledge."

To the squirrel and pheasants, she bowed her head. "Hail, creatures of Awen's glade, may you ever be protected from discovery and harm."

She extended a hand to help Henry up, then swept forward in a curtsy.

"Hail, Henry, Valet of William, Duke of Normandy, and rescuer of maidens from the dungeons of Chateau Falaise."

Straightening, Emily noted the stars in his eyes and lowered her voice to a murmur. "I truly cannot thank you enough. You saved me from sure death at the Duchess's hand."

The valet's cheeks reddened in the growing light. He hung his head. "'Twas my orders, Lady Awen. I would do it again."

The bull stamped and snorted, reclaiming Emily's attention.

"What brings you here, Tarbh?"

"Your presence, Master Druid."

The cranes lifted their eerie cries, raising chill bumps on Emily's arms. "Long have we wandered the fog of the Otherworld anticipating your return." The other animals offered similar cries.

There was a commotion behind Tarbh, then a long, loud squeal. A stout boar accompanied by a sow joined the circle around Emily and Henry. Then, a wolf, a fox, and a giant hare left the bushes. A neighing white horse galloped across the clearing, along with a stag, a hind, and a cow. The semicircle around Emily and the valet swelled.

In awe, Emily thought of the night she had arrived in Atlanta when the Elders had gathered as spirits. She had known nothing of her heritage at the time, but they had channeled Awen's memories and power to her. It had taken much longer to access that power. Even now, it was a struggle.

An owl hooted and landed in a birch. A raven joined it on an adjacent limb. From the canopy came the melodic trill of a blackbird, reminding Emily that twilight was the shimmering, a time of transition between this world and the next, a gateway for crossing over. The animal Elders were doing just that and joining their Awen en masse.

The blackbird fluttered down to settle on the top of Tarbh's head between his mighty horns. An eagle shrieked overhead. Then clashing talons with a hawk, the eagle descended to light on the horse's withers and the hawk on the stag's hindquarters.

Gazing around the Elder circle, Emily realized many had yet to appear. Most notably, Cu and Hope, the four dragon Keepers, and the water creatures. But this was most of them. Her heart filled and overflowed into tears.

"Hail Awen, Queen of the Druids," they cried together.

Henry sputtered and clutched at Emily's arm, then collapsed in a heap to the ground. The animals moved closer as Emily knelt to take his pulse. His heart beat strong. Relieved, she wiped her tears away.

"I think you scared him," she said to the Elders, and laughter rose from the menagerie—low and tinkling, loud and bawdy, melodic and merry.

Henry sat up, then leapt to his feet, appalled that he had left Emily without a guard.

"My apologies, mi' lady. But, am I losing my mind? Animals ain't meant to speak. And there are so many of them."

It took all of Emily's willpower not to giggle.

"No, Henry, you are not losing your mind. These animals are special, and you must be, too. Most people would not understand them."

She turned to the Elders. "Thank you. I am grateful to see each of you."

Tarbh stamped once, then twice. "We are grateful to be reunited with you, Master. But the man must turn back. He cannot advance further."

Henry cleared his throat and bowed slightly. "I should be getting back, anyway. Wouldn't want the guards to miss me and go looking." But he peered uncomfortably at the animals, then leaned close. "Are you sure you'll be okay alone with this lot?"

Emily squinted at the animals who were here because of her. She touched Henry's shoulder tenderly.

"Yes, Henry. I will be okay. Thank you for everything. And, if it's appropriate, please thank William for me."

His Adam's apple bobbed up and down, then Henry reluctantly moseyed toward the trail. The animals chirped, snuffed, neighed, and grunted as he turned toward them and bowed. Then her rescuer slipped silently into the trees.

For a moment, the early morning was still. Then Tarbh lowed.

"Come, dear Awen. We shall escort you to your hut."

NORMANDY

Lugh woke with Cu standing over him, wet nose nuzzling his neck. Light leaked from the edges of the blackout curtains, and the digital clock read 5:22 p.m. He had fallen into bed eight hours earlier.

"What is it, boy?"

Cu whined, but Hope answered.

"It is time to go." She leapt to the bedtable, thick fur bristling and amber eyes wide. "Hurry up, Lughnasadh. We have little time."

"For what?"

He rolled out of bed and yanked his jeans on in one fluid motion. Buckling his belt, he stretched, then rubbed his eyes. His sleep had been interrupted by dreams of a familiar hut in the middle of nowhere. He shuffled past Cu to the bathroom.

"To reach Falaise," Hope said.

Lugh turned to gape at the Scottish wildcat. "Huh?"

"We must go to Falaise. And we must hurry. It is best we get there before nightfall."

"As in William the Conqueror's Falaise?" Chills danced across Lugh's shoulders and down both arms. "Where he lived when he and Awen got together?" The goosebumps spread to Lugh's back. "But why there? Emily is in Wales. Plus, we have a plane to catch."

"No, Lughnasadh, Emily is here," Cu said, breaking his usual silence. "She needs our help."

Lugh stared, dumbfounded. "She told me the dragons were taking her to Beli, not Falaise."

"Remember what you told me on the plane?" Hope meowed. "You had a feeling Emily was in trouble. Well, she is, and she's here. She was waylaid." Leaping to the floor, Hope wove through Lugh's legs.

He pondered the druid Elders' news. Emily was in France, and they were, too. What were the odds?

"How did she get to Falaise?" He fumbled for the map on his cell phone. "And how far is that?"

"I do not know," Hope said. "But I'd wager it has something to do with that rogue fire dragon. Get going, Lugh. We have to hurry."

"Falaise is forty miles south, and according to GPS, it's an hour and fifteen minute drive. Are you sure about this?"

"Absolutely."

Eyeing the oversized tabby, Lugh shut the bathroom door, shucked his pants, and stepped into the shower. Grateful for the hot water and forceful pressure, he lathered his hair and body, then rinsed beneath the heavenly spray.

Toweling dry, he wrapped the towel around his waist. Then he opened the door, and steam billowed past him to cloud the vanity mirror. He threw on clean clothes and stuffed his dirty ones in the laundry bag.

Cu waited by the door, leash in his mouth. Hope perched beside him in Buddha pose.

"Gotta go, pal?"

Cu whined.

Tugging on his jacket, Lugh snatched the key from the dresser and opened the door. Hope ran outside, meowing, followed by Cu. A brisk wind buffeted them as they hurried around the quaint inn. The rainclouds had departed, leaving white wisps and puffs dotting a pale blue sky. The sun dipped toward the west.

While the animals availed themselves of the manicured grass bordering the parking lot, Lugh phoned Jocko's. The day manager was just opening the restaurant and assured him all was well.

Lugh returned calls to both Morgan and Brian, but neither answered. Disappointed he couldn't talk to his nephew, he left a message.

He gazed up at Caen Castle visible in the distance beside the abbeys of Saint-Étienne and Sainte-Trinité. According to the map, the historic buildings perched on a hill at the heart of Caen. Even here on the outskirts of town, the impressive spires soared above the city.

Hope yowled and raced back toward the room. Cu finished whizzing and bounded to Lugh, trailing his leash.

Taking a last look at the view, Lugh hurried to their room, wishing they had time to explore Caen. But Hope's raccoon-like tail twitched back and forth. She glared at Lugh and insisted they get a move on.

SUNRISE HOSPITAL

Juggling her carry-on and purse, Patty followed the other passengers down the stairs to the tarmac at McCarran International Airport. At the bottom, she squealed when a hot gust of wind nearly yanked her carry-on from her grip.

Then, stacking her purse on top, Patty wheeled to the gate, sweat prickling her back.

Her heels clicked smartly through the air-conditioned terminal where she caught the tram to the transportation hub. Patty checked her cellphone, but neither Latoya nor Shalane had responded. She had not expected an answer from Shalane, but Latoya surprised her. She would try again once she got settled.

She exited the terminal, and got a faceful of grit. Sputtering, Patty hailed a cab and directed the driver to Sunrise Hospital on Marilyn Parkway. While they maneuvered evening traffic, Patty grinned. She was genuinely worried about Shalane, but she was in Vegas, baby!

Shalane had brought her to the glittery mecca not long ago for a boob job. Patty cupped her hands beneath her new cleavage and gazed down with admiration. She hadn't wanted a huge rack. Just one big enough to make men stand up and pay attention. And now, thanks to Shalane, women did too.

But Patty was eighteen, and the legal age in Nevada was still twenty-one. That meant no drinking, no admission to the shows, *and* no fun for Patty.

When they reached the hospital, she pranced across the wide, sheltered entryway to the reception desk, pushing the expensive carry-on Shalane had bought her.

It had taken some doing, but Shalane's husband, Cecil Carpenter, persuaded the head nurse of the Critical Care Unit to allow Patty into Shalane's room. Afterward, Patty had talked him into getting some sleep on the travel bus while she sat with Shalane. The man looked haggard and at the end of his rope.

Sinking into the wide, uncomfortable chair, Patty tucked a foot beneath her and studied Shalane. The usually imposing woman lay unmoving. Her complexion was pale and pasty, and her platinum hair feathered around her face. Patty leaned closer to brush it from her brow and jerked away when Shalane's eyelids fluttered.

Chuckling at her jumpy nerves, Patty dragged the chair closer to the bed. She lifted Shalane's hand and threaded their fingers. Disappointed when nothing happened, Patty squeezed and leaned back to wait.

An ashamed tear escaped down her cheek, and Patty dashed it away. She had abandoned Shalane in Nashville, Tennessee, and though her actions had felt justified at the time, part of her had regretted it ever since.

When Shalane's eyes fluttered again, Patty stroked her face, slowly and gently, hoping for a response. None came, and Patty yawned. She hadn't slept much since the nightmare about Ishkur's gory death.

But as the minutes ticked by, not even the fear of nightmares could keep Patty awake. She fell asleep, rear-end in the chair, torso draped across the hospital bed, and her head resting in the nook between Shalane's arm and chest.

☼☼☼

In her dream, Patty was Nergal, and their whole body throbbed. He slumped against a cold stone wall, gagged by the nearly unbearable stench of rotting flesh and excrement. He was not alone, but Nergal had no idea who was beside there him.

Certainly not Inanna. They had dragged the Draca down a different corridor to whatever torment awaited her. His own had been prolonged and severe. But they had wrested no information from Nergal, not even when they flayed open his nearly-healed wounds.

He thought of Magdalena, the Agarthan doctora who had dressed those wounds and nursed him back to life after Mot and Maw left him for dead in a deserted chute. Nergal had protested when a platoon of soldiers marched Magda away, leaving him, Ishkur, and Inanna to fight. And fight they had.

81

Between them, they killed at least twenty warriors. Some were Dracs, but most were Ceruleans and other mercenaries. Then, Mot's lance had pierced Ishkur's heart, and if not for Inanna, Nergal would have met the same fate. He shuddered, remembering how Inanna leapt between them like an avenging angel.

She had slashed at Maw's twin with a sword and machete seized from the attackers, while two Ceruleans grabbed Nergal's limbs. He had struggled mightily, but another merc joined the first two and spread him wide, leaving Nergal open for Mot's killing blow.

Once again, Inanna stood between Nergal and death. She tore into his captors, hacking off legs and arms and heads until it was just Nergal and Inanna back-to-back, surrounded by Mot and his Drac warriors.

The next he knew, Nergal was being dragged through the dark, dank dungeons of Araf. Behind him, a Draco lugged the moaning Inanna. Nergal's chest lay open, and he had cuts on both arms and a shallow slash across the scar on his cheek. But he was alive.

He groaned and heaved into an upright position. Inanna had set Nergal up in Irkalla, to which she claimed to have no choice. But thrice, she had shielded him from Maw and Mot.

By Nergal's calculations, that made them even. He might even owe Inanna now. But first, they must survive to escape the dungeons of Araf.

☼☼☼

The overhead light flicked on, waking Patty from the dream. She stretched and unfurled, back protesting. How long had she been out?

She yawned and rubbed her eyes as a lanky nurse's aide bustled to the bed with a tablet in his hand. The aide grinned, and Patty's breath hitched. She hastily smoothed her hair and straightened her clothes, flashing the dreamy man a demure smile.

"You're new," he said conversationally.

She nodded, mute.

While he recorded Shalane's vitals, Patty studied the man. Brown eyes rimmed with long, dark lashes graced a face that wasn't much older than Patty's. His arm muscles rippled beneath the russet skin exposed by his short sleeves. The aide repositioned Shalane's blood pressure cuff, and glanced at Patty, as if waiting for an answer.

"I flew in from L.A. this evening. Can you tell me about Shalane's condition? Will she wake up soon?"

The CNA typed on the tablet, then looked at Patty.

"That's hard to say. She has been in a coma since the ambulance brought her in. Her vitals are normal, and her brainwaves indicate a high level of function. But she has yet to respond to treatment or stimuli. Maybe your presence will give her a reason to wake."

The aide smiled again, a white, toothy grin, then glanced down at Shalane, who looked small and forlorn in the hospital bed. Shyness crept into the CNA's tone. "I know *I* would wake up for you."

Patty averted her eyes. He was cute and all but now was a bad time. Plus, he was Shalane's nurse, for chrissakes. That made Patty giggle. If Shalane was awake, she would've already seduced him. And likely would as soon as she regained consciousness.

"Is she going to be okay?"

"We think so. Once she wakes from this coma. But the sooner, the better."

There was a sudden groan from the bed, and Shalane's head whipped from side to side. Then her whole body contorted, torso and hips rising and falling as her arms and legs thrashed beneath the covers.

Gasping, Patty watched helplessly as the aide checked the beeping monitor, and administered something into her intravenous line. Shalane calmed right away. The lines on her face smoothed and a half-smile sprang to her provocative lips.

Patty read the aide's name badge. "Thank you, Donald. That was scary."

"No problem, ma'am. Umm, I mean, miss," the CNA nervously corrected. "She's been doing that off and on since we admitted her." He laid his palm gently on Shalane's forehead. "She's quiet now."

Eyeing the chair, he asked, "Would you like a cot to get some sleep?"

Patty started to say no, then changed her mind. Even if she didn't sleep, it would be nice to stretch out. Cecil wouldn't be back until morning.

"That would be nice. Thank you."

"My pleasure." Donald waggled his fingers and left the room.

Patty plopped in the chair and kicked off her heels. Digging in her carry-on, she fished out a pair of fuzzy socks and pulled them on, then found a folded blanket and hard pillow on the metal shelf next to Shalane's bed.

Wrapping her body in the blanket like a burrito, Patty slumped in the chair and held Shalane's hand while she waited for a bed.

84

JOHN BLITHERSTONE

"VA-AAL!" Khenko's father called from the patio.

"Coming," she responded, tone airy. Then, squeezing Khenko's arm, she hurried to the house.

He followed, feet dragging.

"Where's Big Bird?"

The question shocked Khenko. His Pa hadn't called him that in years.

"He'll be in soon. He has a decision to make."

There was a short silence, then his father spoke again.

"He'll make the right one. He always does." Not one ounce of sarcasm colored John Blitherstone's words.

Khenko froze midstride, stupefied. Not since Khenko had declared his preference for boys over breakfast one morning back in high school had he heard his father speak nicely of him.

His mother had thrown her arms around him. His sister, having her own identity crisis in junior high, had sighed heavily and rolled her dark eyes.

"Like no one knew," she'd quipped, then went back to eating her Cheerios.

But Khenko's warm and loving father had stiffened into an ice carving, folded his napkin, shoved his chair from the table, and left the dining room without a word.

From then on, John Blitherstone never mentioned his son's sexual orientation. Their conversations grew short and strained and consisted mostly of disapproving lectures about one thing or another.

As a result, Khenko avoided his father more and more, and at seventeen, he moved in with a friend. That many years and more had gone by, and hearing his father speak of him kindly seemed too good to be true.

He'd told himself it was his father's loss. But it had been harder on Khenko than he cared to admit. His father's rejection was a big part of why he moved to the Bahamas and purchased the Atlantean

Center. It was far, far away from John Blitherstone and his disapproval.

When Khenko reached the patio, his parents had gone inside. He wiped his bare feet on the colorful rag rug, then hurried quietly through the kitchen and dining room, bound for his upstairs bedroom.

He'd almost made it to the staircase when the door to the powder room opened, and his father emerged, as surprised to see Khenko as he was him. There was a momentary flash of joy in his father's eyes, then his heavy, bronzed lids sagged over irises that were a tad cloudy.

"Khenko."

The single utterance, rife with sorrow, stirred Khenko's hope. Then, John Blitherstone cleared his phlegmy throat and ogled his hair.

"Don't they have barbers in the Bahamas?" His gaze trailed down to Khenko's bare feet, then back up to his eyes. "Or shoes?"

Shame coursed through Khenko. Then anger sprang to his defense.

"Yes, Pa, they have barbers in the Bahamas, but I've been busy. Life is different there. It's forgiving of the conventions placed on us here in the states." He eyed the long braid trailing down the middle of his father's back like a fat king snake. "I've been thinking about growing it long like yours."

John's raven hair held no hint of gray, while at thirty-five, Khenko's strawberry blond was under attack. He made it a practice to pull out every gray hair that appeared, not ready to acknowledge his advancing years—particularly with so little to show for them.

His pa eyed him critically. "Then I'll loan you some pomade to slick it down, so it's not so wild. I'll get it for you." He shuffled to the stairs, then pulled himself up slowly by the railings.

Khenko watched from the bottom, wondering what had happened to make his father so weak. Feeling like that seventeen-year-old boy who had needed his father's approval, he followed, knowing his kinky locks would never behave like his pa's straight hair. Nevertheless, Khenko took the container and headed to his room.

"Khenko?"

He turned, ever hopeful.

"If you're going to stay, I would like to call a meeting. The Iroquois council has been inactive for years, but I am feeling uneasy.

Something is happening. Or is about to. I don't know what it is or whether it will affect the Iroquois. But we should be ready, in case."

Khenko's heart settled around his toes. Every fiber of his being protested, but he nodded nonetheless.

"Sure, Pa. Whatever you think."

Patting Khenko on the shoulder, his father shuffled to the stairs. He paused to level a long, penetrating stare at Khenko, then clomped down slowly using the railings again.

Khenko stared after him, turning the jar of pomade round and round in his hands. Since leaving Zephyr Cay, Khenko had been on an emotional roller coaster. And, God knew—he was not fond of roller coasters.

One long-ago day at Six Flags came to mind. Khenko had insisted he accompany his older cousins on Bizarro. He was tall enough, even at that age. But Khenko was too young. His mother would've offered a resounding NO, but she was at home with his new baby sister. Between Khenko and his cousins, they had badgered his pa until he finally relented.

What had started as a thrilling adventure, climbing and descending that first hill, had quickly devolved into a horror story. In the first loop-de-loop, legs dangling, Khenko had spewed his half-digested corndog on his cousins, the people in front of *and* behind them, and of course, himself. When they had exited the ride covered in puke, his horrified father had promptly thrown up, too.

Khenko snickered, then laughed out loud. Tossing the pomade in the air, he caught it deftly and swung down the stairs.

At the bottom, enjoying his own private chuckle, his father looked up in time for Khenko to wrap him in a bear hug.

"Thank you, Pa. *Thank you!*"

When the too-thin arms circled Khenko, his aching heart nearly burst. After a few moments, his father let go.

"All that for some pomade?" The faded eyes crinkled. "Or is that 'thank you' for something else?"

"It's for not being mad that day at Six Flags when I threw up on the roller coaster."

Surprise arched his father's brow. "I was just thinking about that. Your cousins were so mad we had to leave, I had to stop Jere and Josh from pummeling you."

"Yeah, well, they got me back in the years that followed."

They laughed together like old times, then his father sobered. He waved a finger at Khenko's hair, then the pomade in his hand.

"Now go get presentable. The others will be here soon."

It was Khenko's turn to be surprised.

"Others?"

"The Council."

"Already?" Khenko's heart thumped. After running out on his folks and turning his back on the Iroquois Nation, he was nowhere near ready to face them.

UNEASY ALLIANCE

Shibboleth finally found the witch stone. He held it to the light and rubbed vigorously until the black stone vibrated.

The witch appeared before him in a hologram, and Shibboleth recoiled. Her usual dewy features were wrinkled and loose, her voluptuous figure shrunken, gnarled, and ancient beneath a tattered robe.

"Hail, Shibboleth, Ruler of the Draconian Empire." She bowed slightly, took a step toward him, and extended her hand.

"Hail, Bé Chuille, She-Witch and Consort of Lord Enki and his pantheon." Shibboleth reached for her hand, and the hologram wavered. Then it waxed, and Bé Chuille appeared in the flesh.

The witch exhaled a sensuous pent-up breath, then wrapped her emaciated arms around him.

"It's been far too long," she sighed suggestively against his ear slit and rubbed her groin against him.

Her withered appearance repelled Shibboleth, yet heat rose in his loins nonetheless. He unfastened his belt and let it drop to the floor. Then, wrapping a long arm around the withered form, he wrestled the winter hag to the floor.

Her knees came up and her sharp nails clawed at Shibboleth's cloaca. He winced as she pried it open, then gasped when she released his engorged penis from its flap and leaned down to take it into her mouth. Licking and sucking, she slid a spiked phalange up his anal canal.

Shibboleth wriggled and shuddered as she drove it deeper inside him, and the sensations danced through him.

He ripped off the hag's dirty cloak. Beneath it, she was naked, and her loose flesh folded layer upon layer, making him gag. But, knowing the end result, he lifted a deflated breast to his lips and suckled until she moaned and gripped his penis tighter and reamed his anus with her finger.

Convulsing, Shibboleth nibbled at the long, pointed nipple until soon it was as hard as his cock. Then he lifted her flaccid breast and sucked hard. Beneath his lips, it filled with new life. Bé Chuille writhed, trying to guide his cock to her vagina. Denying her the release she sought, he rubbed his engorged member against Bé Chuille's dimpled belly while he continued sucking her tit. She arched in ecstasy as the breast plumped to the size of a ripe melon.

Letting go of that one, Shibboleth took hold of the other and rolled its nipple between his claws. Bé arched beneath him, begging for penetration. He leered down at the repugnant face and drew the pencil-hard nipple into his mouth, suckling with the vigor of a newborn.

As that breast renewed, the hag squirmed beneath him. With the spiked finger far up his ass and a hand clutching his engorged cock, the Cailleach rocked and moaned, feverishly trying to coax his penis to her vaginal canal.

Surveying the mostly renewed body, Shibboleth leaned backward to avoid the sight of the still shriveled face and moved his hips until the tip of his cock tickled the opening of the witch's vulva. Then, with a screech, the Cailleach let go, wrapped her arms around him, and slammed all seventeen inches of his majestic schlong inside her cunt.

Shibboleth's heart raced as he pounded his organ into the witch again and again. Her screech took on an even sharper edge, ending with a shriek as the once beautiful goddess orgasmed. She rocked harder, squeezing his cock with her cunt. When it exploded inside her, her lips and cheeks plumped, and beauty returned to Bé Chuille's face. Her thin, disheveled hair took on its former raven glory.

But that didn't stop the witch's gyrations. She rolled them both over and rose on her knees to ride Shibboleth, moaning and groaning and screaming at the top of her lungs. Eventually, she slowed to a rolling motion and drew Shibboleth's mouth down to hers. Youth fully restored, the goddess kissed him deep and long.

Then, with a heaving sigh, Shibboleth withdrew his drained member and tucked it inside its flap. The witch rolled onto her back. For a moment, he lingered beside her on the floor, then he hefted his long frame upright and ogled the goddess.

"Your years are restored. What news do you bring, Bé Chuille?"

The witch goddess smoothed her long, luxurious black hair and passed a hand over her body. The torn robe was replaced by a soft, black, flowing one that tucked in at a narrow waist and accentuated ripe hips and full breasts.

Feeling his loins tighten again, Shibboleth ignored his nether regions and focused on the snapping indigo eyes. Pleasure time was over.

"Now is the time if you wish to advance upon AboveEarth. I have taken care of the dragons. The borders are no longer guarded."

Shibboleth's ear slits expanded. "That explains how we were able to breach the boundaries in several places. Well done, Bé Chuille. That is good news indeed." He donned his weapon belt. "Come."

Support staff of various species melted into the background as the witch and Shibboleth sauntered through the compound. Many had suffered at Shibboleth's hand. Most stared at the witch, jaws slack.

In the control room, Shibboleth accessed the feeds for his reconnaissance teams. In addition to breakthroughs in California and India, the Reptilians had gained access to AboveEarth in Australia, Japan, China, and Mexico.

Bé Chuille murmured to Shibboleth, "I understand Maw has perished. Will Mot replace him as your second in command?"

A knife twisted in Shibboleth's gut. He had yet to process his rage. "Aye."

He pulled up the coordinates for Maw's twin. Mot had moved the training camp to Irkalla and appeared to be supervising a heated battle between two young officers.

"Mot, report."

Mot's head jerked up. He peered at the camera and straightened to strike his chest with his left fist.

"Hail, Shibboleth! There is little to report since your last briefing. But in this cadre, I have sixteen Dracos and twenty Dracas whose skills are progressing as expected. I also have three other squads of similar makeup. They, too, are coming along nicely." Mot stuck his chest again.

"So that's a hundred and fifty new officers that will soon be battle ready?"

"Aye, sir." Mot's eyes narrowed. "Who is your guest?"

Bé Chuille moved in front of the camera. "It is I, Mot. Bé Chuille." She ran her tongue across her bottom lip and bowed slightly. "It has been a long time."

"Aye, witch. What brings you to UnderEarth?"

Bé glanced at Shibboleth, who spoke into the mic.

"Bé Chuille has brought news. We are free to access the old portals without interference. She has defeated the dragons. Our time has come."

Mot's eyes lit. "Excellent. Well done, Bé Chuille. Has my father promised you a fat reward?"

"Aye," the witch joked. "He has trothed me to you."

Shibboleth's heir stiffened. "He what?"

The witch cackled, and Shibboleth laughed.

"No, Mot. Bé Chuille is teasing."

Mot's posture relaxed, and the panic drained from his olivine scales. "I do not find it funny, Sir." His forehead wrinkled in a frown. "I will wed no one. What is it you seek from me?"

"Your presence. Report to the control room immediately."

Minutes later, Mot swept through the wide door and approached Shibboleth, striking his chest.

"Yes, Sire?"

Pride and elation filled Shibboleth. Their time was nigh. "Bé Chuille has no love for the humans and has aided us many times in our war against them. Now she has rounded up their dragons and imprisoned them in a place where they can no longer hinder our access to AboveEarth."

The witch tossed her raven hair. Then, running her hands over her voluptuous, newly-restored body, she relaxed against the console between Shibboleth and Mot. Smugness played on her arrogant features.

"But, I did not tell you my price, Lord Shibboleth."

Blindsided, he considered the witch. "What do you mean? You would go back on your bargain?"

"Nay, Warlord," she laughed wickedly. "We have no bargain. Not until I name my price and you agree will I help you defeat the humans."

Shibboleth growled and considered snapping her lovely neck in two.

"If you refuse," she continued coolly, "I shall release the dragons. But not merely to block the borders between Above and UnderEarth. No, Warlord. I will set them upon you, your spawn, and your citizenry until there are none of your race left on Earth."

A shiver passed through Shibboleth. Not much struck at his Reptilian heart, but dragons were at the top of that list. He'd had good reason to steer clear of them during his time on Earth—of them *and* the god who had exiled their races to this hellhole.

He leaned toward Bé Chuille and hissed menacingly, "Name your price, woman."

As tall as Shibboleth and heavier of build, the witch pressed back. Her beauty paled and her voice grew deep and threatening.

"I am no woman. I am Bé Chuille, Goddess of Marduk and Dark Witch of Beli." The witch twiddled a long finger.

Mot moved to interfere, but Shibboleth motioned him back. His ears popped as with a pressure change. Then one went silent. All ambient sound switched to the other ear, along with an intense ringing that echoed inside Shibboleth's head. What had she done to him?

"You shall treat me with the respect to which I am due," Bé Chuille jeered. "Or in addition to unleashing the dragons, I shall silence your hearing permanently. Now listen to my price and prepare to accept." She twirled her finger, and Shibboleth's ear unstopped. The ringing subsided.

Clamping down on his temper, Shibboleth worked his jaw. "I am listening, witch. Speak."

Bé Chuille drew to full height. Placing her hands on comely hips, she peered down her regal nose at Mot then Shibboleth. His bones chilled as she uttered her terms.

"Release General Nergal and restore his full rank and privilege."

White heat shot through Shibboleth. "I will do nothing of the sort. That worm is a traitor, a murderer, and a thief. The only privilege he shall be granted is death. And he shall find it at my hand in front of the Reptilian nation."

Shibboleth rubbed his claws together with glee. "I even have a special arena set up for the event. Nergal's death shall be witnessed by his comrades and peers. And you, should you choose to stay and watch."

Bé Chuille sighed heavily. "As I feared, Warlord. You leave me no choice. Prepare to defend your lives and home against the dragons. They will descend through every portal from AboveEarth. Your warriors will know nothing but defeat and death, starting with you and Mot." She lifted her hand to snap her fingers.

"Wait!" Mot cried as Shibboleth recoiled.

The witch's hand stilled.

"My Lord Shibboleth," Mot implored, "allowing Nergal to live might help our cause. Let us hear Bé Chuille out."

Shocked, Shibboleth roared in protest, but Mot continued in a beseeching tone.

"Our ranks have grown dangerously thin, especially those of our seasoned warriors. And despite our mutual animosity, General Nergal has served the Reptilian nation valiantly over the years."

Shibboleth saw red but held his silence to let his second-in-command continue.

"To wage a simultaneous war upon the humans *and* the dragons would tax our limited resources. Let us rescind Nergal's death warrant and restore his rank along with that of my litter-sister Inanna. They are both fierce warriors. And the doctora could care for our workers while we restore and fortify the base in Agartha."

Hatred curdled Shibboleth's insides. He itched to gut Nergal and display the worm's head on a stake as a warning to other would-be challengers. But Mot's reasoning was sound. Plus, the prospect of executing his daughter-spawn had not been sitting well with Shibboleth.

An idea came to him, one he had not entertained in a long time. "Inanna, I will allow to live. But only if she returns to Irkalla to rule beside me." Mot's face darkened, and his forehead twitched. "And when your time comes," Shibboleth clarified, "Inanna will rule beside you." Mot's jaw relaxed but remained outthrust.

Cocking a brow at the back-stabbing witch, Shibboleth continued. "I will allow the doctora to return to Agartha. Besides assisting Nergal, I have no qualm with the healer. But I cannot, *I will not*, allow Nergal to live." To Mot he half whispered, "If you knew what I know, you would not entertain the notion of setting him free, much less give the worm your trust."

But the witch hissed. "My bargain, my rules. Your reluctance to cooperate has steepened my price. Lord Shibboleth, you will set Nergal free, restore his full rank and privilege, *and* you will assign him to lead the fight against the humans, including command of your AboveEarth contingents."

Shibboleth gasped and stared at Bé Chuille. "Are you insane?"

Her cheeks and upper lip hiked, and her nose wrinkled in disgust. "Do this, or I will leave and unleash the dragons. Then you and your issue will die horrible deaths. You will never wrest AboveEarth away from the humans, nor gaze upon Sol or escape to the stars as is your deepest desire." She glowered unyielding, indigo eyes as sharp as daggers.

Mot urged Shibboleth again to concede, and his resolve wavered. But Shibboleth could not. If he allowed Nergal to live, the worm would eventually learn the truth of his origins. Then there would be no stopping the wretch.

The witch's face darkened. She wagged a forefinger, and Shibboleth's ears popped. Her lips moved, but he could hear no sound except a violent ringing. Frantic to hear again, he worked his jaw. Then inside his head came Bé Chuille's chilling declaration.

"I know your secret, Warlord. I know that Nergal is Enlil's direct descendent, making him the rightful ruler of the Reptilian nation. Not you, and certainly not your heirs."

Shibboleth's gaze flew to Mot. From his litter-son's expression, it was apparent he had not heard the revelation. But the witch knew too much.

"You are right to fear Nergal," she crowed triumphantly inside his head. "Once Enlil's heir learns of his blood claim, he will not hesitate to usurp your power. And I shall be happy to join him in that."

"Not if I kill him first," Shibboleth hissed aloud. Mot jerked away, eyes wide. "No, not you," Shibboleth reassured, unable to hear his own voice.

The black-hearted witch advanced. "I tell you now, Warlord, if you do not release Nergal according to my terms, I will reveal your secret here and now. Not only to Mot but to your entire realm." With a sweep of the arm he had helped restore, a vision of Irkalla's stadium appeared, and it was filled to the max with spectators enjoying the post-ceremony war games.

Dread flooded through Shibboleth. His stomach churned, and bitterness rose to clog his throat. If the witch made Nergal's birthright public, the fallout would be disastrous, not only to Shibboleth and his spawn but to the entire Reptilian nation.

Bé Chuille threw back her head and let loose a harsh, victorious cackle that chilled his blood. "Give it up, Warlord. My bargain, my terms."

The mocking words bounced around Shibboleth's skull. After all these ages, how had he underestimated Bé Chuille's depravity? If Nergal learned of his claim, his warriors would thwart Shibboleth and ruin any chance of wresting AboveEarth from the humans.

And if Shibboleth was to get off this forsaken rock, he would have to submit to the witch's demands though everything in him rebelled against it. His lip twisted.

"You win, witch. Restore my hearing. I accept your bargain."

Mot stared after the witch as she flounced from the room. What could she have said to change Shibboleth's mind? In all the years Mot had known his litter father, he had not seen him back down. Not on something he felt as adamantly about as Nergal.

That was another mystery. Mot had never understood why Shibboleth hated the Draconian general so much.

Shibboleth cleared his throat. "You will keep this to yourself. Do not repeat what you witnessed. *Ever.* Understand?"

Mot nodded slowly. "What did I witness, Sir? What did the witch say to change your mind?"

Shibboleth sagged like a bladder losing air. "Nothing I can share. But you get your wish, Mot. Nergal shall live to see another day. And despite my substantial misgivings, he will lead the charge against AboveEarth. I gave the witch my word. Now you shall make it happen. Take the chute to Araf, and release the doctora. Then bring Nergal and Inanna to me."

"As you wish, Sir." Mot strode to the outer corridor.

The witch lingered there, one hand propped seductively on her hip, the other twirling a long lock of raven hair.

Mot stopped to eye her up and down. For a human-like creature, she was quite attractive. He had copulated with an untold number of them over the millennia, but Mot preferred a spicy Draca over the most luscious human. Especially this one. For Shibboleth to back down, she must be evil indeed.

"Bé Chuille, what is it you seek?"

"An ally." She fluttered long eyelashes and fluffed her hair.

Mot knew she was flirting. Her wiles did affect him, but he would be damned if he would let the witch know. When he didn't react, she tried again.

"I fear Shibboleth cannot see past his anger and would be the death of your race. You, on the other hand, are brilliant and wise and forward-thinking." She offered a conciliatory hand. "You will make a fine leader."

Flattered, Mot took it, then jerked away when electricity jolted through his claw and up his arm. The sensation was not entirely unpleasant. He stared at Bé Chuille.

"What was that?"

"What was what?" She grinned lasciviously.

"That spark. What did you do?" Mot rubbed his arm and held it against his ventral plates.

"That was not my doing but yours," the witch chortled. "And it proves you are truly your grandfather's son. What is your wish, heir of Enki? Name it, and I will make it so."

Mot eyed her warily. "And what price would you ascribe to such a boon?"

"The same price I offered your litter father millennia ago when we ended up on this forsaken planet." She examined long, sharp nails, then scratched her nose with one of them.

Wresting an answer from Bé Chuille was proving difficult. But Mot was good at getting to the bottom of things. He would find out what she'd said to make Shibboleth yield to her demands.

"What price is that?"

Bé Chuille smiled and crooked a taloned finger.

Mot recoiled, averse to getting close to the witch. But she leaned toward him.

"In exchange for your help with my quest, I will aid you in yours. Just name what that is, and our bargain will be struck."

Studying her seemingly guileless countenance, Mot's resolve wavered. "What is this quest you speak of? With what do you require assistance, Bé Chuille?"

"I seek the same as you, Death Bringer."

Mot winced at the moniker. Together, he and Maw had been dubbed Shibboleth's Death Bringers. But it had been Maw who delighted in the slaughter. Mot preferred intellect and reason over brute force.

"And that would be?"

"An end to the humans. More specifically, one particular human."

That piqued Mot's attention. He leaned closer, curious as to who had incited the witch's ire. "And who might that be?"

"That is none of your concern." She said it softly, but Mot flinched.

"I will not enter a bargain without knowing what it entails. If you refuse to reveal your target, I shall be forced to decline."

While the witch pondered his ultimatum, Mot withdrew his communicator and rang the commanding officer in Araf. Then turning his back, he conversed with the second and waited for him to locate the major.

When the witch started tapping her foot, Mot raised his brows.

"Your target?"

She growled as the major came on the line.

Mot turned away again and stalked to the lift. "Major, this is General Mot. Warlord Shibboleth has rescinded the orders against General Nergal, Inanna, and the doctora. Please prepare them for transport. I will escort them back to Irkalla."

There was silence on the other end of the line.

"Major? Are you there?"

"Yes, but I am shocked. Lord Shibboleth was adamant about the fate of General Nergal. It was my understanding there was to be a public execution. What happened to that?"

Taken aback by the audacious questions, Mot decided to ignore the affront. "Lord Shibboleth has changed his mind. His why is not your concern. Prepare the prisoners. I will collect them shortly."

Ending the call, Mot glared at the witch who had crept up behind him.

"What?" he demanded, wishing to be rid of her unwanted advances. "Have you decided to reveal the target of your enmity?"

Bé Chuille's expression hardened. Nose in the air, her cheeks reddened, and her dark eyes gleamed, making Mot wonder if he should reconsider. He had heard the stories. It wouldn't do to make an enemy of this one. Still, her hesitancy baffled him.

"Are you afraid I might side with your target? Conspire with them? If so, I have no love for the humans. It is my intention to wrest AboveEarth from them. Same as my litter father."

But unlike Shibboleth, Mot did not wish to exterminate the humans. Instead, he envisioned a future where the two lived side by side. If not as allies, at least not as adversaries. But he dared not share his vision with anyone. Including the witch.

She glared into space, then back at Mot. "I cannot tell you what you wish to know. You may refuse me now, but I foresee you will change your mind in the future."

Mot pressed the button for the lift, and Bé Chuille leaned close. She whispered into his ear slit, sending chills down his spine.

"Goodbye, for now, Mot, Son of Shibboleth and Descendant of Enki."

Striking his chest, Mot stepped inside the open lift. When he turned, the witch had vanished.

☼☼☼

Leaning forward in his captain's chair, Shibboleth adjusted the feed to view the corridor leading to the lift and chutes. Bé Chuille lurked in the hallway and intercepted Mot as he left the control room.

It appeared Bé Chuille was offering Mot a proposition. Vitriol coursed through Shibboleth. How had he missed her subterfuge all these millennia? Had he been blinded by her sensuality?

He thought back to the beginning. He had first met Bé Chuille after their disastrous arrival on Earth. The witch was under the protection of Lord Enki, and Shibboleth had given her little thought. But over the millennia, with Enki out of the picture, the witch goddess had become his familiar. Together, they had collaborated against the druids, the humans, and the gods.

Based on her expression, Shibboleth decided he had nothing to worry about. Still, he would ask his litter son what the witch wanted. It wouldn't do to have Mot conspiring with the enemy.

But could Shibboleth end the alliance with Bé Chuille?

Not without bringing the wrath of the dragons upon the Reptilians. But he could have her executed. That way, she couldn't spill Nergal's secret or sick the dragons on him.

But who would do the dirty work? It needed to be someone he trusted. Shibboleth thrummed his claws against the console. He would have them end Nergal's life too. And do them both secretly. Normally, he would send Maw and Mot. But left to his own devices, Mot would form alliances and spare lives rather than fight.

If only there was a way to contact the Galactic Council. Or the World Alliance. Surely someone had figured out how to resume off-world travel. Most of the trapped gods had managed to escape, either by a freak of physics or powerful spatial manipulation.

But unlike Enki, Enlil, and the other gods, the Reptilians did not possess magical skills.

FRIGHTENING ENCOUNTER

Mitch visited every business in downtown Zephyr Cay. In the Pescadero, he ran into Frederick, his motorboat captain. The fun-loving local was hanging out with friends until their return trip to Nassau.

But every person Mitch showed Emily's picture to, stared at it blankly and wagged their heads. Now his new clothes were clinging, damp with sweat. And he was none the wiser about Emily Hester's whereabouts.

Reaching his last stop, Mitch sighed, discouraged. Then he shoved through the door of the liquor store, prepared to be shot down again. A jumble of smells assaulted his senses. After the bright Bahamian sun, it took a moment for his eyes to adjust to the dim interior. When they did, he was surprised.

This was not your typical liquor store. The shop was crammed from floor to ceiling with merchandise, trinkets, and other wares. It reeked of exotic spices and something else—marijuana.

Ceiling fans stirred the soupy air, distributing the chill from a laboring swamp cooler. Two women browsed racks of folded clothes and a couple more shopped in the back.

Shuffling to the glass-fronted cooler, Mitch grabbed a six-pack of beer and another of Coca-Cola. He set them on the counter and eyed the liquor section for a bottle of Bahamian rum.

A gangly teen squeezed by, barely brushing Mitch. But it startled him, and that surprised the kid, who jumped backward into a velvet-covered table laden with jewelry.

Mitch winced as it tipped sideways, dumping its precious contents, then rammed against a larger table that toppled too. He inched away as the leather-faced proprietress came running from the back.

Dust danced around the boy who stood in the middle of the chaos with a frightened look plastered to his face.

"Estúpido!" screeched the proprietress, slapping at him with a fly swatter. He hunched forward, shielding his face.

A young lady, who appeared to be his mother, righted one of the fallen tables and hastily transferred the items from the floor. Mitch set the other upright and bent to help.

The wizened proprietress ceased flogging the mortified kid but continued her tirade. He fell to his knees and gathered an armful of books, then stacked them carefully beside the jewelry and other wares.

When the floor was clear, the boy's mother and the proprietress, whom she called Madame Bouvee, exchanged words. She must have offered to pay for the damage because Madame Bouvee broke out in a toothless grin. Relief flooded the boy's worried face as they moved to the counter.

Mitch returned to the liquor display, and caught a glint of blue from the corner of his eye. A sunray slanted through a crack in the siding to dance from a pin on the rescued table.

While the woman finished checking out, Mitch eyed the brooch. It was slightly tarnished and looked like genuine gold. But that was ludicrous. Few small shops could afford to carry such an expensive item in inventory, much less leave it out for anyone to steal. Not at today's prices.

Lifting the weighty pin, Mitch studied the blue stone commanding its center. If he didn't know better, he would say it was a blue sapphire. But gems like that were more expensive than gold.

Madame Bouvee appeared beside Mitch, and he nearly jumped from his skin. He hastily returned the brooch to the table. She snatched it up and held it in the air between them. The grayed dreadlocks bobbed vigorously, and the beady eyes twinkled.

"Dis yurz?" she gurgled, peering intently at the stone, then at Mitch.

He wagged his head.

Madame Bouvee lightly touched the brooch to her forehead, sternum, and both sides of her chest in the shape of a cross. Then she held it in the air until the light danced from the stone's many facets.

"No," she croaked ominously. "Dis *Awen's*."

Mitch gasped aloud.

She shoved the brooch in a fold of her thin dress and leaned close to peer into Mitch's eyes. An eerie feeling coursed through him as recognition sparked in the depths of her sunken orbs.

He jerked backward and dug in his pocket for his cell phone. Opening it, he showed the picture of Emily to Madame Bouvee.

Her eyes glittered. She tapped the screen with a sharp nail.

"Awen." Then she prodded Mitch's chest and repeated it.

Sweat trickled down the hollow of Mitch's back. What was the crone trying to say? She pointed at the brooch then at Emily's picture.

He backed away, shaking his head. No way was Mitch helping Emily Hester. But the proprietress moved closer and pressed the brooch into his hand.

The stone tingled against Mitch's palm. He shoved it back at her, snatched a pint of rum off the shelf, and set it beside his items on the counter. But the woman clutched at his forearm with a strength that belied her scrawny frame. Mitch tried to jerk away, but her nails bit into his flesh. Then she pulled him close and hissed in perfectly enunciated English.

"This is not a request. You will take this brooch to your sister. If you do not, you bring destruction upon the world... *and* yourself." With that, Madame Bouvee pressed the brooch into his hand and limped behind the counter.

Near hyperventilating at this bizarre turn of events, Mitch stuffed the weighty trinket in his shorts pocket.

Emily had been here. Madame Bouvee verified it. And she had called her Awen. How could the islander know *that* name? Or that they were siblings? Who *was* this woman? Mitch's heart pounded.

Extracting the pin from his pocket, he turned it over. Brilliant blue rays danced in the sunbeam. He twisted it side-to-side, inspecting the intricate handiwork, then ran his finger over the stone. It was large, at least two carats. This was no ordinary trinket. It was a priceless heirloom.

Making a decision, Mitch pivoted to pay. But Madame Bouvee was no longer at the counter. Nor did he see her among the patrons still browsing the dim store. He rang an old-fashioned call bell, then wandered toward the heavy curtains lining the back of the shop.

A low hum erupted beneath the floor, accompanied by a deep vibration. Then the slats began jittering beneath his feet, and the hum ratcheted up to a roar.

"Earthquake!" one of the women yelled.

"Run!" another screamed.

But before Mitch could do anything, the floor groaned and sagged in the middle, throwing him off balance. He bounced off a rack and yelped when he landed hard on his ass, then slid sandals-first toward the crater opening in the floor. The ancient cooler grumbled menacingly. Then it tipped toward him.

Still sliding, Mitch threw his body sideways as the heavily laden hunk of glass and metal missed him by inches. It landed on its belly with a resounding crash and skidded toward the hole. Trying to stop his momentum, Mitch slid after it, battered by shelving, racks, and tables, and the merchandise stacked upon them.

Suddenly, a tall, human-like creature with green scales rose in the middle of the collapsed floor. It wavered motionless, red eyes fixed on the plunging appliance. Then, the cooler rammed into the beast, spilling its guts.

Unable to stop, Mitch tumbled into the corpse as its purple blood spurted, soaking him and his new clothes. He writhed to escape the reeking mound of entrails, and lost his lunch violently. Never had he seen a more violent death or smelled anything so horrific.

Then two more of the lizard men climbed from the pit.

He froze and nearly pooped his pants. Mitch had seen these monsters in sci-fi movies, but never had he imagined facing one. Then, instinct kicked in, and he scrambled to escape. Getting a foothold in the ankle-deep clutter, he leapt to seize an exposed floor joist, then swung himself up.

Vicious claws tore at his back. Mitch winced and dragged himself higher. Then the hideous creature grabbed his foot and yanked him backward to dangle in the air. The other beasts howled, obviously finding Mitch's situation hilarious.

That pissed him off. He was a US Air Force veteran trained in hand-to-hand combat for God's sake. Anger sliced through his paralysis.

Using his weight to throw his opponent off-balance, Mitch broke free. He landed in the debris, then rolled and climbed to his feet in the rubble to face both of the horn-headed, red-eyed bastards.

They goaded him, licking thin lips in anticipation and clicking sharp claws. He quickly devised a plan to take the evil assholes. Then two more of them materialized, and Mitch reconsidered.

He vaulted to the protruding joist, sending an avalanche of loose items down on the monsters. Then he swung to the top.

Madame Bouvee herded patrons past him out the door. He followed, but hesitated when a blood-curdling scream rent the air.

Peeking over the rim, he gulped. A young woman beneath a table in the fallen merchandise was hauled kicking and screaming from her hiding place.

He glanced at the door and patted his pocket. The brooch and his wallet were safe. But instead of running after Madame Bouvee, Mitch looked for a weapon. A wooden case lay on its side. He put a shoulder to it and inched it toward the drop zone. Then it occurred to him that it might miss the monsters and crush the woman.

He didn't see the scaled arm sneaking over the edge, but next thing Mitch knew he was dangling upside down again. Only this time, the four snarling beasts prepared to draw and quarter him.

INTERVENTION

Never had Mitch seen creatures like these, much less been accosted by one. Now, he dangled upside down in the grip of a monster straight out of a sci-fi movie. Three more just like it, with sharp teeth and ravenous red eyes, prepared to dissect the tasty human.

In desperation, Mitch threw his weight against his captor. One of his legs broke free, but a second beast wrapped a scaly arm around Mitch's neck and slammed him into the shattered wares littering what was left of the floor.

Exquisite pain shot up and down Mitch's back. He arched and thrashed, tearing at the sinewy muscles clamped against his windpipe. Seeing stars, Mitch gasped and went limp, then heaved hard against the monster. It didn't budge, nor did its vise. Mitch's vision blurred as something tingled against his thigh.

Reminded of the brooch Madame Bouvee had forced on him, he gathered his strength. Mitch was not going down without a fight. He struck out with both hands, aiming for the rangy lizard's eyes. One stiffened forefinger found its mark.

The creature howled and let go of Mitch, who sucked in glorious lungfuls of air. But the other three pinned him, pummeling him with blows and kicks.

"Stop!" a voice commanded from overhead.

It distracted the monsters long enough for Mitch to squirm free. He scrabbled backward through a sea of damaged goods and last season's clothes, all reeking of spilled whisky. Then, slicing his palm on a broken liquor bottle, he stood warily, applying pressure to stem the blood. The creatures gaped upward.

It was the wizened shopkeeper. Mitch did a double-take. She floated above the pit in a shimmering orb of white light. She pointed a finger, and the bizarre creatures fell to their knees.

The young woman trembled beneath an upside-down table.

"Pssst," he hissed, and the girl's head swiveled as he inched toward her.

"Go! Get out of here," Madame Bouvee barked, pointing to the door.

But it seemed very far away.

She swished her hand, and the lizard men fell prostrate on the ground.

That's all Mitch needed. He waded through the sea of refuse, grabbed the woman's hand, and dragged her from her hiding place. She stumbled behind him to his escape route.

He quickly glanced at the prone monsters and knitted his fingers into a sling. Then, motioning the girl to step on, he lifted her to the joist. She scrambled from the wreckage with Mitch close behind and was running from the store when he hoisted himself over the edge.

Hopefully, to safety, if there *was* such a thing. Mitch was beginning to wonder. He thought of the crazy histrionics of the Awen Order. He had thought their portents nonsense. But apparently the druids were paranoid for good reason.

"Baby boy."

That voice! The whispered words swirled inside him as Mitch turned toward the voice he recognized from all those years ago. It was the woman who had told him that William Hester was his birth father.

"You remember!" the witch crooned, orb pulsating around her. She smiled sweetly, and though her gums were mostly void of teeth, Mitch wasn't repulsed.

In the pit, one of the creatures stood on unsteady legs.

"Halt!" the woman barked.

"Do not harm us, witch," the monster said. "We will let the human go."

"You will let them all go," her voice boomed. "And you will return to the place from whence you came."

Another monster rose and hissed in defiance. "Or what, *Human?*"

Lightning sparked and danced around Madame Bouvee.

"Or I will strike you dead. All of you. Your choice."

Mitch backed toward the door, eye on the monsters.

The closest roared, "No witch, it is you who shall die!"

"Die! Die! Die!" they chanted, punching the air with clawed fists and pounding the ground with clawed feet that looked like they could tear a person into shreds.

"So be it." The witch cackled gleefully, extending a gnarled hand.

Lightning shot from her fingertips, and Mitch nearly choked when jagged bolts struck the chest of each being. One screeched and collapsed, smoke curling from a massive hole in its thorax. The others groaned and buckled to the ground.

A crashing boom shook the building, rattling the rickety walls and sending more wares into the gaping pit.

Then, frightened cries arose outside.

"Go! Find Awen," the witch shrieked. "Give her the stone. And, baby boy?"

Mitch gazed up at the glowing face and gasped. It had morphed to look remarkably like his own, and intense love pierced his heart. Inside his head, he heard the rest.

"Your driver awaits you at the Pescadero. Speak to no one else. Frederick will get you back to the mainland. But be forewarned. The Reptilians are shapeshifters. Only trust him after he's given the safe word."

"And what is that?" Mitch asked, still basking in the love she radiated.

"Awen Tide."

Then her face twisted. Eyes slanting inward, the witch drew a wand and flew past Mitch out the door.

"*RUN!*" she screeched.

But a new terror confronted Mitch outside. Chaos gripped the small village. Fear-crazed residents crashed into the dense jungle, fleeing creatures that poured from a gash where the laundromat had stood.

Madame Bouvee, or whoever the woman was, flew high above him, cackling and hurling lightning bolts at the green-scaled monsters. She spied Mitch by the wrecked emporium and screeched in his head, "RUN, DAMMIT!"

So, Mitch ran. Past the café and general store he ran, leather Keens slapping the hardpack. He zigged to avoid colliding with a villager and thanked God when his sandals stayed on in the scuffle.

Sweat beaded on every surface of his body. It rolled down Mitch's chest as he passed the boutique where he'd purchased his clothes and shoes. An eerie stillness befell the village as he slammed through the door of the Pescadero.

The occupants eyed him with curiosity, strangely calm. He dodged an older gentleman with flowing white hair who regaled two youngsters with a tale of times past, and hurried to the smoky back room where his driver waved him to a pool table. The lanky islander lowered his cue to line up a shot as Mitch threaded the crowd.

"Dude!" he huffed, reaching the table out of breath. "What the fuck? All hell is breaking loose out there."

Frederick eyed him sideways and lined up another shot.

"Uh-huh."

Mitch surveyed the scene, near hyperventilating. Why did the islanders seem unconcerned? Didn't they know what was happening?

"Are you ready to go? Madame Bouvee said you were waiting for me."

The local's dark eyes regarded him, reminding Mitch of the witch's warning.

"Oh, and what's the password?"

"Chill, dude. It's *Awen Tide*. Now move while I make this last shot."

☼☼☼

Alexis Mayhall flew above the island. As residents ran screaming through the small village, she zeroed in on a Reptilian standing over a downed human, cackled, and threw a lightning bolt.

Never had Alexis experienced the thrill of such magic. She had been a competent druid in her youth, but this was different. This magic was… intoxicating.

She executed a loop in the air and laughed gleefully. Never had Alexis been able to fly. Hell, she didn't know anyone who could.

Then a sobering thought occurred to her. Where had the power come from? The old crone in the store? She highly doubted it. But as she snuffed out the Reptilians one by one, Alexis couldn't help wondering.

Had the snake Elder, Nathair, imbued her with his magic? Could the animal Elders even do this sort of magic? To fly and shoot lightning bolts from the fingers of one's hands? It was exhilarating but terrifying, too.

Below her, Frederick and Mitchell exited the Pescadero, and her mother-heart leapt. Mitchell's head tilted up and he waggled his fingers, then stumbled but continued running toward the pier.

Alexis's breath caught. A brilliant halo surrounded the son Hamilton had taken from her.

She had kept her silence. But Alexis never forgave Hamilton, and had kept an eye on their son from that day forward. When the time was right, she had cornered him and told him about his father. But what she didn't reveal—could not reveal under penalty of death—was that she was his mother. Not Rona, her sister.

All in the name of the Order.

Alexis hurled lightning at two Reptilians lurking by the pier. Her son ran past them and boarded the motorboat with Frederick. Then, they shot through the surf with the westering sun at their backs. By her reckoning, they should make it to Nassau before nightfall.

Meanwhile, she would rout the rest of the Reptilians. What could they want with this tiny speck in the Bahamas, anyway? She zigzagged back and forth, searching for stragglers.

When reasonably sure she had destroyed them all, Alexis peered toward Nassau. Mitch's motorboat was a dot on the horizon. She landed, took a deep, centering breath, and called on her new-found powers to repair the damage to Zephyr Cay.

☼☼☼

The *Sweet Melissa* bounced over the boisterous waves. The sea was even rougher than it had been that morning and that was saying something. Mitch clung to the briefcase he had rescued from the inn.

They slammed into a trough, and his stomach protested. Normally, he didn't get seasick. This time was different.

Keeping his eyes on the horizon, he sucked on the ginger hard candy Frederick had tossed him earlier. Purple blood stains and stench clung to his body, so when spewing monster guts flashed in his head, it was too much.

He convulsed and clapped a hand over his mouth and slithered from the seat to hurl his guts over the side, shocked there was anything left. But with each new surge of nausea, Mitch retched violently.

When it finally calmed, he lay slung across the railing, too weak to get up or raise his head. A lone tear leaked from the corner of one eye as the horrific scene at Madame Bouvee's replayed in his mind. Like a bizarre episode of the Bollywood reality show, *Your Worst Nightmare,* it kept replaying. Only this was real—and it had happened to Mitch.

He stayed that way until the salty spray and brisk wind rejuvenated him. Enough, anyway, to drag his bones back into the seat. Frederick eyed him sympathetically.

"All betta?"

Mitch groaned and wagged his head. "Got any more of that ginger?"

The islander grinned, dug in the console, and passed him a handful of the hard candy.

By the time they made port in Nassau, the sun was sinking into the sea. Mitch felt substantially better. He had decided not to take the brooch to Emily. Instead, he would meet Shalane in Las Vegas before deciding whether to help.

He opened his briefcase and used his tablet to transfer the agreed-upon credits to Frederick, along with a generous tip. Then, climbing from the boat, he staggered on wobbly legs toward the taxi stand.

"Monsieur!" the driver called.

Mitch wheeled, hoping it wouldn't take long to get his land legs back. Frederick loped to him and gave Mitch a long, appraising stare.

"Yinna not gonna 'elp t'e Awen, arya?"

Surprised, Mitch gulped. How did this man know so much about his business?

"That woman has been my enemy since Day One. Why should I help her? What possible motivation would make me change my mind?"

"Yinna be an 'ero!"

"Who cares about that?"

Frederick's lip curled. "Yousa! You care 'but dat. 'Sides, wat ot'er choice is t'ere?"

Mitch pondered the question, then shrugged his shoulders.

"Exactly!" the islander scoffed. He watched the people scurrying around the quay, then lowered his face to Mitch's.

"T'e way I sees it," the dark man murmured, "yinna 'ave two choices. Take t'e pretty pin to Awen and be an 'ero. Or surrender to yer 'ate and be t'e sorry sonofabitch t'at let t'e 'uman race die."

Mitch grunted and climbed into the waiting van. The Bahamian watched him, muttering, and Mitch looked away as guilt twisted his gut. He didn't need a stranger to remind him of his inadequacies.

Finally, the van pulled away from the quay. Mitch wasn't due in the office for a couple of days. He would return to Atlanta, then fly on to Vegas.

That brought him up short. Had he really only arrived in Nassau this morning?

Catching his reflection in the window, he ran a comb through his hair and tried Shalane's number. When it went straight to voicemail, he hoped his message sounded calm and collected, neither of which he was feeling.

He was in line waiting to clear security when Mitch noticed other passengers eyeing him oddly. A young couple edged away, and he looked down and groaned. Dried blood marred his usual impeccable appearance, and he stank of lizard guts. A sink bath in the nearest restroom would have to do. It was too late for a shower or a change of clothes.

As Mitch passed through the scanner, something else hit him. He needed to report the Reptilian attack. But who could he tell? His cheeks burned. He would be labeled crazy and ridiculed just like Shalane's friend Patrika.

His law practice couldn't handle that kind of publicity. Shit, it might even get him disbarred. Without thinking, he tried Lugh MacBrayer. They were no longer friends. In fact, far from it. But Lugh was the head priest of the Awen Order and would know what to do.

Lugh didn't answer. Mitch left a detailed message, then bit the bullet and called Morgan, the Order's head of security. He wondered if she would take his call since he was no longer their attorney.

"Morgan Hester Foster," came the clipped greeting.

Mitch quickly relayed the details of the incident in Zephyr Cay and was shocked to learn his monster sighting was not the first. Brian MacBrayer, Lugh's nephew, had also had a run-in with them. The FBI had been notified and were taking action. Mitch relaxed a little. He had done his part.

Now, he had just enough time before boarding the plane to wash up and buy a ticket to Vegas. Tonight, he would get a good night's sleep and leave first thing in the morning.

But when he finally reached Atlanta, Mitch was exhausted and sick of the horror looping in his head. He took a taxi home, where he laid the sapphire brooch on the dresser. Then, ripping off his stinking clothes, he stuffed them in a plastic bag and threw them in the garbage bin behind the house.

In his walk-in shower, Mitch lathered and stayed beneath the spray until the stench no longer clung to him. Then, toweling dry, he climbed between his sheets, pulled the covers over his head, and passed out.

NOW WHAT?

In the last light of day, Alexis surveyed her work with amazement. Some other power had done this. It couldn't have been her. She had not practiced magic in thirty years and had never been able to do advanced stuff.

The terrified islanders quietly crept from the jungle, coaxed out by the silence that had descended in the aftermath of the brutal attack. Some cared for the injured, others dragged dead Reptilians to a pile. The rest gathered around Alexis as she worked.

Muttering chants and incantations, she lifted the corpses, then floated them to the beach and deposited them on the growing pile.

When the gruesome task was complete, a village elder drenched the pile in oil, and tossed a burning brand on top. The stack caught quickly, and soon acrid flames ascended to the dusky sky.

A sweet soprano broke into song, joined by other voices. The words were foreign, but it seemed to Alexis they were singing praise and gratitude. When they bowed to her, or rather to Madame Bouvee, she returned the gesture, humbled beyond anything she had felt in life.

Afterward, Alexis hobbled back to the emporium, closed the rickety door, and slumped against it. Now what?

She circled the repaired store and stopped in front of a full-length mirror beside a tiny dressing room and stared at Madame Bouvee's image in the dim overhead light.

How would Alexis look had she not died? Certainly not this bad. The proprietress must be ancient. Had Alexis lived, she would only be in her late 50s.

She studied lines etched so deeply that they folded and overlapped like brown leather ruching. Only a few teeth remained in her wide mouth. The silver hair was wound in dreadlocks that gave off a faint scent of musk and rosewood. Hunched and gnarled, her body ached, but her faded blue eyes gleamed.

A sudden pain in her right temple moved to her chest, then spread. Madame Bouvee had been kind enough to allow Alexis entry. Now the wizened islander wanted her out.

A bell jingled, and a couple burst through the door.

"Oh, thank God you're open! We need booze, and we need it now!"

The buxom blond American couldn't be more than twenty-five, thirty tops. A much older man trailed behind her, a rich sugar daddy from his groomed appearance. Eyeing Madame Bouvee with distaste, he wrapped an arm around the blonde's shoulders and pulled her toward the door.

"Honey, we have a bottle of wine in the room."

She shrugged away from him, her pretty face twisting in a petulant glare. "After what we just went through, I need something stronger." She pointed to a bottle behind the counter. "How about a liter of that Jack Daniels. And," she eyed Alexis hopefully, "do you carry Coca-Cola?"

Alexis shrugged, but the woman squealed and pointed to the bright red cans on a shelf near the Jack. "Yes! Look! They have Coca-Cola! I told you I would find some, didn't I?"

Alexis restrained the urge to roll her eyes. How old was this woman? Twelve?

The man groaned but agreed to the whisky and a six-pack of the coveted bubbly. Then, laying a proprietary arm on the woman's shoulder, he purred, "There, Honey. That's everything you wanted."

She batted her long, mascaraed lashes. "How about a couple of those marijuana cigarettes?" The man hesitated, and she nuzzled against him. "Please, Todd?" For a moment, she looked frightened and older, then she fluttered those lashes again. "I mean, shit, we were almost killed by monsters for God's sake!"

Her sugar daddy wagged his head, and Honey thrust out her lower lip.

"No nooky for you, then. Ever again."

But the guy was adamant. "Honey, no. No pot. All I want is to get off this miserable island and back to Atlanta. I need my wits. Just in case." He ventured a worried glance at Alexis, then laid his credit card on the counter. "Thank you, this will be all."

Honey brushed off his arm, huffed, and turned away, then dug a lipstick from the tiny purse hanging against her hip.

They were going to Atlanta. Hmm.

Alexis swiped the card in the gadget she assumed was for that purpose. As the couple left—Honey sulking and the man herding her out the door—an idea hatched.

She was still technically dead, and Talav had not said how long she would get to stay in the real world. The magic was heady, but Alexis couldn't stay in Madame Bouvee's body. Or on this island.

If she transferred into the bimbo, Alexis could be in Atlanta by tomorrow. That would allow her to contact her old friend, Morgan, and hopefully find out why monsters were roaming Zephyr Cay. Was it a coincidence the healer lived here and Emily had just left? Alexis thought not.

Using the key in Madame Bouvee's pocket, she flipped off the lights and locked the door, then stealthily followed the couple to the Seaside Villas.

AWEN'S GLADE

After parting ways with William's valet at the edge of the forest, the animal Elders led Emily to Awen's glade. She stepped through the circle of birch trees into a green sanctuary and gasped as the breath caught in her throat.

It was as she remembered from her dreams. On the other side of the clearing, water cascaded from a rocky outcrop. Below that, a pond glittered in the early morning sun.

These were the fabled Waters of Luftshorne. She owed her life to these waters—to them and her ancestor, the priestess Awen. After receiving a vision, Awen had enlisted the aid of a brave mare to rescue William of Normandy from an ambush, whisking him to this very glade.

He would have died without her timely intervention. Moreover, Awen's actions prevented a chain of cataclysmic events that would have destroyed Earth. Then, Emily would never have been born, much less be here today.

To the right of the pond, beneath the outer branches of a gigantic oak tree, nestled Awen's hut. Its thatched roof and bare-plank walls blended into the surrounding flora. A trickle of smoke rose from the stone chimney to disappear in the breeze.

The slanted morning sun filtered through spring leaves that rustled softly in the breeze. Songbirds gathered on the lower branches halted morning arias to gawk at Emily and her entourage.

Tarbh bugled and stamped the ground as he edged toward the pond. Emily and the Elder host followed.

From the water's edge, Dobhran, the otter Elder, chattered gleefully, "It is Awen, it is Awen! Come see, it is Awen!"

A salmon broke the surface and balanced on its tail. "Hail, Awen," Brayden gurgled, then splashed into the water.

Losgann appeared and hopped to the bank. "Welcome home, Awen. The Elder Host is delighted to stand in the radiance of your presence."

"Hail, Awen," a congregation of crickets sang.

"Hail, Awen!" honked Ella, the swan Elder. She glided to the grass to land gracefully in the midst of a loud bang and blinding flash.

Emily dove for the ground, covering her head. When nothing else happened, she peeked and gulped.

She was on the side of a frozen mountain and below her, a-Ur heaved lightning bolts at a witch. Beside him, Tienu stood frozen in place, encapsulated in a thick layer of ice.

The hag brandished her wand, and ice raced up a-Ur's legs. His shriek pierced Emily's heart, and she bent double, feeling his pain as it reached his chest. She rose from the snowbank and frantically searched for a way down to them.

But, Tienu's voice rang in her head. "Stop! It is a trap. Bé Chuille seeks you. Return to Awen's glade. That is an order."

Since Emily had no idea how she had gotten here, much less how to return, and she was finally in Beli and the twenty-first century, she hesitated.

But Tienu was insistent. "What you see is a vision that has already come to pass. It is a trick. Go back now. Before it is too late."

Then she was on the grass in Awen's clearing with the Elders staring down at her.

"What happened?" Losgann croaked. "Are you okay? You were about to speak, then went into a trance." The worried Elders crowded close.

Standing drunkenly, Emily brushed imagined snow from her cloak, then feeling silly, tossed heavy curls from her face.

"Yes, I am fine. But I was transported to Snowdonia. Tienu was frozen, and Draig a-Ur battled a witch. She was winning, but when I tried to help, Tienu magicked me back here. At least, I think he did."

She eyed the Elder Host. "Does the name Bé Chuille mean anything to you?" Tienu used it both times he referred to the crone.

"That's the winter hag!" Reinu, the ram Elder, bleated. "What is the wicked witch up to now?"

"I do not know." Emily scrubbed her face in her hands. The brief encounter had shattered the tiny amount of peace she had gained in Awen's glade. A deep foreboding crept upon her, and her fear was reflected in the animals' eyes.

"It's okay," she reassured. "I may be young and green and not the powerful Awen you all remember, but I will figure this out. I know there's a way back to the twenty-first century. I just have to find it. Now, where were we, before I was so rudely whisked away?"

Echk, the horse Elder, nudged Emily with her silken white nose.

"We were telling you how happy we are to see you. That stands no matter your age or abilities. We are tied to you in life and death. When you live, we live. When you die, we die and return to the Otherworld until you live again. Your presence has called us to this place and time.

"Our sole purpose, Awen, is to support you in your appointed task as the Peace Maker, Master Druid, and High Priestess—She Who Keeps Earth Safe. We have been with you for eons, much longer than you may remember. In life, we assist you, and in death, we hold your power and your memories until you incarnate once more."

Leaning close, Emily touched her forehead to Echk's and cradled her silken face.

"Thank you, Echk."

She backed away and looked around the semicircle at Gyarr, the rabbit, Faol, the black wolf, Elij, the willowy deer hind, Torc and Muc, the wild boar and sow, Bo, the shaggy cow, and all the others whose names and powers she had learned from Hope.

"I do not know what strength lies within me. But one person alone cannot to stop the dark forces being released into the world. I will need each of you and all the friends we can muster if we are to have a fighting chance. I have seen the enemy. They are a vicious, warring Reptilian race without souls. And now we know they are not the only threat. What else can you tell me about this Bé Chuille?"

Sionnach, the fox Elder, slipped silently from a bed of reeds and stood at the feet of Echk and Tarbh. "The Cailleach is wily, Master. Cruel and wicked. And though Bé Chuille was once a beautiful goddess, thwarted ambition and narcissism blackened her heart." The fox paused. "She never did care about others, only ever thinking of herself."

"But should we worry about her? Is she dangerous?" Emily wound a curl around her finger and nibbled at the ends. She already knew the answer.

"Aye, that she is," Giagh, the goose Elder, honked. "But no one calls her Bé Chuille. Not anymore. All have forgotten that the winter hag *is* Bé Chuille. She was once a valuable member of the Tuatha de Danaan, but her wickedness grew so strong, Queen Druantia banished her to the ice lands. There she has remained, becoming ever more cruel and bitter and gnarled, biding her time until she can bring death upon Druantia's line."

A chill passed over Emily, and her whole body trembled.

Muc, the sow Elder, known for nourishment and abundance, ambled to the front. Her long bottom teeth protruded above her top lip as she peered up at Emily anxiously.

"We are wearing you thin. Come, Awen. Let us get you settled into your hut. You are in need of a good meal and some strong brew. *And* a hot bath." A faraway expression clouded Muc's kindly eyes. Then they refocused on Emily. "Soon your betrothed will join you." The long lashes blinked suggestively. "You don't want to be stinking of feces."

Emily's face flamed. She had been wearing the stench so long she no longer smelled it except for an occasional whiff. But what did Muc mean?

"Betrothed? You mean… like a fiancé? I don't have one of those."

The sow's eyes narrowed. She twisted to peer up at Tarbh, then the rest of the Elder host.

"Never mind that for now." Tarbh stamped his feet. "You will find everything you need in your hut. There is food in the pantry, heated water in the tub, clean clothes in the wardrobe, and fresh bedding on the mattress. The Elder host will take turns standing guard."

The image of the air dragon battling Bé Chuille, and Tienu encased in a block of ice crowded into Emily's mind.

"What about Draig Tienu and the other Keepers? They are in danger."

Tarbh and Echk shared a look, but Elij, the doe, responded.

"That cannot be helped. Not until your preparation is complete. The good news is: Beltane is upon us. But until then, Beli is a death trap."

Emily shivered. Tienu had said the same thing.

THE GREAT PEACEMAKER

Despite his earlier reluctance, Khenko enjoyed seeing the members of the defunct Iroquois Council. Most were kin, including his cousins Jere, Josh, and Johanna. They'd reminisced briefly about the Six Flags incident, then joined the impromptu gathering, listening to his father and two of the more ancient Elders speak of their unease and the uncertain times. Now, he was anxious to get away from them all.

Changing into a pair of old running shoes, Khenko hurried to the gate. He let himself out onto Mercer Avenue with no particular destination in mind. Sweat soon popped out on his brow, but the trees lining the street were full and luscious, shading him from the heat of the evening sun.

Contentment and a sense of belonging coursed through Khenko as he passed the houses he'd known since youth—Mary Beth's, Cynthia's, Billy and Joel's. The old Baxter home was still spooky, even now as an adult in the light of day.

From the outside, the neighborhood looked the same. The homes here passed from generation to generation rarely changing hands. Khenko's had belonged to his mother's people, Dutch settlers instrumental in the early years of Princeton's development.

His mom's ancestor, Pernicia Bloom, had been kidnapped by the Mohawks, as was often the case when a white man's musket killed one of their matriarchs. As was their custom, Pernicia took the place of the murdered Mohawk woman.

Amazingly, she had taken to her new life and flourished. Pernicia's mate, a lusty brave named Two Wolves Howling, eventually became the tribe leader. Their descendants went on to aid in the formation of the Iroquois Confederacy.

Skirting a busy intersection, Khenko cut through an alley and a parking lot and soon reached Princeton Battlefield State Park.

It was quieter here. A man could think. Khenko was no longer used to hustle and bustle and people everywhere. Life on Zephyr

Cay had been laid back. This insane pace and noise level could drive a gentle person insane.

He slowed to a walk, long stride gobbling the asphalt while his mind ran over the events of the last days. That nagging feeling had not gone away. Instead, it continued to grow keener. He still didn't know why he had awakened alone at the vortex on his ferry, rocking in a stormy sea. Nor why he had gone out before sunup. Or why the voices had talked him into returning to Princeton.

Khenko knew the answers were important. And he was pretty sure there was a dragon involved. Or dra*gons*. The image of a multicolored she-drake flashed, and for a moment, he remembered. Then, the thought tendril waned and disappeared.

Frustrated, he focused on his mother's mystery.

A prophecy delivered to the White House by a witch who then disappeared. A god and goddess living inside Earth trying to right a failed experiment. And mysterious goings-on in the Azores Islands, where Khenko was born.

His jaw tightened. That last one really pissed him off. Why would his parents let Khenko believe for thirty-five years that he'd been born in Princeton? He was anxious to hear the answer to that *and* the circumstances of his birth. Then Khenko faltered.

His birth certificate listed Princeton Hospital as his place of birth. If he'd been born in Corvo, how did they pull that one off?

The woods thinned and opened to a clearing with a statue in the center. The sign declared this section was dedicated to the Iroquois Confederacy. Khenko vaguely remembered his mother proudly telling him about the statue and its dedication last year.

He admired the life-sized bronze, and leaned closer to read the placard.

"THE GREAT PEACEMAKER DEGANAWIDA AND HIAWATHA, Cofounders of the Iroquois Confederacy. Their example sparked the spread of democracy across the globe, beginning with the United States of America."

Without warning, Khenko's sight went blurry, and he collapsed cross-legged to the concrete.

In the body of a crane, he soared above a teal ocean with two ibises, one named Druantia and the other Thoth. They soon reached a small island and dove for the grassy crater of an old volcano.

The surface screamed toward him, and Khenko squawked. Then they broke through the Earth and slammed into some sort of energetic webbing. He kept flapping his wings but remained in place.

"What in the world?" he wondered.

"Now, that is the right question," Druantia croaked.

Khenko came to with a start, swimmy-headed and more than a little freaked out. A couple strolling hand-in-hand gave him an odd look and a wide berth. He lowered his forehead into his hands until the wooziness passed. Then he noticed the storm clouds scudding in his direction. How long before the rain arrived?

In an effort to quiet his insides, he breathed deeply, but the snake residing in his gut was restless. It writhed upon itself, and the deep sense of foreboding ratcheted up another notch.

He closed his eyes and the vision returned. Only this time, he descended a narrow tunnel with the ibises until it ended in a deep, dark well. Khenko struggled to come to, then blinked. The clouds had overtaken the sun.

A newly sprung breeze sent leaves and candy wrappers skittering across the grass. Chills roved Khenko's body, making the hairs stand at attention. He knew enough about visions to know that he should relax and go with it. But he was too exposed. He had no idea how deep the vision would take him, or for how long. Plus, a storm brewed.

Lightning flashed on the horizon, barely visible above the trees. Khenko stood and counted five seconds before thunder rumbled in the distance. He had five minutes, max. Not enough time to make it home.

The only pavilion in sight was occupied by a young family with a large brood of kids. Nodding respectfully to the statues of the Peacemaker and Hiawatha, Khenko turned and ran. With any luck, he would find shelter.

But luck was having nothing to do with Khenko Blitherstone.

The clouds billowed, growing blacker and angrier by the minute. Wind whipped through the trees, and lightning bolts split the firmament—one, then another, and another. Their three booming cracks merged to shake the sidewalk.

Khenko ran full out, praying to a God he wasn't sure was there. But the clouds burst, releasing a hard, soaking rain.

Spying a Plexiglas bus stop, he galloped to it and ducked beneath the cover. The others made space for Khenko as rain battered the enclosure and ricocheted off the pavement.

The scent of wet asphalt and earth delighted Khenko. He squeezed water from his hair and grinned from ear to ear. He had always loved Princeton's crazy weather.

Wiping the rain from his face, he beamed at a college kid armed with books and another carrying a musical instrument. Alexander Hall was around the corner.

"Are you practicing, or do you have a performance?" Khenko asked.

The shy brunette blushed and looked away before answering. "We're practicing for a performance."

"Excellent! Congratulations."

The girl's blush grew deeper.

"That means you're really good. Not just anyone gets to play in Alexander Hall.

"T-thank you." She grinned, clutching the case tighter.

The rain showed no sign of slacking. It splashed into the enclosure, and the Plexiglas took the brunt of its force. A loud clap of thunder exploded beside them, and someone squealed. Khenko flushed, not a hundred percent sure it wasn't him.

Then, another storm entered his vision—one that swept upon Zephyr Cay.

Lightning arced overhead, and the fine hairs on Khenko's body danced in response. Then thunder boomed, and the sweet scent of ozone saturated the air. The occupants huddled closer to get as far from the elemental fury as possible.

The storm was directly over their heads now. Lightning sizzled, and thunder cracked. The musician screamed. Behind her, an older gentleman spoke softly in a calm, reassuring tone.

But the snake in Khenko's gut coiled, and a lump rose in his throat.

A redheaded woman ran across the beach to the verandah of the Atlantean Center. Behind her, a dragon scurried into the jungle to escape the downpour, a multicolored behemoth with penetrating gold eyes.

A tug at his shirt sleeve brought Khenko back.

"Sir, are you okay?" It was the brainiac with the books.

The rain had stopped as abruptly as it had begun. A bus waited, its door thrust open, and the shelter was empty except for Khenko, the young man, and his friend, the bassoon player.

Blinking the woman and dragon from his eyes, Khenko thanked the kid and bid the girl a magnificent performance.

Then, with darkness nipping at his heels, he loped through the rain-washed evening, grateful for the streetlights. Like homing beacons, they guided him along the edge of Princeton's Campus and safely home.

CATCHING A BREAK

Metal banged against the bars, rousing Nergal from the trance-like state that helped him bear the pain. Groaning, he pulled himself to an upright position and crouched in the deep recesses of the cell.

The door clicked open, and a guard stood to the side.

"General Nergal, by order of Warlord Shibboleth, you are to be transported to World Headquarters in Irkalla. Your escort awaits."

Staring in disbelief, Nergal hesitated. Was this a trap? Would the guard kill him when he left the cell? Taking his chances, Nergal charged out of the cell and limped as fast as possible down the corridor. A locked gate stopped him. Roaring in frustration, he glanced behind him. The guard was not in sight.

There was a loud snick. The gate vibrated and swung open when Nergal pushed against it. He passed through to the outer room. Two guards waited, weapons drawn.

This was it. Nergal prepared to die. His claws went into the air instinctively, but instead of shooting him, one of the Dracos gestured toward a door leading to the outer corridor.

Keeping his eyes on their guns, Nergal stepped sideways to the door and slipped through, shivering when the guards fell into place behind him. But death did not come. They shadowed Nergal as he hurried down the long hall to an elevator. Then, they entered behind him, weapons pointed at his chest.

When the doors opened, Mot, Shibboleth's remaining Death Bringer, waited in full battle gear. Rage seized Nergal, and he lunged at the loathsome Drac.

"You killed Ishkur!"

"You killed my brother!" Mot bellowed, as Nergal slammed into him, wrestling the younger Drac to the ground.

"General Nergal, cease your attack at once!" Mot gurgled, but Nergal applied pressure to his neck. It was kill or be killed. Then he noticed the six guards surrounding them, weapons pointed at Nergal.

"Nergal, stop!" Mot gasped. "You are to be freed."

"You lie," Nergal hissed. But he relaxed his death grip.

Mot lay still and sucked in air.

"I speak the truth. Warlord Shibboleth issued a stay of execution for you and your comrades. Your rank and privilege will be reinstated upon our return to Irkalla. You would kill me for that?"

"I would kill you for trying to slay me." But Nergal eased up on the force against Mot's chest. "Why should I believe you? What reason would Shibboleth have for sparing me?"

Mot blinked up at Nergal, who still kneeled on his chest.

"Honestly? I have interceded with Shibboleth on your behalf. Too many Dracs have been needlessly slaughtered. We suffer a shortage of seasoned warriors and a dirge of officers that command respect. You, General Nergal, are such an officer."

His explanation shocked Nergal.

"I also believe you to be loyal to the Reptilian nation. It took some doing, but I convinced Shibboleth you would be a valuable asset against the humans. Now, would you mind removing your knees from my chest?"

Nergal rolled off Mot, then considered the Drac's words. Despite Shibboleth's long-standing vendetta against Nergal, his spawn appeared to be telling the truth. Nergal pointed to the weapon lashed between Mot's shoulder blades.

"Will you run me through with that lance when I turn my back?"

Mot withdrew the weapon, pointing its deadly tip toward the ceiling. "In different circumstances, I probably would. But if we are to win our war against AboveEarth, we need you alive. Once that is accomplished, I cannot say. But until our common enemy is defeated, you, General Nergal, are safe from me and Lord Shibboleth."

"And your warriors?" Nergal eyed the Dracs crowded around them.

"They are sworn to protect you and will follow you into battle when the time comes."

The muscles in Nergal's neck relaxed. "And Inanna? I would take her as my second-in-command since you have slain Ishkur."

"Not possible," Mot declared. "Inanna will travel with us to Irkalla. But she will remain in the capitol to rule beside Shibboleth."

Nergal's brows shot up. It was no secret that Inanna despised her litter father. And from what she had told Nergal, Shibboleth felt the same about her. So what scheme was the warlord devising?

Surrounded by guards, Inanna limped into line behind the contingent escorting Nergal. Her body vibrated with hatred, keeping her mind off the pain.

Inanna searched the crowd for the doctora. Not seeing Magdalena, her gaze went to Mot, her despicable litter brother, who stood at the front of the platform. He and Maw had made her life a living hell for five centuries.

Most recently, Mot had murdered Ishkur, her consort. He had also allowed the mercenaries to beat Inanna to within an inch of her life and imprisoned her in the filthy, vermin-ridden dungeons of Araf. Now, she was supposed to forgive and forget. And take orders from the arrogant worm? No way.

Closing her eyes, Inanna imagined the magma scorching Mot and Shibboleth, taking their lives like Maw's. But it changed nothing. Shibboleth had advanced Mot to second in command and intended Inanna to be his third. Over her dead body.

She would not stay in Irkalla with her litter father, even under the penalty of death. But she would play along, then deal with the rest when the time came. Meanwhile, she would use the hour to reach Irkalla to get some much-needed sleep.

Nergal studied Mot, Shibboleth's spawn. On leaving the station, the muscular Draco had fallen asleep sprawled across a bench in the chute car. Unlike his nasty litter-brother, Mot's claws were bare rather than painted red. Mot's distinctive vest was another story. Fashioned from an arthropod's shell, Nergal recognized it as similar to the one Maw had worn.

A despicable Draco in his own right, Mot was downright civilized compared to his brother. He certainly possessed more brain power. Had Shibboleth not groomed Mot as a warrior, he could have made a formidable technologist. Of course, most brainy sorts were short of stature. Not Mot. He was taller and leaner than either Shibboleth or Maw, but his skull was large like Ishkur's. With a brain like that, would Mot make a good leader?

He had a few characteristics in common with Nergal. Mot's scales leaned more toward beige than olive, and his shoulder blades protruded in rudimentary wing nubs. As far as Nergal knew, none of Shibboleth's spawn had inherited his wings. But Mot had inherited his tail.

The chute car rocked back and forth as they rumbled through a station. The lights flashed, and a computer voice rattled off their destination and time of arrival. Nergal stared at the dark tunnels through the chute windows and thought of their fateful flight from Agatha.

Then a conversation he'd had with Ishkur in the lab came to mind. While researching and devising the Human Domination project, the Vice Major had uncovered evidence of DNA tampering. At the time, it had seemed farfetched to Nergal. But after recent developments, he was inclined to embrace Ishkur's theory. Or at least accept it.

Ishkur had claimed the reptilian race had not always been sentient. Or not like now. They had basic communication skills and kept to themselves. Like humans, they had operated within a race mind, living an eat-or-be-eaten lifestyle. But that was before Sumerian gods tinkered with the DNA of both races.

Shibboleth claimed his line hailed from Lord Enki. Nergal, on the other hand, had been born in a pod. But Ishkur's research had revealed that Nergal, too, descended from the gods—possibly from Enki's brother, Lord Enlil.

But one thing Ishkur had been sure about, the Sumerian gods had shaped the Reptilian race, then brought them to Earth. Other than that, their history was foggy.

As the chute car thundered through another station, regret over Ishkur's death assailed Nergal. Or maybe it was sorrow. Nergal was unschooled in emotions, and until recently, had prided himself on the lack of such weakness. But that was before.

Resolving to dig deeper into Ishkur's supposition, Nergal shoved his thoughts aside. He needed sleep. And according to the overhead monitor, they would be in Irkalla in less than an hour.

CHARLOTTE FIELD OFFICE

At exactly 12:00 midnight Eastern Time, Elise Hester Johnson strode into the Charlotte Field Office of the Federal Bureau of Investigations. Flashing her badge to the grunt at the front desk, she requested an audience with the agent in charge. The man raised an eyebrow, then muttered into a phone and pointed to a line of chairs against the wall.

After spending the last hours on her ass, the last thing Elise wanted was to sit. She ignored the peeling brown Naugahyde chairs and leaned against the wall.

The FBI duty station looked as old and small as Elise felt. The walls were a faded Comet-green, and the tan cubicles were scuffed and blotchy. A layer of dirt coated the closed blinds, and a cobweb danced from a lazily revolving ceiling fan. Tattered magazines lay face up on a rickety table beside the chairs.

But at least it was cool. Outside was like a furnace.

A phone jangled in the back room, making Elise jump. Then the front door burst open, startling her again.

A tall, well-proportioned agent juggling an armful of takeout from China Wok strolled into the office. He nodded to Elise as he passed, trailing an aroma that elicited a growl from her belly. The meal she'd had before boarding the plane had been less than appetizing. Between that and the anxiety, most of it had remained on her plate.

Scanning the wanted posters on the wall behind the chairs, Elise raked her fingers through her new short do. Many of the mugshots she recognized from AIA headquarters, but a couple of the faces were new to her. Leaning closer, Elise read the names, aliases, and offenses and nearly leapt from her skin when a burly agent touched her shoulder.

"Holy crap!" she shrieked, shoving her firearm back in its holster. "You almost got shot."

The imposing man introduced himself as Special Agent Charles Timmons. She gave him her name and credentials, shook his beefy hand, and announced she was there to pick up Brian MacBrayer and his companion, Ethnui.

Five minutes of one-upping ensued in which Charles Timmons did his best to forestall Elise. Then, he finally conceded. The transfer was signed by the FBI Director herself, and he could find no fault with the paperwork.

Relaxing infinitesimally, Elise availed herself of the loo while the agent fetched Brian and Ethnui. When she stepped back out, they were walking toward her.

Brian blinked and started to say something, but Elise shook her head inconspicuously. The dark eyes gleamed, and her godson stayed silent as she whisked him and his terrified friend out of the station and into the waiting sedan. When the back door slammed, Brian's usual twenty questions began.

"Shhh," Elise ordered. "All in good time. Now, buckle up."

It was barely morning in the UK, but she sent a quick text to Cybele, letting her know Elise had been successful in springing Brian from the FBI. Now, she had to get them on the plane and back to his mother.

As she pulled from the curb, Brian slapped his hands on the back of the seat. Elise reached for her gun, then glared at him in the rearview mirror. As she backed from the space an older man's voice gurgled with glee.

One hand on the shifter, Elise gasped. The voice was that of her cousin, Hamilton Hester—*not* Cybele's fourteen-year-old son. But Hamilton was dead. She had attended his funeral.

"Elise Hester Johnson, I have never been so happy to see you in my life!"

That was definitely Hamilton's voice.

Swerving to the shoulder, Elise slammed on the brakes and fixed her gaze on the boy in the mirror.

"Hamilton Hester? Is that you?"

Both kid's heads bounced up and down, and Elise's heart leapt.

"Damn you, Hamilton, I thought you were dead. I even went to your freaking funeral." She dabbed at her eyes, thinking of all the tears she had shed. They didn't often talk these days, but they'd been best friends for as long as Elise could remember.

Ham's sonorous voice tumbled from the boy. "But someone did try to kill me, 'Lise. Hell, they succeeded, as you can attest. Lucky for me, I'm a master druid and have the ability to shift bodies."

Elise squeezed the hand resting on the seat. "Thank the goddess Brian was around!"

"My first host was Cu, the Irish wolfhound. You remember him, don't you, 'Lise?"

"With extreme fondness." Elise had last seen the dog Elder on the day of Hamilton's funeral. "But Morgan told me you never regained consciousness. How did you manage the transfer?"

"Do you really think my bossy stepsister knows everything?"

"Good point."

Aware of the tight schedule, Elise activated the grill flashers and stomped the gas pedal, steering the bucking sedan onto the interstate. Then, for kicks, she shoved the pedal to the floor. The turbo kicked in and Elise swerved to the left lane, gleefully threading traffic.

In the rearview mirror, she noted Brian clinging to his shoulder harness. Ethnui's head swung side to side, taking in the terrain. When the girl jerked around to gawk at a herd of Holsteins, her saucy cap tilted, and Elise caught a glimpse of one pointed ear.

The girl hastily repositioned her cap with a guilty peek at Brian. He bumped her shoulder good-naturedly.

"We don't have to worry about Aunt Elise. Welcome to AboveEarth, Ethnui," he cooed with an affectionate grin. "Didn't I say you would love it up here?"

Then his countenance matured, and the voice deepened. "Where are you taking us, Special Agent Johnson?"

It was odd hearing Hamilton's voice coming from the boy who happened to be a miniature version of his father, Jake MacBrayer.

"To the Air National Guard Base. A company plane is waiting." Elise swerved to pass a vehicle on the right, then quickly cut in front of it.

"This is the second wild ride we've had today," Brian laughed, "and I like it. But I think Ethnui might be sick."

The girl had paled, and indeed, looked ill. Elise killed the flashers and settled into the left lane.

☼☼☼

Brian leaned his chin over the seatback. "I'm hungry. Can we stop and eat?"

His godmother eyed him in the rearview mirror.

"We'd better not, Hun. We're on a tight schedule, and I really don't want to miss this plane. No telling what kind of torture trap

130

we would end up in." She checked her mirrors for the umpteenth time as if worried they were being followed.

"What about a drive-through, Aunt Elise? Pleeease?" To prove his point, Brian's stomach growled so loud Ethnui giggled.

"Oh, alright," his aunt conceded. "If there is one between here and the base."

"There's a Chick-fil-A at this next exit." Brian had been keeping an eye on the signs. "I haven't had one of those in ages."

"Nor have I," Elise confessed.

When it looked like they would keep going, Brian sighed loudly and whined, "Aren't we stopping?"

At the last possible moment, they exited and Brian spied the restaurant directional sign.

"Hang a right, Aunt Elise."

The black sedan screeched into the driveway of Chick-fil-A and joined the long line of cars.

"This better not take long," Elise groaned.

But the line moved swiftly, and soon the attendant handed a box with three drinks and a bag of food to Elise through the driver's window. She pulled into a space just long enough to take her food and pass the bag and drinks to the back seat. Then they were on the road again.

Brian wolfed his sandwich, along with his waffle fries and lemonade. Then he unwrapped a second and devoured that as they wheeled into the Air National Guard Base.

ROWDY RANDY

On the cusp of sleep, Khenko startled awake.

He flopped over, exasperated, and fluffed his pillow beneath his head to try another calming technique. Hoping to persuade his anxious body to succumb to sleep's glorious throes, Khenko contemplated his heart.

"The heart is the hub of all sacred places. Go there and roam."

It was one of Khenko's favorite sayings by Bhagawan Nityananda, an enlightened guru from the twentieth century.

But tonight it wasn't working. *Nothing* was working. Not even his mother's pipe. Now, it was just past midnight.

Huffing, Khenko kicked the covers back and climbed out of bed. He grabbed his laptop from the dresser and propped his back against the heavy wood headboard, tapping keys. The air conditioner whined beneath his window, working overtime to cool the thick, damp air left behind by the storm.

Before he had retired, Khenko researched anything and everything to do with disturbances in the Azore Islands. There wasn't much. Now he'd reached another dead end. He groaned loudly in frustration.

Determined to find *something*, he typed "Thoth" in the search bar.

His mother had said he was a Sumerian god. But as Khenko had thought, Thoth was listed in the Egyptian pantheon. He was depicted in their ancient drawings with—HA!—an ibis head.

Responsible for bringing civilization to the world in the form of literature and the arts, Thoth had dictated a book that still survived today. It was said this work outlined the path to ascension and everlasting life.

Khenko took a peek at the online version. But despite his best intentions, he kept getting lost in endless iterations that seemed to take him nowhere.

Still, it appeared Thoth was a god's god. He had intervened in their wars, saving them, and the world, from themselves. He had also brought the great Osiris back to life, and refused to be drawn into the petty grievances of the other gods and goddesses. It was even suggested that the Greek god Hermes and Thoth were one and the same.

Less well-known but equally fascinating, Druantia was a Celtic goddess known as the Queen of the Druids. She was considered a triple goddess who ruled birth, death, immortality, and metempsychosis. What the heck?

Like Thoth, Druantia inspired the study of the stars and their movements. But where Thoth had his eyes on the moon, she was intent upon the earth and physical sciences.

Khenko highlighted the word "metempsychosis," copied and pasted it to his browser, then read the first two results aloud.

"Metempsychosis is the passing of the soul at death into another body either human or animal. – Merriam-Webster"

"Metempsychosis refers to the transmigration of the soul, especially its reincarnation after death. – Wikipedia"

He thrummed his fingertips on the laptop. "That means, Thoth and Druantia were both known for their ability to reincarnate and/or change bodies," he mumbled to himself. This made sense considering gods were supposed to be immortal.

Bookmarking the information for future reference, Khenko closed his laptop and laid it on the bed table. Two minutes later, he was sawing logs.

☼☼☼

Duh duh duh DUH, duh duh duh duhhh…
The opening strains of Beethoven's 5th dragged Khenko from a sinister dream in which he'd been tangled in a spider's web. Unable to escape, he was waiting for an attacker he couldn't see but knew was there.

Shuddering, Khenko snatched his cell phone and peered at the time. It was one a.m. He'd been asleep for all of five minutes.

"Hullo?" His voice was scratchy and gruff.

"CUZ! You're awake! Come over here and party with us." It was Josh. His cousin.

"Dude," Khenko groaned. "Do you know what time it is? I just got to sleep."

"So come on, then," Jere interjected. Apparently they had him on speakerphone.

"Get yo' pantywaist-self out of that bed and get over here!" That voice was a blast from the past.

"Rowdy? Is that you?" Khenko gasped. "Last I heard, your sorry ass was in Kosovo or some such country. Long time no see."

Randy "Rowdy" Kowalski had been a fixture in Josh and Jere's lives, and by extension, Khenko's, until Randy joined the service two years after high school. Then, the rowdiest partier in Mercer County had transformed into a rock-hard, by-the-book grunt. Khenko had seen him only a handful of times over the intervening years.

"Yes, it's me. I just got off tour in Kazakhstan and will soon report to my dream assignment in the Azores."

Khenko sat up in bed. "The Azores? Seriously?"

"Looks like it. I'm their top communications expert, K-Man. They send me to all the sweet spots."

"Yeah, yeah," Josh quipped. "You coming to Jere's or not?"

His feet hit the floor. Rowdy was headed to the Azores, and Khenko didn't believe in coincidences. Everything happened for a reason. And Rowdy was the best computer hacker Khenko had ever known. Maybe his childhood friend could help Khenko crack the Corvo mystery.

"I'm leaving now. See you in a few."

And that's all it took, even on foot. When Khenko knocked on Jere's door, it opened wide and Randy Kowalski's massive frame filled the doorway. He held a beer in one hand and drew Khenko inside with the other, then through the foyer to the den.

Music played quietly in the background. Josh and Jere greeted Khenko with bear hugs, then went back to throwing darts.

Following Rowdy to the kitchen, Khenko accepted a beer. Rowdy eyed him up and down, then nodded appreciatively.

"You finally grew into those feet and ears, huh? You're not the stringbean I remember."

Khenko bobbled the beer and put it back in the refrigerator.

Rowdy's eyebrows arched.

"It's late and I'm not really in a partying mood. But I would like to run something past you." Khenko studied the hard-bodied Marine who had once weighed close to four-hundred pounds. Granted the guy had the skeleton of a giant and stood a full six-foot-seven inches.

"You look good, Randy. The best I've ever seen."

"Where you going, sore loser?" Jere yelled from the living room.

Randy's complexion pinked. "That's what happens when you join the Marines." He proudly tugged the starched tan shirt from his green trousers and patted six-pack abs.

Josh strode into the kitchen and whistled. He lobbed his empty can at the trash and threw an arm around Randy and Khenko's midsections, then drew them together in a grip that surprised Khenko.

Pulling away, he eyed his cousin.

"Been working out, Josh?" A half foot shorter than Randy, the two of them would make a formidable tag team. Randy stuffed his shirt back into his pants.

Josh flicked Khenko's abdomen. "And you *haven't*, have you, K-Man? Still as soft as ever." His lip curled. "But daaamn it's good to see you, bro."

Jere strolled in. Josh's fraternal twin had a more compact physique and was the brains of the two. And while Josh had inherited his father's straight, raven hair, Jere's was muddy brown and kinky. Like Khenko's.

"I'm off to bed," Jere said. "You guys keep the noise down and don't destroy the place." He gave Josh the stink eye. "And *you* need to get home to Layla."

"Naw, I told Layla I'd be hanging with the boys. Hell, it's been nearly twenty years since we've all been together."

"Twenty years? Damn." Khenko snorted. "You three are getting old."

"Especially Randy," Jere chuckled, punching him lightly in his six-pack. "Dude's retiring at the end of the year."

"Not anymore." Randy's head wagged. "They offered me a plum gig, so I re-upped for another tour."

"No way. What did your girl have to say about that?" Jere looked thoughtful.

"She's stoked! We're hoping she can come with me."

"Awesome." Jere clapped him on the back. "You guys can crash here if you want." He glanced at Josh. "Except you. Layla will have your head, so I called you a cab. It'll be here in a minute." He waved and exited, saying over his shoulder, "I'm glad you two are back. It's good to see you."

"Same here, Jere," Khenko called, then rounded on Josh. "You drag me out of bed in the middle of the night then *leave*?"

"It's Randy's fault." Josh waved at their childhood friend. "Ask him." Then he left too.

Which left Khenko and Rowdy staring at one another in Jere and Josh's childhood home, the site of many escapades of the Fantastic Four. That's what they had called themselves.

"Let's sit," Randy said, not seeming all that rowdy anymore.

He led the way to the den and perched on the seat of an armchair. When Khenko sat on the faded floral sofa, Randy leaned closer and lowered his voice.

"Do you know Elise Hester Johnson?"

"Elise Hester Johnson," Khenko repeated, turning the name over in his mind. "No, I don't think so. Should I?" But something niggled.

"That depends. Have you had any dealings with the Alien Intelligence Agency?"

Excitement surged through Khenko. "Dealings, no. But I've heard of the organization. Is it real?"

The lines around Rowdy's lips and eyes relaxed.

"Yes, it's real. In fact, the AIA is the clandestine arm of the U.S. Space Force. It's charged with monitoring alien activity on Earth."

"Whoa." Khenko leaned closer, impressed. "And you're part of that?"

"Remember I said I was re-upping for a plum assignment in the Azores?"

"Uh-huh."

"Well, that's not entirely true. Special Agent Johnson approached me and said that if I could enlist you in the AIA's cause, she would see I get assigned to Lajes Field in the Azores. But she made it clear—she needs you, not me. So I'm only in if you are." Randy peered intently at Khenko, who stared back, dumbfounded.

"I really want that posting, Khenko. My lady finally agreed to marry me and I want this as her wedding gift. Plus, it's the Alien Intelligence Agency, K! Remember how much we wanted to hunt aliens when we were growing up?"

Chuckling, Khenko nodded, remembering the countless hours they'd spent stalking aliens with toy tomahawks and spears.

"Now is our chance. For *both* of us, K-Man." When Khenko remained quiet, Randy's face crumbled a little.

"I get why they want you. You're still active duty, Randy. But, why me? I will be forty in a few years. They don't recruit old farts into the service."

Randy laughed. "No, they don't. But you're apparently special, Khenko." He inspected Khenko's frame and shrugged. "Maybe they need a consultant."

Khenko squirmed, uncomfortable with the thought of working for the government, but intrigued, nonetheless. "What does this Johnson lady want me to do?"

"Hell, if I know." Randy wiped his brow. It was cool, but he was in full military garb and beginning to sweat. "Still, it wouldn't hurt to talk to her. If you don't like her offer, you can refuse." He scratched his nose. "For my sake, I hope you accept, though."

The niggle grew stronger. "What did you say her full name is?"

"Elise Hester Johnson."

"Hester, huh? I might know a Hester." At the edge of his consciousness danced a gamine face with an upturned nose, fascinating green eyes, and red hair tipped in gold. Khenko groped for the memory but it disappeared. He waggled his head. "Nope, it's gone."

Randy glanced at his wrist unit, then at Khenko expectantly. "So, whaddya think?"

Letting go a loud breath, Khenko leaned against the sofa. He didn't like where this was going. "Did you come here just to recruit me for this Johnson woman?"

Randy nodded. "That, and to see my lady." His eyes lit up. "It'd been months, K." He dug into his pocket and drew out a dark-purple velvet box, flipped it open, and passed it to Khenko.

A solitary pink diamond twinkled in the middle of a simple, rose gold setting.

"Very nice. Congratulations. Who's the lucky lady?" He handed the box back.

"Anabeth Swineheart. Remember her?"

"I thought she married Bo Leander."

"She did." Randy smiled. "But they split a long time ago. We've been together for five years." He fiddled with the hat in his lap, then looked up. "Are you in or not? Will you at least talk to Special Agent Johnson?"

Khenko sighed heavily, and wished he hadn't answered Jere's call.

"I guess. You got her number?"

Randy beamed. "Even better."

He whipped out a cell phone and punched a button, engaging the speaker function. It rang on the other end.

"Special Agent Johnson," a no-nonsense voice clipped.

"Colonel Kowalski here. I have located Khenko Blitherstone. He is here with me now and has agreed to hear you out, Special Agent Johnson."

"Excellent. Good work. Put him on, Colonel."

"I'm here, ma'am. Randy has you on speaker phone."

"Hello, Mr. Blitherstone What I have to say is for your ears only. Please take me off speaker."

Randy and Khenko gaped at one other, and Khenko did as the agent asked.

"Yes, ma'am," he said into the receiver.

"We're off speaker?"

"Yes, ma'am."

"Mr. Blitherstone, the President of the United States needs your help and is calling you to duty. Your country needs you."

Khenko nearly dropped the phone.

"You will be classified as a civilian contractor and amply reimbursed for your services. Unless you'd rather be called back to the Guard." Her slight Southern drawl did little to soften the blow.

Sweat popped out on Khenko's brow, and his palms dampened. Frantic, he glanced at Randy who watched him apprehensively. He knew Khenko's stint in the National Guard had been the worst two years of his life.

The war had landed on American soil in 2028. All able-bodied citizens between the ages of seventeen and twenty-five had been drafted for a two-year stint, and the death and destruction had devastated Khenko. He'd blocked those years from his memory, refusing to think about them, much less share them with anyone else.

Johnson's announcement brought the horror roaring back.

"Pack your bag, soldier. Your plane will depart Joint Base MDL Trenton at oh-five-hundred."

Panic washed over him. "Tomorrow?" he squeaked.

"Today," she said, and the line went dead.

Khenko sank to the sofa, not sure when he'd risen. He passed the phone back to Randy and stared at his reflection in Randy's eyes.

"You okay, dude?"

"Not even," Khenko groaned. "I think I'm going to throw up." He bounded for the bathroom.

☼☼☼

With minutes to spare, Elise showed her credentials at the front gate, then gunned the sedan to where the supersonic jet waited. She slammed the brakes, and loose belongings hit the floorboard. Then she hurriedly checked in with the waiting pilot.

Before herding her passengers onto the X-5900, she made sure the coast was clear. Then settling into a seat across from them, she answered an incoming call on her cell.

"Special Agent Johnson."

On the other end, Colonel Kowalski reported about the Blitherstone man.

She spoke quietly into the phone so the others couldn't hear, then unbuckled and rushed to the cockpit to give new orders to the pilot. Then taking her seat, she sighed and sat back as the PA system squawked.

"Buckle up, folks. Our next stop is Joint Base MDL in Trenton, New Jersey. We have a couple more passengers to pick up and a short layover in Trenton before flying on to Europe."

REVELATIONS IN THE NIGHT

Mitch woke in a cold sweat in the pitch dark, convinced his room was crawling with monsters with sharp, pointed teeth and glowing red eyes. He fumbled for the bedside lamp, grateful when its glow proved him wrong.

He was safe at home. No lizard men threatened, but his stomach roiled the nausea hit.

Leaping from bed, Mitch made it to the bathroom and hurled mostly liquid into the toilet. He'd lost his lunch on the turbulent ride from Zephyr Cay. Now the haunting image of slick lizard guts and spurting blood made him puke again.

When the nausea finally passed, Mitch peeled himself from the porcelain bowl and trudged to his bed. It was 3:30 a.m. Sleep meant the nightmare could return, so he plodded to the kitchen instead. He fished a can of Coca-Cola from the refrigerator hoping it would settle his stomach.

Slurping the strong liquid, he let go of a long, satisfying belch. Then, carrying it with him, Mitch padded to his office and powered up his laptop for the first time in a few days. His eyes drooped as he typed 'green-scaled lizard men' and yawned loudly.

Thousands upon thousands of results queued. Narrowing the search, he added 'Patrika Tolbert' to the string, then clicked on the top article, and stared in disbelief.

No wonder Shalane Carpenter hadn't answered his calls or texts. She had collapsed on the stage during her first show in Las Vegas. She was in a hospital in a freaking coma.

Fully awake now, Mitch clicked the news tab. The latest update was from last evening. Shalane was in a coma in Sunrise Hospital in Las Vegas.

Mitch's gears turned. Was Patrika with her? If so, maybe she had access to Shalane's cell. He desperately wanted to quiz the girl about her encounter with the lizard men. He could find out about Shalane at the same time.

Grabbing his phone, Mitch shot a text to Patrika on Shalane's cell, hoping she would read it and respond. But when nothing came back, he continued wading through articles about her and the monsters, searching for the original. Shalane had whined about the reporter disrespecting her. Was that the L.A. Times?

Mitch read the article, amazed at the accuracy of Patrika's description of the lizard men. She had even provided names of the main players, like Nergal, and Shibboleth, Inanna, and Ishkur. The other links regurgitated the original article, adding nothing new.

But he found posts and blurbs all over the net bashing Shalane Carpenter and her loony tunes mistress.

Wondering what else he might find, Mitch returned to his original query about the lizard men. He slogged through article after article posted by people who claimed to have encountered what they called Reptilians.

They spoke of underground bases worldwide and an age-old war between the Reptilians and Humans. The race supposedly thrived on negative human emotions, and had a hand in creating them by fueling wars.

Much of it read like conspiracy theory, or even fantasy. But Mitch had been attacked by the Reptilians. He knew they were real.

Deeper and deeper into the web, he dove until he passed into the dark web, a place he typically wouldn't dare venture. His partner used it to research criminal cases and was a pro. Mitch was not.

He stood and stretched, then checked his phone. Patrika had not answered. But it was the middle of the night in Las Vegas.

He stared at the clock. His partner would shoot him if Mitch called at this hour. He contemplated his closed laptop. Then, intertwining his fingers, he cracked his knuckles and sat back down. What the hell.

"Let's pull this dark thread."

Minutes later, Mitch stumbled into a chat room where the parties claimed to have had an encounter with the Reptilians. He read the comments from the sidelines, fascinated as two people discussed what each claimed had happened recently.

One was in California, land of fruits and nuts. The other was in India. That one had not personally witnessed the lizard men but described what her grandfather had seen. Neither of the parties had interacted with the Reptilians. Both believed they had escaped undetected.

Mitch rubbed his face in his hands, wishing he had been that lucky. Then, his computer dinged, and an odd message flashed across the screen. He quickly severed the internet connection and powered down, hoping a lurking pirate had not singled him out. Then he wandered to the bedroom and climbed between the sheets.

It was 5:15 a.m. Maybe he could get a few hours of sleep before his late morning flight. But his mind wandered to Madame Bouvee shoving the sapphire brooch at him, demanding he take it to Awen. But how could she have known about her unless she'd met Emily?

A sudden rush of guilt nibbled at Mitch. He flopped to his side, punched the pillow, and buried his face, determined to get some sleep. Moments later, his eyes opened. In his line of sight was the brooch.

Mitch reached for the pin and gazed into its dark stone. With the blackout panels engaged, the only light was from the Sound Tower that doubled as Mitch's alarm. But it was enough to make the facets sparkle. He tilted the brooch sideways, and the twinkles coalesced, flowing through the stone like water.

Mesmerized, he let his gaze follow the shimmering waterfall until his lids became so heavy they closed. He fell into a trance-like state, and while he was aware of being in his comfortable bed, Mitch found himself on a frost-bound hillside overlooking an open wasteland.

Below and before him stretched an icy tundra dotted with thousands of pillars. An eerie wind shrieked across the plain, ending in a sinister, familiar laugh. Goosebumps roved his upper body.

He peered down row after row as stinging ice crystals bit at his face and exposed arms. Then, horror of horrors, Mitch was *in* the barrow, stumbling through the rows of frozen megaliths. He slipped and fell against one, then gasped and leapt backward.

Inside the block of ice was a dragon. The size of a small car, its horns, flared nostrils, and ferocious claws were frozen mid-attack. Mitch stared, horrified, then moved to the next monolith, the next, and the next, until he was jogging down the long rows. Each pillar contained a dragon of varying size, fierceness, and color.

Laughter shrieked across the glacial wasteland. Mitch shivered as it multiplied, ricocheting between columns and around the rows until it sounded like many voices laughing. Then they all quieted, leaving the mournful cry of the penetrating wind.

"Help us," came a nearby groan.

Mitch looked about frantically. No one was there.

"Save us," came a keening wail.

He backed away, spooked. Were the dragons still alive? He inspected the nearest one. Its eyes were frozen open, but it seemed not to see.

"Help Awen," begged an eerie voice behind him.

"Take the stone to Awen," another commanded.

"Help Awen, or all will be lost," a third cried.

Freaked to the max, Mitch covered his ears. But the voices bombarded him, anyway, tearing at his heartstrings. Finally, he shook himself from the dream using every ounce of willpower he could muster. But as he came to, he heard Jake MacBrayer hollering as plain as day, "Buddy, wait! I'm here. Save me!"

Mitch woke curled in fetal position, clutching the sapphire brooch. His childhood nightmare had returned. Except for Jake. That part was new.

He ran the details through his mind, sighed, and got up. Then, yanking on a pair of clean jeans and a tee shirt, he shoved the heirloom in his pocket and padded to the kitchen with the creepy nightmare running through his head.

ESPN helped to block it out, but a resounding crack followed by a crashing rumble vibrated the house. Ham sandwich in hand, Mitch hurried to the window, jumping when lightning splintered the sky. Seconds later, another boom rattled the panes.

The New England-style three-story was situated on a hill, giving Mitch an unobstructed view of downtown Atlanta. He ran up the back stairs to the widow's walk, the main reason Mitch had bought the place.

From up there he could watch the spectacular storms that graced Atlanta year-round, as well as seasonal fireworks. But by the time he made it to the top, rain pelted the glass door in sheets. He settled for the view from the sitting room.

Plopping into an easy chair, he munched his sandwich and watched the lightning dance above Atlanta. The trees lashed frantically, nearly bending sideways in the wind-driven rain. Mitch thought of the nightmare and the frozen dragons. What did it have to do with Jake?

The sky brightened as the swift-moving clouds moved on, taking the lightning strikes and thunder boomers with it. Mitch grabbed a rain slicker, willing to brave what was left to watch the storm march toward the mountains of North Georgia. But the doorbell rang, startling him.

Who would be calling at this hour? He certainly wasn't expecting anyone.

He hesitated, then stepped outside, in no mood to entertain guests. If he ignored them, maybe they would go away. Mitch sat on one of the built-in benches and turned his face to the sky. Rain landed softly and rolled down his cheeks. The fierceness had passed.

A low snort sounded behind him, and Mitch whirled, expecting to see a tall green monster. But nothing was there. Chill bumps paraded up the back of his neck and across his skull. Great. Now he was *hearing* the goddamn things.

He crossed the widow's walk to peer down at the driveway. An SUV was parked in front of his house.

The wind and rain stopped altogether, and steam rose from the metal roof. He glanced at the thermometer, then looked again. Unbelievable. It was ninety-two degrees first thing in the morning, and it wasn't yet May.

Mitch snuck a last look at the retreating storm, then ducked inside the house. Whoever was out there punched the doorbell repeatedly. What the fuck?

He tossed the wet slicker on its hook and stomped down the stairs. The doorbell ceased when Mitch reached the entryway, but the offender laid siege to his front door instead.

Peering through the peephole, Mitch sucked in a sharp breath. Arthur Creeley, the Acting Grand Druid of the Awen Order, pounded on his door. What the hell did his old coach want with Mitch?

STORM CENTRAL

Awen's cabin was rough but clean and welcoming. A fire blazed, and there was food on the table—odd considering no one was around but the Elders. Emily turned to ask if they'd used magic, but they had disappeared. Also weird. They'd been right behind her.

She slung her backpack on a cane rocking chair and peeled off the heavy woolen robe. It was toasty in here. Draping it on a hook, she shucked off the soiled boots and wiped a sheen of sweat from her brow.

Unruly curls had escaped her ponytail to cling to her neck. She rinsed the stink from her hands with water from a ewer and removed the elastic band. Then, smoothing hair that grew longer by the minute, she twisted it in a knot on top of her head. She secured it with the band and bobby pins from her pack, then something scraped against the cabin wall.

Cracking the door, Emily peeked out. A stiff wind had sprung up, sending leaves tumbling across the clearing. Then, she spied the culprit. A limb dangled from the oak tree and twisted in the wind, scrubbing against the house.

Taking a firm hold, she gave it a tug. The branch came away as a gust of wind lifted it, and her with it, slamming them both into the unforgiving trunk. Emily shoved the heavy limb off of her, and wailed in frustrated. She had reached her limit of bad shit for one day. And it was still morning.

Stepping into the clearing, she scanned the sky. Above the rustling birches outlining the glade, clouds curled and gathered. Gray and ominous, they billowed across the morning sky, dimming the light in Awen's dell. A storm brewed.

A thrill went through Emily, primal and electric. This was what had driven her to become a Disaster Specialist, though that seemed a lifetime ago.

Lightning streaked across the sky, followed by a faraway rumble. Emily circled the clearing, savoring the feel of the cool grass beneath her bare feet.

But where was Tarbh? The bull Elder had said he would take the first watch. She peered into the thick woods. Maybe he'd taken refuge from the coming storm and watched from there.

Splinters of electricity branched from a stalk of lightning to dance overhead. The electricity washed over Emily, raising the hairs on her arms and sending tingles down the back of her neck. She lingered in the center of Awen's clearing, counting the seconds between strikes and booms, and quivering with excitement at the spectacular display of purple spider webs that lit the heavens.

Then she squealed as the sizzling snap of an electric bolt struck, not once, but twice in rapid succession. Too close for comfort, she ran for cover, pelted by hard, stinging raindrops that soaked Awen's dress. As thunder rolled angrily around the clearing, Emily nipped into the door. She leaned against it, grinning, then ran to the window, not wanting to miss a thing.

The strikes continued hard and fast, to the tune of deep, rolling thunder that resonated in Emily's lower chakras. Reminded of the tale of gods bowling in heaven, she chuckled and caught a flash of purple from the corner of one eye. Then she screamed when thunder exploded beside Awen's tiny shelter to mingle with a long, splintering crash.

Shivering, Emily rushed to the other window and leaned across the bed to shove the curtain aside. The driving rain made it difficult to see, but a birch had taken the strike. Newly green leaves whipped and whirled in the rising gale. Another bolt struck on the opposite side of the hut, and Emily squealed again. A loud thunderclap rattled the door.

Her heart beat ninety miles a minute. Emily usually loved thunderstorms. This one? Not so much.

Saying a prayer for the animals, she drew deep breaths and blew them out loudly, trying to calm her frayed nerves. Then, the wonderful aroma of fresh-baked bread filled the room. Salivating, she glanced at the table. Steam rose from a plate of rolls that hadn't been there before.

What the heck was going on here?

The door slammed open abruptly. Emily ran to shut it and dropped the bar into its slot. Then, panting, she shoved her backpack out of the rocking chair and sank into it to catch her breath and stare at the whipping fire.

Awen's fire. Awen's spells.

That moment of stillness reminded her of the calming spell. Taking three deep, cleansing breaths to steady her nerves, Emily anchored energetically into the earth, connected with the other elements—rain strafing the hut, lightning dancing above the glade, and the wind whooshing through the trees.

Feeling her heart overflow with love and gratitude, Emily murmured the simple invocation and felt the power pour through her and out of her hands and feet. There was another loud rumble, and then everything went quiet, save a gentle patter on the thatched roof.

Relieved and ever surprised when her spells worked, she stared at the fire and rocked back and forth slowly. Her dress was wet and smelled vile, but the wind no longer whistled down the chimney, and the flames had ceased their frantic dance. Little by little, her body relaxed.

Several minutes passed before Emily moved to the front window to lift the thin curtain. A light, steady rain fell on Awen's glade. She spied a few downed limbs, but everything looked as it had earlier.

She crossed to the other window to check on the unfortunate birch. Its trunk was split, and its crown lay against the cabin. Another foot or two, and it would have taken out the roof. That, or the whole side of the little house.

"Thank you, God," she breathed softly, then nearly choked.

Behind the shattered tree, a deer materialized, then morphed into the outline of a woman. She was tall and beautiful, with black, flowing hair that fell below her waist. The light of recognition gleamed in the exotic eyes. Emily started to wave, then thought better of it and retreated from the window.

But something about the apparition seemed familiar. Was it Druantia checking in on Emily and Awen from the Underworld? She peeked again, and the woman was gone, making Emily wonder if she had been there at all. She had seen some crazy things since entering that wonky wormhole yesterday.

Or was it today? She had gained several hours between the Bahamas and Northern France. Now, if she could just make sense of all that had happened.

She was stuck in the eleventh century. The occurrences at Chateau Falaise had convinced Emily of that. Scientifically speaking, time travel was out of the question, so it must be a manifestation of the Otherworld.

The dragons had warned her. Hope had warned her. No venturing off the path. No wandering of intention whilst in the Otherworld. Now Emily knew why—first hand.

But she had no idea how she had entered the Otherworld. She hadn't done it intentionally and had no recollection of crossing over. On every other journey, she had been fully aware. Not this time.

Maybe it had happened in the wormhole on the way to Beli. She had been so puffed up listening to her mother and Bran and then her father going on about her accomplishments. Then Tienu appeared out of nowhere creating new tunnels with his fiery breath and herding her through. Is that when it happened? Had Tienu sent her back here and then abandoned her?

Emily winced, ashamed. Tienu had said a missing component of her preparation would be complete at Beltane, and until then, Beli was a death trap. Was that why he had gone there rather than staying with Emily?

That felt right. She had seen the concern in Tienu's eyes when she told him the Keepers were on their way to Snowdonia. He knew the witch was there and had said so. Tienu had not abandoned Emily. He'd *had* to go.

But knowing that didn't make her feel any better about being shunted off to another time "zone." Especially one not accessible by planes, trains, or automobiles.

Sunlight slanted through the gauzy curtains, and Emily stopped rocking to peer outside. The rain had stopped, and the sun twinkled off the wet grass and trees. Tarbh emerged from the woods and tossed his head at Emily, then crossed to wade shoulder-deep into the pond.

That reminded Emily that her hot bath was probably lukewarm by now. Grabbing a still-warm roll, she ate half, then stuffed the rest in her mouth and lifted a clean gown from a shelf. Then she circled the partition hiding the claw-legged tub.

Poking a finger in the water, she was surprised to discover it was the perfect temperature. Emily said a quick prayer of thanks for magic and magical creatures, then shucked off the smelly dress and her island-bought underwear and slipped into the deep tub.

Moaning in ecstasy, she let her body sink to the bottom. Then, deftly freeing her heavy hair from the bun, she let it fan around her and used her fingertips and a ball of soap from a nearby tray to scrub the stench of Falaise's sewers from her curls and pores.

When she was clean, Emily donned Awen's velvety-soft dress and eyed the tiny bed in the corner. But the boots were still soiled. Promising herself she would sleep soon, she took a rag to the shoes and had removed most of the schmutz when the aroma of roasted meat wafted to her.

Her stomach growled, and Emily glanced at the table. Steam rose from a heaping plate of food. Finishing, she washed her hands and sank into a chair to slather butter on a roll.

"Mmmm." Gobbling a slice of the meat, she moaned again. After weeks of eating smoothies, fruits, nuts, and vegetables, she was grateful for a more substantial meal.

Lifting the cover from a bowl, she spooned vegetables onto the crockery plate. Emily recognized the parsnips and carrots, but not the crunchy stuff, though it tasted a bit like turnip greens. When she finished, she belched loudly.

When a light knock sounded at the door, Emily sucked in a breath. It was unlikely Henry would return to Awen's glade, but had the Chateau guards tortured him until he revealed her location? Or was it the mysterious woman? Emily relaxed. Most likely, it was one of the animal Elders.

Tiptoeing to the front window, Emily lifted the curtain and peered out. There was no one there. Her heart rate kicked up another notch. She stood, staring, not sure what to do. Then the knock came again. Peering out from beneath the gossamer curtain, Emily squinted but saw nothing.

She searched for a weapon and grabbed an old kitchen knife. Then she crept to the door, took a deep, bracing breath, and silently lifted the bar. Easing the door open an inch, she peered out. No one was there but a gentle mist fell.

Emily called loudly, "Who is there?"

No one answered. After a long moment, she called out again. "Anybody there?" Still no answer. Gulping, she yelled louder. "Tarbh? Are you out there?" The bull broke through the trees at the edge of the clearing and galloped to Emily.

"Aye, Master. What is it you desire?"

"Right after the storm, I saw a woman out back next to the tree the lightning struck. I thought I was seeing things because she appeared as a deer, then she changed into a woman and quickly disappeared. But just now, two different knocks sounded at the door, yet no one was there."

The fierce bull hurried around the side of the hut and disappeared. Emily joined him by the fallen birch, but neither saw any sign of the visitor. Tarbh backed away, wagging his head.

"I was guarding the only entrance to the clearing, and no one passed me. But the storm was quite violent and noisy, so I can't say for sure. Even so, I would have seen or heard them leave once the thunder and lightning passed."

Together, they circled the cabin, then walked along the pond's banks and around the edge of the clearing. There was no overt sign of an interloper.

Emily scratched her head. "Could they have come and gone using magic?"

Tarbh tossed his great head. "Not without detection. Our senses are attuned to magic."

"Well, heck." Emily peered into the darkness, weary to the bone. "I think I'll go lay down. I haven't had much sleep in the last few days."

"Good idea. Rest well, Master. I shall rouse a few of the Elders and post more lookouts. We shall keep you safe."

ROAD TO NOWHERE

Lugh called the airline to exchange their tickets for a later flight, only to learn that PetJet didn't fly out of Caen. They would have to settle for a smaller jet with Cu and Hope traveling in the cargo hold or keep the rental car and take a ferry across the Dover Strait and English Channel. Figuring Hope would veto the cargo hold, Lugh left their tickets open until they could locate Emily.

With that decided, he threw his suitcase in the rear of the sport utility vehicle next to the travel cages, then joined Cu and Hope in the front.

GPS said it was fifty-minute drive to Chateau Falaise. But rush hour traffic proved to be snarled and horrendous, with one accident after another.

Cu and Hope fell asleep right away. Hope's black-and-brown-striped bulk overflowed the front passenger seat. Cu stretched upside down in the back, also filling the seat. The whine of traffic and the car's engine barely drowned his snores.

Lugh eyed the big dog in his rearview mirror and his heart swelled with affection. He thought of the night Cu had shown up on his doorstep in the middle of a snowstorm, not long after Brian had come to stay. It was hard to believe Lugh had been against keeping the big galoot.

His phone buzzed. It was Cybele, Brian's mom.

Lugh whipped into a fast food restaurant and joined the long line at the drive-thru. But when Cybele began blurting out her concerns, he pulled into a parking space.

"Wait. Back up. Morgan did what?"

"That dreadful woman turned Brian and Ethnui over to the FBI and won't answer my calls. Something is wrong, Lugh. I think Brian is in danger."

The hairs on Lugh's arms stood at attention, and chills crept up the back of his neck.

"What do you mean the FBI has him?"

Lugh's dealings with Morgan had always been amicable. And until recently, Hamilton Hester had trusted her. It never occurred to Lugh that he should do otherwise.

"Do you remember the family outing at Zoo Atlanta when Brian was four? Morgan told me something that made me leave Jake. At the time, I thought moving away was the answer. But, aww hell, none of that matters now. What matters is Brian. And something tells me he's in grave danger.

"I'm half out of my mind and can't think straight. But I did talk to Elise Johnson, my godmother. She's on her way to North Carolina to rescue him from the FBI. Did you know she's AIA? It's really their jurisdiction anyway, not the FBI's. Did I tell you the girl is a Fomorian?"

As she spilled her guts, the lump in Lugh's chest crystalized.

"Cybele, I don't know what the AIA is, but I do know you have good instincts. Hamilton warned us not to trust Morgan, but I thought he was being paranoid. You did the right thing getting Elise involved. Hopefully she can get Brian from the FBI and on a flight to you."

Cybele let go a heavy sigh. "Brian can't come here."

"Why not?" he asked, surprised.

"It's not safe. I can have her put Brian and Ethnui on a plane to you in Wales. Or wherever you are."

Lugh stared at the cars on the highway, then over at Hope. Her anxious eyes were fixed on him.

"Cybele, I'm not in Wales. There was a horrendous storm and we were rerouted to France. We spent the night in Caen and were supposed to fly out today. But Hope informed me that Emily is in Falaise, so I rented a car and we're driving there now. With luck, we'll find her quickly and can head on to Cardiff. But I don't know how long this will take."

"Shit, shit, shit, shit, SHIT!" Cybele cried, then followed it with a string of more colorful expletives. Lugh held the phone away from his ear until she calmed down. "What are we going to do with Brian, then?"

"I thought you were on a tropical island. Bali or some such. How dangerous can that be?"

There was an audible gulp on the other end. "Umm, well. I am *not* in Bali."

"And?" Lugh prodded.

"I'm in London. But I'm leaving in a few minutes."

Butterflies plundered Lugh's gut. "What the… WHAT? You're in *London*? What are you doing in London?"

Cybele's sigh was long and loud. "I didn't want to tell you in case it didn't pan out, but I'm looking for your brother. I've been all over Europe, and the trail led here."

Something big and hairy unfolded inside Lugh. "You have news about Jake?"

Another sigh. "Yes, a rumor. But it was from a reliable source. So, I started in Egypt, then that led me to France, then London, and now here where the trail has gone cold. I'm off to Glastonbury in a short while."

"Good God, Cybele. I wish you would've told me. What if something had happened to you? What if you disappeared like Jake? It would kill Brian, not knowing. Hell, it would kill me."

"I know, I know. I wanted to. I started to more than once. But—" She sucked in a sharp breath. "Lugh, I gotta go. I'll call you back."

Lugh stared at the phone, then slowly drove around the fast-food restaurant to enter the long queue for the drive-thru. They were still in line when Cybele called back.

"How about if I fly Brian and Ethnui to Cardiff and arrange for them to stay in a hotel near the airport until you get there?"

Lugh ran his hand over his heavy stubble. "That could work. But do you think Elise would be willing to keep them in London for a few days until I locate Emily?"

"Doubtful, but I'll ask. You focus on finding Emily. I'll either get Brian and Ethnui to Cardiff, or settled with Elise. Then I'll call or text you with the particulars. Stay safe, Lughnasadh."

"You too, Cybele. And thanks for taking care of Brian and Ethnui."

"Well, he *is* my son. I felt bad about dumping him on you in the first place, but I didn't know what else to do. Thank you, Lugh. Your help has meant a lot—to me and to Brian. Now I have a train to catch. Talk soon."

Lugh scratched Hope's chin and pondered Cybele's revelation.

"What's wrong?" the cat Elder demanded.

Cu shoved his shaggy head over the back of the seat. Lugh ruffled his wiry hair, and drove forward in line.

"Morgan Foster turned Brian and Ethnui over to the FBI." Lugh snorted in disgust. Nothing good could come from getting the Feds involved. Thank goodness Elise had agreed to step in. "She thinks Brian is in danger and wants him and Ethnui to meet us in Wales."

He pulled forward again. They were next in line.

"She'll buy their plane tickets and put them up at a hotel near the airport in Cardiff. Unless Elise Hester Johnson can look after them."

Cu yipped, and Lu clamped his hand over his ear.

"What did she say about Morgan?" Hope translated.

"Hold that thought." Lugh pulled up to the kiosk.

"I'll have a burger," Cu barked.

Lugh laughed and ruffled the wolfhound's head. "How many? One? Two?"

"Five!"

"How 'bout two big ones?"

Cu hung his head and rolled pitiful brown eyes.

"Hope? Do you want a burger?" The Scottish wildcat shook her head and her tags clinked against her collar.

"Nope. None of that artificial "meat" for me."

Lugh scrunched his nose at her and ordered. At the window, he paid and took his drink and the paper bag stuffed with food. Pulling forward to park, he peeled the wrappers from Cu's bun-free burgers and fed them to him one at a time.

When he was done, Lugh sank his teeth into a cheeseburger, and stuffed a handful of fries in his mouth. He chased it with a sip of coke. He had fed the animals before they left the hotel, but Lugh hadn't eaten since that morning.

"Lugh, we can't miss our rendezvous," Hope said. "It's getting late. We need to hurry." The westering sun seconded her words.

"Okay, okay."

He navigated the parking lot to the street and then entered traffic. Horns blared, and Lugh jerked the steering wheel, barely avoiding a pileup with a tractor-trailer.

When traffic unsnarled, he settled into a steady stream of cars. As he munched the surprisingly satisfying burger and hand-cut fries, Lugh marveled at the beauty of the French countryside.

They were passing a spectacular field of wildflowers that glowed pink beneath the setting sun when Hope, who'd been peering intently out the window for the last several miles, broke the silence.

"We're here."

Lugh glanced at the dashboard.

"GPS says we have a few miles yet."

"We're not going into town."

He shot a questioning glance at the tabby cat, whose black-striped face was close to his.

"We're not?"

"No, Lughnasadh. We are going to Awen's glade. Turn here." She tilted her nose to a tiny lane on the left.

As luck would have it, there was a break in traffic. Lugh hit the brakes and yanked the wheel left. They ended up sliding sideways onto a barely perceptible dirt road overlain with pea gravel.

Cu barked madly, rendering Lugh momentarily deaf, while Hope reared and propped her paws on the dashboard. The animal Elders made interesting travel companions, if not great guides.

"Are you sure this is a road?"

It was rough and narrow, and though Lugh drove slowly, the stiff suspension magnified every bump.

"Appears to be." Hope purred louder as the forest closed in around them.

"Appears to be?" Lugh stopped in the tunnel of deciduous trees. "Where are you taking us?"

"I told you." Hope glared at Lugh, haughty eyes blazing.

"Awen's glade? Seriously? That was a long time ago, Hope. A thousand years. By now, it's probably someone's farm. Or worse, a trash dump or something equally distasteful."

"Trust me. Awen's home is here." The yellow eyes danced. "And she is here, too. I feel her."

Cu's yap ended on a long howl that raised goosebumps on Lugh's arms.

Excitement crept into his voice. "She, Emily?"

Cu threw his head over Lugh's shoulder.

"Yes, the Awen. She's here." The slanting sun filtered through the leaves to reflect off the wolfhound's soulful eyes. "And yet, she is not."

Lugh snorted. "Well, that's about as clear as mud. Just what do you mean? Emily's either here, or she's not."

"One would think that, yes?" Hope purred. "And yet, what Cu says is exactly true. Drive, Lugh."

Giving the animals the side-eye, Lugh eased the car along the rutted lane through woods that grew darker and creepier by the minute.

After what seemed an eternity, he glanced at the dash clock and groaned. It had only been five minutes. The lane was carved into contiguous ruts, and though they traveled at a snail's pace, every jar irritated Lugh's brain and skull.

He thought longingly of the pain meds Finn had prescribed for the head injury he had sustained at Zoo Atlanta. Lugh had thrown them away at Cu's urging but would give anything to have one now.

"Are we almost there?" He rubbed his forehead, nearing the end of his endurance. The washboard road wasn't helping any.

Hope growled, low in her throat, and leaned closer to the windshield.

"Almost." The golden eyes regarded him, as if sizing him up. "What?"

His sarcastic response bordered on belligerence—another sign Lugh had had enough.

Hope settled back on her haunches. "STOP!"

Lugh slammed the brakes, flinging an arm out to keep her from flying into the windshield. Instead, he punched her shoulder, inciting an angry yowl as the SUV skidded sideways in the mud. Lugh steered into the slide, seesawing the vehicle to get it under control.

Then, putting the car in park, he raked his hands through his hair and shouted at himself.

"You idiot! You're going to get us killed. Pay attention, Lugh!"

Cu whined from the back floorboard where he'd ended up again.

Lugh reached over the seat to caress his head.

"I'm sorry, Cu. And you too, Hope."

She meowed and bumped Lugh's shoulder with her forehead.

To gather his wits, he stepped out of the SUV and almost crapped his pants.

In front of the vehicle, loomed a Kodiak-looking bear about ten feet tall. The setting sun backlit its dark fur and the car's headlamps revealed menacing claws and teeth.

Lugh's heart pounded. He glanced about for a weapon. Of course, nothing was handy.

Hope leapt to the ground to bristle beside him while Cu barked frantically from the backseat. Wolfhounds had been bred to hunt big game and drag men off horses and chariots in wartime. But even at a hundred and twenty pounds, would Cu be a match for a bear? Especially one this big?

Easing his hand inside the SUV, Lugh unlocked the doors and inched his hand backward to free Cu. Then, shielded by the open front door, he watched in shock.

The Irish wolfhound hurtled from the car and bounded toward the beast, tail wagging as if it were his best friend.

The bear came down on all fours. "Hello, Cu."

Lugh stared in disbelief. The bear talked. And in a high-pitched tone that belied its enormous stature.

Cu pranced in front of it, tossing a backward glance at the SUV.

Hope yowled and hurried to greet the hulking bear.

"Time grows short, Artis," the cat announced. "Has the new Awen arrived?"

"Aye, Cat," the bear shrilled, and Lugh's heart leapt.

"Then you must take us to her. But first," the Scottish wildcat wheeled to face a still astounded Lugh, "I would like to introduce Lughnasadh MacBrayer. Lugh, meet Artis, the bear Elder."

Lugh nodded warily but stayed behind the car door. The bear's scrutiny jangled his already-frayed nerves.

"This is Awen's, um, friend?" Artis stared, and Lugh could tell he had been judged and found wanting.

"Indeed he is," Hope hissed in Lugh's defense. "Will you take us to Awen's hut? We have journeyed far, and this druid priest is recovering from an injury. He requires rest."

The cat Elder's accent had grown thicker, as it did when she was distressed. "Plus, we all sense Awen is in trouble."

"The Awen is, how do you say, caught? Stuck? She is at the hut, but not."

The bear batted its eyes. "Awen wanders the Otherworld and knows not how to return to this one."

Lugh's heart sank. One could die in that shadowy land between worlds.

"Take us there," he commanded and climbed into the SUV.

The Elders loped behind Artis down the dark washboard lane.

Lugh followed, head aching more with each jarring thump. Finally, when he could stand it no longer, he whispered a soothing spell, and the bouncing calmed considerably.

Annoyed that he hadn't thought of it earlier, Lugh spoke another to ease his pain and prayed to Brigid that they weren't too late to save Emily.

PARDON ME

Shibboleth peered out at the brightly-lit arena, wings tucked against his back. The ceremony would be a far cry from the execution he had planned. He eyeballed Nergal and barely contained his rage. It was a travesty the worm occupied a place of honor on the dais beside Inanna.

Inanna glanced up and caught Shibboleth's scrutiny. Shooting him a murderous glower, she sidled closer to Nergal. Shibboleth hissed. The Draca had always resented his interference—in any matter. But especially when it came to her association with Nergal. She was as stubborn and rebellious as her mother had been.

His offspring's attraction to Nergal had concerned Shibboleth from the start. He had done everything he could to discourage it, including meting out punishment through Mot and Maw. Nothing had worked.

Now, the last thing he wanted was to bestow honor on the Drac that had come between him and his favorite daughter-spawn. But Bé Chuille's alternative, a war against the dragons on Reptilian soil, was unthinkable.

Horns blew, and drums beat. Families and support staff, including the Dracs too young to be drafted, cheered from the bleachers. Troops from all over UnderEarth marched onto the field and lined each side of the broad arena.

Shibboleth blanched. Each had left a skeleton crew behind to guard the bases, but Mot was not exaggerating. Their ranks were much thinner than Shibboleth had expected. Fear mixed with his simmering rage to curdle his blood and threatened to strangle his words.

He stepped to the microphone, and the arena exploded in applause. Behind him, Mot hissed. He had wanted to be on the field with his armed forces.

"Reptilian Nation," Shibboleth began, voice booming over the loudspeakers, "today we gather, not for an execution as was previously announced, but for a declaration of war." Raucous boos and cheers rose from the stands and field.

"Long have we toiled in UnderEarth. While the humans enjoyed the expansive surface world, we have dwelt in the abyss, deprived of the sight of the moon and stars and the feel of the true sun upon our faces." He waited as a louder roar rose from the crowd.

"But no more," he continued when they quieted. "Our ally, the Witch Goddess Bé Chuille, has taken up our cause." He signaled to the witch who joined him at the podium. "Bé Chuille has imprisoned the dragons, clearing our way to AboveEarth." This time, there were no dissenters. "The portals are open and accessible."

Those seated leapt to their feet as the stadium exploded in catcalls and applause.

"In addition," he continued, pleased with their response, "I have advanced Mot to be my Second-in-Command." He nodded to Mot, who took Bé Chuille's place at the front of the stage. "General Mot will coordinate and command our troops from UnderEarth." When the applause petered out, Mot returned to his seat.

Then Shibboleth dropped his bombshell, sweeping an arm out over the field. "But what you see before you is the sum total of our Reptilian forces. Between our infighting and the magma that continues to devastate Agartha and its surrounding cities, our warrior ranks have been severely depleted. And we had only just rebounded from the sonic attacks."

The stadium groaned as one. It had been a century since the infamous attacks, but most remembered. The weaponized sound waves had bypassed AboveEarth, but the result to UnderEarth was catastrophic. Resident Dracs and their ancillary slave races had been wiped out as their main UnderSea and UnderEarth bases were destroyed.

"After those attacks, we stepped up the purebred clone program. But now, even they are mostly gone." An eerie silence befell the crowd. "So, to bolster our numbers and avoid further depletion of our ranks, I hereby pardon Inanna, Shibboleth's Spawn. Inanna will relocate to Irkalla and become my Third-in-Command." Shibboleth noticed Mot's glare in Inanna's direction

This time the crowd remained subdued, though contentious grumbles could be heard. The Reptilian nation had never had a female ruler. But that didn't mean it never would.

"Furthermore," he continued, "I hereby pardon Nergal the Destroyer and all of his Drac warriors and staff." Screeches, hisses, grunts, and roars filled the arena. "Nergal shall resume his duties as General of Reptilian Forces in Xibalba IX and will lead our charge against AboveEarth while supervising the rebuild of Agartha."

The Reptilians went wild. They had come to witness an execution. Instead, they were getting a war.

A NEW ALLY?

Bé observed the spectacle, smug and secure in her place of prominence on the stage behind Shibboleth. Once again, she had played a role in shaping Reptilian history. It was not the first time and likely would not be the last.

Feeling the familiar pull at her groin, Bé searched the faces of the Drac troops, then those in the audience. The sex act with Shibboleth had been necessary to restore her youth. But renewing her tissues and vital organs was always painful and less than satisfying. Bé needed more. And she needed it now.

Her regard went to Mot, standing at attention behind Shibboleth. Bé caught his gaze. A dangerous glint flickered momentarily. Then the snapping red eyes returned to Shibboleth and Inanna.

Bé turned her scrutiny back to the crowd. A young Drac was bold enough to grin directly at her and slid his tongue suggestively over his upper lip. Bé's crotch dampened, but she looked away. He was no match for Shibboleth's son. Mot had experience, nobility, a studly body, and the genes of a god. These were qualities Bé sought in an ally and a sex partner.

Horns blew, drums rolled, and bells rang out as Nergal and Inanna retreated to the back of the stage near Bé Chuille. Shibboleth, always long-winded and more than a little pompous, continued waxing eloquent about other business.

Bé eyed the young Draco. She was thinking about dragging the lewd stud behind the arena to bonk him silly when she noticed Mot watching her. Shibboleth's son let the tips of his forked tongue linger erotically on his lower lip. Then he stood to leave though Shibboleth had not yet ended his speech.

Bé slipped from the stage and through the crowd, catching a glimpse of Mot as he vanished around a corner, tail disappearing last. Then, using magic, she caught up to the virile Draco. Mot was only one generation removed from Enki. With luck, the god had passed his staying power to his issue.

Mot hissed and grabbed her arm to drag her through a long, glistening hallway to a room resembling a staging area. It was empty, but a bank of windows looked out onto the arena where the crowd was breaking up.

"The ceremony is over," Bé mentioned casually, gauging Mot's intent. Would he fuck her? Or attack?

His eyes lingered on Bé's lips—a good sign. Then she had a momentary glimmer of uncertainty when the Draco went for her breasts with claws that could slice them in two. She winced in anticipation, but Mot squeezed gently before clamping down harder, sending a thrill through her. Then the studly Draco lifted her to him. Her toes barely grazed the floor though Bé was the taller of the two.

"Now," he growled, "what bargain would you strike?"

Before she could answer, Mot fluttered his forked tongue in her ear, and Bé moaned as lusty sensations roved her body.

"Bargain?" she sighed, melting into Mot's muscular arms.

Ripping her dress from her shoulders with a primal growl, Mot tossed it aside. Then, lifting her sensitive breasts, the powerful Draco suckled both nipples. Back and forth he went, deepening the pressure until Bé convulsed in an orgasm that didn't quite reach her twat. Groaning, she groped for his penile flap, releasing his member from its prison.

How long they copulated, Bé was unsure. But by the time Mot finished, she was thoroughly sated for the first time since Enki had disappeared. And that had been a millennia ago.

Rolling off, Mot stroked Bé's thigh with the tips of his sharpened claws, and her desire grew strong again. But when she turned toward him, Mot pushed her away and bolted upright. Quickly fastening the belt he'd shucked earlier, the Draco stood by the closed door and regarded her with an odd expression.

Sulking, Bé spoke a charm to repair her gown and refresh her appearance, then stood to face him.

"Now," he said flatly. "Tell me about this bargain you would strike."

THE CONVERSATION

atrika Tolbert studied her pores in a magnified hand mirror, searching for zits. She'd been in Vegas for a full day, but the doctors still had no explanation for Shalane's coma. To Patty, this was both good and bad news. The doctors felt certain Shalane would wake soon, but how could they know if they had no idea what was wrong?

She hid her mirror when someone approached the door. They kept going, but Shalane's phone vibrated on the table by the bed, and she nearly jumped from her skin. Curious, she lifted it and saw red. The text was from Mitchell Wainwright.

Shalane had met Wainwright while they were in Atlanta. They had hooked up after one of her performances and Shalane had been smitten. That had been the clincher for Patty, the she'd reason left Shalane in Nashville. That and Shalane's nasty behavior.

When she realized the text was addressed to her, Patty drew a sharp breath. She stared at the screen, then scrolled backward to read the previous text. It had come through during the night. Both said the same thing.

Shock rocked Patty. Wainwright had seen the news and wanted to speak to her. Yes, about Shalane's condition. But he also wanted to talk about the Reptilians.

She stared at the beeping monitors, face burning. Why would the attorney want to speak to her? She had never met him, so he must be desperate. Otherwise, why text her on Shalane's phone?

Remembering her reaction when she heard about Shalane, Patty felt a pang of empathy and almost called back. But jealousy won. She ignored the message and laid the cell face down.

But several minutes later, she huffed loudly, lifted the phone and copied Wainwright's number into her own cell. Then stepping into the hallway, she called. He answered on the second ring.

Once convinced it was Patty, Wainwright launched into a series of questions about Shalane. She answered each one as best she could, trying not to sound resentful. But when he quizzed her about the Reptilians, she had had enough.

"Look, I am not having this conversation with you. I'm sick to death of people ragging me about the lizard men."

"No, no!" the attorney said. "I didn't call to mock. I called to compare notes with the only person who might believe me. I saw them, Patty. They almost killed me."

She nearly dropped the phone. "You *did?* What happened? Where were they?"

When Wainwright didn't answer, Patty shuddered. She whispered into the phone, "Please tell me they haven't found a way out."

Wainwright groaned. "I want to, but I can't. I'm sorry."

"Holy fucking mother of God." She swallowed hard. Then all hell broke loose on the unit. She nodded as an aide hurried past with a crash cart. "Are they here, Mitch? If so, we're all doomed."

"God, I hope not," Wainwright said. "I saw them in Zephyr Cay in the Bahamas. When Shalane left yesterday, I stayed to search for Emily."

"Uh-huh," Patty said as if she knew what he was talking about.

"I didn't find Emily, but the Reptilians found me."

That, she understood. "What do you mean they found you?"

"I mean, they blew a hole in a store's floor, and five lizard men came pouring out. One got crushed by a cooler, but the other four tried to kill me. Or eat me. Or something. I'm not sure. But I know I would be dead now if it weren't for the owner."

"Omigod!" Patty exclaimed. But for the first time since the dreams had begun, she felt less alone. Someone believed her. And that someone had even seen the monsters. Still, she needed to know for sure.

"So, you believe me, then?"

"Believe you?" There was a heavy sigh. "Of course I do. I fought them and nearly died."

"Do you think you can get someone to listen and do something? The FBI doesn't believe me. They laughed me out of the interrogation room. Then they denounced me to the public, making my life even more of a living hell than it already was. I get prank calls about the mothership. And when I'm recognized in public, people whisper and point like *I'm* the alien.

"Worse," she continued, "the dreams have come back. I experience every excruciating detail of what a Draco named Nergal seems to be living. It's freaking awful, Mitch." She sagged against the wall. "Can I call you that?"

"Of course, Patrika."

"Call me Patty."

"Will you tell me about your dreams? What happens in them?"

Patty pivoted to survey each end of the hall. Nurses and aides bustled from room to room on morning rounds. The earlier emergency must've been handled. No one paid attention to Patty.

In a low voice, she poured out the details of her nightmares in order. She did *not* mention the problems they had caused between Patty and Shalane. Mitchell remained silent and respectful throughout, interrupting only twice to ask pertinent questions. It felt good knowing someone finally believed her. So much so, that Patty actually relaxed.

"But the thing I've been most worried about," she said in conclusion, "is those monsters breaking out. Now you tell me they have." She paused, recalling the bloody slaughter she had witnessed, and a shudder seized her. "They will kill us all, but the FBI refuses to do diddly."

"What do you expect? They're assholes," the attorney growled. "They don't know their asses from holes in the ground. Or should I say lizards in the ground?"

Patrika snickered.

"But I have it on good authority that they *are* taking the threat seriously now. You spooked someone. Good job, Patty. Also, someone else I know was captured by the Reptilians and escaped to tell the tale."

"Really?" Goose bumps danced up and down Patty's body. "I cannot imagine. My dreams are scary enough."

"You said that in your dreams, you *are* one of the monsters. That you feel its injuries and experience its pain. Can you access their thoughts? Or contact them?"

Patty recoiled. "God, no." Then she mulled it over. "At least, I don't think so. I mean, I wouldn't even know how to try. But why would I want to? I want them *out* of my head."

"Yeah, I'm having nightmares, too. Sleeping *and* awake. But your dreams might come in handy. Maybe you could keep an eye on them. See what they are up to?"

"Yeah, no, I don't think so." Patty shuddered hard. Mitchell Wainwright wasn't so bad after all, but she'd be damned if she would willingly participate in her own mental torture.

SHOCKED TO THE CORE

Patty stared at the television above Shalane's bed. Stations around the country were airing footage of the lizard men attacking people. One showed a shopping mall in Denver, another a college campus in New Jersey. People in both places ran every which way trying to escape the green monsters, while law enforcement faced them down.

Patty wasn't aware of the tears sliding down her face, only of the terror that gripped her soul. Her heart pounded. She wasn't dreaming. But this was real.

She flipped channels and stopped when a news camera arced slowly over a thick forest. It focused in on a dark-skinned officer in plain clothes leaning over several bodies. The closest had been mauled, cheeks laid open and skull smashed in.

The officer looked up, and Patty leapt to her feet. FBI Special Agent Derek Jeter blinked at the camera, then down at his partner.

Becket Warren lay dead at his feet.

"No! It can't be." She sobbed and collapsed into the Naugahyde chair.

Patty stayed there, crying and rocking back and forth, arms wrapped around her shoulders. Then deciding she needed to talk to someone, Patty called Mitchell Wainwright. It went straight to voice mail. Patty next tried Latoya, who didn't pick up either. She left a message, then leaned over to shake Shalane gently.

"Shalane, I need you, wake up!" But of course, she was still in a coma.

Turning off the television, Patty padded quickly to the nurse's station, surprised to find no one there. She hurried up one hall and down another. Dinner had been delivered and the trays collected. Few were about.

"I wonder," she murmured to herself.

Taking the elevator to the bottom floor, she hurried toward the emergency room. The closer she got, the more chaos she encountered. When she reached a set of double doors with

EMERGENCY emblazoned across them. Patty shoved through and gagged.

The waiting room was filled to overflowing with victims of the lizard men. Near hyperventilating, she sobbed and ran back to the elevator, punching the button repeatedly until it arrived. Then she hurried to Shalane's room, tears flowing, and turned on the TV.

The Reptilians had infiltrated the elaborate maze of tunnels running beneath Las Vegas. They had decimated the homeless and forgotten souls living there, then poured from the entrances into the closest hotels—the Rio, Caesar's Palace, the Flamingo, and the Orleans—tearing humans to shreds with an eagerness that was as terrifying as their claws and teeth.

Switching back and forth between local stations, Patty watched for the next hour. The Las Vegas Police Department, joined by agents of the FBI and a federal agency she had never heard of, the Alien Intelligence Agency, had routed the attackers.

Breathing easier, Patty tried Mitchell Wainwright again. Her call rolled to voice mail.

THE SITUATION ROOM

Elise's cell phone warbled the moment they touched down at Joint Base MDL Trenton. The face of her childhood friend filled the screen. Katarina Hobbs was the current head of the Federal Bureau of Investigations, and she looked hopping mad.

Elise disengaged her seatbelt and slipped into the command center to answer the call.

"Elise Hester Johnson," Kate howled, "what in God's name do you think you're doing interfering in an official FBI investigation?"

Elise held her friend's laser-beam gaze for a long, fraught moment. "Your FBI made a mess, Katarina. I am simply cleaning it up for you. That girl, Ethnui, is a Fomorian. She should have been turned over to the AIA immediately along with the boy. You know the FBI has no jurisdiction in alien affairs."

Kate's cheeks pinked. "That girl is no Fomorian. My agents would have informed me of that."

"Not if they missed it." Elise sent a picture of Ethnui. One pointed ear peeked from beneath the girl's thick brown hair.

"Well, shit," the FBI Director snapped. "Now I have to tell the Attorney General." She shouted to her assistant to get the AG on the phone, then growled at Elise, "Dammit to hell. God knows how long I'll have to endure bullshit from the man herd for this."

"That man herd is to blame. *You* didn't blow this. Agent Beckett did."

Kate glared. "Same diff. But I refuse to face *der Führer* alone. I'll schedule the briefing. You get your bony ass to Washington, stat."

"Fuck you, Katy Kat. You are not the boss of me. I'm on a tight schedule. And I'll have you know, my butt has not been bony in years."

Elise had purposely used the nickname Katarina hated, and she looked ready to explode. Suppressing a smile, Elise checked the time. It was 0307 ET.

"Stand by while I talk to the pilot."

The young captain was amenable, and the briefing was set for 0530.

More than a little annoyed at this turn of events, Elise sighed heavily and texted her new recruits, moving their departure to 0800. Then, returning to her seat, she tilted it back as far as it would go and fell fast asleep.

☼☼☼

It was pitch dark when they landed at Andrews Air Force Base. Elise instructed an Airman to keep an eye on the groggy Brian and Ethnui, then poured a steaming cup of coffee and amply laced it with stevia and half-and-half before exiting the plane.

She tossed her briefcase into a waiting sedan and climbed inside to sip her coffee. As they neared the Department of Justice Building, Elise placed a quick call to her boss in London. Director Wansley wasn't available, so she left a detailed message on his voicemail.

When the driver bypassed the Attorney General's Office and dropped her at the White House, Elise's heart beat faster. She passed through the outer door, and a cacophony of specters' voices hit her at once. Doing her best to ignore them, she signed in, and passed through security only to find that Kate had yet to arrive.

Instructed to wait in the gleaming lobby, Elise settled in a thickly padded leather chair and pressed her hands to her ears. Boisterous ghosts crowded the rotunda dressed in attire that spanned the history of the White House. They chatted to one another, remarking loudly, and often rudely, about the passersby.

A few minutes later, at 0517, and not a minute too soon, Katarina Hobbs exited security. The leggy bombshell strode toward Elise and passed right through a translucent gentleman with a bushy beard and expressive eyebrows. The ethereal column of smoke from the ghost's stogie trailed behind Kate as her stubby heels clicked across the gleaming floor.

Then Kate did something unusual for both of them. She enveloped Elise in a bear hug.

Easing up on the pressure, the FBI Director murmured in Elise's ear, "You are my *SHE-RO*." Then squeezing again, rather spitefully this time, Kate let go and growled, "What were you thinking, Special Agent Johnson?"

Elise blinked at the rapid change.

"I was thinking my childhood friend usurped the authority of my agency."

"Seriously? You still on that? I swear I didn't know. But, you forged my name on an official transfer order. What the fuck, Elise?"

"Just getting you back, *Madame Director.*"

Kate's face blanched. The director had done something similar to Elise the year before. Something that had earned Kate the nod for the director's chair.

"Touché," she mumbled. "But, before we go in, what are your plans for Brian MacBrayer and the Fomorian?"

"Her name is Ethnui." Elise's tone was frigid. It irked her that Kate and her cronies treated intraterrestrials like lesser beings.

"Whatever. What's your plan?"

"I am taking them to AIA Cheltenham to be debriefed. After that, who knows? Brian has seen the Reptilian compounds. Or one of them. And as Ethnui rescued him from the Reptilian dungeons, it's likely she has knowledge of their inner workings. Plus, those two need protection. *And* containing. We don't want their stories leaked to the public and causing a mass panic."

Kate nodded approval. "Perfect. Come with me."

They reached the lower levels and entered the Situation Room a few minutes later. Their bosses, the Secretary of Defense and Attorney General greeted them, and Elise and Kate snapped to attention. Moments later, the President of the United States strode through the door with his Chief of Staff, and everyone stood.

"Be seated," President Chopin intoned. "Secretary Davis, why are we here?"

With that, the meeting came to order. First, Secretary Davis introduced Kate and Elise, then brought the President and Security Council up to speed. Elise added details when necessary. Once the cards were on the table, President Chopin approved the plan, and Kate and Elise were dismissed.

Alone with Kate in the long hallway, Elise resisted the nervous urge to giggle and was glad she did when Secretary Davis strolled from the Sit Room.

"Special Agent. Director." He nodded stiffly.

"Sir," Elise began, but he held up a hand and waved them into a nearby room. It appeared to be a storage area with boxes, bins, and random furniture piled high.

"Do either of you want to add anything to your earlier statements?"

Elise's face grew warm. She had a long and passionate history with SecDef, most of it rocky.

"Yes, Sir," she said respectfully. "Kate, would you give us a minute?"

The FBI Director eyed her up and down, then slipped from the room.

"Sir, I should brief you on Operation Corvo."

The ice-blue eyes glittered. "Go ahead."

"I have enlisted Colonel Kowalski and the civilian, Khenko Blitherstone. We were leaving MDL Trenton at 0500 until Director Hobbs insisted on this detour. We shall return to Trenton to pick them up, then depart for Azores Lajes Field before continuing to Cheltenham with the two subjects."

"And what do you plan for the boy and the Fomorian?"

"They will be recruited by the AIA to help neutralize the Reptilian threat. Hopefully, for good this time."

"Very well. Keep me apprised." SecDef's eyes softened and lingered on Elise's lips before he strode from the room.

Slightly breathless, she joined him and Kate in the hall, grateful he hadn't mentioned their last meeting. Then, the three of them returned to an outer lobby still teeming with snarky, snippety ghosts.

"Director Hobbs, thank you for your insight." SecDef shook her hand. "Special Agent Johnson." He hesitated, then reached for Elise's. "Try not to piss off any more of your superiors. I don't appreciate being roused from bed after only an hour's sleep."

Elise felt her blush all the way to her dyed roots. Normally such ribbing didn't bother her. She even expected it. But the United States Secretary of Defense was another matter. He was a narcissistic asshole, but he had been the love of Elise's life. The one she hadn't been able to get over.

"Yessir."

He sauntered from the building taking Elise's sparkle with him. Feeling a colossal letdown, she shook Kate's hand and held on when she would leave.

"Kate, Morgan Hester has been compromised. She is not to be trusted."

Shock rippled through the director's usual deadpan expression. "I don't believe that."

"Believe it or not. But the information comes from a reliable source. Be on your guard. And do not share sensitive information with Morgan."

"And your source on this is?"

"Secret. For now, anyway. But impeccable. And since it's a matter of national security, hell, international security, please trust me on this."

Kate eyed her suspiciously, then conceded. "So, what do you suggest I tell Morgan when those kids don't show up in Atlanta as expected? She *will* call, you know."

"Tell her the truth. They are being detained and will be returned to the family as soon as practicable. Or make something up. But Kate, don't trust Morgan. Our lives and that of the world may depend on it."

☼☼☼

Elise was boarding the jet at Andrews when her phone jingled. The clone she'd installed on Kate's cell was doing its job. The FBI Director had texted Morgan Foster.

Elise knows.

And that was it. No explanation or instruction. No return message. Just "Elise knows."

EN ROUTE TO THE AZORES

Khenko Blitherstone tore his gaze from the girl sleeping in the opposite seat. Six hours ago, he was with his friends. Now he was on a sleek, low-slung jet enroute to Terceira Island in the Azores. Under orders from the President of the United States, no less. And though he had quizzed Agent Johnson upon boarding the plane, Khenko still had no idea why he was here.

His childhood friend, Marine Colonel Randy Kowalski sat on one side of him, Special Agent Johnson sawed logs on the other. Across from them, two teens sprawled across several seats, sound asleep.

His gaze kept drifting to the girl whose pointed ear peeked from brown hair and a pink ball cap, proof that there really were aliens on Earth. The world governments had gone back and forth on the subject. Until now, Khenko had been undecided.

But if they didn't exist and live on Earth, there would be no government agency dedicated to tracking aliens. And, the tall, thin girl snoring quietly across from Khenko would not have ears that would do an elf proud.

According to Agent Johnson, the girl was a Fomorian. The race had once thrived in the English Isles until forced underground by the Tuatha de Danaan—whoever that was. Seems Khenko had some research to do when they reached their destination.

The cabin pressure changed, clogging his ears. The stealth jet had begun its descent. The engines' hum was barely discernable. Propulsion had come a long way in the last few decades, burning cleaner and quieter and for longer distances. But this jet was light years ahead of everything else on the market.

It was a breed of its own, engineered by Lockheed Martin for NASA and first revealed in 2024. Since then, the innovative aircraft had come a long way. It boasted both stealth and supersonic capabilities, and the interior was more luxurious than most military craft. The X-5900s could cross the Atlantic from New York to

London in about an hour, twice as fast as the supersonic liners that had replaced the old fleets.

Khenko yawned and glanced at his phone. There was barely enough time left for a nap. They had traveled close to three thousand miles in forty-five minutes. Good thing he had slept in yesterday morning.

THE WHITE HOUSE

After several grueling hours coordinating the Bureau's efforts against the Reptilians, Katarina Hobbs returned to the White House. Unfortunately, the lizard men were popping up faster than her agents could contain them. Now the NSA, Homeland Security, and even the National Guard had been called into action.

When the call came in from Morgan Foster, her oldest friend, and longtime crush, Katarina Hobbs put the call on hold to step from the Situation Room.

"How're things in Washington, Kate?" Leave it to Morgan to toss pleasantries aside. "My team has notified and rallied the druid nation."

"You've activated your entire network? Worldwide?"

"Yes, ma'am," Morgan chuckled. "You sound surprised."

Kate peeked into the teeming Sit Room, where generals, admirals, and the National Security Chief barked orders into phones, at computer screens, and at one another.

"I'm sure it helps not having to deal with the political implications. If you could see the chaos here, you would understand."

Snorting, Morgan growled. "Yeah, like there's no politics in the druid nation, a secret society in which every Order is as different as the next. Not to mention language barriers, cultural hurdles, and petty personality conflicts. But it does help that we have a common enemy."

"Yeah, well, I might be the Director of the Federal Bureau of Investigations, but here in the Sit Room, I'm a peon—and you can better believe they're all peeing on me. You would think my agency was responsible for the attacks rather than being the first to identify the threat. Idiots, every one of them."

Morgan guffawed, and Kate's heart back flipped.

"Whip 'em into shape, Katy Kat. No one's better at that than you."

"Yeah, well. Tell *them* that."

The Sit Room door opened, and the Attorney General's head poked through the crack.

"Israel's on the horn. We need you, Kate."

RECONNECTION

When the ceremony was over, Nergal stopped by the infirmary. The doctor who had tended his wounds before the spectacle prescribed him a pain blocker, then Nergal caught the first chute back to Xibalba IX.

On arrival, he breathed a sigh of relief. He considered retiring for the night. He could sleep for a year. But Nergal was eager to salvage his Human Domination Project, so he strode to the lab adjacent to the command center.

Little had changed since he had last been here, except Ishkur would not be returning. The stab of regret surprised Nergal. Was it due to Ishkur's loss or because Nergal could not yet avenge his death?

Tossing his bag next to the console, Nergal bent to inspect the Fomorian. It lay unmoving behind the glass partition, with the leads still connecting it to Shalane Carpenter. According to the briefing, both the creature and Shalane were in a coma and languished at death's door.

Ignoring two Drac scientists he did not know, Nergal crossed to the main keyboard and pulled up the stats. As he perused the target's vitals, Nergal's gut twanged. The scientists were correct. Shalane was in a coma and, like her Fomorian Connector, appeared to be teetering between life and death.

"Has the status changed since these stats were updated?"

The scientists gawked at Nergal, then at one another.

When neither spoke, Nergal growled, "Who is in charge here?"

"Why, Major Azi," the tallest muttered, cocking an insolent eyebrow. "I believe he has retired for the evening, Sir. Would you like—"

"Get him in here, *now.*"

The tall tech moved to the intercom. The other kept its head down, watching Nergal from beneath lowered lids while her claws clicked across the keyboard.

Several minutes later, a scientist hurried through the door. He looked much like Ishkur, and, like the deceased major, his large head barely reached Nergal's chest. Well-developed muscles rippled beneath a scarred vest, and his belt was slung low across powerful hips.

Out of breath, the Drac struck his chest in respect.

"Major Azi, reporting for duty."

"What happened to the Fomorian and its target?"

The scientist looked sheepish, but didn't back down.

"When we initiated the first phase of Project Takeover across the globe, four of the targets and their connectors died. The Fomorian," Azi motioned toward the glass, "and its target lived. But they collapsed and have languished in a coma ever since."

"Have you tried to revive them?"

"The Fomorian, yes. But without him we have no way to reach the target."

"They are dying."

"Yes." The scientist's dismay was apparent. "They are."

Nergal's gaze flit from the Fomorian to the readout. Shalane Carpenter's vitals were dangerously low.

"Detach him and connect me to the target."

"Sir, no!" Azi gasped, horrified. "Commander Shibboleth spared you because we need your expertise. Connecting you to the target is much too risky. The others were lesser beings. You, we cannot afford to lose."

Considering the major's words, Nergal hesitated. Maybe Azi was right. He scrolled through Shalane's feed, searching for answers. When he reached the data from the failed Project Takeover, Nergal cast it to the overhead screen and searched for the startup log for comparison. It wasn't there. He side-eyed Azi, who watched him work.

"Where is the startup log? Have you compared it to the Human Domination data to see if anything was amiss?"

"Sir?"

"The startup log. Ishkur's documentation containing our data from the original test run? It included the parameters and datasets from every trial, including the successful one between the Fomorian and the Reverend."

"Ahh, yes. May I?"

Nergal ceded the keyboard to Azi. The scientist quickly located the elusive log and sent it to the overhead beside the other data. Then, together they perused the two files.

"There!" Azi exclaimed and zeroed in on a line of code in each file. They differed by one character. "That's it?" he groaned. "That one little tittle caused the entire project to fail? To kill eight beings?" Azi rubbed his face in his claws. "How did I miss that?"

"It happens to the best," Nergal allowed. "And from what I gather, with Ishkur gone, you are the best scientist in UnderEarth. No?"

Azi's face scales darkened. "Yes, I am. But I cannot defend this novice mistake. Warlord Shibboleth will have my head."

"Only if he finds out. I will not tell him. Will you?" Nergal directed the question to the other two scientists.

"Tell who what, Sir?" The Draca asked, owl-eyed.

"No, sir," the other said. "But I wasn't paying attention. What did you say?"

"Not a thing. You are both dismissed for the evening. Go back to your quarters. We'll take it from here." Nergal waved toward the door, and they scurried from the lab.

"Correct the coding, and hook me up," Nergal directed. "I would save this target if at all possible. She is perfect for our project."

"Are you sure, General Nergal?"

"Positive." Nergal opened the glass enclosure and pressed a button. A partition slid open, revealing a second onyx slab. "Once my connection is active, you can uncouple the target from the Fomorian and let him die in peace. Or save him if you wish."

"But what if something happens to you?" The distraught scientist twisted shiny claws together.

"Then you will save me, Major. After all, you are the best scientist in UnderEarth, right?"

Azi sputtered, then swallowed hard. All business now, the scientist's claws clattered as he corrected the coding error. Then Azi joined Nergal at the enclosure.

Nergal lowered his long frame to the bench and stretched out, then waited for Azi to secure the connections. But, when he aimed the lead at Nergal's groin, Nergal blocked it with his claw.

"No, not there. Go through my armpit. Or my neck."

Azi eyed Nergal speculatively. Then moving to the top of the bench, he palpated the artery beneath Nergal's collarbone and connected the lead.

A stinging pang shot through Nergal's neck, down into his chest, and up into his head. His teeth clenched, and his body arched as excruciating agony seized his body, knocking him out cold.

Azi watched in horror as the general flopped for several seconds before finally stilling. The computer hummed, doing its thing, until Nergal's vitals appeared on the screen. They spiked dangerously, and Azi held his breath. Then, his heart rate slowed, and his numbers settled into a normal rhythm. Azi studied the legendary warrior's face.

General Nergal appeared half starved. His eye sockets were sunken, his cheeks hollow. One was traversed by a long gash that sliced across an older, jagged scar and ran from one arched brow to a strong, pointed chin. Battle wounds and scars covered much of the general's body. From the evidence, Nergal was lucky to be alive.

A low tone sounded, and Azi hurried to the console. Nergal was making contact. The target was rousing. A thrill coursed through Azi. He watched eagerly as the human's low heart rate and pulse climbed, then normalized. A glance at Nergal and his stats confirmed the general was fine. The tone sounded again, louder and shriller. The woman was stirring.

THE PAST IN THE PRESENT

From the waning light, it was getting late. Emily climbed from the surprisingly comfortable bed, and searched the hut for a bathroom.

There wasn't one, so she donned Awen's supple dress and the dried boots, added a cloak from a peg by the door then slipped outside.

The sun had dipped below the trees, and it was quiet in the glade. The ram Elder, Reinu, grazed near the pond. Elij munched tender grass nearby.

Emily rounded the corner of the small hut, and circled the house, searching for an outhouse or something that might be used as a toilet. Spying nothing, she ducked into the trees and squatted to relieve herself.

"SQUEEE-uh-squee!" came a sharp squeal at her elbow.

Emily yanked up her panties and bolted from the woods, nearly falling face-first when she stumbled over Muc, the sow Elder.

"Oh, no! I'm sorry!" Emily gasped. "Are you okay?"

"Fine," the Elder snorted. "You were squatting near a hornet's nest. I thought you might like to avoid getting stung."

"Amen to that." Emily shuddered. "But why is there a hornet's nest so close to Awen's cabin? Aren't they dangerous?"

"Not usually. Unless disturbed, they leave others alone. If it's a privy you seek, there's one over there." Muc pointed her nose toward the spot where Emily had seen the mysterious woman. It would be in the one place Emily had avoided.

Picking her way past the lightning-scorched birch, Emily spotted what looked to be a low bench hidden by undergrowth. After the scare with the hornets' nest, she approached with trepidation.

The privy was positioned in such a way as to be hidden by trees and undergrowth. From here, Awen's cabin was no longer visible. Emily pulled ivy and brambles away from the wooden bench and spied what appeared to be a hole in the ground covered by leaves.

She brushed these away and found another wooden slat with a hole cut in the middle. Below it, she could hear water gurgling.

Gross. Was she supposed to pee into a creek?

Afterward, Emily wandered to the pond and gazed into the peaceful water. The privy must empty somewhere else. She knelt and washed her hands in the clear, cold water. Curious, she brought a handful to her nose. Finding no smell, she touched her lips to it and found the taste refreshing and clean.

Then, thinking of giardia and all the other bacteria likely polluting the pond, she spit it out. Of course, she was in the eleventh century, so the water was likely unspoiled. Plus, it was supposed to be magical. Surely magical water wouldn't be polluted.

But Emily had to find a way back to her own time. She needed to talk to someone who could tell her how.

She approached Reinu. He baaed and said, "Good evening, Awen. Did you sleep well?"

"I did, thank you. You're standing guard?"

Reinu tossed his horns in affirmation and continued grazing.

"Where are the others?" she wondered aloud, but if Reinu heard, he didn't answer.

She slowly walked the length of the clearing, then circled the birches outlining it. When she came to the path they had followed that morning, she could barely make it out, so well was it hidden. Suddenly, the direness of her situation registered.

She was alone in another time, one thousand years in the past. That rarely worked out well for characters in books and movies.

Tears pooled and trickled down her cheek. Was she stuck here forever? What good was knowing magic if she had no idea how to get back to her own day and time? Surely the animal Elders must know something that would work.

She called to the ram, symbol of sacrifice, breakthrough, and achievement. Surely he would have an answer to Emily's dilemma.

"Reinu, how do I get back to the twenty-first century?"

The ram tore grass and chewed for a moment then lifted his head to study Emily. "I do not know. You always take care of such things. I can help with others, but time and spatial travel are beyond my ken."

Emily gazed at the dusky skyline and shook her head.

"Maybe one of the dragon Keepers can help?" Reinu suggested. "They do that sort of thing all the time.

"Maybe. But the dragons are where I need to be. Are you sure none of the Elders in Awen's glade can help?"

Reinu shook his head. "None that I know. That doesn't mean there isn't one, but I do not know. Maybe Tarbh or Echk might be able to help? Or Mu, the she-cow?"

As she talked, Emily's heart pounded her world teetered. Insides quivering, she sucked in a breath. An anxiety attack was the not what she needed. Drawing another breath, she blew it out.

"And how would I go about asking the Elders?"

"Well. You could wait for them to show up for their turn at guard. Or you could call them. That's usually how it's done."

Her grateful nod to Reinu had her world spinning precariously. Holding her head steady, Emily wobbled back to the cabin to dig in her backpack for the natural remedy Khenko had given her.

The Iroquois medicine man, had rescued Emily from Draig Talav's cave after the earthquake. Then, he had spent several weeks nursing her back to health at his Atlantean Center, a facility on the tiny Bahamian island of Zephyr Cay.

He had stuffed a bottle of the smelly pills into her bag before Emily left with the dragon Keepers. A combination of valerian root, passionflower, and magnesium, he'd said they were natural muscle relaxers. But they also helped conquer the anxiety.

Swallowing one with water, Emily settled into a chair and laid her head on the table. The motion caused a wave of panicked vertigo. She retched and focused on the smoldering fire.

"I am safe," she whispered, trying to prevent a full-blown attack. "No harm will befall me. I am safe. No harm *can* befall me. I am safe. I am sheltered. I am protected. I am loved. God is holding me in the palms of his hands, keeping me safe."

She continued repeating the affirmations taught her by a therapist and kept her eyes fixed on the flickering fire. Soon, the spinning eased. The thought of a juicy burger with salty French fries and a fizzy Coca-Cola flashed in her head.

Her mouth watered. What wouldn't she give to be sitting down to a meal in a twenty-first-century eating establishment? Even if it was a fast-food joint. At this point, nothing sounded better. She settled for a cold roll from that morning's meal.

Pondering what to do next, she ate the roll and sat very still, waiting for the vertigo to pass. When she could close her eyes without the room spinning, she decided to try contacting the dragons. She started with Talav.

When a few minutes passed, and the earth dragon didn't answer, Emily tried Ooschu with the same results. Which left a-Ur and Tienu.

Feeling out with her senses, Emily thought of the day a-Ur had blown into Zephyr Cay on the skirt of a storm. What had been a peaceful few days at the Atlantean Center, lazing on the beach and drinking Khenko's healing smoothies, had morphed into a strenuous training regimen spearheaded by a-Ur.

The air drake had been driven by the need to get back to the Isle of Beli to call a dragon meet. And while he had pushed Emily relentlessly, a-Ur could be surprisingly understanding and gentle. She couldn't reach him, either. Or Tienu.

Emily's frustration grew as she tried Lugh, then her Da, whose hitchhiking spirit had attached to Brian MacBrayer when Cu fell at Zoo Atlanta. But no matter how hard she concentrated, all Emily could hear or see was silence and darkness. No dragons. No Lugh. No Da. Nada.

She even tried Hope and Cu. Still nothing.

Adrenaline and cortisol coursed through Emily's body in spite of Khenko's remedy. Why could she not reach anyone? She had caught on quickly when the dragons taught her how. Why couldn't she do it now?

Huffing, Emily stood cautiously, and felt only a tad dizzy. She slipped outside and tramped around the perimeter of the darkening clearing. Crickets and frogs chirped loudly. She reached in her pocket and withdrew the hard, ridged, gray stone Losgann had given her the day she met him on Zephyr Cay.

Holding it to her mouth, she breathed warmth on the stone, touched it to her lips, and called on Losgann.

The frog Elder appeared instantly with a ribbit and a croak.

"Good evening, mi' lady. Losgann at your service."

Emily bowed to him and explained. "I must get back to the twenty-first century. How would you suggest I do that?"

The frog Elder hopped closer and gazed up into Emily's eyes.

"I do not know, ribbit. Have you tried using your light body? If it's not working, maybe the dragon Elders could help."

"My light body? What is that?"

Losgann's throat ballooned with air, deflated, then puffed up again.

"Beats me. I've seen you use it. I've even traveled with you. But I do not know how you make it happen."

Emily didn't confess she had no concept of a light body. Nor could she conjure one or use it for interdimensional travel. But at least there *was* a way back. She just had to find it.

And she would. She had gotten here, hadn't she?

AWEN'S CABIN

wen's glade turned out to be in the middle of a dense, dark wood. Leaving the SUV tucked into a sycamore thicket, Lugh walked the last fifteen minutes. The narrow path was hard to make out, but Lugh's eyes soon accustomed to the dark. The silent Elders led the way with Lugh bringing up the rear.

When they burst into what he assumed to be Awen's glade, the only light remaining was starlight. Either the moon had set, or it had yet to rise. He wasn't sure which. Not that it really mattered.

He hoped there would be electricity in the hut, though it loomed dark against the aubergine dusk. The glade appeared deserted. Artis lumbered to the door and stood on hind legs to push against it. Cu barked when it creaked open. Hope rushed inside first, followed by Cu. Artis gestured for Lugh to enter next. He ducked through the doorway and hesitated, jaw agape.

Though the outside looked rather ramshackle, the rustic inside glowed in the light of an array candles. A wonderful aroma filled the room; that of warm baked bread and roasted meat. Glancing at the table, Lugh was shocked to see a full spread, including a clean crockery plate and silver utensils. A ceramic pitcher cozied between two leaded glasses.

Pouring himself water, Lugh downed it, then had another as he examined the room. There was a lone, narrow bed in one corner. A rocking chair sat in front of a blazing fire.

Hope yowled and paced the room. "Emily is here, I feel her."

Cu yipped and settled on a colorful rag rug with his back to the fire. Artis's massive chest filled the doorframe.

"She *is* here," he gurgled in that shrill tone. "But, as I told you, she is stuck in the Otherworld. She's gone back in time to the eleventh century."

Cu's howl was deep and bordered on mournful.

"Yes, Cu," Artis snarled. "We must get her back. And soon, before she is stuck there forever."

Lugh had reached for a roll, but that brought him up short. Bread in hand, he rounded on the bear.

"You mean, that really can happen? It's not just hearsay?"

Artis eyed Lugh. "Of course it can happen. And often does."

Lugh wilted into a cane chair. "How do we get her back?"

He buttered a warm roll and shoved it in his mouth. He had eaten a burger an hour ago, but the delicious aroma had gotten the better of him. That reminded him of Brian, who was always hungry and had atrocious table manners. Lugh chewed thoughtfully.

When neither of the Elders answered, he realized Cu and Hope eyed him hungrily.

"Care to share?" Cu whined.

Their food was still in the rental car. Lugh held out a roll, and the hound wolfed it down. The thought of slogging to the sycamore thicket and lugging his suitcase back in the dark made Lugh groan out loud.

Shoving from the table, he opened a small cabinet to scrounge for bowls. Tonight they would eat table food. He would schlep to the car tomorrow after daylight.

"How about you, Artis? Are you hungry?"

The bear wagged his head.

"From the looks of this cabinet," Lugh remarked, removing a plate and a bowl from Awen's meager store, "Awen must not get much company."

The Elders' eyes followed Lugh as he divided the meat into three portions. He gave two to the animals and sat down to devour his own as a cold wind whistled through the cabin.

Artis no longer filled the open doorway. Lugh gazed out into the dark clearing and sighed. He hadn't "heard" this much silence in… he thought for a moment. It had been a very long time. So long, he couldn't remember. Then, looking up at the sky, his breath caught.

With no moon or city lights, trillions of stars winked against an inky sky. He had only seen the Milky Way once while vacationing at the Dark Sky Reserve in Ketchum, Idaho.

"Artis?" he called quietly into the night.

The bear didn't answer.

Lugh ducked inside and barred the door. Cu had gobbled his food and was sprawled in front of the fireplace licking his privates. Hope's head was in her bowl. Lugh settled at the table to finish his simple yet tasty meal and wondered who had prepared it for them.

ALEXIS MAYHALL HESTER

The heat was oppressive, ninety-six degrees at 9:00 a.m. with a predicted high of 107. Add ninety-two percent humidity and the air was so thick it was an effort to breathe. At least the Bahamas had had a breeze.

Alexis parked Honey's Porsche in the Foster's driveway. As soon as she stepped from the cushy, air-conditioned interior, Honey's expensive outfit clung to her, and beads of sweat collected on her lip.

Fanning her face with one hand, Alexis jabbed an impatient finger against the doorbell. Grandfather clock tones echoed through what she knew was a marble entryway.

Twenty seconds passed, thirty, a minute.

She peeked through the beaded glass and considered ringing the bell again, then thought of pounding on the door. But if Morgan hadn't heard the deep, resounding bongs, she was either deaf or not home. What now?

Remembering the druid knock, Alexis rapped sharply on the glass three times, paused for three counts, then rapped three more. This time, she heard the clickety-click of high heels crossing the entryway.

Alexis blotted sweat and oil from her make-up with a tissue and smiled serenely when Morgan Hester Foster opened the door. But Morgan's smile was less than welcoming. She looked to the right and left of Alexis, then behind her, as if Alexis wasn't there.

"Hello, can I help you?" the Hester matriarch finally asked. "I recognized your knock, but I don't believe I know you."

Alexis chuckled, a pleasant, rolling chortle that was nothing like her own laugh. She reached out a hand, and in a firm, no-nonsense tone, said, "I hope you do, Morgan. I am your old friend, Alexis. Alexis Mayhall Hester."

Morgan let go of her hand abruptly. Her expression remained blank for a few seconds, then her face reddened, and her eyes narrowed.

"Alexis is dead. I don't know who you are, but you are *not* Alexis Hester. My friend is dead." She tried to slam the door, but Alexis pushed against it.

"I did die, Morgana." The tall druid started at the use of her nickname. "Hell," Alexis continued, needing to convince the Hester matriarch. "For all intents and purposes, I'm probably *still* dead. But a dragon found me in the Otherworld and enlisted me to help save Emily."

Morgan raked Alexis up and down, eyes stern.

"No, I don't think so. Who are you, really? And why are you impersonating Alexis Hester?"

Digging in Honey's tiny purse, Alexis removed her driver's license, and handed it to Morgan.

"This says I am Honey Dewars."

Morgan snickered. "Honey Dew? Honestly?" She slapped her thigh and peered at the official Georgia driver's license, turning it from side to side, holding it to the light, then tilting it back and forth to view the metallic hologram. When she looked up again, confusion and doubt had replaced the anger.

Morgan had been one of Alexis's dearest friends. More so even than her sister, Rona. Of course, Alexis and Rona were raised by different mothers and rarely saw one another. Then there was their friend Katy Hobbs, but that was another story.

"So your name is Honey Dewars, but you claim to be my dead friend Alexis." Morgan shook her head sadly, then said in a menacing tone, "Look, you've had your sick fun, *Ms. Dewars*. Now what do you really want?"

Sighing, Alexis said, "Morgana, it really is me. What can I say to make you believe me?" She shifted on the landing, high heels pinching her toes and sweat puddling between Honey's ample breasts. Desperate, she tried again.

"You helped me leave Hamilton on Emily's fourth birthday. Hell, you *planned* most of it. All I had to do was get Emily to the park and then on that bus. You arranged the rest." The dark eyes flickered but continued boring a hole through Alexis.

"Then, you cut me off, though we promised to stay in touch. Why, Morgan? Can you imagine how hard it was to get by alone with a four-year-old? With no job and no money?

"Why wouldn't you return my calls? Or my texts or emails? I was devastated, having to raise that precocious child on my own. And she wasn't even *mine*. And yes, dammit, I am dead. But that girl is in danger, Morgan. And inhabiting this stranger's body is the only way I can help."

As Alexis talked, Morgan's face changed from pink to red to pasty white. She opened the heavy door the rest of the way, took Alexis by Honey's elbow, and pulled her into the blessedly cool house through the foyer to the den.

"Sit," she commanded. "I'll be right back."

Breathing a sigh of relief, Alexis sank into a worn armchair and dabbed at the sweat with another tissue. The furnishings and décor had changed in the last twenty-five years, but the room still retained the homey feel it had had when they were children and the house had belonged to Donald Foster's parents.

The clicking of high heels across the gleaming hardwood signaled Morgan's return. She handed Alexis a tall glass of iced tea crowned with a large lemon wedge, then settled on the sofa and leaned toward Alexis.

"So. You really are Alexis Hester?" Her brows disappeared under a fringe of hair. "Back from the dead?"

"I really, really am."

They sat that way for a long moment staring at one another, Morgan speculatively, Alexis hopeful. Surely her old friend would believe her and help.

"Then, who is this woman you have taken hostage?"

"Does it matter?"

"Only if you've harmed her."

"Why would I? Honey allowed me entry. I'm not sure she knew what she was getting into, but her relationship was souring and she saw it as a way to get away from that troglodyte, Todd."

Alexis shifted uncomfortably in her chair when Morgan continued to stare. Finally, the Head of Security for the Awen Order sighed loudly and stood to cross the room, coming back with a framed photograph. She thrust it into Alexis's hands.

"Tell me about this."

Alexis peered at the picture and an invisible hand squeezed her heart. It had been taken their senior year at Druid Hills High School.

"Wow. Look at us. We were so young." Whisked back in time, she gently traced the faces of the three girls who had planned to change the world. "This is me, you, and Kate Hobbs. Katarina. We were the sole members of the Katy Kats, our not-so-secret club."

She glanced up at Morgan, whose expression never wavered, then back at the photo.

"Who took the picture?" That steely gaze was unremitting.

"Elise Hester. She wanted to be in the photograph, but you made her take it instead."

Even back then, Morgan had been bossy and overbearing, especially to the flighty, brilliant Elise. She had barred Elise from the Katy Kats and forbade Alexis and Kate from hanging out with their druid classmate. Alexis had always suspected Morgan was jealous. After all, Elise could see dead people. The self-righteous Morgan couldn't do anything that cool.

While Alexis waited for a reaction, she sipped her tea nervously and smoothed wrinkles from the pale yellow skort outfit she had selected from Honey's closet. The styles hadn't changed much since her death. But as the silence stretched out, she became more uncomfortable.

Alexis had expected Morgan to be wary. But she had hoped she would be excited to see her once convinced of her sincerity. Happy even. But from Morgan's brooding expression, that was far from the case.

Feeling the need to escape the thick tension and gather senses that had scattered to the far corners of the room, Alexis broke the ponderous silence.

"Could I use your bathroom?"

Morgan stood. She anchored her hands on her hips, thinning lips pooched out resentfully.

"Why did you come back, Alexis? You made a vow. You swore you wouldn't."

Standing slowly, Alexis squared off with the formidable woman.

"You are not supposed to be here," Morgan spat. "Why did you come back?"

Heat coursed through Honey's body. Alexis hadn't wanted to believe it, but the understanding she had gained doing penance was true. Morgan Hester was a bad person—and always had been, even as a child.

"Because death has a way of showing you to yourself. You shaped me, Morgan. You goaded, demeaned, and bullied me like you did all the other kids. You convinced me to do awful things I never wanted to do. *You* made me suspicious of Hamilton. And when that didn't get you what you wanted, you turned me against my own daughter. How could you, Morgan? I trusted you. *I trusted you.*"

"Oh, boo-hoo," the bitch cackled. "Poor baby. You never did anything you didn't want to do."

The deep bong of the doorbell startled them both.

TWO SIDES OF THE VEIL

A quiet knock sounded at Awen's door.

Lugh's sharp intake of breath had him coughing helplessly as a chunk of beef lodged in his windpipe. He hacked like a madman while Cu barked. Another rap sounded—three taps, silence, then three more—and Lugh regained his breath.

That was a druid knock. Could it be Emily? Or had Artis returned?

He snatched a sip of water and hurried to the door, where Cu barked frantically. Hope had transformed into a growling ball of whoop-ass with an arched back and hair on end.

Putting a finger to his lips, Lugh lifted the bar. Then, inching the door open, he spied a tall woman with long, black hair— *not* Artis or Emily. The woman's back was to the door, and her hair cascaded below her buttocks.

"Hello?" His greeting came out as a squeak. Embarrassed, Lugh cleared his throat and tried again. "Can I help you?"

The caller swung around, and Lugh's body went to jelly. Before him stood the most beautiful woman he had ever seen, her dark eyes tilted slightly upward, as did her narrow nose. Wide, plump lips painted an enticing shade of scarlet parted in a slight smile. The thick lashes batting seductively at Lugh were so long they swept the woman's carved cheekbones.

Flabbergasted, he stared open-mouthed at the mysterious visitor whose ornate dress barely covered her breasts. Who was this woman, and what was she doing in Awen's supposedly secret glade? Was it she who had provided the food?

"Who are you? And what do you want?" Lugh demanded, ignoring the tug at his groin.

The full bottom lip protruded in a pout. "Is that any way to greet a lady? I could ask the same of you."

Lugh studied the dark eyes to gauge the beauty's intent. They were void of guile, but his gut told him she was dangerous.

"Maybe. You seem harmless. But you could be a demon spirit sent to harm me."

Hurt marred the attractive features. The luscious lips pursed. Laying a finger against her chin, the woman murmured something too low to hear. Lugh leaned closer and asked her to speak louder.

Again, her mumble was unintelligible. But this time, it was accompanied by a flash of light and a loud boom. Recoiling swiftly, Lugh slammed the door and jammed his foot against it, shutting the mysterious woman out.

☼☼☼

"What do you mean there's no way back?" Emily snapped.

A fat lot of help the animal Elders were. She had assembled them hoping one would know a spell that would get her back to her own time.

"There has to be. I was transported there without even trying, so there *is* a way. I just don't know what I did to make it happen." She scrubbed her face in her hands, frustrated.

"Perhaps if you got quiet and looked back, you would see the answer," Giagh honked.

"Yeah, I tried that."

"And?"

"Nearing the end of her patience, Emily shoved away the curls tickling her face and glared at Giagh.

"No luck. Why do you think I asked you?"

"Can you show me the magical stones?" Losgann croaked.

Emily drew out the Frog stone and the Otter stone.

The frog Elder nosed them. "This is the one I gave you, and this is from Dobhran." He shook his head. "No, these will not do. You need the other stones. The wandstones."

Emily held out her right hand. The emerald ring her Da had passed to her glittered on her index finger.

"This is Aóme, one of the wandstones." Then, Emily lifted the chain and drew the ruby pendant from inside Awen's dress. "And this was given to me by a woman on Zephyr Cay. I believe it to be a wandstone, too." She held it next to Aóme for Losgann and the others to see.

"I suspect you are right," Druid Dhubh, the blackbird Elder squawked. "But where are the others? You need all four. Preferably attached to the wand."

Despairing, Emily hung her head.

"I do not know where the other stones are."

Sionnach, the fox Elder, asked the blackbird, "Why can't you take Awen across? Do you not straddle the gateway between worlds?"

"Aye, but so does Corr," Druid Dhubh retorted. "Where is the crane? He is the one who should take her."

Emily had met Corr in Zephyr Cay. But the crane Elder had not made an appearance in Awen's glade.

Druid Dhubh ruffled his ebony feathers and fixed golden eyes on Emily. "It is true I have the ability to walk both worlds at the same time. But I have dwelt in the Otherworld for a long while, so long my powers have yet to fully return. I dare not attempt to shuttle you anywhere, Master, lest I lose you forever in the mists of the Otherworld."

Emily heaved a loud sigh. "It can't be worse than being stuck in the eleventh century."

The blackbird squawked and fluttered its wings. "Yes, Master Druid. It could be *much* worse. I will not risk your life." He cawed and scanned the circle of magical animals. "Where is the wolfhound?"

"Cu is in the twenty-first century, where I belong."

"That is unfortunate. As the Guardian of the Mysteries, the wolfhound could easily shuttle you to your proper time. Assuming your intentions are honorable. And that you maintain tight control over your unconscious mind."

Frustration trounced Emily's growing hope. "The definition of 'unconscious' is that one *has* no control."

"Plus, Cu is not here," Faol, the wolf Elder, added. "So that plan will not work."

Shevug, the hawk, swooped closer. "Why not call Cu to you? Or the dragon Keepers? Any one of them could transport you between time and space."

The other Elders clamored in agreement. "Yes, call Cu." "Call the Keepers." "They can do it."

Emily's scant hope vanished, and her exasperation soared. She reminded them she had tried that—several times.

Bo, the shaggy cow Elder, stopped grazing. "Where *are* the other Elders? Why are they not here with us now?"

Gyarr, the lanky hare, hopped to the front of the Elder host. His ears pointed at Emily. "They are not here because of this one. She has no faith in her abilities or herself. I sense you are new to your powers, young Awen. Am I right?"

The Elder's tone was gentle, not accusatory, but heat suffused Emily's face and neck. Starlight revealed her shame to all within sight.

"Yes." The admission came in a strangled whisper. "I am embarrassed to tell you that my mother made sure I knew nothing of my powers or my druid heritage. My father found me after she died, but that was only recently. You're right. I *am* inexperienced, weak even. I do not know what I'm doing, where I'm going, or how all this will play out. But I *am* trying, I promise." She buried her face in her hands, then looked out at the Elders, miserable.

"The Awen Order and Cu and Hope did their best to train me in a short time. Then, I spent a few intense weeks with the dragon Keepers." Emily sniffed back tears. "Of course, I was recovering from near-fatal injuries at the time. But you all knew about my lack of training. You were at my initiation. I saw you there."

The Elder host agreed they *had* been there. But never in memory had the Awen been denied her destiny, and the Elders had not understood the ramifications. It did not follow the natural order of things.

Gyarr, the rangy hare, pounded the grass with his hind foot, and the Elders quieted. "This explains a lot. It is a wonder you have made it this far, child."

The hare's ears pricked skyward. He tested the wind with his nose, then twisted to survey the path at the edge of Awen's glade. A startled look crossed Gyarr's face, then he bounded to the forest and disappeared as if pursued by demons.

Chills danced over Emily's body.

Sionnach tossed his head and stepped closer. "Might I offer a suggestion?"

"Please do."

Druid Dhubh and the others crowded near.

"You said you have attempted to reach Cu and the Keepers. Now that you have a little more information, maybe you could go inside the cabin, get quiet, and try again?"

Emily's exasperation nearly spewed out, but the fox's eyes shone with such belief, she sighed and muttered, "I have. But I will try again."

Squatting, she gazed into the Elder's eyes. "I have been dying to feel your fur, Sionnach. Would you mind?"

He lowered his head. "I would be honored, Master."

Emily touched it tentatively, then ran a gentle hand down Sionnach's back to the tip of his bushy tail. Stroking his neck, she sank her fingers into his thick ruff, and the fox gurgled deep in its throat.

A quick longing for her cat, Ralph, engulfed Emily. It deepened, and a tear gathered in the corner of one eye. Then she shook it off, sat back on her heels, and considered the Elder Host.

"Does anyone else have a suggestion for getting me back to the twenty-first century? A *different* suggestion?"

"Us, Awen. Get *us* back to the twenty-first century," Sionnach yipped. "Where you go, we follow."

The words were a punch to Emily's gut. "Then Cu and Hope should be here."

She tilted her face to the moon behind the treetops. It hid behind a cloud, and she nearly sobbed. Would she ever be a worthy Awen? She couldn't even draw her most beloved Elders.

Dejected, she flounced inside, chilled to the bone. Adding wood from the rack, Emily stoked the fire until it blazed, then gazed into its depths. There was a way out. She just had to find it.

A knock startled her from her reverie. Emily opened the door cautiously, expecting to see one of the animal Elders. No one was there.

A brand exploded behind her, then sizzled, ejecting a stream of whistling fire. She swallowed hard, and the lump of dread that had lodged in her throat traveled to her chest, then settled like a brick in her midsection.

She knew what she had to do.

Sighing heavily, Emily peered out at the now empty clearing, secured the door, and settled in the rocking chair. She had tried everything else. It was time to ask Awen.

Shuddering at the thought of giving up control, she stared into the fire and drew a deep, raggedy breath.

✹✹✹

A pounding commenced outside the door, and Lugh's heart raced. He peered through the window, expecting to see the mysterious woman, but she wasn't there. Lifting the bar, he cracked the door but still saw no one. Then he threw it wide, and the woman appeared, gown billowing in the wind.

This time, Lugh was ready.

197

"Who are you?" he demanded, blocking the doorway. "And what do you want?"

The woman laughed, a sharp, caustic cackle that chilled Lugh's blood.

"I am Bé Chuille, goddess of Marduk, consort of Ogma, daughter of Flidais, and Elder of the Tuatha Dé Danann. As for what I want, I seek the one who lives here, a druid witch by the name of Awen. Now," her eyes narrowed, "I have answered your questions. You must answer mine. Who are you?"

Hope and Cu growled behind him, and Lugh drew to full height.

"The one you seek is not here. I am Lughnasadh MacBrayer, Head Priest of the Awen Order of Druids."

The lovely face contorted in anger. "The druid whelp who killed Beli-Mawr bore a similar name. Are you Lughaid's spawn? If so, I shall take pleasure in returning the favor." She raked Lugh up and down with a contemptuous glare. "But, that is not likely. You are a mere mortal. A handsome one. But you are dark and swarthy and of average build. You bear no resemblance to the once mighty King of Tara.

"Now, out of my way. I have business with Awen, and you shall hinder me no more." She flicked her wrist, paralyzing Lugh before he could react.

Limbs frozen by his sides, Lugh strained to summon a spell that would stop her. But this was no mere woman. She was a wicked witch and a powerful one. While he strained to break free, she strode through the door. Then, shoving him aside, the witch advanced on Cu and Hope.

Helpless to intervene, Lugh watched.

"Well, well. If it's not Awen's beasties." Bé Chuille cackled merrily. "Where is your master?" She twirled a finger. "You shall spill your secrets."

But, rather than obeying, Hope gathered on powerful haunches and leapt into the air. She landed on Bé Chuille's head and wrapped her forty-pound body around it, claws digging in.

She shrieked and bucked like a wild woman, then spun in a drunken circle to dislodge the cat. Lugh watched in astonishment as Hope persisted, claws deep in the witch's skull. Blood ran down Bé's temples, and her black hair whipped as she gyrated.

Then, Lugh heard Cu inside his head. "Hope, jump on Lugh's back and hang on tight."

The wildcat yowled gleefully, and using the witch's head as a springboard, she leapt, propelling a screeching Bé Chuille in the opposite direction.

Lugh's knees bent under Hope's weight. Fortunately, his leather jacket took the brunt of her claws, and she landed squarely without toppling him.

The witch deftly flipped to her hands and knees, then rose from the floor with blood flowing down her face and a murderous gleam in her eyes.

Cu barked at her menacingly. Then, wrapping a paw around Lugh's leg, the wolfhound howled, long and plaintively, as the witch reared back to hurl a curse.

Lugh winced and tried to duck.

TOGETHER AGAIN

Emily settled deeper into the rocking chair.

Breathing in and out slowly and rhythmically, she focused on the flames dancing in the fireplace. Soon, her body relaxed and her mind emptied. Then, closing her eyes, she filled her lungs completely, let the air out, and called to Awen inside her head.

"Awen, if you are here, can you help me? I'm stuck in the eleventh century and don't know how to return to my own time. The Elders mentioned a light body, and said a few of them, including Cu, could transport me across. But they're not here, and Druid Dhubh fears he will lose me in the mists of the Otherworld. Can you help me, Awen?"

A sudden commotion rose behind Emily. She leapt from the chair into a defensive posture and gasped aloud.

In the middle of her ancestor's tiny domicile crouched Lugh MacBrayer and the two animal Elders. Hope rode astride Lugh's shoulders, and Cu was glued to Lugh's thigh.

"Lugh! Cu! Hope!" Emily gurgled. "You found me!"

But something was wrong. Lugh's eyes lit, but he was apprehensive. Where is the witch?" He wheeled to face the door with Hope still clinging to his shoulders.

A chill rippled through Emily. "You mean the winter hag? Is that who knocked at the door and disappeared?"

"Yes, the winter hag," Cu howled. "But fear not. She is back where we left her."

"What do you mean?" Lugh and Emily asked together.

"We didn't go anywhere," Lugh added, puzzlement etched across his brow.

Emily was equally mystified.

"Did you switch places with the witch?"

She eyed Lugh uncertainly. "Me? No, I've been here. Where did you come from?"

Hope jumped down from Lugh's shoulder to address Emily. "Relax. Cu brought us here." Then, the wildcat gazed up at the worried priest. "Lughnasadh, the witch will not find us. We are safe for now."

Going down on her knees, Emily hugged Hope close, keeping a shy eye on Lugh, who peered out the window. Cu danced around them, nails clicking, and Emily pulled him into a three-way hug.

"God, I've missed y'all," she gushed. "Cu, last I saw you, you were flying down the slope at Zoo Atlanta with Da onboard." Cu's wet tongue found Emily's cheek, and she wiggled away. "How did you find me?"

"I'm pretty sure it was the other way around," Hope meowed. "You found us. We were flying to Wales per your request, when a nasty electrical storm forced our plane to land. As soon as we touched down in Caen, I locked onto your energy signature."

"So did I!" Cu barked, not to be outdone.

Emily grinned, fascinated.

"Lugh rented a car and drove us to Falaise," Hope added. "We were almost here when Artis, the bear Elder, intercepted us. Artis told us you were stuck in the Otherworld. And in the eleventh century."

"That's right. He did." Lugh smiled at Emily for the first time, a quick, sloppy grin that sent shivers skittering over her body.

Nervous now, she broke eye contact and settled in one of the cane-back chairs. The sexy druid priest had pushed her buttons with nothing but a grin. How did he do that?

Then something occurred to Emily.

"If Artis is in the twenty-first century, how did he know that I am not?"

Hope's eyes took on a faraway glint. Cu wagged his head, and Lugh plopped into the opposite chair.

"The bear did not say." The pirate-priest reached for Emily's hand, dark eyes sparkling. He turned it over and caressed the back of her fingers, seeming to be as happy to see her as she was him. "But wouldn't your connection have clued him in?"

"Hmm? Clued… huh?" Emily tilted her hand and intertwined their fingers. Lugh's grin grew wider, making it difficult to think.

"You asked how Artis knew you were in the eleventh century. I thought maybe it was because of his bond to you."

"Oh. Yeah." Emily's color rose under Lugh's scrutiny. She asked Hope and Cu, "Did either of you know I'd been sent back in time?"

"No," Hope murmured. "I knew you were in Falaise. And I knew something was wrong. But not what."

"Same here," Cu barked, then lowered his head. "But to be honest, I was busy enjoying the ride. So what?" he demanded when Hope glared at him. "I'm a dog. What do you expect? At least I'm honest."

While they sparred, Emily noticed how well her hand fit inside Lugh's. Then something struck her, and she pulled away.

"You know, of the animal Elders I met before coming to Awen's glade, I've seen only one in the eleventh century. Until you arrived, anyway." She tapped her chin, thinking. "And Losgann only appeared after I used his amulet to call him. Oh, wait. Dobhran is here."

Her mind returned to those first anguished days in the carriage house at Wren's Roost. The night before her initiation, Dobhran, the playful otter Elder, had come to Emily in a dream. She slid her free hand into the pocket of Awen's dress to cradle the talisman he had left under her bed and remembered Artis.

"Oh, yeah! Artis was in my dreams, too. He chased me." Emily shuddered, remembering. "I wonder... Maybe the animal Elders are drawn to me wherever I am? And then stay there unless I call them? But that doesn't explain how Artis knows I'm here.

"Unless..." Her eyes widened. "Surely he didn't have anything to do with sending me back here." Then she shook her head. "No, I'm pretty sure that was Draig Tienu."

"I have another question," Lugh said. "If we are in the eleventh century, how can that be? Time travel isn't possible." He drew out his cell phone and then waved it in the air. "But when I checked this before meeting Artis, it had full bars. Now, it has nothing. 'No service,' it says." Lugh's gaze roved the table, then the floor.

"And our dishes. They're not here either." He blinked at Emily, then at the animal Elders. "Cu, how did you get us away from that witch?"

The wolfhound laid his chin on the table next to Lugh. "My spell was designed to reunite us with Awen while hiding us from Bé Chuille."

"Bé Chuille? The winter hag?"

"Yes, she was here searching for you," Hope growled. "Or rather, she *is* here. But thanks to Cu, she is on the other side of a time veil one thousand years in the future."

The cat twisted to look up at the wolfhound. "Was that you that blocked the witch's curse?"

"Of course," Cu yipped. "And hid our destination so she could not follow or trace our path."

"Smart," Hope purred.

"What is the date?" Lugh demanded.

"It is Beltane," Cu crooned.

"2042?"

"No. We have crossed into Awen's time." Cu scratched his shoulder with a hind leg, and his eyes rolled back.

Lugh huffed loudly and laid his forehead on the table.

They sat in silence for a long minute until he looked up and wagged his head as if clearing cobwebs. Then, resting his strong chin in cradled hands, he peered at Emily.

"It's good to see you. Your hair's gotten long."

Delighted, her gaze swept the priest. "Yours too."

His hair was even shaggier than when she'd last seen him in the Otherworld. He had a Band-Aid on his forehead and a new scar across one eyebrow. But he was as handsome as ever.

Returning her perusal, the druid priest grinned, sending electricity sizzling through Emily.

When he stood and pulled her into his arms, grateful tears filled Emily's eyes. For the first time since the earthquake in Atlanta, she felt safe. Contentment washed over her, and she relaxed and melted into Lugh's embrace.

Cu danced around them, barking like a loon. Hope settled on the rag rug in front of the fire to groom her fur while Lugh rocked Emily back and forth.

"It's you, it's really you," he whispered in her ear. "I have waited so long. I was beginning to wonder if I would ever find you. How did you get here, anyway?"

Emily reluctantly disentangled from the priest's arms. "It was Draig Tienu."

She settled in the chair and quickly recounted her adventures in the wormhole, her troubles at Chateau Falaise, and their harrowing escape and flight to Awen's glade.

"So that's how you knew you were in the eleventh century," Lugh murmured once she'd explained about Duchess Matilda's soldiers and the gallows.

"That, plus Awen's glade. It is exactly as I see it in my dreams and in the snatches of Awen's memories."

"What do you mean?"

"Come see."

Taking Lugh's hand, Emily led him outside. The moon had climbed higher, and the clearing was quiet. The only Elders in sight were Cu and Hope, who trotted ahead to the water's edge.

"These are the Healing Waters of Luftshorne." Emily gazed into the pond, and a deep reverence filled her. Ripples formed as the animal Elders lowered their heads to drink.

Lugh whistled, impressed. "There was no water when we arrived."

"How sad."

"So we really are in the eleventh century."

"Yes, we really, really are."

They stood in silence, gazing into Awen's starlit pond, and Emily was acutely aware of Lugh's shoulder grazing hers.

After a while, the gurgle of water bubbling from a crevice in the rocks induced a trance-like state, and Emily's eyes grew heavy. Her next yawn was louder and longer, breaking the spell.

Lugh yawned, too. Emily chuckled and sank into the grass cross-legged. Around the pond and in the trees, frogs and crickets struck a chorus.

Lugh joined her on the grass, stretching out on his back.

"There's Orion's Belt." He pointed.

Emily scooted closer until their bodies met. Then she laid her head on his shoulder and sighed. "Aren't the stars magnificent without the light pollution?"

"Yeah. Kinda makes you want to stay here, doesn't it?" Lugh rolled to face Emily.

She turned her head toward him. "Yeah, kind of. As long as you're here." Then she shuddered, remembering the soldiers guarding Chateau Falaise.

Turning her face to the night sky, Emily sighed. "No, not even then. As afraid as I am of facing witches, calling dragons, and saving the world from aliens no one knows about, I am more afraid of staying here." She rolled to face Lugh.

"William's wife wants me dead. Well, not me—Matilda wants Awen dead. That's reason enough to get out of here. But the twenty-first century needs us, Lugh. We can't let the Reptilians exterminate Humanity."

She shivered and crowded closer. "Not when we were chosen to protect them. We can't let them down."

"Them *or* the Order," Lugh agreed fervently and entwined his fingers with hers.

They stayed that way for a long time, holding hands, talking quietly, and gazing at the stars. Lugh related what had happened after Emily disappeared into the ground that day at Zoo Atlanta. Emily described her traumatic confinement in Earth's dark underbelly before being rescued by Draig Talav.

They forgot about Cu and Hope, who had wandered off, and about everything and everyone else. As the full moon neared the peak of her arc, Emily curled into Lugh. His arms encircled her and drew her close. And there, on the banks of Luftshorne, Emily drifted to sleep in the druid priest's arms.

ARTIS TAKES A STAND

Bé Chuille unfastened her cloak and crouched to face off against Artis. The insolent bear had ambushed her after Awen's animals disappeared.

"I should've killed you the last time you got between me and my prey," she snarled, letting her wrap fall to the ground. "Now, where did that man and Awen's beasties go?"

Artis huffed and pounded the ground with his paws. "Witch, I have endured your wicked ways for millennia untold, controlling my instinct to end your miserable life. No more. I know not what the goddess saw in you, but your past association with Brigid will not save you this time."

The bear charged, and Bé feinted sideways. He barely missed, then whirled to strike out with a vicious paw that slashed Bé's face and catapulted her to the dirt.

Temper flaring, she staunched the blood with a spell and glared at Artis, whose massive bulk, all ten feet, and nine hundred pounds, towered over her.

"What happened to you, anyway?" the bear taunted, saliva dripping from its jaw to slither down Bé's cheek. "You were such a bright, charming girl. What rotted your heart and turned it black?"

That struck a chord. A dangerous one.

Livid now, she used her sleeve to wipe the drool from her face and sprang up to throw a curse. The self-righteous bear cartwheeled backward, and Bé cackled with glee.

Too quickly, it scrambled to all fours and charged again. Bé hurled a stunning spell. This time, the bear squealed and fell short, writhing in the grass. Then, with a bellowing roar, he struggled to his feet and advanced again.

Bé crouched, waiting.

When Artis leapt, exposing his soft belly, she made a slicing motion in the air.

Unfortunately, the bear was too close. It slammed into Bé, knocking her to the ground, then collapsed on top of her, spewing hot guts and slippery blood. His slimy entrails clung to her with horrible sucking sounds. Then, the repulsive stench overpowered her, and she retched and nearly vomited.

In agony, the dying bear bellowed "I will be back, witch. And next time, it shall be *you* who dies. No more winter hag, no more Cailleach, no more Bé Chuille."

Gagging violently, Bé struggled to wriggle away from the heavy bear and its foul-smelling guts. But his mass kept her pinned there.

In his dying throes, the bear swore, "You cannot kill me, witch. As long as Awen lives, I shall return." Then Artis gurgled and gave up the ghost.

Bé Chuille took a moment to collect her wits, then freed herself with a spell. Rolling away from the disemboweled bear, she stood, wobbling like a drunkard, and prodded the carcass with a toe.

A nervy laugh escaped into the twilight as Bé moved away from the stink. Then she collapsed in the weeds, laughing like a mad woman.

She had not intended to do battle with Artis. In fact, Bé had always been in awe of the druid Elder. Why had he goaded her like that?

Her laughter died, and she thought of what Artis had said about returning. So what if the damn bear came back. Bé would kill him again. And she would keep killing the effeminate asshole until his precious Awen was dead and he could no longer return to mock Bé Chuille.

Casting about the lifeless clearing, Bé growled. The man and Awen's beasts were gone and Artis had refused to reveal the Awen's location. Her last resort was torturing Draig Tienu, but the dragon king would likely prove most difficult.

As the Beltane moon peeked through the birches, the stench of death drifted to Bé. She spoke a quick spell to cleanse the gore from her clothes and body. Then, waving a hand above her head in a circular motion, she activated her light body and set her intention on the Stygian Plains.

COMING TO

Shalane breathed deeply, relishing sweet air and the bloom of warmth against her face. She floated on a cloud, no longer bound, and the pain was finally gone.

Moving into a much-needed stretch, she opened her eyes and immediately squeezed them shut against the blinding light.

Patty could not get through to Mitchell or Latoya, so she called her mother, needing someone to talk to. They chatted about this and that for a while before Patty asked if they had seen the news.

"*Yes,*" her mother gasped. "Oh, Patty, I'm scared stiff. We haven't left the house since we first heard."

A loud moan came from Shalane's hospital room.

"Hang on, Mom." Patty hurried inside. She smoothed the hair from Shalane's forehead and sucked in a breath when the blue eyes opened.

"Shalane?" Patty whispered, leaning closer.

But the eyelids closed. Beneath the covers Shalane's ample chest rose and fell as she expelled a great, sighing breath.

Excited, Patty rang the button for a nurse, then chirped into her cell, "I think Shalane is waking up. Let me call you back."

She tossed the phone on the chair and crowded closer to the bed.

When her eyes could handle the bright light, Shalane opened them fully. She was definitely in a hospital. Machines beeped behind her, and her head ached. Other than that, there was no pain.

"Shalane?" Patrika Tolbert huddled next to her, youthful face inches from Shalane's.

"Patty?" She had rescued the Marilyn Monroe lookalike from a bar in San Diego, but Patrika had returned to California during their stay in Nashville. Shalane wanted to ask why the girl was there, but could only managed a gruff, "water."

Patty quickly held a cup with a straw to Shalane's lips.

She slurped a small amount and squinted at the girl.

"Whu 'u here?" She sucked down water and said more clearly, "Why'm I here?"

Donald burst into the room. "Well, looky here," the CNA cooed, reaching for Shalane's wrist. "The queen is awake." He took her pulse manually, and Patty leaned closer to answer Shalane's question.

"They said you passed out during your performance in Las Vegas. They couldn't revive you, so they brought you here to Sunrise Hospital. You've been in a coma." She swallowed the tears gathering in her throat.

"I flew out as soon as I heard the news. I'm sorry, Shalane. I should never have left. Can you forgive me?"

"Get me out of here, and I will forgive anything." Shalane gingerly raised on one elbow.

"Easy, dear," Donald warned good-naturedly. "I'll let the doctor know you're awake. She will want to give you a once-over to make sure everything is working properly. *Then* you can think about leaving."

Shalane rolled her eyes, and Patty grinned. It was good to have her back.

☼☼☼

Many hours later, the doctor gave Shalane the news she didn't want to hear. She must return home. The tour would be too stressful for her overtaxed system.

Outraged, she protested, but the doctor stood firm. She would not release Shalane until she promised to follow up immediately with her primary care physician to rule out underlying issues.

The cute CNA rolled Shalane to the limo. Shalane fanned her face as a hot, dry wind sucked the moisture from her pores.

How could anyone live in this hellacious heat?

She reached for Cecil's hand, and declared for the third time, "You *have* to get me back on tour. *Now.*"

He buckled her into the cool interior. "Honey, are you sure? The doctor says no."

"I'm positive. I've been away too long already, Cecil. We have work to do."

Both he and Patty stared at Shalane through the open door, then at one another.

"What? I'm all fragile now?"

They closed the door and climbed into the limo, careful not to poke the snarling bear.

Shalane ignored them both and dug a mirror from her handbag. In the room, she'd been too groggy to care. But seeing her reflection now, she groaned. Snapping her fingers, she smiled as the lines disappeared around her eyes and mouth and the mottled redness evened to a healthy glow.

She looked ten years younger and the picture of wellbeing. An urgency overpowered her then, so strong it nearly took Shalane's breath.

She must get back on the road.

"Look, we missed the Vegas show. I cannot afford to skip another. Where is our next one, anyway?"

"In Portland, Oregon." Cecil squeezed Shalane's hand and laid it in his lap. "We have notified the promoters, but nothing has been canceled yet. We were hoping you would pull out of it, Babykins. And it seems you have. But the doctor is worried about your prognosis, baby. I am, too."

A silent Patty smiled sweetly from the opposite seat.

Shalane's pulse quickened. She hadn't expected to see the girl again. "You came back."

Patty squirmed and red suffused her face. She sat up straight and smoothed her stylish linen trousers. "I did."

They locked eyes. "I'd hoped you might."

They reached the Bellagio and the limo stopped at the front door. Night had fallen, and the porte cochère was alive with revelers coming and going. As Shalane climbed from the back seat, her waiting team applauded and crowded around her, welcoming their leader.

"The end is near."

Startled awake, Shalane lifted her head. Archangel Michael sat next to her in a chair. He straddled the seat, leaning his arms on the back to study her. The light seeping from around the hotel curtains was enough to illuminate the angel's handsome face and rugged, shockingly studly physique.

He reached out a hand to stroke Shalane's face like a lover would, a first for her. Typically, the archangel imparted information in no-nonsense terms. In all the time she had worked with Michael as a spirit guide, never had he appeared to her, much less touched her physically.

The apparition peered into her eyes. Her twat tightened, and a lovely, sensual warmth spread from her belly to her groin, awakening her lust. Groaning, she pulled the angel to her, gasping at the size of his engorged penis.

When he raised on his elbows to penetrate her wet pussy, an exquisite orgasm rocketed through her. It ricocheted all around her body, from one cell to another, until she arched in an ecstasy Shalane had never felt.

As the orgasm faded, she heard a gravelly chuckle. Archangel Michael was gone. In his place was a lizard-faced monster with horns and a livid gash across its cheek. It leered down at Shalane for a long moment, then disappeared.

Erotic chill bumps roved her body. Everywhere they skittered, an orgasmic thrill raced over her, and for the next several moments, Shalane relished the decadent sensations.

Then, rolling over, she woke Patty with a long kiss and made slow, sweet love to the young woman before drifting off to sleep.

AZI INTERCEDES

"**G**eneral Nergal, Warlord Shibboleth is on the hologram for you."

Nergal didn't rouse, so Azi stepped to the general's side and prodded his shoulder.

"General Nergal? Can you hear me?"

When there was still no answer, Azi interrupted the connection between the general and the human target.

This time, Nergal's consciousness returned to his body and he gasped for air.

"Why did you pull me out?" he growled.

"It's Warlord Shibboleth. He's on the hologram demanding to speak with you." Noting the general's agitation, Azi averted his gaze to study the readout.

"It appears the target's vitals have stabilized. And while you were under, I managed to duplicate the method used by Vice Major Ishkur. I believe we can bypass your input by connecting the target directly into the mainframe. Which means you would be able to communicate with the target via your handheld without being connected."

Nergal rolled gingerly from the onyx slab with an almost sorrowful expression. Then he straightened, stretched, and shuffled to the console.

"This is the only viable target we have left. Are you sure about your bypass?"

"Not one hundred percent. But I am certain of my calculations. I can show you the algorithm once you have met with Commander Shibboleth."

Nergal hesitated, contemplating the image on the screen. The Reverend Shalane Carpenter slept peacefully.

Worried they were taking too long, Azi said, "We shouldn't keep Commander Shibboleth waiting, Sir."

Nergal glared at him. "No, we wouldn't want that, would we? Lead the way."

☼☼☼

"General Nergal, what is the status of your search? We are amassing troops and need officers to command them. How many have you assembled?"

Nergal groaned inwardly as Commander Shibboleth's hologram wavered, then grew strong again. Being forced to report to him was demeaning, and for that reason, Nergal had avoided contact. Glancing at Azi, he cleared his throat, then addressed the despicable warlord.

"We have four surviving officers at Xibalba IX, but my feelers have yielded no further results."

Shibboleth's angry roar gave Nergal a jolt of satisfaction.

"So, it's only you and four more? What is the holdup, General?"

"Beside the fact that you killed most of my officers when you stormed Xibalba IX? If any are left, they have scattered and remain underground." Nergal scowled at the arrogant warlord.

"Your Vice Major Ishkur did the same in Agartha," Shibboleth rejoined. "Yet, I still have officers. Yours were not all in Xibalba that day. Some were stationed at other bases. Mot tells me they are many."

Nergal struggled to keep his tone civil. "Aye. They were. But none remain. You wiped out the bulk of them in Xibalba IX, in essence declaring war on me and my Dracs. Is it any wonder they have gone into hiding?"

Shibboleth bared a full complement of razor-sharp teeth. "Scum! I will not be lectured to by the likes of you. Be grateful to my litter son and our present crisis for shielding you from my wrath. Otherwise, I would end your maggoty existence. Now, go. Find your officers. You will comply within two AboveEarth days or meet my vengeance." Then Shibboleth's hologram faded and was gone.

"Sir?" Azi's eyes narrowed. "*Have* you tried to contact your officers?"

Nergal bobbled his head. He had not. He had been connected to Shalane Carpenter since his arrival in Xibalba IX, taking no break to eat or drink or use the facilities.

He studied the impertinent scientist. According to Shibboleth, Azi's intelligence was superior to Ishkur's. He also seemed to have no fear of Nergal, and that was refreshing. But the last thing Nergal needed was a Shibboleth loyalist to report his every move.

"I spoke the truth. I do not know which, if any, of my Drac officers survived. Nor do I know where they would be hiding, much less how to contact them. I'm sure the typical channels are monitored. They wouldn't risk being found out."

"But they might be watching and listening."

Nergal shrugged, not comprehending.

"Your officers could be tapping into the networks. Let's put you in front of the camera, Sir. You can announce to your Dracs and support personnel that all have been pardoned, then command them to report to duty."

Nergal regarded the scientist. "That's a brilliant idea. I believe Vice Major Ishkur would have liked you."

"Sir, I am unworthy of your praise. I have wanted to meet Vice Major Ishkur for as long as I can remember. It saddens me that his brilliance will no longer benefit our nation." Azi wagged his head, chin drooping. "So much loss."

Then, striking his chest in salute, Azi wheeled and strode to the door.

"Let's get you to the Control Room to deliver that message."

Within a few hours of Nergal's announcement, several Dracs that had been in hiding made contact. Officers Kaijin, Mokele-Mbembe, and Nahuelito were among the first to arrive, and with their assistance, Nergal devised a battle plan.

Then he assigned regiments to each of the seventeen officers before contacting General Mot to coordinate the fight against AboveEarth.

LAUREL CANYON

"Shalane, wake up."

Groaning, she turned away and snuggled into the pillow. "Shalane, we have to go." The voice was more insistent and a hand shook her shoulder gently.

Opening one eye, Shalane peeked at its owner. Patrika Tolbert was fully dressed and made up to a T. The blonde's lower lip protruded, the way it did when she wasn't getting her way. Shalane rolled to her back and stretched between the luxurious sheets.

"What's your rush, sweetheart?" Shalane patted the covers and beckoned to the woman. "Come back to bed." She lowered the sheet to expose her naked breasts, and cupped them together to point her nipples at Patrika. "We've all missed you so much."

An adorable shade of pink colored the blonde's cheeks accentuating the blusher she had dusted over them.

"I've missed you all, too. But Cecil called. He said we have to hit the road to reach Portland in time to make your show."

Shalane stretched again, pulled the covers to her chin, then over her face.

"No. I don't want to. I need to sleep. The doctor said so. Can't we fly tomorrow and meet them there?"

"Cecil said no. The flights are booked." Patty tossed a terrycloth robe on the bed. "I let you sleep as long as I could. The bus will be here soon." She drew the blackout shades, and sunlight flooded the suite.

Growling, Shalane rolled out of bed.

Patty eyed her naked body, then touched Shalane's cheek. "Last night was nice. Raincheck on the sex?"

Shalane shuddered. If she'd had sex with Patty, had the dream also been real?

Not noticing Patty's sunken eyes or the haunted look that had been there for weeks, Shalane stepped into the shower, turned the water on hot, and lathered her hair.

☼☼☼

They were almost to the Barstow, California, cutoff when Shalane woke from a dead sleep. She sat up in the queen bed.

"Stop! We have to go back!"

Patty looked up from the ezine she'd been reading.

"To the Bellagio?"

Shalane looked about frantically. "No! We have to go home. To Laurel Canyon. Where's Cecil? We have to go home. Go get him. I have to tell Cecil."

"He's driving, Shalane. Can I tell him for you?"

Shalane seemed to have a hard time focusing, then zeroed in on Patty. "Driving? Isn't that what we pay the driver to do? Go get Cecil, Patrika."

Huffing because she knew it would be futile, Patty hurried to the front.

"Cecil, Shalane is asking for you."

"She's awake?" Brows raised, he eyed Patty in the rearview mirror. "It's only been a couple of hours. The medicine Dr. Acharya prescribed was supposed to knock her out for longer."

"I know, but she's awake and wants you."

Keeping his attention on the road, Cecil took the exit for Highway 58 towards Bakersfield.

"I'm kinda busy. Can you find out what she wants?"

"She says we have to go back."

"Back? To the hotel? Did she leave something?" He glanced up again. "Just call them, Patty. I'm sure whatever it is they'll be happy to mail it."

"No. Back to Laurel Canyon. She says she has to go home." Nervous now, Patty studied her nails. She had only seen pictures of Cecil and Shalane's mountaintop mansion and wasn't sure she would be welcome there.

Cecil shifted gears and laughed heartily. "Well, hallelujah! That's one problem solved. I thought she would be furious when she found out we canceled the road tour."

"Yeah, well, she probably will," Patty muttered, and Cecil nodded.

"Yeah, you're probably right. Tell her I'll be back there in a couple of minutes. Jorge can drive us the rest of the way."

When the tour bus parked in front of their house, Shalane made a beeline for the wet bar. She poured a hefty glass of Glenlivet and took it to the terrace to look out at the ocean.

This sight would never grow old. The sun was low over what was left of the Channel Islands and an onshore breeze ruffled Shalane's fine hair. She brushed it away. Now that they were back, she could get an appointment with her own stylist.

She rounded the terrace to the other side to look down at the San Fernando Valley. As usual, traffic clogged the freeways. Shalane lowered her bulk into her favorite chair and nursed her scotch, wondering where Patty had gotten off to. Cecil had said he'd show her to the guest room, but they both knew the girl would likely sleep with Shalane.

Remembering the last time she had been up here, Shalane thought of Ebby Panera, whose name had turned out to be Emily Hester. The woman's rejection, then disappearance, had angered Shalane.

But she had run into Ebby in Venice Beach. Or rather, Ebby had run into her, knocking Shalane over and giving her a mild concussion. That night, Shalane had been so livid she'd sent a storm from up here to punish the woman.

She sighed and sipped her Glenlivet. Now, she no longer cared. When had her obsession with Ebby disappeared?

She thought of Ebby's brother, Mitchell Wainwright. Her preoccupation with him was gone, too.

In fact, Shalane felt nothing, just a laissez-faire attitude toward everything—including her First Evangelical Tour of America.

At least Cecil was on the ball. He had her staff making arrangements for Shalane's remaining contracts. Starting with the Portland show, they would broadcast Live via Zoom. It wasn't the same as being there in person, but it was the next best thing. Her loyal followers would understand. The rest? As Cecil said, fuck 'em.

"Shalane?" Patty called from behind her.

She twisted in her chair to motion the girl over, and Patty plopped in another chaise lounge.

"It's pretty up here."

"Yes, it is. It might be my favorite place in the world. Did you see the ocean?"

Patty popped up to look, and Shalane joined her as she ooo'd and ahh'd.

"I can see why. But how do you afford all this?"

"Dontcha remember? I told you I was as rich as the Pope."

Patty's tinkling laugh rang out. "That you did." She turned to Shalane, all earnest now. "Are you sure you don't mind finishing your tour from here?"

Shalane nodded to the Pacific churning in the distance. "With a view like that? Nah. It beats watching real estate pass by outside a bus window, hands down."

"But you were so gung-ho before."

"Was I?" Shalane had wondered about the same thing, but she found she was no longer attached to the whys and wherefores—of anything.

"Yes. You were. What happened when you were in that coma, Shalane?"

She stayed silent, wondering whether to tell Patty or not.

"I was tied down inside a glass cage with alien creatures poking and prodding me. There was so much pain I didn't know where it ended and I began."

Patty stilled. "Did they have lizard faces and scales?"

Shalane's heart beat faster.

"And big red eyes?"

She nodded, afraid to speak in case her voice shook.

"Those are the Reptilians I told you about. They're loose, Shalane. I saw it on the news. And at the hospital, the emergency room was filled with people they had maimed and killed."

A horrifying thought seized Shalane. Had one of them been in her room last night instead of Archangel Michael?

ILHA DO CORVO

After arriving in the Azores, Randy and Khenko had been fed and put up in base quarters, where Khenko slept like a baby. Then midmorning the next day, they boarded a helicopter for Corvo.

Freya Satterfield, a scientist from New Mexico who was an expert in crystals and microchip technology, joined them for the ride. Khenko soon found out that Freya was not a woman—or not a human one. Instead, she was a Fomorian, the same species as the girl on the flight from New Jersey.

That gave Khenko pause. How many Fomorians had he encountered over the decades without knowing?

As the North Atlantic Ocean spread before them, a smile tickled Khenko's lips. The blues contrasting and complimenting the greens of the archipelago had his heart soaring.

Flores Island was lushly appointed and dotted with flowers in varying stages of bloom. As they passed over, their destination loomed before them. Like the other islands of the archipelago, Corvo was the last vestige of a once-active volcano. Its flattened caldera jutted half a mile into the sky.

Excitement coursed through Khenko. For as long as he could remember, he had believed the lost continent of Atlantis lay somewhere in the Bahamas. But recent research, done after his mother's revelation, suggested that the Azores was another possibility—one he fully intended to investigate.

The pilot had said the island was usually swathed in clouds, but on this day, the blue was uninterrupted. No matter which direction Khenko twisted his head, the sun shone brightly against the azure canopy. It reflected off the water and highlighted the time-worn features of Corvo Island, the smallest of the Azores.

They landed at Vila do Corvo, the one village on the tiny island. As they climbed from the helicopter toting their sparse luggage, Khenko ducked beneath the rotors and bumped into Randy when the Marine stopped to greet a swarthy man in a straw hat and island garb.

Antonio Delgado introduced himself and told them to use the next few hours to enjoy the island. He would be their driver, but someone else was flying from the mainland to join them.

"Would you mind securing our bags?" Randy asked. "I'd rather not have to lug them around."

"Of course." Antonio waved to a nearby van, then gave them each a small map of Corvo. As he tossed their bags in the back, Khenko, Freya, and Randy huddled together to inspect the map.

"There's a swimming hole," Freya pointed to a spot near town. "And a museum and a gift shop. Oh, and the old windmills." She pointed them out on the map, then turned to wave toward the airstrip. "Those are over there."

"Is there a coffee shop?" Khenko wondered. "I could use another cup. And maybe something to eat? My breakfast has already worn off."

From the van, Antonio called, "The Caldeirao has excellent food and coffee. It's over there."

At the end of the airstrip, fifty yards away, a long white building with a red clay roof nestled beside the windmills. The Caldeirao faced south toward the sea and Flores Island.

"That sounds good," Freya said. "I'll join you for a soda, but I would love to explore the town a bit." Sweeping her dark hair into a ponytail, Freya fastened it against the strong onshore wind. If she was a Fomorian, Khenko wondered, why weren't her ears pointed like Ethnui's?

Deciding he would save the question for later, Khenko eyed Randy. He'd been reticent since leaving Lajes Field.

"Coffee and early lunch or exploring with Freya?"

Randy's gaze roved the small town and followed the hills to the top of Monte Gordo. "What I really want to do is climb up there." He glanced at Antonio still perched in the van. "Do you think we have time?"

"No." Freya studied the map. "It's four steep miles up and the same back down." Randy's face fell, and Freya added, "Maybe we could do it another day? I'd love to climb to the summit, too."

"Will we be here that long?" Khenko groaned. The lack of information was typical for the military, but annoying, nonetheless. "Do you know what they want us to do?" He directed the question to the perky Fomorian.

"Nope. No one told me either. But this is way better than being in the office." She peered up at Randy, slightly smitten. "Do you know anything?" Rowdy shrugged his wide shoulders, grunted, and continued staring at the summit of Monte Gordo.

"What's wrong, Rowdy? You're quiet this morning."

But Randy merely shook his head. Khenko knew from years of experience not to push. His friend would spill his guts when he was good and damn ready and not a moment before.

☼☼☼

Colonel Kyle Reinosa dragged himself from the disheveled bed. Wobbling precariously, he grabbed a fistful of covers and collapsed against it, waiting for the dizzy to pass.

He could tell without a corpsman pointing a thermometer at his forehead that the fever still raged. He'd been as sick as a dog for the last three days since they had chugged into port in Rota, Spain, en route to the Azores. No food, other than liquids, had passed Kyle's lips since the day before that.

Now, he was kitten weak, and on top of everything else, it appeared the corpsman and the other sailor who'd been in sick bay with him had cleared out, leaving Kyle alone to fend for himself.

The alarm klaxon sounded, flooding Kyle with dread. Twelve years in the Navy and such alarms had been rare. He stood tentatively, expecting an announcement to explain the nature of the emergency.

It didn't come. Kyle plopped back down, heart pounding. Unsure of what to do next, he rang the call bell, fighting a deep foreboding. Moments later, boots scraped outside the door but didn't enter. What was going on out there?

Rising unsteadily, he managed to wrench the door open, but the long corridor was empty. Now, the klaxon ah-ooh-gahed nonstop. There was still no announcement, just the spine-tingling urgency of the alarm cycling through its phases.

Fear pierced Kyle's feverish fog. He fumbled with the locker containing his belongings and fished out his uniform and sidearm. Then carefully shimmying into his clothes, he dragged his trembling body to the open door. There was a grunt, then a wail, and a flash of green separated from a fallen sailor. Horror wiped out all else.

Kyle stared, trying to understand what his eyes were seeing. A lurid humanoid with the face of a snake, scales and all, stepped over

221

the sailor and stalked toward him. Kyle clutched his Sig Sauer as its eyes flashed red.

Shivering violently, Kyle pulled the trigger, and the creature slammed backward into others that poured from the upper deck. He sprayed the invaders with everything he had, praying it was enough as purplish-black blood stained the bulkhead and coated Kyle.

When his round was spent, the roars had subsided. Kyle swayed, retching. The hallway reeked to high heaven, and bodies lay mutilated atop one another.

Collapsing in the doorway, Kyle spewed vomit, and everything went black.

AN AUSPICIOUS NIGHT

L ugh MacBrayer woke abruptly. Something was happening. And he was missing out. He reached for Emily, but she was no longer there. How long had he slept?

He rolled to his knees and stared in amazement. In the middle of the meadow was Emily Hester, swaying to the melody of a Beltane song. A ceremonial fire danced at her feet, and her voice rose and fell to the simple tune.

Lugh's heart raced. Beltane heralded renewal, and Brigid knows, they needed that. Beltane marked the beginning of summer and the opening of mating season—not only for the animals but for the druids themselves. Many a druid couple had met and married during a Beltane ceremony. The wind gusted, whipping the bonfire higher.

The Beltane fire was a large part of the ritual. Long ago, it was used to renew the fires within each druid household and to bless their livestock before they returned to pasture. And while Beltane celebrations were more modest in the twenty-first century, the intent remained the same—to celebrate Earth's awakening and invoke blessings for the coming season.

Clouds scudded swiftly overhead, parting to bathe the clearing in mystical light. The full moon wove in and out, and Emily's voice rose. The verse was unfamiliar, but the tune was ancient. Lugh hummed along.

Mother, Goddess, queen of night and earth
Father, God, king of day and forest,
We celebrate your union.
Nature rejoices
In a blaze of color
And life thrives.
Please accept our gift
In honor of your union
Dear Mother Goddess
Dear Father God.

Emily tossed a handful of something that must have been flower petals into the air. They fluttered to the ground, and the earth pulsed beneath Lugh's knees.

That wasn't a coincidence.

Leaping to his feet beside the Waters of Luftshorne, he gasped and nearly choked on his saliva. The low clouds were passing on, revealing a phenomenon so rare no living druid had claimed to have seen it.

It was the legendary tri-moon.

Lugh stared at the formation in shock and disbelief.

In the center of a cosmic bullseye was Luna at her fullest, riding high overhead. A circlet of clouds surrounded her, then a band of starry sky bounded by another ring of clouds. Then, the pattern repeated—a starry sky and a circle of clouds. Beyond the third ring, a more nebulous cloud circle stretched as far as Lugh could see.

Perfectly framed by the formation was Awen's glade. And in the middle of that swayed Emily. Or was it Awen?

Lugh guessed the latter. He doubted the Order's new Grand Druid knew the melody, much less the words. This was her first Beltane. There had been no maypoles or flower crowns for young Emily.

She began another song, even sweeter than the first. As the melody rose skyward to join the divine formation, emotion welled so strongly inside Lugh that he fell to the ground. He thanked the One God and the other gods and goddesses for the miraculous tri-moon. Then, he thanked them for bringing Emily back from the almost-dead and delivering her to him—or him to her, whichever it had been.

Her voice, musical and clear, wafted through the meadow.

Dear God, Goddess,
The winds blow sweet and pure
Beneath your heavenly altar
Where mating creates new life.
Dear God, dear Goddess,
Oh, Ancient Ones,
We celebrate you.
And with you
Life springs anew.

Her arms reached for the rare tri-moon that pulsated in the center of its heavenly rings. Then, Emily's Beltane song ended.

Lugh wiped away the tears of gratitude with his sleeve and climbed to his feet. He approached the Order's newest Awen, the woman he had loved since first sight and meant to marry. He just had to keep them both alive until then.

The wind gusted, whipping the fire into a frenzy, and Emily leapt backward into Lugh's open arms.

Exactly where she wanted to be, Emily sighed and hugged Lugh's arms to her midsection. The rising wind swirled, fluttering the oak leaves and inciting the skirt of Awen's gown to flap around her ankles. The birches around the clearing joined in, creating a joyful cacophony that waxed and waned with the intensity of the wind.

The unusual cloud formation that had taken Emily's breath grew more prominent, and thunder rumbled off in the distance. A blackbird trilled. Druid Dhubh performing his Beltane aria for an audience of two? The heat between them intensified, and Emily turned to bury her face in Lugh's chest.

He tilted her head back with a finger under her chin, and a sudden shyness seized Emily. Then he cradled her face between his hands, and she held her breath. Slowly, tenderly, Lugh kissed her in the way of the Druid—on the forehead, nose, chin, eyes, and both cheeks. Finally, he claimed Emily's lips, soft at first, then deepening the kiss until she nearly swooned.

Lightning crackled nearby, and the hairs on Emily's body stood on end as ozone washed the air, and Lugh kissed her silly. Thunder reverberated, low and long, and the wind whipped the flames at their feet. Then everything faded into the background when he drew her with him to the grass.

Leaning on one elbow, Lugh caressed Emily's face and neck with butterfly kisses until she sighed. Then she moaned when his lips moved to the swell of her breasts and back to her mouth for a long, all-consuming kiss.

Emily dragged her soft dress up to her chin, and Lugh lifted it gently over her head. Scarlet curls cascaded to her naked waist, and

Lugh drew a sharp breath. Only a month ago, it had been shoulder length.

The last of the tri-moon formation had dissipated, blotted out by the approaching storm. In the sporadic moonlight peeking between clouds, Lugh's eyes feasted on Emily's curves.

He traced quivering fingers down her neck to one breast and then to the other. Emily moaned. Lugh lifted them gently, gathered them together, and ran his tongue over their velvet underbellies. Her breath hitched. Finally, his mouth found her firm nipples, and Emily groaned and dragged his head to hers.

"Take me," she breathed.

A lightning bolt hissed past, so close its reflection flickered in Emily's eyes. They jumped, clinging to one another, as thunder cracked, deafeningly loud, followed by a long, angry rumble.

The storm was close. Should he carry her inside?

In answer, the Order's new Grand Druid claimed Lugh's mouth with a dizzying kiss. Then she rolled him over to straddle his waist, and he forgot all about the thrashing trees, the restless thunder, and even the lightning as Emily pried his shirt open and covered his face, neck, and chest in slow provocative kisses.

Lugh writhed now, cock straining against the confines of his pants. She ground against it as a crack of thunder exploded above them, and it was Lugh's turn to groan. He had waited for this moment for so long. The aftershock rolled around the clearing, and Lugh could feel it in his bones.

Emily struggled with his zipper, then his penis was free. Her victorious gaze held his as she stroked it, grinning when it jumped in her hands. Then, slowly, seductively, she wrapped one firm fist around the base and the other above it.

With a smirk that was both sexy and self-assured, she peppered soft kisses all over his cock. That drove him wild. Then, her tongue explored its tip, and he shuddered, pelvis arching.

A splat of rain struck Lugh square on the forehead. He sighed and tangled his fingers in Emily's curls. When she peeled back his jeans to tease him with her tongue, he reveled in each exquisite sensation until another fat drop struck his cheek.

Lugh pulled Emily's face up to his and ravaged her lips, then flipped her over as the clouds let loose, pelting the Earth.

Raindrops hammered Lugh's back as he slid inside her, but his body shielded Emily from the worst of the deluge. Lightning danced around them, just above the ground. It electrified the clearing and unleashed a continuous rumble of thunder and the sweet scent of ozone.

Emily trembled and writhed beneath Lugh. Her hungry lips took them deeper into the coupling trance, two lovers discovering the joys of one another, two souls blending and merging as one.

As their ecstasy mounted, Lugh smiled into Emily's dewy eyes and thrust slowly and sensuously until she moaned beneath him.

"Yes, Lugh, yes, yes… oooh… yes! Yes, do that. Yes, yes, I'm there, oh, God… YEEESSSSS!"

Her throbbing pussy clamped down on his cock, and a powerful orgasm rocketed his world. Suddenly, he was William looking down at his Awen and loving her with every ounce of his being.

Theirs was no ordinary love. It was a love that spanned lifetimes—a love for all ages.

Soaked but sated to the core, Emily lay panting in Lugh's arms. Then, shoving Awen's thoughts and feelings from her, she held him tight, and squealed when a bolt of lightning sizzled past to strike the oak. It split with one long horrendous crack as the side of the trunk peeled away in slow motion. Thunder roared as it hit the ground, and the earth shivered.

Lugh rolled to one side and yanked up his khakis. Emily scrambled to her feet, jerking Awen's gown over her head. It settled around her ankles as a masculine voice boomed above their heads.

"Hail, Awen. Long has it been since last we met."

Beside the fractured oak, scarlet and yellow flames outlined a hologram of the thunder god, Taranis.

Emily gasped and reached for Lugh's hand.

"Your return is greatly anticipated," Taranis boomed, "not only here, but in the Otherworld and the Underworld. Earth is in danger, and you have been called to action. The time approaches when gods, dragons, druids, and men must join forces to protect our fair planet. The battle for Earth has commenced.

"Rise, Awen!" the flaming god commanded, sweeping his powerful arms into the air.

Terror struck at Emily's heart. She wasn't ready. Her knees literally knocked together.

Thunder boomed and rolled around the clearing, and sparks shot from the hologram. Taranis grew to the height of the oak, blazing hotter and brighter.

Emily cowered, and Lugh squeezed her hand as the Elder host appeared.

They crowded near, and Hope slipped between Lugh and Emily to snug up against Emily's leg. Cu leaned against her outer thigh. Wedged between them, her trembling quieted.

Then the hologram thundered, "The Reptilians receive aid from this world. The druids will fail unless you do the same." He paused a long moment before continuing. "Your formal training is complete. Now, only a few tasks remain. Master those, and your aid will be forthcoming."

Taranis then spoke to the Elder Host. "Stay close to Awen. Be ever ready to aid when needed."

Then, fixing his fiery eyes on Emily, Taranis uttered, "But know this: Humankind's hope depends on you, Awen." His gaze shifted to Lugh, then back to Emily.

"Go. Bathe in the Healing Waters of Luftshorne. Linger there. Discover your next steps. But be not afraid. If you remain pure of heart, help will be yours. And with luck, you shall prevail. Now, go!" The fire waned around him.

"And be forewarned. There is more than humanity at stake. You must obey whatever instructions you receive from the Waters, or all will be lost. The gods, angels, and all of the worlds depend upon you." And with that, Taranis, the thunder god, faded and disappeared, as did the storm's remnants.

The Elder Host came to life—bawling, baaing, mooing, screeching, booming, growling—each adding to the raucous roar. Emily stared at them, open-mouthed, then at Hope and Cu, who gazed up at her adoringly.

Lugh tugged at her hand, gently drawing Emily toward the pond. Dazed, she plunged into the inky depths after him. As the water enveloped her, her insides calmed, and a deep sense of love and belonging settled upon her.

When the water all but reached her chin, Lugh gathered her in a passionate embrace, kissing Emily until her body was a mass of quivering, rapidly-firing neurons. Then, as the full Beltane moon continued its overhead arc, they made slow, tender love, sealing their union and fate.

☼☼☼

Lugh's orgasm faded, but his delight in Emily did not. They bobbed in the water, gazing into one another's eyes, needing no words. Her legs were wrapped around his waist, and her arms circled Lugh's neck. Without plan or forewarning, he leaned his forehead against hers to whisper his deepest secret.

"I'm in love with you, Emily Hester."

"I know."

Lugh's heart contracted. That was not the answer he had hoped to hear. Then, in the recesses of his mind, he heard her plain as day.

"I love you, too, Lughnasadh MacBrayer."

The silent words landed, providing an entryway into her dazzling green eyes. Lugh peered deeply, seeing a series of images of Emily in action—vibrant, alive, effervescent, and still annoyingly salty and stubborn.

☼☼☼

Thunder rumbled off in the distance. The storm had passed, and the pond was alive with the light of a million stars. A wave of shivers skittered over Emily. According to Taranis, it was time to learn what would happen next. She gazed into Lugh's eyes, seeing the reflection of the ripples from the pond.

Then that disappeared, and a series of visions took its place, each lasting an instant before the next crowded in—the peaks of Snowdonia, a desolate expanse of tundra lined with rows of icy menhirs, a circle of stones that may or may not have been Stonehenge, then the face of a friend—the tall medicine man who had rescued Emily.

Deep in the forest, Faol howled, dragging Emily from her reverie. A shooting star blazed a trail across the heavens, and the Elder Host joined Faol's haunting serenade. Chills roved up and down Emily's spine.

Beyond words, she sighed, then sputtered when she breathed in water. Lugh lifted her higher until her coughing fit passed. Then Emily tightened her legs around the priest's waist and, acting on impulse, drew him with her underneath the dark surface.

They continued staring into one another's eyes as they descended the short way to the bottom. Down here, the darkness obscured all but Lugh's silhouette. And though Emily had no idea why, she held them both captive in the soft silt.

Soon, the whites of Lugh's eyes grew wider, but he did not resist. Instead, he sighed, sending bubbles rushing to the surface. Then his eyes rolled backward, and his head jerked. Emily kicked off the bottom as her oxygen ran out and propelled them to the surface.

They gasped for air, then Lugh looked about wild-eyed before grabbing Emily and planting a wet kiss on her lips.

"Omigod!" he crowed, bouncing up and down in the water like a kid. "You did it. You did it! Omigod, Emily, you did it! Thank Brigid, yeeehaaaa!"

She grinned, surprised by his rebel yell.

"Did what? Nearly drown us?"

He grabbed her face with both hands and gave her another kiss before sloshing from the pond.

She laughed and paddled behind him. "What's gotten into you?"

Cu and Hope rushed to the water's edge, where Lugh leapt gleefully from one foot to the other. Then the priest strutted around the clearing, shuffled backward, turned a one-handed cartwheel followed by a somersault, then landed on the grass in front of her.

"It's gone, Emily. The pain. It's gone! For the first time since the earthquake, I have zero pain. None. Zero. Zip. Zilch. NADA! It's a miracle!"

She grinned and whooped, "Hallelujah! But it wasn't me. It was the Healing Waters of Luftshorne." She looked to the Elders for confirmation. "Right?"

Tarbh bugled, "A miracle is a miracle. You were the instrument, Awen."

Emily's heart swelled. Taking Lugh's face between her hands, she kissed him gently in the way of the druid. Then, ogling the bags beneath his eyes, she kissed them again, adding, "Whatever the reason. I am overjoyed. But you need sleep." She yawned loudly, overcome by exhaustion. "And so do I."

☼☼☼

Bé Chuille strode along the rows of dragons until she reached those in front. Then, extending her cane, she tapped the ice covering Tienu's face.

"Wake up, dragon."

This particular one had caused Bé a load of grief over the years. He had even ended her life once. But Bé Chuille was immortal. Or had been until she migrated to AboveEarth. Up here, the harsh conditions stripped eternity from gods and men alike. Those who remained on Earth's treacherous surface lived short, desperate lives.

All except the ones who learned the secret of maintaining their immortality as Bé had.

Yes, AboveEarth was beautiful, breathtakingly so. But long ago, something or someone had tampered with her energetics, and there were none now left who remembered what was altered or how to reverse it. Not even Earth herself, though the coding was embedded in the planet's intelligence.

Tienu blinked, then opened his great, scarlet eyes. When they focused on Bé Chuille, Tienu recoiled. Or he would have had he been able to move.

"Where is Awen?" Bé Chuille demanded.

Blink, blink. A scornful scowl. But no answer.

Bé growled, touched her cane to Tienu's frozen midsection, and chuckled when the dragon roared in pain. She held it there until his roar petered to a squeal, then waved it in front of the dragon king.

"Tell me how to find Awen, or there's more where that came from."

A flame flickered from Tienu's snout, falling short of Bé Chuille.

"Is that all you've got, old lizard? I expected more from the King of Dragons."

This time, she placed the tip of her wand against the dragon's chest, cackling in glee when the light went out in Tienu's eyes.

Only Bé was no closer to finding Awen.

Frustrated, she scanned the vast Stygian Plains, then felt for Awen's energy signature. Five minutes later, she was no wiser. Her only alternative was to return to Awen's cabin and wait.

Waving her wand, Bé cackled as the ice reformed over the dragon king.

ANOTHER HURDLE

Emily stared at Awen's ceiling in the early morning light. She traced the outline of a long-necked fish, and another figure that resembled a tortoise ambling through the coarse thatch. Then, snuggling closer to the still sleeping Lugh, she studied his features.

Her heart contracted. The druid warrior's face was still drawn. She hadn't realized how severe his headaches had been until last night. It was one of many things Lugh had shared in their talks by Awen's pond.

She traced a forefinger over where a scar had been on his left brow, hesitating when Lugh stirred. But, he snorted and turned into her, burying his face against the pillow they shared.

The bed was too small for one, much less two. But they had piled into it after witnessing the rare and auspicious Beltane tri-moon. Emily had sensed the moon was special, and after Lugh's explanation, she knew they had been divinely blessed.

Cu whined, and Emily peeked over Lugh's shoulder. Seeing her face, he woofed quietly from his post by the door.

"Shhh," she whispered, not wanting to disturb Lugh. Poor thing needed to sleep.

Slowly and delicately, she extricated her limbs. Then, because she was sandwiched between him and the wall, she scooted to the bottom of the bed and padded to the door. Cu wiggled and greeted her with a wet kiss. Emily hugged him and buried her face in his wiry hair, then lifted the bar.

The wolfhound bolted outside with a joyful yip. Hope slipped out behind him, and a cold wind snuck in through the crack. A chill had descended upon the clearing. Emily shivered and closed the door.

She grabbed the heavy cloak from the peg, settled it over her shoulders, then peered through the window and gasped. Beneath the wounded oak tree, Cu was bumping muzzles with an enormous bear. Hope wound between the bear's legs, meowing.

Slipping her feet into Awen's boots, Emily hurried outside.

"Artis?" she said tentatively.

The beast wheeled and loped to the porch. "Hail, Awen, Queen of the Druids," he intoned shrilly.

"Hail, Awen, Queen of the Druids," Cu and Hope echoed, and Emily's face warmed. Would she ever get used to that greeting?

The wooden door creaked, and a tousled Lugh stepped onto the porch. Emily's heart thumped when his arms coiled around her midsection and drew her close. She snuggled against him, and blushed when she realized how happy he was to see her.

"We meet again, Priest," Artis bugled, lowering his head in respect.

"Hello, Artis! Have we made it back to the twenty-first century?"

Lugh's optimism buoyed Emily's spirits. But her hope was quickly dashed.

"Based on the appearance of Awen's glade, I am afraid not."

In the same high-pitched tone, Artis related all that had happened with the winter hag after Cu transported Hope and Lugh. When he got to the part about Bé Chuille delivering the killing blow, Emily shrank into the circle of Lugh's arms.

"And then, I woke up here." Artis looked around Awen's lush glade. "But everything looks much different."

"It does, doesn't it?" Lugh agreed.

Emily ducked under his arm to face him. "Besides the water, how is it different?"

"It's much cooler, for one," Lugh said. "The temperature in Caen was 95F yesterday. It can't be more than 50 or 60 here. The grass is green, whereas yesterday, the clearing was dry and overgrown with weeds and briars. And Luftshorne was just a pile of stones."

Emily sagged beneath the weight of disappointment.

"So we're still not where we are supposed to be." She sighed, then brightened. "At least y'all are with me now." As she spoke, the Elder Host materialized from the woods, and her smile widened to a grin.

They crowded around Artis, who roared in greeting. Then the bear Elder addressed Awen.

"Master, Cu transported the priest and Hope to you. He can shuttle you to your proper time. But be forewarned. You are safe from the winter hag in the 11th Century. Once you return to your own time, Bé Chuille will be waiting.

"I know from experience that witch will do anything in her power to kill you. And her powers are substantial. But the fate of the world is riding on you, Awen. When dealing with the witch, beware."

The Elder Host voiced agreement.

But, Emily needed the nightmare to end. And Cu was the answer. She wheeled to the Irish wolfhound.

"Do it, Cu! Take us back to the present."

A ray of morning sun broke through the trees to sparkle off the Waters of Luftshorne. Sadness tugged at Emily's heart to war with the thrill of going home.

An idea bloomed. "Can you take the Waters and lushness with us?"

The lanky hound wagged his head. "No, mi' lady, I cannot. I am not even certain such magic exists."

A commotion rose in the woods. Gyarr, the hare Elder who had disappeared the day before, bounded from the forest.

"Run!" he screamed. "They are coming, hurry! Hide!"

As a body, the Elder Host turned toward him. But before they could react, a loud twang followed by several more whistled through the forest. The animals nearest the treeline fell to the flying arrows, and the clearing filled with cries of anguish as chaos ensued.

Lugh's hand found Emily's.

"Hide," she screamed. "Matilda's soldiers have found us!"

She pulled Lugh toward the woods behind the hut. But before they could take more than a few steps, a loud twang sounded, and a projectile crashed through the trees.

"Get down!" Lugh yelled, pulling her to the ground beneath the injured oak as a boulder arced overhead and crashed into Awen's pond.

Then men shouting orders in French poured into the glade and formed a barrier, bows raised.

The animal Elders had scattered and disappeared. Only Cu, Hope, and Artis remained. But it was Emily they were after. She had completely forgotten about Matilda's soldiers, but they had not forgotten about her.

A stout soldier in a plumed hat led the charge. Behind him, two others dragged William's valet to the front of the formation. At a nod from the leader, they shoved him forward and Henry slumped to the ground.

Emily gasped and threw a spell of protection around the kind elderly man who had helped her escape Chateau Falaise. Lugh tugged fiercely at her arm, but Emily shook him loose and stepped forward.

"Hold your fire," she commanded in her sternest voice. "We have not harmed you." It came out in French, a language Emily did not speak. But when the soldiers clamored for Awen's death, she understood their cries.

"Capture the witch. String her up," they yelled in unison.

The leader held up a hand and they fell silent.

"Come quietly, and the others shall be spared." He pointed at Lugh. "Except for him. He will be taken to Duchess Matilda and hang beside you at dusk."

Emily shuddered and let Lugh pull her back to him. But her heel caught, and as she stumbled into his arms, a bow twanged. Artis leapt in front of them, then slumped backward, taking the arrow meant for Awen.

"Go, Cu!" the bear Elder bellowed. "Get them out of here! We'll find you in the twenty-first."

There was a flash of cyan blue, and for a moment, everything went dark. Emily thought an arrow had found her, and she was dead. Then she was in Lugh's arms in the center of Awen's glade with Cu and Hope glued against them.

"Yeehaaa, we're back!" Lugh rejoiced.

Emily peered around him. There was no one there. No soldiers, no Henry, no animal Elders. She twirled toward the pond and sucked in a breath.

Weeds, bushes, and blackberry brambles had overtaken what had been a lush meadow. And where the Waters of Luftshorne had freely flowed, a dry lakebed abutted a stone wall and a jumble of rocks.

"Omigod, omigod, omigod," she cried as tears sprang to her eyes. "Awen's glade. It's, it's… Oh. My. God!" She wheeled toward Cu and Hope. "Who did this?"

"You did," a menacing voice growled.

Emily snapped to attention. Chill bumps raced across her body.

"You and your infernal humans," the voice added.

Then, Emily spied the woman. She was statuesque, with flowing raven hair and snapping eyes. And she advanced toward them.

"You should know better, Awen. Your 'noble' humans have raped, pillaged, and plundered the Earth. Once again, you have brought this planet to her knees. Your filthy humans will never learn."

Emily trembled, both angered and frightened by the imposing figure she knew was Bé Chuille.

"Earth may be in danger, but we are sworn to save her. What will you do to help?"

Hope stepped between them, hackles raised. "Stay behind me," she commanded, erecting an energetic shield.

The woman laughed and tossed her hair. "Earth does not need your help, *Druid*." She took a threatening step closer, and Hope's yowl raised the hairs on Emily's arms.

"Begone, witch," the cat commanded. "You are not welcome here. Earth shall prevail. The Druid Nation will make sure of that, starting with vermin like you."

Electricity shot from Hope's raised paw, striking the woman in the chest. She cartwheeled backward, and Hope hissed, "Get to the car! We will hold the witch off!"

Shocked to see the Elder do magic, Emily hissed, "Take care of Lugh and the others should we get separated."

"I'll be okay," Lugh yelled, dragging Emily toward the trail as the witch scrambled upright. "Just keep Awen alive."

They made it to the trees as a curse struck a nearby birch. Behind them, the Elders battled the witch, herding her away from the path as Emily plunged into the woods beside Lugh.

Branches slapped her face, and briars tore at Awen's cloak. Emily shucked it without stopping and used it to wipe the sweat from her brow. The heat was oppressive.

Lugh glanced over his shoulder, and his alarmed expression had Emily looking, too.

The witch gave chase and was gaining ground. Emily pointed at a limb above the trail, and it crashed down onto Bé Chuille. She screeched, and lightning sizzled toward them. Emily shoved Lugh aside, and it sizzled past, but another crackled behind it, catching her in the shoulder.

Icy fire bloomed raw where the curse connected. The sensation spread across her shoulders and arms, then up Emily's neck and down her back to her legs, arresting her flight.

"Lugh, help!" But the ice was quickly spreading through her body, and all she could think of was Lugh and Brian.

Lugh stood over her, frantically throwing curses and blocking the witch's.

As the light faded, Emily called out to the Elders, "Take care of my men!"

IRKED IN IRKALLA

Inanna paced the richly appointed quarters, alternating between anger, delight, and disgust. The suite was heavenly compared to the dungeons of Araf. Hell, it was more divine than *any of* her past living arrangements. But its opulence made her uncomfortable.

From the bank of windows, Inanna beheld the city she had called home for the first years of her life. That was before Shibboleth relocated them to the Southern Hemisphere and left on a mission to AboveEarth. It was after that that Inanna first met Nergal.

She'd been traveling UnderEarth on an extended vacation. A band of mercenaries had accosted her in a slimy dive in lower Morocco. Nergal had muscled in. He'd made short shrift of the mercenaries, then bedded Inanna, beginning their long and rocky relationship.

Over the next many years, Nergal had advanced through the ranks while Inanna continued her travels. They met up frequently for lusty interludes. Then Shibboleth returned from AboveEarth, a changed Reptilian.

Before, he was a doting father. But when Inanna introduced Nergal as the Draco she planned to mate, Shibboleth went ballistic and ordered Inanna to stop seeing him.

She refused. When his subsequent arguments could not change her mind, Shibboleth sent Mot and Maw to discourage Nergal and chastise Inanna. Caught off guard, they had both nearly died.

After that, Inanna went into hiding. Exiled by Shibboleth, wounded and terrified, Inanna was consumed by fear and rage. For five centuries, she retreated deeper and deeper into the shadowy belly of UnderEarth, hiding from Shibboleth and his Death Bringers and using her rage to fuel her flight. She had not seen Nergal again until recently when Mot and Maw found her and forced Inanna to set him up.

A knock sounded, startling Inanna. She crossed to the door and stared at the clothed creature standing in the opening. With a bosom and shape similar to Inanna's, the being was much shorter, barely reaching Inanna's chest. Choppy white hair framed a smooth, pale face and eyes as violet as the flower of the same name.

Inanna stared. She had seen eyes that color only once—on the doctora.

"You are human." There were many in UnderEarth but never in Shibboleth's palace when Inanna lived here. Of course, that had been millennia ago.

"I am." The violet eyes regarded Inanna intently. "We have not met. I am ShaRhea, your father's hand servant." The human's voice was soft and soothing. "With so many preparing for war, I have been pressed into service in other areas." ShaRhea shifted from one foot to the other as if nervous.

"Shibboleth has requested your presence in the command center." ShaRhea crossed her arms over her ample chest. "Please follow me."

☼☼☼

Irkalla's command center was massive, with data and communications hubs occupying the bulk of its area. Drac scientists operated various consoles, keyboards, displays, and wall screens. Scenes from UnderEarth played out silently.

Shibboleth and Mot stood before a large monitor in the center's heart. On it, General Nergal addressed a contingent of Dracs and support staff. Inanna's humanoid guide instructed her to join them, then beat a hasty retreat.

Acknowledging Inanna, Shibboleth turned back to the screen. "General Nergal, report."

Formidable, even swathed in bandages, Nergal faced the camera and struck his chest in respect. Inanna and her kin returned the gesture, and the general clasped scarred arms behind his back.

"Sir, per your command, the planning for our invasion is complete. As you see, I have divided the territory into quarters. Within each, there is a multitude of access points that lead to the surface. Probe drones are mapping the most strategic routes and calculating feasibility while our scouts reconnoiter and report back."

Troop assessments and an impressive array of maps replaced Nergal's image. Views of the various access points flowed over to adjacent wall screens as Nergal continued his report.

239

"Utilizing Mot's roster of available commanders and worldwide troops, officers have been assigned to each quadrant pending your approval. Once the plans are authorized, our contingents can begin deploying to AboveEarth."

His face reappeared. "Sir, I am seeing reports of rogue Dracs attacking AboveEarth."

"Yes," Shibboleth acknowledged. "I have seen the reports, too. But I believe this will work to our advantage, giving the humans a taste of what is to come."

Nergal nodded. "So be it. Lord Shibboleth, with Ishkur gone, I need an officer to direct the rebuild of Agartha and lead in my stead while I am gone. Do you have someone to fill that role?"

Inanna sucked in a breath. This could be the answer to her plight and get her away from Irkalla and Shibboleth. "I will go, Sir. At least until the war with the humans has been won."

Mot's eyes widened. He nodded approval, but Shibboleth just glared.

"General, I will review your data and consider your request. Meanwhile, Mot will lead the first wave of troops, with you and the others following."

Shibboleth cut the feed and turned to Inanna.

"You will stay here until I say otherwise."

Mot waited until Inanna stalked from the room, then turned to his litter father.

"Sir, I was thinking. Agartha is one of our most strategic bases. If General Nergal is in AboveEarth fighting humans, he will not have time to complete the rebuild."

Shibboleth's lip curled. "That is General Nergal's problem, not ours." He moved briskly toward the door, and Mot followed.

"But it *will* be our problem. If Agartha is gutted, how will we defend it against the humans or their dragons should they invade?"

Shibboleth peered at Mot intently, then expelled a long breath.

"It has been a difficult day. I need a drink."

Mot followed his litter father to the nearest Reptilian bar, a short walk from the palace. Typically bustling with Dracs, mercenaries, and officers of the guard, today, it was quiet. The beings were likely at home saying goodbye before tomorrow's muster.

Upon seeing Shibboleth, the patrons scuttled out of the way, striking their chests in respect. The bartender followed suit.

"Warlord Shibboleth," the Pharechi shrilled, and Mot resisted the urge to clap his claws over his ears. "Long has it been since you honored us with your presence. And welcome to you, General Mot. It is good to see you in our fair city. What can I get for you?"

"Furroot. Your largest mug," Shibboleth growled, straddling a barstool and resting his elbows on the counter.

"Same." Mot settled on the next stool. "I need food. What do you have that is fresh?"

The bartender blanched. "I am not sure. Let me check."

The weasel-like creature drew two furroots, set them on the bar, and scurried to the back.

Shibboleth lifted his, chugged the contents, then slammed the mug on the bar, letting go a long, drawn-out belch.

"Mot, you are right. Agartha must be reinforced against attack. But were you suggesting I send Inanna for that task? Your litter sister has never led a regiment, much less a base. Especially one as large and critical as Agartha." His eyes roved the bar.

"Aye," Mot agreed. "But who would we get? Inanna is the only one left. Our Dracs will all be fighting the humans."

The bartender returned with a bloody slab of meat on a tray. He laid it before Mot.

"Our selection is slim today, but this haunch is from a freshly slaughtered Ecthelion. Will this do, General?"

"Aye." Mot tore off a chunk with his teeth and chewed thoughtfully. His litter father eyed the meat with distaste.

"Do you not like Ecthelion?" Mot mumbled, mouth full.

"Not raw," Shibboleth admitted. "I prefer it cooked these days."

Shocked, Mot asked, "Doesn't that destroy the texture and flavor?"

"Not at all. The cooking makes it easier to chew, and seasonings intensify the flavor."

Mot shuddered and took another bite as Shibboleth called for a second furroot.

He downed it while Mot finished his meal, then burped and said, "What if Inanna fails?"

"Then you can bring her back and train her up the way you did me and Maw."

"But you and your brother were easy. Inanna was trained, if you'll remember. But your sister is like her mother. She balked at every opportunity and questioned everything."

Mot laughed, remembering. "Yes, she is a hellion. But didn't you send her away early? I don't remember her being in my later classes."

"Aye, that was her mother's doing." Shibboleth ordered another furroot and stared into its depths.

Lifting the one he had yet to touch, Mot washed down the Ecthelion and swished the fizzy brown liquid through his teeth.

"You have changed my mind," Shibboleth declared. "I will delay Nergal's first incursion and send Inanna to Agartha. He will brief her there before he leaves for AboveEarth."

Mot kept his expression neutral as Shibboleth sucked down his third furroot and stood to leave.

"How much?" the warlord asked and belched.

"It's on the house, Sir," the Pharechi squeaked. "Yours, too," he shrilled to Mot, who stayed seated.

Shibboleth left, and Mot sipped his now lukewarm furroot and puffed on a cigar. His plan was unfolding nicely.

ICE BOUND

Emily came to, shivering so hard she bit her lip. The forest had disappeared, and its oppressive heat was a memory. Instead, ice nipped at every inch of Emily's body. When she tried to move, she couldn't.

Had the witch bound her? Or worse, paralyzed her? She blinked and rejoiced. At least her eyes moved. But where was she? And why was she encased in a cold, hard cocoon?

It took several moments before the answer came. Emily was in the vast field of frozen menhirs. Fear seized her. The closest were dragons wrapped in icy tombs. As the sensation drained slowly from her body, leaving her numb, Emily knew she, too, would soon be dead.

The ice seeped deeper into her bones, and the pain eased. Emily tried to fight the death sleep, but she soon drifted off.

A little while later, how long she didn't know, she came to again, still frozen inside a cocoon of ice. But at least there was no pain.

This should have scared the bejesus out of her, but Emily felt nothing, only a peaceful bliss. The fear and dread that had been her existence for the last several months was gone. She felt freer than she had since finding out about her heritage and the destiny that had been chosen for her at birth.

Blue sky stretched as far as she could see, the deep blue of an arctic sky free of moisture and humidity.

The sunshine offered no warmth, sparkling off the frozen dragon menhirs like a field full of Swarovski crystals. A light breeze played with drifted snow, sending flakes fluttering into the air and across the icy expanse.

A deep yearning to see the landscape unencumbered by her prison filled Emily. Without knowing how, she slid from her body into the air. Wonder filled her.

From this vantage point, the entire tundra became visible, and Emily gasped. In every direction, as far as she could see, were rows and columns of frozen dragons. So this was why the Keepers couldn't find the dragons. They were here in this frozen wasteland.

She was pretty sure she wasn't dead. Were they?

Emily peered closer and noticed a silvery cord running from her spirit down to the center of her icy prison. In awe, she realized there were thousands of other cords, and they were attached to the lightbodies of the dragons.

"Hail Awen, Queen of the Druids," the spirits cried in unison.

A wave of love washed over Emily, and she could feel Awen stirring, not as an interloper but as an equal. It was a curious sensation.

"Awen?" she breathed aloud.

"Yes, Emily?" The whisper came through her own lips.

"What do we do now?"

"Now," Awen said, "we wake the dragons and end this age-old fight. But first, may I help you remember?"

Emily acquiesced, and Awen said, "Hang on, here goes."

The memories began flowing. As a world of knowledge opened before Emily, her etheric body glowed brighter.

The sky became dark, filled with stars more numerous than in Awen's glade. Then, the void expanded to infinity and coalesced on a planet—a verdant oasis in space.

At first, Emily thought the planet was Earth, but in a startling flash, it exploded. Then, a planetship shattered nearby, littering space with escaping pods and wormholes as two disparate civilizations fled for their lives.

The darkness spread, and Emily found herself hurtling through one of the wormholes. Then, abruptly, she was inside Earth. The interior's wonders flashed before her—grand palaces, giant beings, gods, goddesses, angels, and humans—all inhabiting lush, verdant landscapes. But there were others, too. Aliens of every shape, size, color, and ilk lived inside the planet known collectively as Terra or Inner Earth.

Then, a Reptilian race came into focus, and Emily recoiled. Alongside the Druid refugees, were thousands of tall, thin, muscular beings whose scaled bodies ranged from pale cream to crocodilian green. Some had angelic wings, but most did not.

Then, the Sumerian gods duped the mighty creatures, and Emily wept. Their brutal captors forced them to mine for gold in caves beneath towering mountains. The Reptilians with large heads and black eyes were treated slightly better. These, the gods forced to develop vast computer networks and design an organic, self-repairing chute system that connected their military bases.

The Druids, on the other hand, were greeted with respect. They were granted generous land allotments and gifted residences built by the angels and gods. But even they were deceived.

Awen showed Emily how the humans had also suffered rape, torture, enslavement, and murder at the hands of the Sumerian god named Enlil and his vicious Asag.

Her unbelieving eyes filled with etheric tears as she witnessed the debauchery of these supposedly benevolent beings. Then, when the tide turned and the Druids waged war to free Humanity and the enslaved Reptilians, Emily's heart nearly burst.

Her spirit zoomed forward, and Emily witnessed the exodus of the Druids and Humans out of UnderEarth. But though they migrated to be free, they didn't realize and were never told that they traded their hard-won immortality for this so-called freedom.

Finally, Emily experienced the loss and heartache of war after war after war, waged between the descendants of the Druids and Humans and the soul-less Reptilians that followed them to the surface. Time and again, the vile creatures sought to eradicate humans and take Earth for themselves.

The memories flooded Emily's being until she saw everything everywhere all at once, from long before Awen's birth through today.

"Emily Bridget."

She tried to ignore the lyrical voice and stay in the flow of recollections, but Awen was firm.

"Focus. Come back. We have work to do."

Reluctantly, she returned her attention to the plain where she bobbed from a silvery thread. Beside and around her were hundreds of rows of frozen dragons. Emily blinked and refocused.

Was she seeing things? Was that Lugh down there?

But Awen demanded her attention. "Emily, if you still doubt that you and I are one, look down at your physical body." Emily did.

"Now, look at our light body."

There was only one.

"If we were separate beings, you would see two cords and two light bodies. But you see we only have one. Do you understand?"

The sensation of chill bumps danced across Emily's etheric body. "Yes, I think so."

"Good," Awen said. "Now, how about we return to our physical body and call that dragon meet?"

A thrill skittered through Emily. But she still wasn't sure she was prepared. "Don't we need the other wandstones to call the meet?"

"To call it? No," Awen purred. "That part is done. The dragons are here."

THE SUMMONS

Mitch stomped through the foyer of the Foster estate house. He resented being summoned, especially since he was no longer employed by the Awen Order. Emily's first official act as Grand Druid was to fire him.

Arthur Creeley crowded in behind Mitch, bumping into him when he stopped short. In the living room stood the golden-haired heartthrob Mitch had seen in Zephyr Cay. What were the odds? He clamped his jaw shut and stepped into the cavernous room. It was pleasantly cool after the sticky humidity.

"Morgan," Arthur rumbled and shook her hand.

Mitch ignored her and approached the blonde.

"Hi, I'm Mitch Wainwright. You'll probably think I'm crazy, but didn't I see you in Zephyr Cay?"

Pleasure pinked the pretty face.

"Why, yes," she drawled, "I believe you might be right." She fluttered long lashes and offered her hand. "Honey Dewars. Nice to meet you, Mr. Wainwright."

"Please call me Mitch." Something other than her looks seemed familiar, but he couldn't place what.

"Mitch." She beamed and turned to Arthur. "And you are?"

"Arthur Creeley, ma'am. At your service."

Morgan moved between them. "Arthur is our Acting Grand Druid until Emily returns. And it appears you already met Mr. Wainwright. You all have a seat. Honey was about to share some news with me."

The blonde looked startled but recovered quickly.

"Yesterday evening, while in Zephyr Cay with my significant other, we witnessed and barely escaped a monster attack."

Mitchell gasped. "You saw it, too?"

The woman nodded and swallowed hard. "Saw it. Experienced it. Was terrified by it. What do you think they were, Mitch?"

"Lizard men."

Morgan and Arthur blinked, looked at one another, then back at Mitch.

"Go on," Arthur prompted.

"Since returning to Atlanta, my research has revealed they are known as Draconians, Dracos, or Reptilians. Some can shape-shift and masquerade as humans." He shivered.

"I've read about them," Arthur said. "But I thought it was just a conspiracy theory."

"Isn't that what they call everything they don't want us to know?" Honey said.

"True." Arthur nodded. "But this cat's out of the bag. I saw it on the news."

"The news?" Mitch shuddered. "Did they show what they look like? The ones I saw were extremely tall, covered in olive-greenish scales, had flashing red eyes, ferocious claws on both hands and feet and stunk like a sewer." He gagged, remembering the spurting guts, and fought to hold it together.

"You okay there, Mitch?" Arthur laid a meaty palm on his shoulder, and Mitch's stomach calmed substantially.

"Yeah, thanks for that. But, sheesh, Coach. From what I experienced, these creatures are not enemies we want to fight."

Morgan tsk-tsked and wagged her head. "You men are such pussies."

Eyeing her with scorn, Mitch growled, "Look, I don't need to take your abuse. I don't work for you or the Order, and I have a flight to catch. Why did you insist Arthur drag me here?"

Morgan eyed him with disdain. "To give the Order a formal report of your Reptilian sighting, of course. We have called a meeting, and you shall attend."

Like hell, Mitch thought. He glanced at the grandmother clock, whose quiet ticks had punctuated their conversation.

"They should be gathering at Wren's Roost. Since you were instrumental in finding our grand druid the first time, Arthur and I decided you should help again. We need to counter any upcoming Reptilian attacks, and Emily is missing. It's up to you to find her."

Mitch's jaw fell open. Was Morgan inviting him back into the Order?

Honey cleared her throat and ignored Morgan's headshake.

"I shall attend as well." Animosity passed between the two druids, and Mitch couldn't help staring. When Morgan looked away first, he was shocked. Who was this blonde bombshell?

Morgan grunted, "If you must," then addressed Mitch.

"I contacted the FBI after you called yesterday. Katarina Hobbs, their director, has taken a personal interest in squelching any Reptilian attacks. Director Hobbs asked that we report any new developments. She, in turn, will have her office pass us news from around the world.

"She also informed me of other sightings reported in the last two days. A few were here in the U.S., one in India, and most recently, near Shropshire in the U.K."

Honey sucked in a breath. "Shropshire? Isn't that near Wales and Snowdonia? Didn't you say Emily was heading there?"

Mitch gasped out loud. Had Morgan told the goddamned stranger everything?

There was a sudden tickle in the back of his throat. He tried to clear it, coughed, then coughed some more. When it wouldn't stop, Morgan hurried to the kitchen for a glass of water. Grateful, Mitch slugged it back and set the glass on the end table.

"Baby boy."

His head snapped up. The whispered endearment had sounded in his head. He stared side-eyed at Honey Dewars. Was she—? Could it be?

"Shhhh," she hissed in his head. *"Don't say anything."*

There was a sudden tingle against Mitch's thigh from the sapphire brooch. Madame Bouvee had insisted he take the heirloom to Emily. Or rather, to Awen. But had it been the old, leathery proprietress who had given it to Mitch? Or had this woman inhabited her skin? Honey's eyes and everyone else's were trained on him.

"What?" he hiccupped. "Did I miss something?"

"What is in your pocket, Mitchell?" Morgan asked, apparently not for the first time. He started and realized he was fingering the brooch.

"Have you shown it to her yet?" Honey asked aloud.

Taken aback, Mitch glared and shook his head almost imperceptibly. But Morgan wouldn't let it go. Her eyes narrowed, and she leaned so close that Mitch could smell her cloying perfume.

"Show me what?"

Glaring at Honey, Mitch pulled the brooch from his pocket and held it up. The brilliant blue stone glittered in the light, and Arthur and Morgan gasped.

"Where did you get that?" Morgan screeched, yanking the brooch from his hand.

"Give it back." He snatched it and moved away.

But Morgan launched her substantial frame at him. Mitch sidestepped her and scrambled for the door. He'd almost made the foyer when Morgan tackled him from behind.

Luckily, they landed on a wool runner rather than hardwood. He flipped to his back, trying to hoist Morgan off, but her elbow crashed into his nose.

Yelping as his blood spurted, Mitch bucked the bitch off and sat on top of her, prepared to mount a full-scale attack. But before he could do any damage, Arthur's arm closed around Mitch's neck and dragged him off the spitting, clawing matriarch.

"Druids! Please!" the mammoth bellowed, reaching for the trinket.

But Mitch would be damned if he'd let go of it again. Madame Bouvee had given the sapphire to him, not to them. He backed away, stuffing it in his pocket.

But Morgan loomed between him and the outer door—all six feet, one-hundred-and-eighty pounds of hopping mad druid witch.

"That brooch belongs to the Hester family," she hissed. "You stole it."

"No, he didn't." Honey Dewars was nearly as tall as Morgan. She stationed her body between him and Morgan, then stared the startled matriarch down.

"I saw the woman in Zephyr Cay give it to Mitch. She told him to take it to Awen, *not* to you."

Morgan went wild. She screeched and snaked an arm around Honey, trying to grab Mitch's arm. She had almost pried the brooch from his fist when Arthur hauled her off him.

She swung and connected with Arthur's jaw this time, snapping his head back. He groaned and wobbled, then sat down hard in a nearby chair, clutching his bleeding mouth.

Morgan lunged at Mitch again. Her face twisted in fury when Honey tried to stop her. Using a forearm, she batted the blonde away and descended on Mitch, knocking him to the floor. He bucked and twisted but could not wriggle out from beneath her or get his hand away.

One by one, she peeled Mitch's fingers from the brooch. With an enormous effort, he ripped his hand from the Order's Head of Security, shoved her off him, and scrambled up.

"Bastard!" Morgan yelled, slapping his face and grabbing at the brooch. When she came up empty-handed, she swished her wrist and muttered a curse.

Mitch tried to roll out of the way, but it slammed into him. The next he knew, he shivered uncontrollably, encased in a solid block of ice. And horror of horrors, he was smack-dab in the middle of one of his nightmares, surrounded by popsicle dragons.

Only this time, Mitch was one of them, and he couldn't move, flee, or escape.

Terror turned his insides to liquid. How had Morgan sent him here? His eyes would not obey when he tried to blink, but at least the brooch was still clutched in his hand. A fat lot of good it would do him now.

☼☼☼

Alexis watched as they wrestled for the brooch. Then, Morgan slung a curse, and Mitch disappeared. Alexis gasped.

Staring at her empty fist with a flushed and wild expression, Morgan wheeled on Alexis. "You meddling bitch. How dare you interfere with family matters? You know that brooch belongs to the Hester family. The heirloom dates back to the original Awen. The sapphire is one of the jewels from Awen's wand."

She swung toward Arthur. "And you. Who do you think you are manhandling me like that?"

"Your boss," Arthur said flatly, thick brows arched. "What's gotten into you, Morgan? I have never seen you act like this. Bring Mitch back. Now."

"Me?" Morgan feigned innocence. "What makes you think that thief didn't escape on his own? And with my brooch?!"

Anger bubbled up in Alexis, and Honey's body trembled. She stared at her old friend.

"You know that brooch is not yours, Morgana. It belongs to the Awen." Morgan laughed, pushing Alexis to her breaking point. She leaned in, fists clenched, and muttered beneath her breath, "You are an evil witch. Bring Mitch back now. Or else."

"Or else what?" Morgan cackled, putting distance between them. "What will you do to me, honeydew? Drown me in sweetness? Spit seeds at me?" She snorted and laughed at her hilarious joke.

And Alexis snapped. She reared back and slung a tongue-tie curse, but Arthur stepped between them, and it struck him instead.

Muttering something incoherent and eyes hopping mad, the man made a swishing motion and mumbled something that sounded like, "Morgan, calm down!"

That did it. Wagging her head mournfully, Morgan trudged to the living room with Arthur and Alexis trailing behind. She sank into the couch with a faraway look clouding her eyes.

"Where did you send Mitchell Wainwright?" Arthur demanded, standing over the Order's Head of Security.

A blank expression echoed Morgan's silence until Alexis sidled up and pinched the back of her arm.

Morgan jerked away. "Keep your hands off me."

"Where did you send my son?" Alexis whispered in Morgan's ear. She restrained the urge to bite it off when Morgan hooted, a high-pitched, jittery laugh that bordered on hysteria.

"Answer her," Arthur commanded in a steely tone, and Alexis's blood ran cold. She hadn't meant for him to hear. "Where is Mitchell Wainwright?"

But Morgan laughed harder until tears gathered and rolled down her cheeks. Alexis and Arthur stared, first at her, then at one another, shaking their heads.

When she finally calmed down, Morgan dabbed her eyes with a tissue she yanked from a nearby box. Then Morgan leveled them with a brittle glare.

"I have no idea what happened to that Wainwright man." Then, she sniffed and blew her nose loudly.

Alexis didn't believe her. "Sure you do. Just tell us where you sent him. Or better yet, bring him back!"

The regal head wagged back and forth. Then Morgan slumped and stared off into space. "I can't. I don't know where I sent him. Or how to get him back."

"How can that be?" Arthur asked. "I saw you sling the spell."

Bitterness pinched Morgan's fine features into sharp angles.

"Yes, you did. Only I have no idea what that spell does. I saw my mother use it once when I was little. The man disappeared, and she swore it didn't kill him, but she never told me where he went. I don't use it for that reason. But I was so furious, the words popped out before I could stop them."

Alexis settled into an armchair, anger dissipated. She had finally connected with her long-lost son. Now, he had vanished to God knows where.

She stared at Morgan and Arthur. Then, hiding her face in her hands, Alexis mustered all of her power to keep from breaking down in tears.

253

MEETING OF THE AWEN ORDER

The meeting had begun over an hour ago and Alexis was bored to tears. She hid behind a glass of sweet tea provided by Wren's Roost's caretakers Simon and Mary Cobb. The couple had been around the estate for ages and had taken care of Emily when she was little. Of course, they didn't recognize her in Honey's body.

She had remained silent as the Awen Order hashed out defense logistics and named leaders for each district drawn on the vast world map in the library. As head of security, Morgan would coordinate their efforts from Atlanta.

Then, Katy Kat, their old friend and now FBI director, appeared onscreen to update the Order on defense proceedings. The druids' plan of attack coincided with the government's, with little duplication.

When they finally spoke about the location of Emily and Lugh MacBrayer, Alexis straightened. The last Morgan knew they were both in France, most likely in Falaise at Awen's glade.

That was news to Alexis. No one paid attention to her, so Alexis closed Honey's eyes to feel for Emily's energy signature. Finding nothing, she focused on Lugh. Alexis had only met him once or twice when he was a boy. She remembered his hair had been jet black, and his eyes were dark, intelligent, and kind. She wondered if that had stayed with him in adulthood.

But she had no luck finding him either.

Alexis jumped and opened her eyes when Morgan said her name. Everyone was looking at her.

"Could you repeat that, please?"

Morgan sighed so loud that several druids chuckled.

"Would you share what you saw in Zephyr Cay?"

Alexis stood and looked around the cozy room filled with the highest-ranking druids of the Awen Order. She recognized many of the older ones. And though they had no clue who she was, all gave Honey polite attention.

Clearing her throat, Alexis thanked everyone for allowing her to attend their meeting, then described all that had happened on Zephyr Cay. She left out her true identity and most of the part she had played in thwarting the Reptilian attack.

When Alexis finished, the meeting resumed, and by the end of the next hour, the druids had cemented their plan of attack.

WAKING THE DRAGONS

Waking the dragons and freeing them from their icy cocoons was an experience Emily would long remember. Never had she felt so exhilarated or so powerful, even when she had calmed the storm over the Bahamas.

Awen spoke to each dragon, calling them by name, and Emily's heart swelled. The tundra came alive as each of the grateful dragons hailed Awen and thanked her profusely. But when it was time to wake Lugh, Emily stared, disappointed. It wasn't him.

But if not Lugh, then who? She studied the face. It had to be Jake, Lugh's brother. She'd been told they looked alike, but Jake had disappeared the year before. Lugh thought he'd been on a mission to find the dragons, but had Jake been frozen here all this time?

Emily spied another ice-bound human next to Jake. She leaned closer and let go a whoop, then a resounding "YES!" This one *was* Lugh. But there was another dark-haired man beside him. She peered closer. Was it… Mitchell Wainwright? No, that couldn't be.

But the handsome face and scowling blue eyes belonged to Mitchell. How had the ass-hat attorney ended up here? Bé Chuille's curse transported Emily and Lugh. Had Mitchell and Jake somehow run afoul of the winter hag? Had she sent them here?

That didn't make sense, but what other explanation was there?

Tossing Awen's long, bushy hair over her shoulder, Emily moved back to Lugh. She laid a palm against one frozen cheek, and celebrated when tiny cracks radiated through the ice sheath. She placed her other hand on the opposite cheek, and the ice shattered, leaving Lugh's face and head free. Moments later, his icy tomb shattered and fell away from his body with a crashing thump.

Leaning close, Emily touched her lips to Lugh's frozen ones. His eyes fluttered and his lips warmed, but he remained unconscious.

She moved on to Jake and cupped her hands on the ice covering his face. When his ice cocoon crumbled, she repeated the steps with Mitchell. Then, she went back to Lugh.

She touched his cheek, and Lugh's eyes opened. Realizing who she was, he grabbed Emily and drew her close.

"Thank God, you're safe!" He shivered against her. "I thought I'd lost you again."

She pulled back and pointed him toward Jake. "Is this your brother?"

"JAKE!" Lugh enveloped the wobbling man in a bear hug.

Then Jake pulled away to retch into the ice while Lugh rubbed his long-lost brother's back.

Meeting Emily's gaze, he mouthed, "Thank you," eyes glistening.

Jake wiped his mouth and locked Lugh and Mitchell in bear hugs. Then Lugh presented Emily to Jake as his future wife. As the men commiserated, Emily reveled in Lugh's bold proclamation.

The wind shrieked, strafing them with stinging ice crystals. Emily threw up an arm to shield her face and wished she hadn't shucked Awen's cloak in the heat of her 21st Century glade.

"Awen," she urged. "It's f-f-freezing. Can we get out of here?"

"No, not yet," her ancestor purred. "Are you ready to address the dragons?"

A thrill raced through Emily. She wrapped her arms around her shoulders and squeezed Awen tight before moving to the front where Tienu and the Keepers celebrated with their brethren.

Awen faced the dragon host and called them to attention. Then, she chanted in a commanding voice that echoed over the plain.

"Oh, ye dragon kind of old,
I, Awen, dragon master
And leader of the druids,
Call you to fulfill your oaths.
Put aside the curse
That held you captive
And return to your lairs
In the Mountains of Snow.
Fly fast to Yr Wyddfa,
Cadir Idris, Crib Goch.
Find your way to Glyder Fach,
Moel Siabod, Glyder Fawr.
The peaks of Tryfan,
Carnedd Llewellyn,
And Y Garn

Call you to return
Oh, ye dragons of old.
Fly now, ye faithful
Fly now to defend Earth.
Make haste to Beli
To the land of your birth.
There we'll gather again,
Before standing together
To battle the Reptilians
And defend Earth."

With that, the magnificent dragons took flight in droves. Creatures of all shapes and sizes filled the crisp, stinging air. They roared, screeched, shrieked, and sighed in a euphoric release.

Emily marveled as the sun glinted off their scales, creating a kaleidoscope of colors in the clouds and on the snow below. She and the men watched, awestruck, as the dragons entered a wormhole and vanished, all except the four Keepers—Talav, Ooschu, a-Ur, and Tienu.

They crowded close, congratulating Emily and thanking Awen. They eyed the men as Emily introduced them and requested they be allowed to remember the dragons, at least until they had defeated the Reptilians.

They agreed, though reluctantly, and then Tienu's keen eyes peered off into the distance where the horde had disappeared. He bugled loud and long, and his eerie, metallic, almost challenging shriek put Emily on edge. When it faded, the only sound was the frigid wind sloughing over the ice.

A squall rose, shrieking in reply.

Chill bumps ran up and across Emily's shoulders as black clouds materialized to fill the heavens. The wind gusted, lifting the remains of the cairns into a sky gone slate. She leaned against Lugh for warmth and shelter as the ice crystals pelted them. The wail rose in volume and pitch to echo around them.

Shuddering, she shouted, "Let's get out of here."

"Where to?" Lugh asked.

Awen answered. "*We* are flying to Beli with the Keepers, but it will be dangerous. Especially when Bé Chuille learns the dragons are free."

A fierce gust of wind yanked Emily from Lugh's arms and tossed her on the ice several yards away. She clambered up and clutched the bodice of Awen's freshly-ripped gown. The temperature had plummeted so fast that her breath froze, and its icy feathers disintegrated in the wind.

"Where should we send them?" Talav nodded toward the men.

"To AIA, the Alien Intelligence Agency in Cheltenham," Jake said, shivering. "I need to report in. My superiors will know what to do next." He swung toward Lugh. "How long have I been here, anyway?"

"More than a year. We thought you were dead."

"Th-that long, huh?" Jake wagged his head woefully. "It s-seemed like an eternity to m-me." He drew his jacket tighter and huddled between Lugh and Mitchell. The men crowded close, shoulders joining.

"I don't care where we go. Just get us out of here," Mitchell said. Then his eyes got big, and he turned to Jake. "You're saying there's an agency dedicated to tracking aliens?"

Jake nodded.

"Jesus Frickin' Christ." Mitchell rubbed his face in his hands and looked up at the ominous sky. "Until a couple of days ago, I thought aliens and UFOs were a load of horsecrap. Then I was attacked by lizard men on Zephyr Cay."

Emily gasped. "You saw them? They attacked you?" Then something struck her. "Why on Earth were you in Zephyr Cay?"

"Looking for you."

His answer shocked Emily. "But why?"

Another gust of wind nearly sent her flying again, but Lugh and Mitchell snagged her and held on.

"Let's go. I'll tell you later," Mitchell yelled over the howling wind. "I'm f-freezing, and this place gives me the creeps."

Jake craned his neck up at the scarlet dragon. "Are you the fire Keeper?" The enormous head bobbed, and Jake's eyes shone.

"I am Jake. I have waited to meet you my whole life. Could you take me and my friends to AIA Headquarters in Cheltenham, England?"

"Of course," the dragon rumbled.

But Lugh protested. "No way. I'm not going anywhere. I'm staying with Emily." He leaned down to murmur, "I lost you once. I'm not losing you again."

But the dragon king seconded Awen's refusal. "I am afraid not. You are needed elsewhere, young raven. If things proceed as planned, you shall see your beloved soon. But for now, your path lies with these two." Lugh's lip protruded, but he didn't argue.

It was now or never.

"Alrighty, let's d-do this thing." Emily shivered violently, and it occurred to her she should renew her protective spell. She did and cast it over the men and the dragons, then relaxed inside a heated cocoon.

"Wow, it got warmer," Jake exclaimed. "Much warmer."

Tienu said, "You can thank Awen for her protective charm."

"Good lord, why didn't I think of that," Lugh groaned, shaking his head.

"Are you ready, young sirs?" Tienu asked, then stared long and hard at Mitchell Wainwright.

He stared back defiantly before lowering his long lashes. But when Mitchell looked up, there was a new gleam in his eyes, and Emily wondered what had transpired between them.

"I'm ready," he said, beaming sincerely at Emily.

She was taken aback. Mitchell Wainwright had been nothing but nasty to her since she had arrived in Atlanta.

"I'm ready," Jake declared.

But Lugh hesitated. He pulled Emily to him. "I love you, Emily Hester. And when we get through all this, I promise I will show you just how much." Then he let her go.

"I'm ready."

Tienu opened a wormhole above their heads, and Emily yelled over the wind, "I'm going to hold you to that promise. Be safe."

Then, Tienu explained about wormhole mechanics and cautioned the men to keep AIA Cheltenham at the forefront of their thoughts.

They moved to the wormhole, and disappeared one by one. A few seconds later, the portal disintegrated, and Emily was alone with the Keepers in the blinding squall.

"Are we traveling by wormhole?" Emily shielded her face from the blasting ice crystals.

"We could, but wouldn't you rather ride?" Awen said.

"Ride?" Emily's gaze swept the vast terrain, bare except for collapsed ice cairns. "Ride what?"

Awen's excitement reverberated in Emily's heart. "Why, Tienu, of course."

"Oh. No, thank you." Emily shuddered. "Once was enough. I don't fancy dangling from a dragon's claws ever again."

Awen laughed, and it was Emily laughing. Then Awen's memories filled Emily, and a thrill flickered through her.

"Oh, on Tienu's back." She giggled, embarrassed. "I guess I'm game." Still, she hesitated, not sure whether she trusted the cantankerous dragon.

He sidled up to Emily, splayed his front legs before him, and lowered his shoulder. She stared, wondering how she was supposed to get up there.

"Climb," Awen said. "Grab one of his horns and shimmy up. Or you can use his scales for handholds."

Emily eyed the sharp tips skeptically, but her body obeyed. She crouched, sprang into the air, and caught hold of a horn. Then, using Tienu's red scales for footholds, she scrambled into the dragon's natural saddle, squealing when the faceted gems drew blood.

"I forgot to tell you to set another protective spell," Awen moaned.

Emily did and felt her body relax. As Tienu instructed the other Keepers, she wondered if Talav and Ooschu would be okay. They had recently begun flying and neither were strong aviators.

"We will not be going far," Tienu rumbled, reading her mind. But he posed the question to the dragons, who agreed they were equal to the task. Then, they all took flight together.

☼☼☼

When Bé Chuille heeded her preset alarm to return to the Stygian Plains, it was too late. The dragons had disappeared, along with Awen and the other humans.

"Nooo," she screeched, thinking of the hours, days, and years she had spent finding them all, then battling each before banishing them here.

Her second thought was that Shibboleth would be furious. When the dragons returned to guard Earth's access points, Bé would have reneged on their deal.

As enraged as she had ever been, she waved her wand, and clouds appeared on the horizon. They picked up moisture from the North Atlantic, multiplying and gathering upon themselves. Then Bé Chuille waved her wand again, and a fierce northeast wind swept the clouds overhead.

Lightning sizzled and struck at her feet, raising the hairs on Bé's body and filling the plain with the sweet scent of ozone. When thunder cracked and boomed, shaking the ground, Bé Chuille sent the storm to find Awen and kill the bitch once and for all.

YR WYDFFA

Exhilaration shot through Emily as they ascended the buffeting airwaves. A vast white plain spread below them as far as she could see.

"Where are we?" she shouted to Tienu, but her words dispersed in the relentless wind. She asked again, telepathically.

"I believe we are above the Arctic Circle," the fire dragon answered inside her head. "But we are still in the Otherworld. Hang on."

They entered an air pocket and dropped straight down. Emily clung to Tienu's horns, relieved when the wind caught beneath his wings. Then Talav zipped in front of them, and the other two dragons changed positions, guarding Tienu's flanks as they climbed higher through the wet clouds.

Soon, they broke free, and Emily gasped. The land was so far away she could no longer make out the terrain. So why wasn't she having trouble breathing?

Tienu answered inside her head. "It's the protective charm."

Then he dove toward Earth, and Emily clung tight. The wind screamed through his sharp horns and scales, and her kinky hair whipped frantically. It slapped her face and stung her eyes as a-Ur assumed the lead.

They were nearly on top of the air dragon when Tienu zigged abruptly, and her bottom half left the saddle. For a moment, Emily was terrified, then Awen took over.

Holding tight to Tienu's horns, she soon laughed as they hurtled toward Earth with her legs dangling freely behind them.

Then they leveled off, and she regained her seat.

The wind was calmer at this elevation. Emily could see the mountains and vegetation, but they were above a churning sea dotted with ice floes.

Soon, they circled the rugged land.

A dusting of snow-topped mountains and mounded ledges that marched away toward infinity. Moss-covered boulders with white blankets loomed like eerie giants frozen on an afternoon stroll. Evergreens and recently leafed trees bordered greening grasses littered with scree, limestone pavement, and boulder fields.

When the sea came into view again, Ooschu trumpeted gleefully. Talav and a-Ur joined in. Tienu remained silent as they glided to a mountaintop covered in snow, and the others landed nearby.

Meadows inhabited by long-maned ponies were visible in the distance, and the faint melody of baaing sheep floated to Emily. But what she saw below troubled her.

People were everywhere—climbing trails, perching on boulders, and taking pictures of the government-protected park. Emily shimmied from Tienu's back, wondering how they could call a dragon meet with so many prying eyes.

On one side, a long building surrounded by people occupied a mountaintop. It was likely the visitor's center she had discovered in her research. A sudden longing for hot tea made Emily weak at the knees. Loosely stacked stones formed a fence that led away from the building at a sharp angle, then disappeared behind a jagged peak.

To their left, two hikers with a dog neared the top of a tor while a tourist train chugged up a steep incline, heading for the visitor's center. Emily watched it reach the summit, bell clanging. Then, passengers poured out while others boarded.

A feeling of defeat crept over her as Emily rotated slowly in a tight circle. In every direction, people occupied the rugged terrain. Most crowded along the lower elevations and near the seaside, but many had flocked to Eryri that day.

Emily wished she could remember the names of all the peaks, but Yr Wyddfa, the pyramidal mountain hosting the visitor's center, was the only one she could recall. Of course, the older, more common name was Mount Snowdon.

Then, something occurred to Emily. "Where is Beli's castle?"

"The ruins are down there," Talav pointed with a forepaw to grounds crawling with tourists.

"We can't have a dragon meet with all these people," Emily whimpered.

"They won't be a problem," Awen murmured. "The dragons are here. We can thank Bé Chuille for gathering them."

The heat of righteous anger bubbled inside Emily. "The winter hag? You talk as if you know her."

"Know her?" Awen sneered. "Bé Chuille has been a boil on my buttocks since the day I was born. My mother is gone because of that witch. But that's another story.

"We must get the dragons back to their posts. The Reptilians are on the warpath."

"Can we at least wait until nightfall?" Emily asked. "I wonder what time the park closes."

The Keepers eyed her curiously.

"What do you mean?" a-Ur rumbled.

"The people. When will they leave?"

The air dragon wobbled his head. "Oh, we never worry about people. Even if they see us, they forget."

"And the forgetfulness curse always works?"

The dragons blinked at one another, then at Emily.

"How would we know?" a-Ur asked.

"Good point." Emily shuddered. Her bad feeling grew stronger. "I still think we should wait until dark. By then, the park should be empty." Then, something else occurred to Emily. "Does the forgetfulness curse extend to me?"

The air dragon's eyes widened to plate size, and Talav wagged her head.

"So those people can see me and report anything I do to the authorities?"

"Yes," Ooschu admitted. "I never thought about that."

"I did," Tienu snarled. "I charmed you before we left the tundra."

Relieved, Emily let go a sigh and wished Tienu had allowed Lugh to come with them. The Keepers were good company, but having a wiser, more experienced druid here would be nice.

"So now what?" she asked.

"Now, we go down to the castle," Awen said matter-of-factly, and Emily chuckled.

She had forgotten about Awen. No living druid was more experienced than her.

Emily pointed to the overgrown ruins. "Should we fly?"

"Aye, climb aboard," Tienu rumbled.

Moments later, they touched down next to Beli Mawr's crumbling castle, and five minutes later, they were surrounded by thousands of dragons of all shapes, sizes, and colors. As the last landed, Awen instructed Emily to stand on Tienu's saddle.

"Umm, sure," Emily mumbled, wondering how she would accomplish that feat.

She slowly drew her legs up beneath her, then straightened to balance precariously atop Tienu's saddle. Awen lifted her right hand to the field of dragons.

Aóme glittered on her first finger, sending a brilliant green beam that connected with the ruby pendant against Emily's chest. The diamond and sapphire were still missing, but when Emily raised her left hand to form a V, the dragon host bowed as one.

A light show ensued as colored sparks flew between the stones and shot into heaven to rain back down upon Emily and the dragon host. Sacred, effervescent light showered them as the energy expanded to encompass the land they stood on. Then Awen broke the silence.

"Dear mighty dragon warriors. For ages, you protected the Druids and our home world of Marduk. Then, for millennia, you have done the same here on Earth. Now, the Reptilians, that warring band of lizard people we swore to contain, have once again declared war on Humanity.

"Oh, ye creatures of a more glorious day, rise to defend Earth. Return to your posts around the globe. Guard the access points between our worlds with your very lives. Root out any Reptilians that have made it through and send them back to the interior from whence they came. The Keepers will join you soon. Now, fly, fly, fly away home."

The dragons roared in unison and took flight in a kaleidoscopic whirlwind to scatter to the four corners of Earth.

Now, Emily and the four Keepers—Talav, Ooschu, a-Ur, and Tienu—were all that remained.

"What do we do now?" she asked.

"What did Druantia advise?" Tienu prompted.

The answer had been heavy on Emily's mind. "That we, or rather, I, should go to Stonehenge while you and the dragons guard our borders."

"Then that's what we shall do," Tienu ruled.

The Keepers lowered their heads to say goodbye, then took to the sky. As the last one disappeared on the horizon, it occurred to Emily that she was stuck on Yr Wyddfa with no way down.

"Way to go." A sinking feeling rifled her gut. "Now what?"

A bolt of lightning sizzled past, barely missing her. Emily squealed as the clap of thunder shook the ground, and a second lightning bolt struck near her feet. Dancing away, she shrieked in terror.

DRAGON ATTACK

Inanna slid onto the bench beside Nergal. He was deep in conversation with Doctora Magdalena. At Nergal's suggestion, they were meeting for lunch at the joint where they had eaten before fleeing Agartha. As usual, Inanna was late.

"Greetings, Inanna," the petite doctora purred. "Nergal and I were reminiscing about the last time we were here."

"You mean the night we had to flee or die?" Inanna snorted. "What's good today?"

"The meatballs were fantastic," Magdalena said, violet eyes glued to Nergal.

"Is it too early for a drink?" Inanna signaled the server.

After arriving in Agartha, Nergal had attempted to teach Inanna what he had learned over several millennia. Now, two days later, it was apparent to Inanna she was in over her head. What had made her think she could rule a base and its city? Especially with Nergal leaving to catch a chute to Xibalba IX.

Inanna sipped her drink and ate silently, noticing Nergal's manner with Magdalena. Instead of his usual stern and angry demeanor, he was calmer, softer, and more forgiving.

A thought formed, followed by a jab of jealousy. Since Inanna had met Nergal, she believed she was meant to be with him. She was wrong about that, too, apparently.

Shoving her plate aside, she ogled Magda as Nergal strode from the bar bound for Xibalba IX.

"You love him, don't you?" Inanna said quietly.

The doctora's eyes widened, then narrowed to study Inanna over the rim of her glass.

"I am drawn to Nergal, yes. I may even love him. But Nergal is royalty and not for me." Magda held Inanna's gaze. "He is, however, for you, Inanna Shibboleth's Spawn."

Not expecting that, Inanna sat very still. The Draca's message was as unmistakable as it was unsolicited.

"Are you implying that Nergal descends from royal blood?"

"I am implying nothing. I am telling you. Nergal is royalty."

Inanna hissed and glanced around to make sure no one paid attention to them. "And how would you know this?"

The doctora thoughtfully swirled the liquid in her glass. Then, she, too, scanned the crowded bar before focusing on Inanna.

"I saw it."

Inanna recoiled. "What do you mean, you saw it?"

"Remember when we were fleeing from Maw and the magma?"

Inanna nodded.

"After Maw shot me, I hovered at death's door, and saw many things. But this one revelation was most vivid."

Chills rippled up Inanna's torso and down her arms.

"You have the sight?"

The doctora stiffened and looked as if she might bolt. Inanna could relate. She knew that feeling well. She touched the claw clenched tightly on the table.

"The sight is uncommon among our race. By law, it should be registered. But your secret is safe with me, Magdalena. Both of them. I have more important issues to manage, anyway." And, boy, did she.

Across the table, Magdalena relaxed. She squeezed Inanna's claw, and leaned closer to whisper, "Yes. I see things. It seldom happens, but all I have seen has come to pass."

Inanna pondered the healer's words. "Are we littermates, Nergal and me?" As if that mattered in the scheme of things.

"No. Nergal descends from a different line."

Thinking of Shibboleth's hand servant, Inanna asked, "What makes you think *you* are not royalty?"

It was the doctora's turn to snort. "Because I am a half-breed thrust upon my mother by a human in AboveEarth. The woman dared not keep me and feared for my life since I look like my father. Apparently, half-breeds are treated badly there, too." Misery marred her kind features. "Did you know Nergal despises half-breeds?"

Inanna's communicator tweeted. She held up a claw and accessed her unit while Magdalena shoved scraps around her plate.

It was Nergal's assistant in Xibalba IX.

"What is it, Azi?"

"I cannot raise Nergal or my contact in Irkalla." From the background came a loud commotion. The scientist's head swiveled, terror reflected in his dark eyes.

"What is it, Azi? What is happening?"

"It is a dragon. Somehow it infiltrated our base in Xibalba IX."
There was a loud, metallic screech, and Azi took off running. In the
background, an enormous red glittering dragon strafed the base.
There was an awful scream, and the screen went blank.

"Did he say a dragon?" Magdalena gulped.

"He did." Inanna reversed the feed, and they watched it
together.

"That looks like the same dragon that attacked Agartha after the
magma erupted," Magda said. "We were escaping the city, and
Nergal stopped to challenge him. But he was near death and
realized he was too weak. After that, he couldn't escape fast
enough."

Inanna stood. "I must return to the base. Go back to your office
and stay off the streets. At least until I determine whether Agartha
is in danger."

Throwing credits on the table, Inanna sprinted to the nearby
chute station through streets crowded with residents and workers.
After the swift pace of Irkalla, Agartha's citizens seemed to move
like snails.

Her chute arrived quickly and soon she strode through a sea of
workers. Construction was well underway on the base, put in place
by Nergal. All Inanna would have to do, or so he said, was keep
them on track and order materials when the supervisor requested.

She reached the control room, one of the only areas not
demolished by magma. The wall screens displayed varying stages of
construction and scenes of the rebuilds going on in town.

Inanna called up the stream for Xibalba IX while trying to hail
Azi on her wrist unit. No one answered. She tried Nergal with the
same result.

Next, Inanna checked in with Mot, who was too busy to talk.
Finally, in desperation, she contacted Shibboleth. He answered on
the first ring.

"Yes, Inanna. Report."

"Sir, I assume Mot informed you of the situation in Xibalba IX.
The dragons have somehow breached the portals, and a fire drake
is terrorizing the base. I am unable to reach Mot or Nergal. What
orders do you have for me?"

"I am aware of the dragon." Shibboleth glanced away and
nodded to someone. "Mot is investigating, and Nergal is on his way
to Xibalba IX. For now, do nothing. I believe the drake to be a
rogue. Bé Chuille assured me she neutralized the dragons.

He ended the call abruptly, and Inanna snarled, "Yes, *sir*, Asshole."

Annoyed at the dismissal and feeling more helpless than ever, Inanna plopped into the captain's chair and tried unsuccessfully to reach Nergal again. Thrumming her claws on the console, she pulled up the feeds for Xibalba IX and shuddered. Residents ran screaming through the streets of a city ablaze.

"Inanna, come in," a scratchy voice urged.

"This is Inanna."

"The drake has disappeared. The base is unharmed, but the wind has shifted, spreading flames throughout the city. Local teams are working to contain the fire, but it appears out of control."

"Nergal should be there soon. Is there anything I can do from here?"

As Azi wagged his oversized head, she realized with a pang he looked much like Ishkur.

"I do not think so. I will make contact if so."

Not knowing what else to do, Inanna raised the alarm for Agartha, notifying residents, workers, and the skeleton crew of Dracs to be alert for dragons. Then, she contacted the other bases. Most operated without protection but had not been attacked.

Exiting the feed, Inanna noticed the center had emptied. She allowed herself a moment of panic, wrapping her wiry arms around her trembling body. Her teeth gnashed as she let the helpless and hopeless wash over her.

Then, remembering Nergal's lecture, Inanna gathered her wits and hurried to her bunk to throw a few things together.

The supervisors didn't need her here. Inanna would go to Xibalba IX. She may not know how to lead troops or subjects or rebuild bases and cities, but she *did* have an in with the dragons.

THE ALIEN INTELLIGENCE AGENCY

The wormhole deposited Lugh, Jake, and Mitchell in a tangled heap. There was just enough light for Lugh to tell they were in a closet or a tiny office. Mitchell lay motionless in a fetal position. Jake unwound his knobby limbs and scrambled to his knees to hurl in a handy metal waste bin.

The sound of Jake heaving had Lugh gagging, too. He dragged himself up using an old office chair wedged between a dusty file cabinet and a small desk, then sneezed and poked Mitchell with his toe. The attorney groaned.

"Good. You're alive. For a minute there, I wondered."

Mitch flopped to his back, knees in the air, taking up all the available floor space. Jake squinted at their old buddy from the trashcan, then buried his face to barf year-old food.

Lugh fumbled for a light switch but found none. "Any idea where we are, bro?"

Jake lifted his arm behind him between yaks and pointed at shelves built into the wall. Over the top was a sign Lugh could barely read in the dim light.

"Lost and Found, HA! That's appropriate. Your guts might be turning inside out, Bro. But you're alive, and we're not stuck in the arctic tundra."

He examined shelves littered with items one would expect in a Lost and Found. Two cell phones were among the sweaters, scarves, books, keys, and other paraphernalia. Lugh tried each, hoping for light, but the batteries were dead.

Finally, he growled, "Did we at least make it to Cheltenham?"

This time, Jake's answer was an incredibly juicy *BLE-EECH* that had both Mitchell and Lugh gagging in reflex.

Mitchell groaned and curled back into the fetal position, where he rocked and moaned in time to Jake's retching.

"You okay, dude?" Lugh asked the attorney.

"*Okay?*" Mitchell's wail bounced off the walls. He came up on his knees, face flushed, and looked like he would either puke or kill someone. Instead, he screeched.

"WHAT THE EVERLOVIN' FUCK? You stand there like nothing crazy just happened to us and ask me if *I'm o-fucking-kay?* Hell, no, I'm *not* okay. What the fuck is wrong with you? I did not agree to any of this—not flying in cloud tunnels, canoodling with dragons, or getting frozen in a block of ice. I want no part of your druid insanity. Send me back home to Georgia. Now."

"Pussy," Jake scoffed, wiping his mouth with his sleeve. "Big whoop, man! What about me? I've been struck in that ice hell for over a year. You don't see me blubber—" Then he yakked again.

Mitchell belched loudly, and they both started laughing.

Without warning, the door jerked open, and Lugh nearly fell out.

"What's going on in here?" a female voice demanded as the overhead light blazed to life.

Lugh squinted through his hand to shield his eyes.

"Cybele?"

She was the last person Lugh had expected.

Jake snapped to attention. "Cybele! I think I'm—" His eyes got big, and his head went down in the trashcan.

This time, Jake muscled in. "Move over, bruh."

While they retched in harmony, Lugh hugged Cybele and gave her the short version of how they'd ended up in the Lost and Found at AIA Cheltenham.

"But what are *you* doing here? I thought you were searching for Jake."

"I am," she admitted with a sheepish grin. "And it looks like I found him." She snaked her arms around Jake's back and laid her cheek on his shoulder. "Hello, lover," she whispered loud enough for everyone to hear.

Jake turned in Cybele's arms. "I would kiss you, but...."

"Eeew," she laughed and wiggled free. "But, I AM happy to see you. I searched Europe, Africa, and parts of Asia. Now, here you are. Without my help."

"That's not true," Lugh protested. "You did a lot. Hey, where's Brian?"

"Not here yet. They'll be landing in a few hours."

"Ethnui's with him?"

"Yes, and Elise."

Mitchell lifted his head from the metal can. "Could I get some water?"

"Of course! You guys come with me."

Cybele backed out of the tiny closet, pulling Jake with her. Lugh and Mitchell followed. The few people roaming the hallway eyed the unkempt vagrants emerging from Lost and Found and gave them a wide berth.

Lugh spotted a bathroom and hurried toward it, but Mitchell beat him to the door. They wrestled over the handle, then Lugh stepped back to let him go first. Inside, he confronted his once-friend.

"I know how I ended up on that tundra, but how in the hell did you get there?"

A toilet flushed. Patent leather shoes peeked from the bottom of a stall. The owner ripped off a long, sloppy fart, and they eyed one another comically. Then, a foul stench wafted to them, and Lugh nearly lost it.

Slapping his hand over his nose and mouth, he picked a stall and did his business, washed his hands, and snicked out the door as quickly as possible.

Seconds later, Mitchell stumbled into him, and they roared, laughing, clutching at one another in the middle of the hall. When he realized Jake and Cybele watched with snarky grins, Lugh sobered. But one look at Mitch's contorted features had him laughing again.

Throwing an arm around the man who had been his friend at one time, Lugh hugged Mitchell sideways.

"I've missed you, man."

That startled the attorney mid-laugh, and for a moment, Lugh thought he would pull away. Instead, Mitch snaked an arm behind Lugh and squeezed.

"I missed you, too."

"*Boys.*" Cybele rolled her eyes to the ceiling. "Are you ready to meet the boss?"

Mitchell protested. "What? Why? Look at me." He ran his fingers through his uncombed hair, embarrassed by his appearance.

"Because Assistant Director Elise Hester Johnson thought you might show up here and left specific instructions for you to be debriefed."

Cybele beamed at Jake. "Want to use the head before I take you up?"

"Don't, man," Lugh warned, struggling to keep a straight face. "A fellow just died in there." Then he met Mitchell's eyes, and they snickered like middle-schoolers.

"Can I use the loo on your floor?" Jake chuckled.

To which Cybele chirped, "Of course."

Upstairs, they were introduced to Rupert Wansley, the new, and rather young Head of the Alien Intelligence Agency. Then they whisked Jake away to be debriefed, and Mitch began sweating bullets.

He drew deep breaths as Cybele relayed her part of the tale, then kept breathing rhythmically while Director Wansley listened to Lugh describe the vast, icy wasteland and the blocks of ice in which they had been imprisoned.

When Lugh left out the thousands of dragons Emily had released into the wild, Mitch's heart pounded. Sweat dampened the front of his shirt and a ringing commenced in his ears. The room tilted slightly and closed in on Mitch, and it felt like he was in a well.

He gripped the arms of the office chair and sank deeper into its fake leather, sucking in air as the unfamiliar sensations bombarded him.

Then Mitch realized they were all looking at him. As his panic soared, his heat level rose. Fanning his shirt collar, Mitch asked the director to repeat his question, then haltingly relayed the details of the Reptilian attack on Zephyr Cay.

Oddly, describing the incident seemed to calm him rather than making it worse. He was pleasantly surprised when the AIA Director listened attentively, never looking at him sideways or blinking in reproach. When he congratulated Mitch on being brave enough to report the incident, profound relief washed over him.

Then, the director shared that the AIA was following up on the report from Zephyr Cay. They had also dispatched teams worldwide to cover similar sightings as they poured in. Mitch asked if they were investigating Patrika Tolbert's claim, but the director declined to disclose specifics.

Feeling somewhat better, Mitch trailed Lugh and Cybele MacBrayer to her office on the same floor. He wondered if they knew how close he'd come to losing it. Between the monster attack, the witch claiming to be his birth mother and his childhood nightmare coming true, something had happened to Mitch.

And that was *before* he'd been sucked through cloud tunnels from God-knows-where to England. As to what had happened to him, Mitch was clueless. He just knew he no longer felt the same.

"How long have you been working here?" he asked as they entered Cybele's tiny office.

Like the MacBrayer boys, she and Mitch had been friends. But he had not known they worked for a secret organization, much less one that oversaw alien activity.

Chill bumps brought an unsettling certainty. His old friends might be his only hope. And that had him shvitzing again.

Why was it so fricking hot in here? Mitch wiped his sweaty palms on his britches and flopped into a chair as Cybele slid behind her desk.

"I've been here for years," she answered with a wry smile.

Mitch's shoulders relaxed when Jake appeared at the door. His escort leaned inside. "He's all yours." Then, the crisply-clad woman turned and left down the polished hall.

Jake flopped into the only other available chair. Lugh propped on the corner of Cybele's desk. She shoved him off and went to find another.

☼☼☼

Lugh straddled the chair Cybele wedged beside Jake.

"Everything okay?" He punched Jake's shoulder. "They didn't demote you, did they?"

"Oh, don't you worry about me. I'm just peachy. But Agent Sorrell told me about you and the Order's new Grand Druid. And my son, too. She said y'all were in an earthquake. What the heck, Lugh? She said Hamilton Hester is dead and that all hell is breaking loose. Are Brian and some alien girl flying here with my boss? Is that all true?"

"Every bit." Lugh glanced at Cybele who nodded confirmation. "There's a lot more to it but we can catch up later. From what I hear, Brian came through with flying colors."

Jake beamed, then sobered. "And Hamilton Hester? He's dead, and we have a new Grand Druid?"

Lugh nodded. "Also true. Remember Emily? The one who freed us from the ice."

"The one you said you're going to marry?" Jake grinned. "Is that the girl who was kidnapped when we were kids?"

"One and the same."

"*I* found her," Mitch said smugly.

Lugh's mind wandered. Had Emily made it to Snowdonia? How long would it take for the dragon meet? It chaffed that he couldn't be there with her. But first things first.

"Mitch, you still haven't told us how you ended up as an icicle." Lugh clamped down on a yawn. "Sorry, I need sleep." Then, his stomach growled so loud everyone in the office heard. "*And* food." He grinned. "I'm starving."

"Me too," Jake moaned.

Cybele leapt from her chair. "Crap, I didn't even think about that. Shall I order us a pizza?" Her face scrunched. "No, not pizza. The pie here isn't nearly as good as Jocko's. Though there is this one place owned by a family from the Bronx. Theirs isn't half bad."

Lugh's mouth watered. "How about a nice, juicy steak? A really big one with a buttery baked potato and an enormous salad with bleu cheese dressing."

"And warm bread," Jake groaned.

"And a cold beer," Mitchell chimed in. "Quart-sized."

"You okay there, Mitch?" Lugh asked. The attorney looked a little pale.

"Yeah, just freaked out. And hungry. Steak sounds good to me."

"Alrighty, then. Steak it is." Cybele rescued her purse from a drawer, then squeezed by Lugh to get to the door. "But I can't guarantee the beer will be cold. Oh, wait."

She slid back around the desk to open a drawer, flashed them a big grin, and produced a package of Biscoff.

All three men lunged for it, but Lugh was closest. He peeled back the plastic, extracted a lone cookie, and chomped into it. Then, taking several more, he passed the sleeve to Mitch, who repeated Lugh's actions and passed it to Jake, whose stomach growled loudly on cue.

☼☼☼

Over dinner, they shared what had transpired in their lives, hitting the high spots since last seeing one another. Now stuffed to the max, Lugh sipped warm beer and laughed at Cybele's imitation of the ongoing battle between Elise Hester and the rude sergeant in her office.

Lugh had stayed close to his brother and looked forward to reuniting with Brian. But Cybele had stuck closer, barely taking her eyes from her ex since opening the door of Lost and Found and finding him puking his guts out.

Lugh had been shocked to learn Jake had gone to work for the AIA after graduating Georgia Tech. He'd been searching for clues about the dragons for the covert agency when he'd disappeared. Cybele started at there around the same time as Jake. And to think Lugh had just learned of the agency.

He guessed that was the whole point. The AIA was a secret organization formed toward the end of World War II, and according to Jake and Cybele, it recruited graduating druids from high school and college. From Mitch's reaction, Lugh could tell this was all news to him, too.

Lugh studied the attorney. He was regaling Cybele and Jake with details of his search for Emily Hester and how the previous firm had looked for twenty years to no avail. Why was his once-friend being so friendly? What had gotten into Mitch?

He hadn't sneered once since they'd landed in Lost and Found. Plus, he was being oddly clingy. He didn't seem to want to be alone without Lugh or Jake. Very different from the man who had avoided Lugh for years.

Mitchell looked up just then and caught him staring. A quick grin flashed, and Lugh instinctively smiled back. Then he looked away and stuffed a cold roll in his mouth. Not that he was still hungry. He just couldn't figure out what Mitchell was up to.

THE DOUGHNUT

The pilot's announcement woke Brian MacBrayer from the soundest sleep he'd had since the earthquake.

He yawned and sat up. Ethnui was awake, cap turned sideways, exposing her pointed ears and giving her a somewhat comical appearance. He laughed and pointed. She reddened and reached up to set it straight, then refastened the pins to hold it in place.

"How did you two sleep?" Elise asked from the opposite row.

"Like a log," Brian replied.

"Good, you may not get another opportunity for a while. We have work to do when we reach headquarters."

Ethnui stretched, one of those long, luxurious stretches accompanied by a shrill, squeaky exhale that sounded like pure bliss.

"And you, Ethnui? Did you sleep well?" Elise smiled.

The blue eyes widened and flitted to Brian, who nodded encouragement. Ethnui bobbled her head.

"I did, yes. But I have a kink in my back." She wiggled her rump in her seat, then wrapped both arms around her shoulders and slowly bent forward until her chest was in her lap. From that position, she rolled side to side, and after a loud pop, straightened and said, "There. That got it."

Brian unbuckled his seat belt to stand and stretch. But Elise shot him a stern look and shook her head, so he sat back down.

He was beyond excited to see his mother for the first time in months. Plus, according to Aunt Elise, his Uncle Lugh would be there, too.

The intercom crackled. "Please fasten your seat belts. We have clearance to land."

Twisting to stare out the window behind him, Brian cautiously moved to another seat to see the landscape better. He buckled in, ignoring Elise's stink eye, and waved to Ethnui, who scurried to join him.

Below them, the vast, sprawling metropolis stretched for miles and miles and miles and miles.

"That's London, England," he explained to Ethnui. "It's my first time here, but I've heard it's one of the most amazing cities in the world."

"It is *the* most amazing," Elise corrected. "Bar none." She sighed wearily, and Brian could tell she was exhausted, though she didn't look like it.

Ethnui sighed, suitably impressed. "Wow, it's so big. And beautiful."

Brian interlaced his fingers with the pretty Fomorian's and leaned his head close to gaze out the window beside her. In the distance, imposing mountains rose from the sea. Their soaring peaks brooded above small villages that dotted the valleys in between. One chain towered above all the rest.

"That should be Snowdonia," he murmured to Ethnui. "Home of the mythical Isle of Beli. That's where Emily will call the dragon meet." He wondered where she was and whether she'd made it to Europe.

As they descended, he pointed out Big Ben, Trafalgar Square, Buckingham Palace, the Thames River, and London Bridge, along with a few other places he recognized from history class, the news, and the internet.

They hit turbulence then, and the flight turned bumpy. Ethnui squeezed his hand tightly and Brian leaned close to whisper reassurance. She'd said they had flying vehicles in UnderEarth, but it was her first flight. He was a bit nervous, too. But he pretended to be okay for Ethnui.

The aircraft landed so softly and quietly Brian didn't realize they were on the ground until the pilot hit the brakes. Then, the ultra-sleek jet taxied to the gate. When Brian popped his seatbelt this time, Aunt Elise herded them off the plane toward a waiting van.

"Uncle Lugh!" Brian yelled, spying his face in the side window.

The door slid open, and his uncle climbed out. He threw his arms around Brian, and as they hugged, Brian spied something much unexpected. His heart skipped a beat. Could it really be?

"Dad!" he squealed, flying into Jake MacBrayer's open arms. "I knew you didn't leave us, I knew it, I knew it."

Then his mother wrapped her arms around them.

"Didn't I, Mama?

She beamed through tears and rocked him back and forth.

"Didn't I?" he said again through tears of his own.

"Yes, baby," she laughed, "you certainly did."

Then his dad engulfed both of them, and they cried, laughed, and rocked together. If he lived forever, Brian would never forget the details of that moment—the hot wind scouring the tarmac, the stench of burnt rubber, the horizontal windsocks, the thick, oppressive air that made it difficult to breathe, and his mother's eyes sparkling into his dad's.

Even his Uncle Lugh's eyes were misty. So were the guy's standing behind him. Brian did a double-take. Was that Mitchell Wainwright, the asshole attorney Emily had tossed from Wren's Roost?

Brian backed out of the hug and pointed at Mitchell who now peered at the oddly shaped Stealth Jet.

"What is *he* doing here?"

"It's a long story, Bri," Lugh murmured, "but we have to get you and Ethnui—"

Ethnui! Brian didn't hear the rest. He swiveled to find the Fomorian standing to the side, clutching at her cap in the strong wind. Her enormous blue eyes telegraphed shyness and a touch of fear. He extended a hand to his savior and crush and pulled her into his circle of humans.

"Mom, Dad, Lugh, meet Ethnui, the girl, umm…" Brian could feel his cheeks heating as Ethnui smiled and reached out a long arm to shake their hands.

"It's nice to meet the parents of such a remarkable young man." She glanced at Brian shyly. "He saved our lives more than once. Without Brian, I would still be in UnderEarth in a Reptilian prison."

"It was you, Ethnui. You saved me from becoming lizard food. If you hadn't rescued me from their dungeon—"

"Zip it," Elise interrupted, laying a hand on Brian's shoulder. "This is not runway conversation." She glanced around anxiously, assessing an invisible-to-Brian threat, then shooed them into the unmarked van.

Once inside, they all eyed one another. Brian broke the silence.

"I'm hungry."

Laughter exploded, and Brian winced. His appetite had always been a source of amazement to the people in his life.

His Uncle Lugh held out a triumphant hand. "See? What'd I tell you? Pay up, big brother."

To which Jake laughed and replied, "Okay, you were right. But I'll have to owe you, little brother."

"There's a steak dinner waiting for you at the Doughnut," Brian's mom interjected.

"The what, who, huh?" Brian squeaked. Ethnui giggled and scooched a hair closer to him.

"The Doughnut. That's the affectionate term for AIA headquarters."

"Why doughnut?"

"You'll see when we get there," Aunt Elise said mysteriously from the front seat. "Now, hush. I think someone is following us. Can you lose them?" she asked the driver.

Brian held on as the van made an abrupt right turn, then a two-wheeled one-eighty in a roundabout. Then, they zigzagged through traffic until the driver and Elise were sure the tail was gone.

"Why would anyone want to follow us?" Brian asked. "Who knows we're here? Or cares?"

In the back of his mind, Hamilton Hester hissed, "Are you kidding? It could be anyone. The enemy is nigh, young raven—in human form and Reptilian."

Chill bumps raced up and down Brian's back. He huddled lower, took his mom's hand, and pulled Ethnui close. The two of them had already escaped a living hell. This time, they had help. Adult help. People he trusted and who knew way more than Brian. But he sensed Ethnui's fear and distrust of the adults. She had retained her human-like form, but had drawn inside.

"It's okay," he whispered close to her ear. "We're safe with these guys. I promise." But the tightness around her eyes told Brian that the Fomorian remained wary and uncertain. And why wouldn't she? Hadn't he been in the same situation not long ago?

Yes, Brian had. And despite his terror, they had made it out. Together. Sliding his arm around Ethnui's narrow shoulders, Brian stayed that way until they pulled into the parking garage at the doughnut-shaped complex of the Alien Intelligence Agency in Cheltenham.

NOT EVEN SEX

Shalane guzzled her cooled coffee and poured another, adding a generous spoonful of sugar and an enormous dollop of whipped cream. They'd recorded her first Zoom show last night, and Shalane was playing it back and critiquing her performance.

She noted some things that needed improvement—mainly to do with her engagement. Playing to an onscreen audience had been odd, but that wasn't it. It was obvious to Shalane that her heart wasn't in it. She paused the playback and stared.

Yes, that was it. Shalane had not been able to summon even one ounce of give-a-shit. And not just about her First Evangelical Tour of America. *Nothing* seemed to interest Shalane. Not even sex.

It started after they checked out of the hotel in Vegas. On the way back to L.A., Shalane had come down with a mysterious fever, providing the final nail in the coffin of her tour. Her illness clinched the decision made by Cecil and her manager. Shalane would perform the remaining dates on Zoom rather than at the individual venues.

There was a quick knock, and Cecil poked his head in her office door. "My love, are you hungry? I was thinking of grabbing barbecue from Shirey's, but I'm open to suggestions if you'd rather have something else."

Shalane wagged her head woefully. "Honestly? Nothing sounds good. Just bring me whatever."

No, not even food, her first and most faithful love, could lure Shalane into giving a shit.

"I'll bring you a plate, then. With luck, you'll be hungry by the time we get back." With a lingering, slightly pitying look, Cecil ducked back out.

Adding a large shot of Kahlua to her coffee, Shalane savored the bite and relished the feel of it puddling on her tongue. With a few exceptions, she had shied away from liquor for much of her tour. Her failed tour. Now, it provided a modicum of comfort.

A quick spurt of shame heated her face. Some bigshot she turned out to be. She couldn't even complete a lousy 20-week tour. Of course, her puzzling collapse onstage in Las Vegas had put a monkey wrench in the works. And then there was that whole Reptilian thing.

Checking the time, Shalane switched on the television, tuning to CNN. Once the world had realized the monsters were real, Patty received invites to every talk show imaginable. Between Shalane and Patty's actress buddy, Latoya Cloud, they had culled the marginal ones and lined Patty up with the more well-known news and talk shows.

Latoya was with Patty today. Oddly, not even that had provoked Shalane's jealousy. For the first time in more years than Shalane could remember, nothing drove her. Not one fucking thing.

She felt oddly empty. For once, her mind was clear, unclouded by lust, greed, or ambition. The constant need for self-aggrandizement was gone. Shalane was free.

Even her guides had disappeared. Archangel Michael had not been back since that night in Vegas. And though Shalane had believed it was him making passionate love to her, in retrospect, she was no longer sure. She had a chilling memory of a Reptilian face leering at her afterward.

Chancy Transom's afternoon news show started, and Shalane increased the volume. Patrika appeared calm and collected, answering the host's questions with grace and humor. When she completed the ten-minute segment, young Patty glowed as the audience applauded, howled, and catcalled.

Weirdly, Shalane couldn't be happier. Patrika was getting her opportunity to become the "someone" she craved.

SECOND THOUGHTS

Nergal huddled in a shallow indentation beneath a stand of yucca and pinyon pines. He had known the humans outnumbered his warriors, but their plan of attack had considered that.

At twilight, he and Azi had shape-shifted into officers, then let the others in once night fell. His Dracs had worked their way through the barracks, killing every human they encountered.

Then, a dragon appeared, and all hell broke loose. It picked his warriors off as they exited the buildings. Nergal's disguise had saved him, but he was uncertain about Azi, who'd yet to join him in the desert.

He rolled to his back in the uncomfortable uniform, unwilling to return to his own shape until he was sure the danger had passed. The sharp scent of pine rosin and desert grit penetrated his nose slits, and he stifled a sneeze. Groaning, Nergal twisted back to his belly and crawled through the sand for a better view of the installation.

The dragon had departed, and several armed guards returned from scouring the desert. Now, the lights in the barracks they had failed to reach went out one by one.

After the spotlight passed over his hiding place, Nergal inspected his leg by starlight. The razor wire had ripped through the uniform, drawing blood. The wound stung, but it was superficial and had stopped bleeding.

He blinked at the stars dotting AboveEarth's sky, and the uneasy feeling he had had since leaving UnderEarth struck him full force. What in Enlil's name was he doing up here? Nergal had forgotten how uncomfortable being on the surface made him feel.

The desire to conquer humans no longer drove him. All he wanted was to return to Xibalba IX and escape the vast openness of Earth's surface. How did they stand it up here? Especially when the harsh conditions robbed millennia from their lives.

The bloodlust that had been Nergal's lifelong companion seemed to be gone, replaced by a plague he could only describe as conscience. Not long ago, he had been arrogantly immune to such emotions. Now, he dwelt in them—an alarming prospect for a Draco of his caliber.

The vengeance he felt for Shibboleth was still there. Nergal wanted the warlord dead. But the humans had done nothing to deserve the systematic cleansing his race would deliver.

Each time Nergal cast about for an answer to his change of heart, he returned to the same conclusion. Somehow or another, the doctora had cast a spell on him. Or it could have been Ishkur. Or Inanna. Regardless, ever since the day Nergal sought aid from the doctora, something had shifted inside him. And not necessarily for the better.

A late-rising moon peeked over the horizon. Azi should have been here by now. A coyote wailed behind the undulating dunes, and a tingle ran up Nergal's spine. He flattened to the ground as others joined the eerie chorus.

Behind him came a crunch, and Nergal froze. He moved his head slightly to follow the sound, then relaxed. Inanna Shibboleth's Spawn stalked silently toward his hiding place, looking none too pleased.

"Get down," he hissed as the spotlight circled closer.

She crouched low until it passed, then closed the gap to squat beside him.

"Where is the dragon?"

"Gone."

"And your Dracs?"

"Dead."

"Azi?"

Nergal kept his attention on the base. "We were to retreat before moonrise, and he is not back. You tell me."

The spotlight passed over, and they hunkered in the sand.

"We must return to the caves." Inanna rose to her feet. "Azi knows the way. He will join us if he can."

There was a snap behind her.

Inanna wheeled, drawing a blade from her belt and gutting the man in one fluid motion.

A shudder passed over Nergal. He peered around them into the dark desert, searching for other would-be assassins. Then, with one last glance at the military installation, he loped with Inanna to the caves.

RENDEZVOUS AT JOCKO'S

Alexis bit into a slice of pizza and made pleasure noises while her rear end did a happy dance in the padded seat. For twenty-five years, she had searched for pie rivaling Jocko's, but none had come close. She sighed and took another bite, savoring the flavors bursting on her tongue.

Like its pizza, Jocko's décor had changed little. The owners had reconfigured the storefront but retained the large bank of windows. Today, drawn shades blocked the scorching midafternoon heat.

The door jingled, and Alexis sat at attention, hoping the summoning spell she had performed before entering had produced her sister Rona.

But it was a couple of women with two pre-teen girls. Alexis relaxed and munched her pizza. Another twenty minutes passed, her head jerking each time the door jingled. Rona had never been one to leave the house without makeup—or to arrive on time. Alexis ordered a refill of sweet tea with lemon and settled in to wait.

Humming a James Taylor tune playing overhead, Alexis was wondering if she should cast a more potent spell when a crack of thunder startled her.

Then the doorbell jingled, and Rona Wainwright bustled in. Alexis's heart thumped. She scanned the overflowing dining room and turned to leave. But Alexis stood and beckoned to her.

Puzzlement deepened the lines across Rona's forehead. When had her twin gotten so old? She glided toward Alexis, who lowered Honey's frame into the chair and waved to the open bench.

"I have room. Please, join me."

Wary, Rona scanned the dining room again, then sighed and sat. "Hi. Are you sure? I don't mind coming back later. Or waiting."

"That's okay. I called you here, Rona."

Shock tightened the familiar features. "Do I know you?"

"Yes. You don't remember me, but I have the information you seek."

Rona's brows knit, and she searched Honey's face. "About my son? Do you know where he is? Are you his friend?"

Alexis relaxed. Maybe this wasn't a bad idea after all.

"I know what happened. But I do not know where Mitch is now. I'm looking for him, too."

The waitress interrupted, handing Rona a menu and a glass of water. "Could I get you something to drink?"

"No, water's good." Rona handed the menu back. "But could you bring me some lemon? I'd like your chef salad, please."

"What? No pizza?" Alexis teased when the waitress retreated.

Rona sipped water, waved at an acquaintance across the dining room, then eyed Alexis.

"No, I had pizza the other day, and that's my limit for the week. What did you say your name is?"

"Honey. Honey Dewars."

"And you're Mitch's friend?"

Alexis hesitated, then blurted, "Sort of. I have something very important to tell you, Rona. But first, you have to promise not to freak out."

Rona's face went white. She gripped the shellacked table and leaned toward Alexis.

"Where is Mitch? What happened? Tell me!"

"It was Morgan, Rone."

Rona's head snapped up at the pet name. "What did you call me?"

"Morgan did it."

"Morgan did what? Who are you?" Thunder boomed, drawing both women's gaze to the windows. The storm had moved in fast.

"The name on my driver's license is Honey Dewars. But I am a druid spirit inhabiting Honey's body. I am Alexis, your sister. Alexis Mayhall Hester."

Rona recoiled as if slapped.

"Alexis is dead." Red mottled her face and neck.

"Yes. I was. But death isn't what we thought, Rone."

Unwavering, stony eyes glared at her. Alexis looked away and sipped tea to steady her nerves. Then, with a deep breath, Alexis spilled her guts.

"After I died, I wandered the Underworld for what seemed forever. Then, a dragon appeared. She offered me redemption if I would do as she bade. After all those years of torture and misery, I jumped at the chance. But when I completed the task, the dragon was gone.

"I ended up on an island where I saw your Mitch. He went inside a shop, and I was curious, so I followed. But something weird happened. Against my will, my spirit was drawn into the old shopkeeper."

Alexis shuddered, remembering. "She had this sapphire brooch and kept shoving it at Mitch. When he finally took it, there was an explosion, and a hole opened in the floor. Then these scary, lizard-like monsters poured out."

Rona's eyes had filled with contempt. Before she could say what she was thinking, Alexis added, "I swear, Rona. I'm telling you the truth. That shopkeeper must have known magic because my powers were stronger than in real life. I could even fly. I know it sounds unbelievable, but I stopped those lizard men from capturing Mitch. He can confirm what I'm saying."

Her twin was nearly vibrating now. She ignored the rumble of thunder, leaned across the table, and said quietly, "Worse than crazy. You sound like a raving lunatic. But we'll come back to that. What kind of pet did I have as a child?"

Sadness squeezed Alexis's heart. She sucked in a breath and looked down at her hands. "I don't know, Rona. They separated us. We didn't grow up together."

The guarded eyes narrowed. "And how did you come by that information?"

Alexis sighed and threw her hands in the air. "I told you. I am your sister, Rone. I'm Alexis." She suppressed a sob. "Your twin sister, though not identical. May I finish the story?"

Rona nodded reluctantly.

"Once I defeated the monsters, I was able to leave the proprietress and transfer into Honey. I knew she was returning to Atlanta, so I hitchhiked here. With her permission, of course."

"And Mitchell?"

"He returned as well."

The server delivered Rona's salad, then retreated discreetly. Slowly and deliberately, Rona lifted her cutlery, shredded the salad into bite-sized pieces, and then poured dressing over part of it. When she finally looked at Alexis, her face twisted in a sneer.

"As you can imagine, I'm having a hard time believing you. What did you mean about Morgan?" "I know you remember how much I worshiped Morgan," Alexis said softly. "She told me since she couldn't be the Awen, I would be next in line as Hamilton's wife. Of course, that didn't happen. Morgan blamed it on Hamilton and the Order. Then, she drove a wedge between me and Emily.

"You tried to tell me, Rone. You said she was spouting lies. But I believed Morgan and quit speaking to you. For that, I am sorrier than you could know."

"And what does Morgan have to do with my son's disappearance?"

Alexis swallowed hard and glanced at the door. The sun shone again. The storm had passed. "The two of them fought over the sapphire brooch. Morgan swore it belonged to the Hester family, and Mitchell insisted he had to take it to Emily. When he wouldn't let Morgan have it, she flew into a rage and hurled a curse. Mitchell disappeared holding the brooch she wanted."

Rona leapt up and gripped the table as her chair toppled. She leaned toward Alexis and growled in a low voice, "Look here, you cheap floozy. Tell me where my son is before I call the police."

"You don't want to do that, Rona. They'll say we're both crazy. Sit down, and we'll figure this out together."

"You *are* crazy," Rona spat through clenched teeth. Then, noticing the prying eyes, she set her chair upright and plopped down.

"Look," Alexis said, knowing Rona was about to bolt, "There is something only you, your husband, me, and Hamilton knew. Emily is your daughter, and Mitch is my son. Ham needed a girl to be his precious Awen, so he switched our babies at birth. His betrayal was the last straw. Between that and Morgan's smear campaign, it broke me. And you know it, Rona. I *am* Alexis."

As she talked, the color drained from Rona's face. She wrung her hands, then planted her face in them and sobbed quietly.

Alexis glanced around anxiously. "Rona? People are staring."

"You should've thought of that before you dragged me here with whatever spell you concocted." Rona sniffed. "What do you want from me, Alexis? After twenty-five years with no word from you, I'm supposed to jump for joy because you've returned from the dead? You made my life miserable before, and now you're at it again."

That took Alexis aback. "What do you mean?"

"You and your precious Katy Kats bullied me through high school. Then, I loved your son as my own and had to watch you ignore my Emily, helpless to interfere. When you kidnapped her, part of me died. Yet I couldn't grieve. Not like a mother or sister should.

"Now you're telling me that Morgan Foster, a woman I've come to trust and respect, is responsible for Mitchell's disappearance? I just can't, Alexis."

She hung her head, mortified. "I'm sorry, Rona—for all of it. My actions were unforgivable. But Morgan is the real instigator, I promise." Desperate tears filled her eyes, and Alexis dashed them away. Though the memories were painful, they were way beyond tears.

"And I promise you, cross my heart and hope to die," she traced an x on her chest, "Morgan's spell disappeared Mitch. You can ask Arthur Creeley. He saw it, too."

Emotion clouded Rona's eyes. "I didn't know if my little girl was alive or dead. Or you, either." A tear slid down her cheek. "We searched and searched. Hamilton never gave up. On Emily or you."

A warmth bloomed in Alexis's solar plexus. "He didn't?" Without meaning to, she exclaimed, "I still love him, Rona. I messed up big time. With Ham. With you. And with Emily."

"You can say that again." Rona picked up her fork, stuffed salad in her mouth, and chewed, looking thoughtful.

"So, you believe me?" Alexis held her breath. Her plan hinged on Rona helping.

Finally, Rona swallowed. "I reckon," she mumbled before forking another bite. They eyed one another across the table, and Alexis held out her hand.

"Truce?"

"Truce." Rona's eyes blazed. "But if I get one hint that you are playing me, I will reveal your secrets to the Order."

"Fair enough." Alexis tossed Honey's thick blond hair, heart thrilled. "Will you help me find Mitch and Emily? And bring those monsters down?"

"Not that last part," Rona said through a mouthful of salad. "But I *will* help you find our kids."

☼☼☼

Rona was still skeptical of the woman claiming to be Alexis Mayhall Hester, but when the blonde named Honey finished bouncing in celebration, Rona asked, "So now what?"

"Now we find our kids."

Shivers galloped up Rona's spine and skittered across her scalp. "Alrighty, then."

They sat quietly, long enough for Rona to finish her salad and the nearby tables to clear. Her friend Juanita waved on the way out. Rona nodded with a smile. Honey observed everything with keen interest and chatted candidly with a handsome man who was obviously an ex.

It occurred to Rona that maybe Honey and Alexis were finding their bearings, too. It couldn't be easy sharing a body. She signaled the server to pay the check.

"I need to change clothes and grab some things for the trip," Rona finally said. She was loathe to delve into the traumatic depths of her childhood. But her twin sister was back, literally from the dead, and had a chance at redemption. Apparently, this was her only path. And, bonus, she would help Rona find Mitch.

Plunking an azure blue Birkin bag on the table, Honey chirped, "Should I follow you?" Just shy of neon, the purse highlighted Honey's eyes. Still, the Druid Hills Shelter could've helped many homeless with that fifty thousand dollars.

"Nah." Rona dug into her low-level designer purse and laid enough cash to cover both checks plus a generous tip down near the Birkin. Honey protested, and Rona waved her off.

She cocked an eye at the busty blonde. "Maybe I could hitch a ride? I walked over."

"No wonder it took you so long to get here." The snorted quip was classic Alexis.

Rona grabbed her forearm and searched the blue eyes. Sure enough, her sister was in there, the one who had kowtowed to no one. Until she did.

"Well, it wasn't like we had an appointment." Rona let go and stood to leave.

"If I thought you would come, I would've tried that." Honey rose and stretched, drawing the eye of every male left in the place. Then she tucked the Birkin beneath her arm. "But for the sake of urgency, I resorted to magic."

Oppressive heat greeted them outside—so much for the storm cooling it off as Rona had hoped. The sun beat down, and steam curled from the sidewalk. Sweat popped out on her lip, and her linen slacks and blouse clung to her frame. Whistling appreciatively, Rona tried not to groan as she lowered her body carefully into the passenger seat of Honey's Porsche.

"Nice ride," she commented, stopping herself from sniping, 'though not built for people my age.' She fumbled for the shoulder harness and buckled in.

Then Honey peeled out onto North Decatur Boulevard. Rona grabbed the chicken strap when she cut off an SUV whose driver was less than delighted. He laid on his horn and threw a one-finger salute.

Honey hooted with laughter, a deep-throated, delightful cascade of merriment, and returned the gesture. Then she popped the clutch, shifted gears, and sped down an open side street.

Rona gripped the strap as they took the turn too fast, and the opening strains of Helen Reddy's classic *I Am Woman* wafted from the radio. Honey cranked it up, and between there and Canongate, they belted out the words of their childhood anthem. The sporty Porsche wheeled into Rona's front drive with no prompts from her, and she got another rash of chills.

"The place looks good, Rona," Honey drawled, cutting her eyes sideways. Alexis despised the Wainwrights and had disapproved of Rona's courtship and marriage to Mitchell Junior.

Instructing her to park in an empty stall in the main garage, Rona led Honey/Alexis to the kitchen. Luckily, her live-in housekeeper was out doing the marketing, and her husband was in Spain doing God knows what.

She wheeled and demanded, "Are you really who you say you are?"

"Druids' honor." Alexis crossed both arms over her heart.

"Why do you think I can help you find Mitch and Emily?"

"Not help me, Rone. Do it." Alexis leaned her elbows on the luxurious granite counter.

The kitchen was enormous and, like the house, bordered on tacky. The Wainwrights had helped settle Druid Hills—the mansion and sprawling grounds dated back to Olmsted's day. Unfortunately, the family had raised snobby children, and their IQs, while adequate, left much to be desired. Rona's husband was different. Yes, he exhibited the same arrogance and had passed it on to Mitch. But he was brilliant and dashing despite his tendency to wander.

"What do you mean by 'do it'?" Rona wondered. "How?"

"By using your mother mojo. Mine's not working. On either of our children."

Rona nearly choked on saliva, but she grabbed Honey's arm when she could breathe again.

"You really are Alexis, aren't you? Who else would know this stuff?" She hugged her long-lost sister close. "But how is you being here even possible?"

"Right?!" Alexis crowed. "I've been wondering the same thing. It's mind-boggling. Yet here I am. Yes, I have to share a body. But I'm alive, Rone. I'm alive!"

Rona groaned and slumped into a chair. "Please tell me Honey is okay with you taking over her body."

The blonde struck a pose, fluffed her big hair, and drawled in a strikingly different voice, "Hell yeah! I've heard rumors about druids all my life. But damn, you all are the real deal, magic and all. I'm in, Miz Rona, I'm in!"

Alexis grinned and gurgled in her own voice, "See! Now will you use your mother mojo and find our kids?"

"Come."

Marching to her office, Rona let Alexis enter first, then locked the door of her private sanctum. She breathed in the spicy odor of incense and ancient manuscripts and removed the small chest from its hiding place. Then, settling into the chair opposite her twin, Rona opened it with a spell.

She removed her scrying ball and unwrapped it with reverence, gently setting it on its velvet square. Then, speaking another, more complicated spell, she trained her eyes on the quartz sphere and let her vision go soft. Her attention was instantly drawn inside the globe, and a scene appeared, too far away to make out the details.

Closer and closer, Rona zeroed in until her heart thumped wildly. Mitch was not in sight, but Emily traded curses with what appeared to be a witch. Snow-covered mountains surrounded them.

Then, Emily went down, and an icy wind shrieked, blowing through Rona. Chills bent her double as ice ran up her spine. Then, strong arms closed around her and dragged her back. She came to, wrapped in Honey's arms.

"What happened?"

"I saw Emily. It's worse than we thought, Alexis."

"Worse than monsters killing us and taking over the world?"

"Maybe. Emily needs our help. There's a witch. A powerful one."

Rona might be back in her home, but the chills lingered. She grabbed a thick throw and wrapped it around her shoulders, then let her body shake until the worst of it passed. Honey held her hand, rubbing it briskly, eyes as big as Wales.

"Wales!" Rona gulped. "Emily is in Wales. Below the summit of Yr Wyddfa. We vacationed there a few years ago."

Hot now, she tossed the blanket aside and retrieved a frosty, long-necked Budweiser. Handing it to Honey, Rona popped the top of another, guzzled half, and belched like a carbon-emitting road hog. Then she swiped her chin with the back of her hand.

Honey had whipped a tablet from her Birkin bag and searched for flights to Wales.

"The soonest we can get there is tomorrow afternoon. We'll need to rent a car and drive to the park. If we're lucky, the train is running, and we can take it to the summit."

Urgency overcame Rona. "Emily will be dead by then."

"Why? What did you see?"

"Our daughter alone battling a witch. And Alexis, Emily is way outmatched."

Alexis shivered visibly. Then, a speculative glint crept into her eyes. She lowered her voice to a conspiratorial tone.

"Can you think of a faster way to get us there?"

Rona hesitated, and Alexis pushed. "Do you remember what Awen taught us when we were little? About moving from place to place using magic?"

"That was a long time ago."

"Yes. It was. So long, I don't remember. But I think you do."

Rona smiled. She reached into the bottom of the small chest and pulled out a slip of papyrus. Quickly scanning it, she folded it and placed it back in the chest, wrapped the crystal ball, and secured it atop the papyrus.

Then, sealing the box with a spell, she put it away, locked the cabinet, and surveyed the room, letting her gaze linger on her beloved druid keepsakes and artifacts.

Out of the blue, Honey chirped, "Does Mitch make a habit of dating floozies?"

Rona chuckled. "Not a habit, no. But he does on occasion. Why?"

"You called me one," Honey drawled. "Do you really think I look like a floozy?"

Rona burst out laughing.

When the red lips pooched in a pout, she grudgingly admitted, "Honestly? I think you look like a million bucks."

THE INFIRMARY

Mitch kept an eye on Jake MacBrayer. His old friend had been throwing up off and on since they'd landed in AIA's Lost and Found. But Jake seemed to be getting worse. Mitch shoved his chair from the table and pulled Lugh to the side.

"I think something's wrong with Jake. He's still throwing up, and look," he eyed Jake over his shoulder, "he's disoriented." They watched him shake his head, not comprehending the agent's question.

Lugh eyed Mitch with curiosity, and Mitch chuckled. He had been an arrogant asshat ever since learning Hamilton Hester was his father. But since the world's existence apparently depended on it, he'd decided it was time to let bygones be bygones.

Lugh scrutinized his brother with concern. "After being frozen for a year, it's a wonder he's alive. But I don't feel that great either. How are you feeling?"

"I'm fine," Mitch said, then thought of the blood in his puke. "Well, mostly. I have a raging headache and could sleep for a week." Then purple blood and stinking lizard guts swam before his eyes, and Mitch gagged.

Concern clouded Lugh's expression, but Mitch shrugged it off. "What do you think about Jake? I'm worried."

Lugh gave him that odd look again. "I'll talk to Elise. After what we went through, I'm surprised they didn't give us a once over like Brian and Ethnui."

Upon arriving at Cheltenham, the two youngsters had eaten steak meals then were whisked to the medical unit. Brian had since been released and declared free of contagious UnderEarth illnesses, at least as far as they could tell. The girl had yet to return.

While Lugh went to consult with Elise in a quiet corner, Mitch surveyed the activity in the large room. They were on the top floor, only four flights up, but had an excellent view of London and its Gloucestershire suburbs. In front of a large screen depicting maps and charts, Brian MacBrayer worked with Agent Rancone to identify the Reptilian base where he'd been held.

Cybele joined the agent talking to Jake. At dinner, Jake had told the group he remembered nothing except hiking to the summit of Yr Wyddfa while searching for dragons. Then everything had gone black until Emily released them.

Mitch found this odd, considering he remembered exactly how he had gotten there. So did Lugh. He and Emily were cursed by a witch named Bé Chuille and then found themselves frozen in the middle of the dragons.

Had Jake somehow stumbled across this Bé Chuille and been sent there unawares? Had she used the same curse Morgan used on Mitch? And if so, was this witch somehow connected to Morgan?

A chill went through him. Were Morgan and the witch colluding with the Reptilians and conspiring against the Druids?

An agent escorted the Fomorian into the room. She looked more like a girl than an alien—tall and thin with long arms and legs. Her hair was a thick mass of straight brown hair. It covered her pointed ears, as did the cap she wore. Her eyes were prominent, more so than any human's eyes. Then Mitch remembered Shalane's. Hers were also larger than life.

Holy shit. In the craziness, Mitch had forgotten about Shalane. He didn't usually go for older women but had a bad itch for this one. He fetched his cell phone from the charging station and stared at the screen. There were nine voice messages and twelve texts. Several were from Rochelle, his legal assistant. The rest were from Patty and Shalane's phones.

Stepping into the hallway, Mitch accessed his voicemail as Elise, Cybele, and Jake emerged and headed for the elevator. Elise asked Mitch to join them in the Infirmary when he was done.

He nodded and listened to Rochelle's messages. When she hadn't heard from Mitch on Monday, she had rescheduled his meetings. But a court hearing needed to be addressed.

He rang her number back and left instructions on her voicemail for the next several days. His partner could handle any court appearances or have them delayed. Then, Mitch went through the rest of the messages and texts.

He was about to call Shalane, who had awakened from the coma when the elevator doors opened. Elise appeared and crooked a finger to Mitch.

"The doctor wants to see you."

Mitch followed the fascinating old bat to the Infirmary.

As it turned out, they had a full hospital ward with a doctor, nurses, and aides. Mitch was happy to see Jake confined to a bed, where IV fluids dripped and machines beeped. They were in the middle of doing a workup on him, complete with EKG, CT scans, bloodwork, and other labs.

So far, they'd found a low body temperature, severe dehydration, and out-of-balance electrolytes, but they'd ruled out anything more serious. A Bair Hugger piped warm air around him to heat his core.

A perky redheaded nurse named Flo—short for Florence because she had been born there—settled Mitch in a private exam room. Flo recorded all his personal information and then took his vitals and several vials of blood. After that, she had him pee in a cup in a bathroom that smelled strongly of bleach, then escorted him to Imaging, where he changed into scrubs.

As he shucked his pants and folded them across the chair, Mitch was careful to make sure the sapphire brooch was secure. Then, feeling a pang at parting with the heirloom, he donned the maroon scrubs and waited for Flo.

Soon, she collected Mitch and led him to the Imaging Department. They met Lugh on his way out.

"All clear?" Mitch asked.

Lugh shrugged, and his aide replied, "The radiologist has to read the images first." Then she herded Lugh away, and it was Mitch's turn.

By the time they were done examining him, Mitch had been thoroughly poked, prodded, and photographed. Then, the sparkly Flo took him to a quiet ward.

Jake was asleep in one of the beds. Lugh sat in a chair facing him, talking quietly on his cell. He watched Flo seat Mitch in the chair on the opposite side and connect an IV to his arm.

"To help with the dehydration," Flo explained.

Mitch gave Lugh a thumbs-up, and the druid priest smiled thinly. Then Flo told Mitch to close his eyes and rest.

"What? No bed for me?" He flashed his most charming smile, and Flo batted her eyes suggestively.

"Do you think you need one?"

For a half second, Mitch considered her offer, then shook his head and grinned. "Not to recover."

"As I thought," she quipped. "If you need anything or change your mind, just press this button. I'll be back in a bit to check on you."

☼☼☼

Lugh ended the call with his manager and scooted his chair closer to the bed to face Mitchell.

"So. Morgan Foster turned you into a popsicle, huh?"

A vein bulged in the attorney's neck. He took a deep breath and blew it out, then nodded.

"Morgan threw the curse. But not for nothing. It wasn't the first time I was there. Remember?" Mitch's hopeful gaze jarred loose a memory that had been niggling at Lugh.

Chill bumps danced along his shoulders and arms. For years, his old friend had had awful nightmares—always about being frozen in an icy wasteland of what he had called dragon popsicles. Lugh's chill bumps grew more intense.

"I do remember. Who would've thought your old nightmares would come to pass?" He gazed over Mitchell's shoulder, thoughtful. "Or that it would be Morgan who did it?"

"Did what?" Puzzlement crinkled Mitch's eyes.

Lugh shook his head. Fog had plagued his brain since the earthquake, and it'd worsened since waking up on the tundra. To buy time, he sat up straight, glanced at Jake's monitors, then back at Mitch.

"Did what, Lugh? It would be Morgan who did what?"

Resting his chin in his hands, Lugh propped his elbows against his abdomen and sighed heavily. Then, staring into Mitchell's ice-blue eyes, he confessed something he probably shouldn't.

"Someone poisoned Hamilton Hester. He thought it might be you." He watched as shock rippled through Mitch.

"Me? Why would I poison Hamilton? I've been angry at him for years, but he's my father, Lugh. My birth father. Why would I want to kill him?"

"I don't know. But Ham suspected you. Maybe because you were so arrogant and bitter. Did you ever talk to him about it?"

Mitchell snorted. "Seriously? The man barely spoke to me. When he engaged my law firm to find Emily, I thought that would change. Then, when I found her, I thought, 'Now, Hamilton Hester will acknowledge me.' But he didn't, Lugh. Now he's dead, and I'll never have that."

Agony twisted Mitchell's features, and Lugh finally understood what had driven him. Then, the attorney's mask fell back in place.

Lugh was asleep when Mitch realized something. The animosity he'd felt toward his old friend was gone, which was good because Mitch needed his help.

Part of him wondered why he bothered, but the rest knew he had no choice. A shriveled old woman named Madame Bouvee had taken the matter out of his hands.

Lugh slept in his chair, and Jake sawed serious logs, but Mitch could not get comfortable. When he closed his eyes, the sinewy creatures with snakelike heads, glowing red eyes, and vicious teeth were there, along with the horrid stench of lizard guts.

Rising from the Naugahyde chair, Mitch crossed quietly to the bathroom. Lugh snorted and rolled his head to the side, but neither man woke. Latching the door, Mitch stared at himself in the mirror.

Despite the bit of color he'd picked up in the Bahamas, his face looked pale in the blue fluorescent light. He rubbed his palm over the thick stubble that was rapidly growing into a beard. His corneas were shot through with red squiggles, and eyes that receded into purpling sockets stared back at him. Mitch splashed cold water on his face, weary to the bone.

Then, slicking his normally-groomed hair back with water, he felt the familiar outline of the brooch where he leaned against the sink. Madame Bouvee's demanding face flashed before him, and Mitch clutched the sink, trembling.

The moment the heirloom had been in his hands, the floorboard had caved and the lizard monsters had appeared, sending Mitch's world into a tailspin. It had not corrected since, and deep inside, Mitch knew it never would.

He thought longingly of his casual conceit and self-absorbed sense of entitlement. What he wouldn't give to turn back the clock, to unsee the horror, and walk away unscathed, lack of conscience intact. But he was beginning to understand that to escape this endless loop of terror, he would have to do what Madame Bouvee had commanded.

It was time to stand and fight. Unfortunately for Mitch, that meant helping the one he despised the most—the twin sister who'd been handed the acceptance, power, and position Mitch had long desired.

Emily's image appeared in the mirror, voice taunting. "You know, you could've given the sapphire to me when I freed you from the ice." Fury seized him.

Barely restraining the urge to slam his fist into her perfect teeth, Mitch seethed. Then her face was gone, and his own stared at him.

"Why didn't you think of that, dumbass?"

Someone rapped on the door, and Mitch nearly jumped from his skin.

"How long you gonna be in there, dude? You okay?"

Mitch scrubbed his face in his hands. He really should ask for a shaving kit. Then an idea came to him. He opened the door and dragged Lugh inside.

The druid priest ogled him, sidled to the toilet, and let go of his bladder.

"Lu-Mac, I need your help. I wish I'd thought to do it when I had the chance, but…" Mitch slid the brooch from his pocket and stared at the mesmerizing stone. "I have to get this to Emily right away. It's important."

"What is it?"

Mitch held the sapphire brooch so that it sparkled blue in the harsh light. Lugh rolled his eyes.

"A pin? Isn't it a bit late for Christmas presents? And early for Emily's birthday?"

Mitch splashed water at him.

"Heeey!" Lugh hissed, finishing his business. "Not funny." He wiped his face on his sleeve.

"Neither is your wit. I'm serious, Lugh. Madame Bouvee insisted I get this brooch to Emily. She even implied that world-ending shit would happen if I don't. And based on what I saw in Zephyr Cay, I'm inclined to believe the old coot."

Lugh stared at the brooch and lathered his hands. When he finally said, "Well then, I guess we better get it to her," Mitch relaxed a little.

"But how?" Lugh added, and Mitch's shoulders inched back up toward his ears.

✧✧✧

Lugh pondered Mitchell's bombshell. He was shocked the attorney had gotten his hands on one of Awen's wandstones. He was even more surprised Mitch would relinquish the stone to Emily.

"I hate to tell you, but in case you weren't paying attention, Emily is on a mountain in Wales. It's not that far as the crow flies. But assuming Elise would let us out of here, by the time we catch a flight and find transportation up the mountain, Emily will likely be done and gone from there."

"Can she call the dragons without all the stones?"

How many times had Lugh wondered the same thing? "I don't know. But we should get going. The Reptilians have begun their invasion, so we don't have the luxury of time."

"What's the quickest way to get there?" Mitch rubbed his stubbly chin, then his eyes lit. "Do you think Elise could get us on that stealth jet?"

"I doubt it." A vision of Cu transporting him between centuries flashed in Lugh's brain. "Cu!" he exclaimed, and nearly swallowed his tongue when the dog appeared in the bathroom.

"At your service," he barked.

"What the—?" Mitchell tried to flatten his body against the tile as Cu wagged his tail and wiggled ecstatically. "Where the hell did you come from?"

Cu barked and licked Lugh's face.

"I think he heard me call his name. The Elders typically only answer to the Awen, but you came, boy, you came!"

Mitchell reached for the doorknob, and Lugh grabbed his elbow.

"I think Cu is our transportation to Emily. If it works, that is."

The attorney jerked his arm away and eyed Lugh as if he'd gone mad.

"Seriously? That dog can take us to Emily?"

"I think so. He's done it before."

Mitchell shook his head doubtfully. "If you think it'll work, I'm in."

"We have to tell the others first."

"They'll try to stop us."

"Or maybe they'll help us," Lugh countered.

DR. HANNAH NOLAN

Hannah crouched in the dark behind a counter, clutching an open scalpel. Whether she dared to use it was another matter. She was a healer, not a fighter. Still, the attackers had killed Airmen in their beds. Hannah had heard the commotion and ran to the barracks. But if the DAF Police Force had not arrived, Hannah, too, would likely be dead.

She retched and clapped a hand over her mouth. Never had she seen so much gore in one place, even during the war.

Footsteps sounded outside the lab. Then the lights blazed on. A Department of the Air Force Policewoman entered, weapon raised.

Relieved, Hannah folded the scalpel and stood, hands in the air. "It's just me."

The policewoman swung the weapon toward her. "Anyone else in here?" Hannah wagged her head, and Sergeant Dahl yelled into the hall, "All clear!"

Then, she holstered her weapon and saluted.

"Thank you, Lieutenant Colonel. We're sweeping the compound for stragglers now."

"Has the th-threat been neutralized?" Hannah stammered. "Are there any survivors?"

"If so, they would be in sick bay."

"I'll check." Hannah slid the scalpel into her jacket pocket and rounded the counter. "If that's okay."

"Of course, Ma'am. But be careful. If you see any red-eyed monsters, give us a shout." Then the woman was gone, and Hannah hurried to sick bay.

Two medics and a nurse worked over a bloody Noncom whose skivvies were slit, revealing a gash across his chest. The man's face was white, his breathing shallow.

The medics parted for Hannah, who consulted the beeping monitors. His blood pressure was dangerously low. He'd lost a lot of blood.

"They brought him in just after the alarms went off," Medic Arnold reported. "Palmer started him on an IV and a broad-spectrum antibiotic while Ulster and I stopped the bleeding. That's all we've done so far."

"Let's get him on the operating table. That wound needs closing. And start him on a liter of blood." They prepared to wheel the victim to an operating room.

"Have there been any others?"

Medic Arnold answered. "No, Ma'am. This is the only one."

Sighing heavily, Hannah closed her eyes to think, then startled awake. She had pulled two doubles with little shuteye in between. Now, Hannah was passing out on her feet. If she didn't get some sleep soon, she would be of scant use to anyone.

But first things first.

☼☼☼

Surgery complete, Hannah washed up and hurried to the small house at the edge of the desert that had been her home for the last couple of years. Shucking her doctor's jacket and uniform in the clothes bin, she stepped into the shower, groaning with fatigue as the hot water beat against her.

The bloody scene in the barracks flashed before her as she toweled dry. A sob escaped. Then she emptied her mind, lotioned up against the desert air, and blew her hair dry.

She longed to climb into her bed but the growl in Hannah's stomach had turned to an ache. She had not eaten in—she thought for a moment—eleven hours. No wonder she had nearly passed out.

Padding to the kitchen, she retrieved the leftover Shepherd's Pie, nuked it, and dove in. Through the window, she spied several military police and shuddered. They were still sweeping the grounds.

Nerves stretched to the breaking point, Hannah opted for a mindless rerun. She carried her bowl and a glass of Cabernet to the living room, and nearly dropped them on the floor. An Airman sprawled in the middle of Hannah's grandmother's rug, a dark stain spreading below him.

The bowl of Shepherd's Pie and wine goblet clattered against the glass-topped table, and Hannah kneeled to feel for a pulse. It was thready and fast, but the man was alive.

The patches on his uniform identified him as a colonel. Hannah turned his face and gasped. It was Colonel Mabry, her commanding officer. She had had a crush on him since Day One, but what was he doing here?

Then the source of the blood became apparent—a gunshot wound to the left shoulder. She probed the area gently and Colonel Mabry moaned, then she reached behind him. The bullet had passed through. The entry and exit wounds were consistent with those of a Sig Sauer, the standard Air Force service revolver. Had Mabry taken friendly fire?

Wiping her bloody hands on the colonel's pants, she drew her phone from her robe to dial 911 for the base ambulance.

Then it struck Hannah. The blood was too dark. The man was not human. A chill passed over her.

"Are you a Reptilian?" Hannah knew some of them could shape-shift. It was either that, or Colonel Mabry was a half-breed like Hannah.

Miraculously, the blood flow had slowed to a trickle. Hannah grabbed her doctor bag from the dining table and poured bleed-stop powder into the wounds front and back. While the powder did its work, Hannah took his blood pressure. It was through the roof, another indication this man might not be human—or not completely.

Hannah was a mixed breed, a condition that had caused her much angst over the years. Luckily, her blood ran human red, so rarely had anyone guessed her heritage. Of course, most didn't know Reptilians existed, and Hannah had been happy to keep it that way. Now, thanks to the unprovoked attack, that could change.

She sat back on her heels and decided not to call for assistance. Colonel Mabry didn't seem to be in immediate danger, and if the service learned of his heritage, it could be the end of his career. She would clean his wounds, administer an injection of antibiotics and a painkiller, then watch and wait. If his condition worsened, she would cross that bridge then.

She retrieved washcloths and hand towels, drew a pan of hot water, and cleaned and bandaged the gunshot wounds as best she could. Then, she quickly checked for other injuries. Finding none, Hannah covered the doctor with a blanket and gently stuffed a pillow beneath his head.

She longed for bed but couldn't leave the colonel alone. So, she grabbed her pillow and a comforter, turned the TV on low, and stretched out on the sofa. Within minutes, Hannah was sound asleep.

☼☼☼

Azi woke with his shoulder on fire and a raging thirst. He tried to roll stand, but excruciating pain shot through his upper torso and down his arm. On the edge of panic, he looked around. Where was he, and why was he in pain?

He remembered charging the barracks with Nergal and his warriors, then being shot. That explained the pain. He also remembered running, crawling, and finally dragging himself into an unlocked house at the edge of the desert because the patrol had nearly spotted him. He'd crawled inside, then must have passed out.

In full-blown agony, Azi pulled himself up using the nearby chair and nearly fainted for his efforts. When the fog cleared, he realized someone else was in the room.

A human with kind eyes watched from a platform. She calmly stood, and a light flickered on.

"How are you feeling?"

Her voice was soft and comforting. She placed the back of a cool hand against his forehead. "I would call you Colonel Mabry, but I don't think that's your name. *Are* you Colonel Mabry?" The mesmerizing eyes probed Azi's, and he found himself confessing.

"No, Miss. I just look like him. My name is Azi."

"Well, Azi, I am Dr. Nolan. But call me Hannah. How did you come to be in the colonel's body? Were you part of the attack?"

Ashamed, Azi turned his head away and felt nauseated. Before volunteering to help General Nergal, Azi had worried he might not have the stomach for war. He was right. On seeing the violence and bloodshed, his stomach had revolted. Then he'd taken a bullet.

"It's okay," the soft-spoken doctora said. "I won't tell anyone. But did you hurt the colonel?"

Azi shook his head and the motion made the room spin. Gagging, he said, "I'm going to be sick."

The doctora slid a hand behind his back, lifted his head, and shoved a plastic receptacle against his face. With her watching, Azi spewed his guts. Every time he retched, pain shot through his shoulder, making him retch again.

The pretty doctora took it in stride. When he was done, she wiped his mouth with a damp cloth, then settled Azi back against the soft chair.

"Did you hurt Colonel Mabry?" she asked again.

"No. When I left, he was alive and well."

"Then I'm afraid you're stuck with me until you recover. Or at least until you're stronger. I will do my best to conceal you and your identity, but beware, Azi. If the guards find out, I won't be able to protect you from them."

She removed something from a bag. "I'd like to take your temperature, if that's okay. Can you tell me what your normal should be?"

He stared, surprised. "Same as yours, I think. 37 degrees centigrade."

She swiped the thermometer across his forward. "You're at 38.2. Let's get another round of antibiotics in you." She reached in the leather bag and drew out a syringe and bottle. "How's the pain?"

"Awful," he moaned.

She fished for another bottle, filled the syringe with the first, lifted his torn sleeve, and stuck it in Azi's arm. He watched through a haze as she did the same with the other bottle.

When the second injection entered his bloodstream, a sense of calm washed over Azi and the pain lessened considerably.

"Were you with the Reptilians that attacked the base?'

Embarrassed, Azi nodded, eyes on hers.

Sadness and horror dragged down the corners of her mouth. "Why would you do that?"

A rush of sorrow overcame Azi. He shoved it aside. "We were ordered to do so by Warlord Shibboleth. He wishes to add your surface world to our territory."

"So you live inside Earth?"

"Aye."

"Are there many of you?" Fear flickered in the steady eyes.

Azi pondered her question. "To be honest, I am not sure. We once held most of UnderEarth, but our population has been depleted."

"Will the others come looking for you?"

"I doubt it." Azi closed his eyes. It was too much effort to keep them open. "As a species, Reptilians aren't known for looking out for one another."

"Then I will take care of you until you are better. Or as long as I can." She laid the soothing cloth across Azi's brow. "Do you think you can make it up to the couch if I help?"

Azi heard her as if from a far distance, then passed out.

Someone pounded on Hannah's door, and her heart lodged in her throat. Turning off the lamp, she threw a blanket over Azi and the blood stain, then hurried to the peephole. It was Sergeant Dahl.

"Ma'am, I hate to bother you," she said when Hannah opened the door, "but is Colonel Mabry with you? A Noncom thought they saw him heading this way."

Hannah slowly wagged her head and yawned. "No. Did you check the mess? That's usually where we find him when he's not on rounds or in sick bay."

The policewoman peered past Hannah, and her anxiety shot through the roof. The last thing she needed was a court martial for harboring the enemy.

"I hope you find him soon," she said in the middle of a big yawn. "I need to hit the rack. I'm coming off two doubles with no sleep in between. And tomorrow, assuming all leave isn't canceled, I'm driving up to the Kern River."

Sergeant Dahl hesitated, then tipped her cap. "Thank you, ma'am. I'm sorry to have bothered you." She descended the steps, then looked back at Hannah, who leaned against the doorframe. "Enjoy your trip, Lieutenant Colonel. From the looks of it, you need a rest. But get some sleep first. You look awful."

Hannah snorted. "Thanks a lot, officer. I hope you find Colonel Mabry soon."

Back in the house, Hannah reheated her Shepherd's Pie and sat in the dark to wolf it down. She stared at the lump beneath the blanket, wondering how a USAF officer had been shot by a military-issue Sig.

A chilling thought had goosebumps dancing on the back of Hannah's neck. Had someone used the attack to commit a crime of opportunity? Maybe Mabry had been the target all along and Azi got in the way. But if that was the case, where was the real Colonel Mabry? And what if the killer came back to finish the job?

Heart pounding, Hannah hurried to the bedroom and dressed. She would head on up to the river tonight and take Azi with her. Assuming she could get him in the car. She added toiletries and a few other things to the bags she'd packed several days ago and threw them in the Jeep beside the other supplies she was taking to the cabin.

She checked Azi's wounds, roused him from a sound sleep, and helped him crawl into the back seat. She piled tarps and blankets on him, then climbed into the driver's seat.

Hannah held her breath as she approached the gate. Would whoever was on duty try to keep her from leaving?

But, she caught a break. She had recently treated the guard for a bad case of jock itch. He waved her through, and Hannah threw up a hand when he yelled, "Bring us back some fresh fish!"

A groggy Hannah turned into the long driveway north of Kernville two hours later. This far from town, it was pitch dark. There were no street lamps, and the only light was a nearly full moon, a zillion stars, and her Jeep's high beams.

They bounced over the rutted dirt road, and Azi groaned. Checking her rearview mirror, Hannah nearly swallowed her tongue. Two vertically-slit eyes blinked owlishly. Azi must have resumed his own form at some point.

"Where are you taking me?" the Reptilian whimpered. "Are we almost there?"

"Yes, almost." Hannah looked back and caught a glimpse of scales shining in the moonlight. "Do you need to stop?"

Azi slumped back against the seat. "No. I can make it." The pain and shock evident in his voice hinted otherwise.

Minutes later, they pulled up in front of a simple cabin. Hannah had inherited it years ago after her mother died in a motorcycle accident. Now, it was the one place she could go to escape the world. She hurried inside, turned on the lights, and returned to the Jeep to fetch Azi.

Hannah settled the Reptilian in a chair in the front room to check his wounds. There was seepage, so she replaced the bandages, gave Azi another injection of painkiller, and then helped him to the extra bed before unpacking the Jeep.

Once Hannah put everything away, she took a wine cooler from the stocked fridge, twisted off the top, and carried it out back to sit by the river. Crickets and frogs sang a lullaby, accompanied by a hooting owl. A mile or so away, a coyote howled. Another answered.

After a while, the night noises and the water running swiftly over the rocks calmed Hannah's anxiety. She sucked in pine and juniper-scented air and felt her body relax. For the first time since the attack, her pulse returned to normal.

She almost nodded off, and Hannah yawned and went inside. She steeled herself against Azi's frightful appearance and checked his temperature. It still hovered at 38.2C, but he slept comfortably.

Dog-tired, Hannah peed and climbed into her bed without bothering to undress.

AMASSING THE TROOPS

Elise had learned the history of Awen and her wand long ago in druid school. So when Lugh and Mitchell announced plans to take a brooch containing one of the missing wandstones to Emily, Elise gave them her blessing. Cybele seconded her decision.

They offered to fly them to Yr Wyddfa via helicopter and drop them at the summit. But after a brief discussion, they opted for a less noticeable entrance. The druid Elder, Cu, would transport them instead.

So tired she could barely see straight, Elise left the druids to their preparations and retreated to her office. She closed the blinds and door, donned her noise-canceling headphones, and sank into her raggedy but comfortable armchair to snatch a thirty-minute nap. It would take her agents that long to rouse the worldwide directors.

She was dosing off when her door slammed open, and Sergeant Banner bawled, "Johnson, get your lazy arse down to the war room. Director Ferrigno from Utah requires a word with you." Then he pivoted on his heel and was gone.

With a deep stretch and a wide yawn, Elise dragged herself up and peeked at herself in the mirrored door frame. Her unkempt appearance was beyond help. She fluffed her hair, pinched her wan cheeks, downed an entire glass of water, and slipped into the bathroom before taking the elevator to the fourth floor.

The doors opened, and Cybele MacBrayer materialized. She handed Elise a tablet along with a steaming cup of black coffee. Scanning the tablet, Elise gratefully slurped the strong liquid and strode into the busy command center.

Computer screens lined every inch of the walls. Some displayed feeds from around the world, while others linked AIA Cheltenham with its international centers. Those were primarily blank, but Juanita Ferrigno's strained face filled one screen.

Elise stepped up to it, and the Utah director bleated, "Sir, we have a situation, and it can't wait."

Ferrigno glanced off-screen, then switched the camera to show a live feed of green-scaled monsters terrorizing the Denver Airport.

Elise gasped. Panicked humans raced to and fro while armed guards shot at monsters. But the guards were outnumbered and systematically targeted and killed by the Reptilians. As much as Elise would like to, there was no denying the threat.

Shuddering, she barked, "Are your forces on the way?"

"Yes, one unit just arrived. Two others will be there in five. Plus, the FBI and local LEOs will converge on site. We're also mobilizing units along the U.S. west coast."

"And the east coast? Midwest? Great Plains? Any word from those regions?"

"They have been quiet so far. But the west side of the country is crawling with lizard men, so we're focusing our efforts here. Any hope of getting reinforcements? We're losing agents faster than we can replace them."

A chill gripped Elise. She stepped to the side, away from the camera, not wanting to record the terror that threatened to empty her bowels. Knowing they were under attack had been bad enough, but seeing the Reptilians killing helpless people with no remorse or emotion chilled her blood.

She knew in her gut that if they didn't get the attack under control quickly, they might as well admit defeat. Physically, humans were no match for the wiry, vicious beings that had no qualms about ending the human race.

"Assistant Director Johnson? Are you there?"

Elise glanced around the war room. It buzzed with activity. Director Wansley had appeared and conferred with other directors as they came online. Elise stepped in front of the camera.

"Yes, Director Ferrigno, I'm here. But will you hold a moment? The other regions are checking in. With luck, they can route personnel your way."

But the story was the same worldwide. While Director Wansley coordinated with the U.K.'s Secretaries of State, Scotland Yard, MI5 and 6, and the other agencies, Elise assisted the agents operating AIA's phones and screens. Over the next few hours, they roused world leaders, scrambled troops, and coordinated defense efforts around the globe.

Elise yawned and glanced at the clock. Her third cup of strong coffee was wearing off. The Alien Intelligence Agency's network of agents had been notified and activated, and the threat at the Denver Airport was neutralized.

Now, there was little else for Elise to do, at least for now. Director Wansley had gone home to see to his wife and kids' safety, and Cybele had left several hours ago to get some sleep.

Weary to the bone, Elise dismissed all but a skeleton crew, then hit the head and descended the stairs to her office. Halfway there, she encountered several Fomorian ghosts on the landing. They discussed the girl from UnderEarth, who was rumored to be in the building.

Chuckling, Elise passed them, then decided to check on Ethnui before returning to her office for some much-needed sleep. As if sensing her intent, the curious spirits followed. She settled in the chair beside Brian, and they crowded around Ethnui's bed. The girl's tortured expression was gone, and one of her arms was slung above her head.

"Oh, blessed Thoth, it is Ethnui! She's alive!" one of the women exclaimed. She bent forward to hug the girl, and her ghostly arms passed right through.

"Your daughter, Ethnui?" another trilled.

"Yes!" the first crowed. "My Ethnui."

The Fomorians cheered and gazed down at the girl.

Elise smiled, then realized they were the first wraiths she had seen or heard since leaving the White House. Being wired had the added benefit of keeping the spirits at bay, and adrenaline and caffeine had Elise cranked to the max.

Brian rolled in his sleep. Elise leaned closer to study her god-nephew's face. He grew up so fast and had experienced things no young person should.

When his eyes opened abruptly, and Hamilton Hester's voice rasped, "'Lise. You look awful. Are you okay?" she leapt from her chair, heart pounding.

"Ham, you scared me!" she laughed, plopping back down. "Oh, I'm just dandy. But guess what? I may look bad, but *you* don't have a body."

"Ouch!" Her best friend groaned. "That's a low blow. But can I talk to you about that?"

Suspicion raised Elise's hackles. "The answer is no."

"You don't know what I want."

"Yes. I do. And the answer is no."

"Elise, I need you. When my body perished, I transferred into Cu. Then he died in the earthquake, and I almost went, too. I barely had time to transfer into Brian. But that was weeks ago, and I promised the kid I would leave as soon as possible."

"No," Elise said flatly.

"We've done it before. It wasn't that bad."

"Speak for yourself, Hamilton." A shudder worked its way through Elise. They had studied transmigration in Druidry classes. But their teacher had not been big on practical application. She had warned them against trying it alone, but Hamilton had been fascinated.

At the same age, Ham and Elise had been inseparable through middle school. He didn't think her weird for being sensitive to what was on the other side of the veil and never ridiculed or belittled her. He even defended Elise against those who did. And though Ham couldn't be there to protect her all the time, she had always felt safe with him.

So, after he hounded her for days, Elise finally caved and agreed to try. Mamó Awen lived in the carriage house at Wren's Roost, the Hester estate, and wasn't home that day. So after school, they hid in her library to try the spell.

The act of transmigration had been easier than either of them had suspected. They slid in and out of each other's body without mishap, but Elise found it creepy. After that, she chose to stick to her own.

Ham, however, got a kick out of it. He practiced slipping into whatever form he could and even tried it with insects. But after almost getting stuck in a Hercules beetle, he confined his practice to humans and pets.

Now, it seemed his obsession had held Hamilton in good stead. Most humans got one life. By transmigrating, Ham had secured himself a second chance. Maybe Elise should loosen up. After all, it had been a thrilling, if eerie, experience.

"Oh, why the hell not?" she said, shocking herself. "Truth be told, I've been as bored as a dead tree at a woodpecker convention." She grinned, and Ham let go a belly laugh.

Then, Ham's voice mellowed. "These two need their privacy. I am going to miss this kid, though. I'd forgotten how good it feels to be young and foolish."

Elise snort-laughed. "You? Forget how foolish feels? I can't imagine. You are the most spontaneous, least stodgy person I have ever known." They laughed together because it was true. Then Hamilton sobered.

"Let me wake the kid, and we can do it now."

"Or you could let him sleep and just do it."

"No, he'll want to know. Psst, Brian," Ham hissed. Then his face changed to that of a sleepy teen yawning and stretching awake.

"What is it, Ham?" It was the boy's voice. He sounded worried.

Elise shook her head. The difference was striking.

"Ready for a bit of wish fulfillment?" Hamilton said.

"Huh?" Brian rubbed his eyes, starting when he saw Elise.

"Remember how I promised I would transfer out of you as soon as I could?"

Brian sat up.

Ethnui stirred and woke, too. "What is it?" she slurred, fishing a long, dark hair from her mouth.

"You mean I finally get to pee alone?" Brian chuckled.

"Yeah. And defend yourself against lizard men," Ham reminded.

"Oh. Yeah. That." Brian nodded thoughtfully. "I'll miss that for sure. Thanks, old man. You taught me a lot."

"It was a pleasure, Bri. You're a quick study. And I'm not old."

The boy's eyes misted. He blinked away tears, and his youthful features hardened. "I'll miss you, Sir. But go on, get outta here. I'll be fine. You take care of yourself. Where are you going, anyway?"

Ham thrust his chin at Elise, and Brian nodded satisfaction.

Still not a hundred percent sure she wanted to do it, Elise sucked in a breath, reached out her hand, and brushed Brian's cheek. Warmth ran up her arm and spread, Ham's spirit leaving Brian and easing into her.

"Damn," Hamilton said in a deeper version of Elise's voice. "It sure is cluttered in here." Then he spied the ghosts lounging on Ethnui's bed and did a double take. "Holy shit! When did they get here?"

Sensing someone outside the door, Elise warned, "Shhh, zip it."

The door opened, and Director Wansley's face appeared. His groomed brows hiked to his bangs.

"I thought you were getting some shut-eye, Johnson." He scanned the room. "Didn't I just hear guys talking?"

Crossing to him, Elise lied. "No. Just me and Brian. I stopped to check on the kids before taking a nap." Brian waggled his fingers, then flopped over to bury his face in his pillow.

"How are they?" The director asked with genuine concern. One thing about Rupert Wansley—well, two, if Elise cared to admit it—he was wicked smart and had a heart of gold.

"A lot shaken and a little beat up. But they are ready to help get the Reptilians back in UnderEarth where they belong."

Wansley smiled, pleased. "Good, good."

He directed his infamous laser beam gaze at Elise, and her gut contracted. There was no way he could know what she was thinking of doing. But, still.

"I know we've had our differences, Johnson, but I admire you. And to be perfectly honest, you scare the hell out of me. That said, there is no one in the Agency I would rather have my back."

Wansley's hazel eyes bored into Elise's. His praise was difficult for her to hear, especially under the circumstances. She blushed, uncomfortable.

"Yessir, we have. I was thinking something similar about you. You are what is known as a genuinely good human. Umm, let me rephrase—a genuinely good being. I find that refreshing." Then, Elise chuckled. "Do you really find me scary?"

"Ohhh, yeah. Scarier even than these creatures." The director waved his tablet in the air.

They chuckled, and Hamilton railed inside Elise's head. "Oh, *hell no*, dude. I can assure you that E is not nearly as scary as those soulless creatures."

"Shhh!" she warned.

Wansley smirked and glanced over at the beds. "Are there spooks here now? Are they talking to you?"

Harrumphing, Elise glared down her nose. Maybe Wansley wasn't so charitable after all. Or selectively so.

Hamilton agreed.

"Sir, I'm going home. Other than catnaps on the plane, I've had no sleep in thirty-six hours." She tried to pinpoint the exact number, but her memory was fuzzy. "Maybe more."

He leaned closer and wrinkled his nose, and Elise sighed.

"And as you not so graciously point out, I need a shower and a change of clothes. Permission to leave for as long as it takes to revive myself? Special Agent MacBrayer will assume point while I'm gone."

The expressive brows went solar this time.

Elise persisted. "Sir, you underestimate Cybele. She is a good manager."

Still, Wansley balked.

"Come on, Director. Cut her some slack. If your spouse disappeared, I'm sure you would do the same as MacBrayer. She's back now, and so is Jake. *And* her son. I'd say she is fully committed to the AIA."

Wansley eyed her for another beat, then relented. "I'll give you twelve hours."

Elise almost protested it wasn't enough. But why bother? She would likely get canned for whatever Ham had concocted. Or at least reprimanded.

She lied again. "Works for me."

Then Wansley left. When the elevator dinged, Ham propelled Elise back to the bed. They hugged Brian and Ethnui goodbye, and Elise's heart filled with such tender emotion that she thought it might burst. Hamilton's feelings for the boy and girl ran deep. He squeezed Brian the hardest.

"Y'all take care of each other, and we'll see you soon. I promise."

"Shhh, Ham," she warned in her head. "You don't know that."

"Yes. I do," he hissed back.

In her office, Elise tucked her Glock in her shoulder holster and stuffed extra magazines in the side pocket of her go bag. She debated whether to leave her badge in her desk drawer, but she was taking her gun, so technically, she needed her credentials, too. She had no idea where she and Hamilton might end up, but there was a good possibility she would need both.

On the quick trip home, Elise called Cybele to inform her that she was now in charge. Her goddaughter fired off many questions, but Elise explained little. There was no need to get Cybele in trouble, too.

Then, eating cold leftover Thai, she repacked her bag with fresh clothes and showered quickly.

Weary to the bone, Elise climbed between her sheets and used a druid meditation to slow her galloping brain. She was sliding into the blessed embrace of theta when Hamilton whined, "Eli-iiise."

"Shh," she commanded. "I have to sleep. Otherwise, we'll be dead before nightfall."

Four precious hours later, Ham woke her from a dead sleep. "Elise, wake up. I have a bad feeling. We have to go."

TRADING PLACES

As it turned out, Hamilton was right. Reptilian soldiers had materialized in the London underground, and it was taking the government's available firepower to drive them back down.

While Ham watched the breaking news, Elise unplugged the coffee maker, toaster, lamps, and other assorted appliances, programmed the lights to turn on and off at predetermined times, and arranged for a neighbor to water the few plants she had managed to keep alive.

Then, strapping on her Glock and sliding her personal Sig in her purse, she tossed it and her bag on the passenger seat and peeled out of the neighborhood. Five minutes later, they wheeled into her favorite American diner.

"Why are we stopping?" Hamilton had been pushing her to hurry since shouting her awake.

"I thought you were hungry," Elise told Ham in the rearview mirror. Then she chuckled at herself. "I wonder if this is what schizophrenics look like when they talk to themselves."

"Have you ever wondered if schizophrenics were cases of nonconsensual possession?"

Shuddering at the thought, Elise stopped on the steps of the diner. "No. Not until now. But thanks a lot, Hamilton. I won't be getting that out of my head anytime soon."

Catching the glorious scent of American bacon, she followed her nose and let her oldest friend order the heftiest breakfast on the menu. Then, amid his sighs and groans of pleasure, she helped Hamilton devour it.

Most of it, anyway. He had ordered so much that she had to stop or barf. Leaning back, Elise hitched a thumb and forefinger under her pants button and released it. Then she burped as politely as possible behind a disposable napkin.

"Mm-mm-mmm, that was good. Thank you, Elise. I never knew you had such a hearty appetite."

She inhaled and held it for a count of three before retorting, "No, *that* was you. *I* was merely helping a friend." She belched again. "I think I might pop." She sipped her coffee and sighed.

"Okay, Hamilton. What's our next move? Shall we go help Emily save the world?" She worried a piece of bacon that had gotten stuck in the pocket between her molars.

"This is a long shot, Ham. Space Force has lead on the project, though AIA and the military is involved. We have the nation's best, most talented minds and technicians working on the problem, plus outside experts that surpass anything we can match. I'll do my damndest to get us in, but I have nothing to bring to the table."

"Nothing to bring? E, if I remember correctly, you once told me you speak or understand every language spoken by the aliens on Earth."

"The known ones, yes. Your point?"

"How many others can do that, AIA or otherwise? Until now, most of Earth had no idea aliens live here, much less speak their language."

The light turned yellow, and Elise zipped through. "You have a point." At the next red light, she programmed Birmingham Airport into her nav system.

"We'll fly commercial. Wansley will pitch a bitch when he finds out, but that will give us some lead time. Plus, I might get a bit more sleep." She checked her rearview mirror and changed lanes to turn onto Tewkesbury Road toward the M5.

Elise sighed. "The fallout from my last rogue incident landed me at a desk and almost cost my job. After this, I will be canned for sure. With luck, they'll let me keep my pension."

When Ham scoffed, Elise explained. "I might be tenured, but let's be honest, Ham." She glanced in the mirror. Once-tiny lines carved deeper in her face. "I'm no spring chicken. And there are plenty of agents jockeying to take my place."

"Then we'll show them what you're made of, Elise. None of those agents can hold a candle to you."

"Still," she said, voice trailing off.

Taking a sip of cooling coffee, she gunned her coupe past a line of slow cars and settled into the rhythm of the road.

THE KERN RIVER

The silence was deafening when Azi woke, the dark complete. Was he dead? He tried to stand, and pain shot through him, reminding Azi of what had happened. For a moment, panic seized him.

Had General Nergal's Dracs made it back to the cave? Had Nergal? They had torn through one building unhindered. Then, in the next, they were met by a squad of uniformed humans. When the Dracs tried to leave, a dragon attacked.

The last thing Azi remembered was Nergal sounding the retreat. Then Azi must've lost consciousness because he woke under a pile of dead Dracs. Only then did he realize he was shot.

In agony, he had crawled toward the rendezvous point. But a patrol appeared, so he hid in a building. Lucky for Azi, it had belonged to the doctora. Otherwise, he would be dead. Or dying in a human prison.

It had been unbearably hot in the desert. But cool air circulated, and Azi could hear the babble of water. Curious and needing to empty his bladder, he rose gingerly from the soft bed and made his way outside.

The sight of the night sky and its millions of stars took Azi's breath. This is what made him volunteer for Nergal's army despite his dislike of violence. He leaned against one of the evergreens and pissed, then settled on the bank of the narrow river.

This must be where the doctora caught the fish she had forced him to eat. Her scent lingered on the nearby chair. Lying on the ground, Azi peered up at the stars and sighed. His shoulder throbbed, but the fever that had raged for days had finally broken. Now, he was weak and shaky, his head thick and fuzzy.

He stayed there for a long while, listening to the burble of the river and watching the moon and stars traverse the sky. Then, a twig snapped. Azi tensed, ready to run or pounce depending on the threat. In his current state, he hoped he had to do neither.

"There you are." It was the doctora. Azi relaxed. "When you weren't in your bed, I thought something had happened."

"Did I scare you, Dr. Nolan? I heard the river and was curious. Plus, I needed air."

"Please, I told you, call me Hannah." She settled on the ground beside him. "Isn't it glorious here, Azi?" She laid back. "When I was little, my mother taught me the names of every major constellation and star. Now I barely remember them, but I cherish the memories of Mama."

"She's gone?"

Azi flattened his back to the pungent, moss-covered bank and turned his head to study Hannah. She was unlike any female he had ever known, though he'd not met a human one. Hannah was strong and capable, with nerves of steel, yet had a gentle, soothing way that made him want to be in her presence.

"Yes. This place was Mama's. She bought it with the divorce settlement after Daddy left us."

"So, was it just you and her?"

Hannah went quiet, then expelled a deep breath. "At the end, yes. Before that, my older brother lived here."

"Where is he now?"

Sitting up, Hannah wrapped her arms around her knees and rocked back and forth. Her expression took on a faraway quality. So did her voice.

"I wish I knew. Boyce left a few years after Daddy. He wasn't lucky like me." Hannah turned to regard him with eyes that held back unshed tears.

"Boyce inherited Mama's form. She was a Reptilian or a half-blooded one, and she looked like you rather than me. Boyce did, too."

That explained a lot. "Did she live up here disguised as a human? In AboveEarth, I mean. How did she manage to pull that off?"

"She was very good at shapeshifting. My brother wasn't. He left to search for access to your world, and we never saw him again. Or, I didn't. I'm pretty sure Mama didn't either. She would've told me."

Azi thought about Boyce. "I wonder if he made it and if he changed his name. Boyce would be unusual for a Reptilian. And as a species, they don't take kindly to half-breeds. I know. I'm one."

"I know," Hannah said, and Azi sat up so fast his head swam. He grabbed her arm to anchor.

"You okay?" She peered intently at Azi. In the moonlight, she reminded him of the angels that had once populated UnderEarth.

"Thanks to you, yes." He let go of her arm and took her hand. "What made you save me, Hannah Nolan? Why didn't you call the guards?"

"Honestly? I almost did. But I thought you were Colonel Mabry. The dark blood told me he was part Reptilian, and I didn't want to get him in trouble. Bad things happen to mixed breeds up here."

"Well, thank you. I would be dead or in one of your prisons otherwise." Azi breathed in the sweet night air and expelled it noisily. "If I lived on the surface, I would never leave this place. It is the closest thing to heaven I have seen."

"Me, too," Hannah sighed. "I wish I didn't have to go back to the base."

They stayed that way for a few minutes, her rocking and Azi watching from the corner of his eye. Then Hannah leapt up and reached a hand down to him.

"We'd better get you back inside. The fever has broken, but it's time for another round of antibiotics."

FACING BÉ CHUILLE

mily yanked her hood over her curls and dodged a searing lightning bolt. Black clouds gathered and mushroomed, and a gentle rain fell. This time, she was ready for the intense clap of thunder and didn't scream as it crashed and echoed off the tors of the Eryri.

An eerie cackle swept the clearing, but the winter hag was nowhere to be seen. Awen spun Emily in a barrel roll to avoid another lightning bolt. Thunder rattled the ruins of Beli's Castle, and she leapt to her feet.

Wind shrieked down from the mountaintops, driving icy crystals that stung her exposed flesh. Emily drew her wrap closer and renewed the protective spell, amazed to feel excitement rather than fear. The presence of her ancestor had everything to do with that.

The sleet turned to snow and fell faster. Fat, wet wads clung to the grass, covering the ground. Emily craned her neck, feeling the witch's malevolence, but the thick snowfall obliterated all else.

She was about to ask Awen, when the snow parted, and Bé Chuille descended to hover before her. Corrosive evil poured from the witch.

A deep shiver ran through Emily. "Awen, are you there? What should I do?"

"Fight!" Awen hissed.

The winter hag descended to the snow-covered ruins. With a shrill cackle, she raised a crooked wand and struck the Earth. Ice spurted from the tip. It fanned out across the clearing to coat the snow, then raced up the surrounding mountains. The wind howled, whipping the snow into a white-out.

Emily could see nothing now. Sensing this was the battle the druids had prepared her for, she reinforced her protective spell just in case and prayed to God. Not the ones she had learned of in druid classes, but the one she had relied on since childhood.

Her least-favorite scripture sprang to Emily's lips, least favorite because her stepdad used to spout it when he was shit-faced drunk. She smirked at the witch, and let it roll off her tongue.

"God forgive her for she knows not what she does!"

The smile vanished from Bé Chuille's face, replaced by shock and dismay, then determination. She reared back and rained curse after curse upon Emily, keeping her too busy to conjure a curse of her own. She was preparing to project a paralysis curse, when an invisible net settled upon her and Emily could no longer move.

She strained to wiggle her arms, but they were pinned against her sides. Her legs felt like thousand-pound weights. Instinctively, she called out to the dragon Keepers, but they had left to defend Earth against the Reptilians. Then the vitality left her body, and Emily collapsed in the snow.

※※※

Gwynfor Fearnley removed the metal coffee can and dropped his pack beside the summit marker. He had reached the pinnacle of Yr Wyddfa for the three hundred and fifteenth time. Gwyn had hiked alone.

On the other three hundred and fourteen climbs, his partner, Mark, had summited with him. Now Gwyn was here to spread his ashes.

A tear escaped and Gwyn dashed it away. It was a year to the day since Mark's passing. A year since Gwynfor had had the heart to make the climb they both adored.

He had wanted to release his lover at sunset, their favorite hour. But the light had vanished, blotted out by sudden unforecast clouds. They boiled and thickened over the Eryri as if summoned by the magical Elves of Tylwyth Teg or the once noble Druids of Gwynned.

A bolt of lightning sizzled toward Llyn Llydaw, followed by a resounding crack of thunder. Working quickly, Gwyn removed the lid from the coffee canister, and planted his legs against the rising wind. He said a last goodbye to his beloved Mark, and with an agonized sob, emptied his ashes over the side.

But, Mark wasn't ready to say goodbye. A gusting updraft sent his cremains back up into Gwynfor's face. He sputtered and spit ashes and bone bits, then laughed at Mark's insistence on having the last word.

326

Brushing them away as best he could, Gwyn replaced the lid and stowed the can in his backpack as a light rain began to fall. He was grateful he'd chosen the Rhyd Ddu path rather than Llwybr Cwellyn. The trail would be difficult to maneuver on the way down.

He retrieved the slicker from his pack, slid it over his head, and tied the hood beneath his chin as lightning zinged past. Thunder cracked, so close Gwynfor jumped. Saying a prayer to Brigitte, his patron saint, Gwynfor slung the pack over his shoulders and carefully navigated the stepped approach. Soon, the rain turned to snow, and the footing became even more perilous.

"On your left."

The gruff warning startled Gwyn. He scooched to the right, and two hikers he had seen at the top of Yr Wyddfa passed quickly.

"Stay safe," he called as they scampered past.

Gwyn descended another half meter. Then A cackling shriek floated on the wind, and his head snapped up. Gwyn could just make out two women in the valley below. Then lightning danced through the cloud layers and thunder reverberated across the Eryri.

He shivered and wondered if the women were okay, then tying the plastic hood tighter over his ribbed beanie, he swept snow from his coat and pants as another eerie shriek rose.

Shuddering, Gwynfor decided he should get off the mountain fast. Wiping snow from his goggles, he buried his pole in a deepening drift to creep carefully around an exposed outcrop.

But, a gust of wind slammed Gwyn in the back. His poles flew in one direction and Gwyn tumbled in the other. He bounced down the icy rocks, trying desperately to stop his momentum. Then, Mark materialized to whisk him to safety.

COLONEL MABRY

The vast desert was dark beneath the star-studded heavens. Hannah dropped Azi near the entrance to the caves and then drove slowly to the base. His fever had broken two days ago, and his wounds had completely healed since then. In Hannah's eyes, that was a miracle.

Azi had explained that some Reptilians, and in his case, hybrid Reptilians, had retained this ability. Others, like Hannah, had not. He had promised her he would isolate the gene. She hoped a simple splice could transfer the ability to humans.

But first, they had to stop a war. Or rather, Azi did. He had political influence in UnderEarth. Hannah had none.

They had talked nonstop over the last two days, discussing the differences and similarities between their species, mainly the soul and whether Reptilians—and every human, for that matter—had one.

Since the Anunnaki gods were their mutual ancestors, why wouldn't they all have inherited a soul? And why didn't that soul override their instinct to fight?

So they made a bold plan. Azi would return to UnderEarth to convince his boss they could reach a mutually agreeable settlement with the humans. After all, there was no real reason the two species couldn't coexist, be it on AboveEarth, in UnderEarth, or both. Wouldn't it make sense to let individuals decide for themselves where they wanted to live?

While there, Azi would reverse engineer the cell phone Hannah had given him. He believed once he boosted the signal enough, they could establish communication between worlds and speak to one another. Meanwhile, Hannah would resume her duties at the base and discover what had happened to Colonel Mabry.

As she unloaded the perishables from the Jeep, the wind shifted, and the temperature dropped dramatically. Soon, fat globs of sticky, wet snow began falling. Shocked, Hannah dug her thick robe from the back of the closet, switched the thermostat to heat, and found the national weather channel on the TV. Then, hugging the robe closer, Hannah stared in disbelief.

A mammoth storm was sweeping down from the Arctic and settling across the Northern Hemisphere. Previously-scorching temperatures had dropped precipitously around the globe. What could have caused such weather? It was May, for godsakes.

Brewing a steaming cup of ginger tea, Hannah sipped it while meteorologists on another channel explored options before chalking it up to climate change—like every other odd weather event since Hannah had been a kid.

She knew there was no way Azi had time to do anything, but she checked her cell phone anyway. Then, she turned off the television and climbed into bed. She had a twelve-hour shift starting in the morning, and after staying up talking to Azi for the last few nights, she badly needed sleep.

The thought of the Reptilian scientist put a smile on Hannah's face, and she drifted off to dreamland.

Morning came much too early. Hannah hit the snooze button and dozed until the alarm blared again. Swearing at it, she dragged herself out of bed and wondered about Azi. Had he made it back to his lab? Would he stop the Reptilian attacks?

Security was amped up, but the base had mostly returned to normal. Hannah stowed her purse inside her desk drawer and went to the mess. She grabbed a bagel, smeared it with cream cheese, and poured a large cup of coffee.

Then, sipping the strong brew, she strode back to sick bay and nearly fainted. Her commanding officer, Colonel Mabry, reviewed case files at a desk.

"Nolan," he acknowledged.

She stared open-mouthed from the doorway. "Sir?"

"What is it, Lieutenant Colonel?" Mabry looked up, brows raised.

Gathering her wits, Hannah entered the room and set her bagel and coffee on a counter.

"Nothing, sir. Just surprised to see you."

He peered at her intently through wire-rimmed glasses. "What do you mean?"

"Only that, well… I thought something might have happened to you. You vanished after the attack. I was worried."

The handsome face blanched. Mabry removed his glasses and looked away with a loud sigh. Then, wiping beads of sweat from his forehead, he cleared his throat and stared at the charts.

"Colonel?"

This time, when he looked up, Mabry's face blazed red.

"What?" she coaxed.

He glanced at the open door and blinds, then back at Hannah. Finally, her C.O. mumbled, "You promise you won't tell?"

"Tell?"

"Yes, tell. I freaked out, Hannah. I was trying to save an Airman in the middle of that bloodbath when I saw—" Another spurt of red colored his cheeks. "Dammit, Hannah. I saw ME!"

She stared at the Colonel. "What do you mean you saw you?"

"I mean, a man was there and looked just like me. I knew he had to be one of the monsters. I panicked and grabbed the Airman's gun. I shot him, Nolan. Then, I hid and didn't come out for hours. By then, you had gone off duty."

Well, that explained that. Colonel Nolan was alive and well. And it was he who had shot Azi.

Everything inside Hannah screamed, but she assured her C.O. his secret was safe. Then, gathering charts, she hurried to complete the morning rounds.

RAPID DESCENT

nticipation had Elise buzzing as the helicopter descended to the airstrip in Corvo. The project had been active for several years, but Elise had only visited once. Her hitchhiker was seeing it for the first time.

Chuckling at his salty quips inside her head, she hefted her pack and joined the group on the tarmac. She had previously met each new team member—computer genius Colonel Randy Kowalski, his friend Khenko Blitherstone, and Freya Satterfield, an American-born Fomorian and harmonics expert recruited by Cybele.

Freya was young but the best in her field. Her parents, both AIA agents, had died on a mission when Freya was eight. The agency had adopted, schooled, and trained her.

The group climbed into the waiting van, and Antonio Delgado, their island liaison, drove them two miles out of town. Pulling to the deserted roadside, he parked the vehicle.

"We're here." He regarded them in the rearview mirror.

"Here where?" Khenko snorted, taking in the sparse landscape bordered by a restless sea. Grazing cows raised curious heads from rocky vegetation to eye them.

"Our destination." Elise slung her duffel bag over one shoulder, secured the floppy hat on her head, and exited the vehicle.

The others followed suit. Once they unloaded, Antonio pointed to the mountain looming on their left.

"Follow me."

They walked a short distance to an entrance obscured in the mountain. Elise dropped her heavy bag and moved aside to make room for the others.

Antonio tapped jangling keys against a nearly invisible metal plate. There was a click and a whir, and a section slid away, exposing a computer screen.

"State your business," a voice commanded.

Antonio motioned to Elise. She stepped to the screen.

"AIA Assistant Director Elise Hester Johnson, here with the recruits as requested."

"Assistant Director," the voice mellowed. "Welcome to Corvo. Someone will be up to fetch you momentarily."

There was a deeper whir, and Elise glanced at the others. Khenko and Freya's eyebrows soared, but Elise thought she caught a glint of mutiny in Kowalski's eyes before his lips flattened into the semblance of a smile.

Then, a portion of the mountainside slid sideways, revealing double steel doors. High and wide enough for an armored tank to pass through, they opened slowly, and a tall, thin officer with gray eyes greeted them with a brisk salute.

"I'm Lieutenant Evans, Ma'am. Please step inside."

Returning the salutation, Elise and the recruits followed the lieutenant across a gigantic chamber to enter an oversized lift. The doors clanged shut. Then, the car lurched and moved slowly downward, picking up speed as they descended.

On her first time down, Elise nearly peed her pants. This time, she couldn't shake the feeling they were hurtling toward hell.

The Fomorian's eyes were closed, face serene. Kowalski nodded to Elise nonchalantly. But Khenko was another story. His face had turned pale green, and when the lift finally stopped, he gasped and gripped the rail, looking faint.

Elise prodded him with an elbow. "Are you okay?"

The tall man rolled his eyes upward and took a deep, settling breath. "You could've warned me. I'm not keen on any scenario in which I plummet to my death." He rolled his eyes again and muttered sullenly, "And I prefer to be able to see the sun and sky."

"Well, get used to it," she snapped. "Your home will be down here for the immediate future. At least until we complete the mission."

"What *is* our mission?" Kowalski inquired.

Elise sensed a storm brewing beneath that calm exterior.

"You will be briefed soon," the lieutenant answered. "Please follow me."

The elevator opened on an expanse of what appeared to be hardened magma. Khenko gulped and followed the lieutenant and Assistant Director Johnson from the elevator.

Freya twirled to take in the well-lit surroundings and trilled in obvious delight, "We're inside the volcano. I thought we must be."

"Thank God it's extinct." Randy hefted his pack on his shoulder and surveyed the wavy walls warily.

"That doesn't mean it can't come to life," Khenko said, almost tripping over his feet. Randy stopped and stared open-mouthed, and Khenko hurriedly added, "But the possibility is next to nothing, so no worries, Dude." He bumped the burly Marine's shoulder with his fist for good measure.

They walked to the far side of the vent, where another set of doors waited. These opened to a second lift, which descended even more rapidly than the first. Claustrophobia threatened, and Khenko shoved it down with the other mental monsters that nipped at him.

He closed his eyes and breathed in and out, emptying his mind. Then, a scene popped into Khenko's head.

He was on a beach, *his* beach at the Atlantean Center on Zephyr Cay. An aqua dragon lolled on the white sand, a multicolored one frolicked in the shallow surf, and a silver drake circled low overhead. They surrounded a woman. And not just any woman. Someone Khenko had rescued and nursed back to health.

The vision faded, but the elevator still whirred. How far had they descended? How much farther would they go? And why couldn't Khenko hold on to the memories of the redheaded woman with the laughing green eyes?

Finally, the car slowed and stopped, and Khenko met the gaze of the other passengers. Agent Johnson's knowing smile spoke volumes. Then the doors slid aside, and Khenko gasped.

A tall, thin being with nearly translucent skin and large, compassionate eyes was waiting outside. Agent Johnson stepped from the car, conversed with the being in another language, and then turned to Khenko's group.

"White Star asked that we follow her."

Khenko trailed behind, gaze darting everywhere. The sky extended for miles overhead, and if he didn't know better, he would guess they were on the surface of Earth rather than deep inside. Only the light source was larger and glowed a pale, smoky red.

The terrain was just as astonishing. Giant vegetation covered the landscape in myriad shades of green. And in the center of all that lusciousness rose a watery island that seemed to float in the air. Concentric circles framed a soaring city, and water flowed through and around the rings to cascade over the edges of a translucent outer basin.

White Star leaned close to confide in English, "Only a privileged few are allowed entrance." Then she bowed and warbled, "Welcome to the Queendom of Atlantis."

Khenko's heart leapt.

So, this was Atlantis. A wave of profound love washed over him. Khenko fell to his knees and touched his forehead to the grass, sobbing silently.

He recognized this place. He had seen it in his dreams, and now he knew why. It was Khenko's heart home. He belonged here. His mother had said so, and now Khenko knew it too. Like always, Val Blitherstone had spoken the truth. His wonder knew no bounds.

"Um, K-Man?" Randy prodded his rear with a booted toe. "Are you okay?"

Khenko stood and could feel ecstasy radiating from him.

"Never better," he purred with an enormous grin.

An odd-shaped vehicle zipped silently overhead, then descended to land in front of them. The top opened like a clamshell, and a stocky pilot jumped out and removed his helmet.

"Climb aboard," the being said, loading their bags in the back while Khenko, Randy, Freya, and Agent Johnson said goodbye to White Star and piled into the plane.

ATLANTIS

In the middle of the Atlantic Ocean, eight hundred miles west of Lisbon, Portugal, and tens of thousands of fathoms beneath the Azorean Isle of Corvo, lay the lost continent of Atlantis.

The pilot had flown Khenko and the others from the island's outskirts to the central city. Now, he led them to a large, richly appointed hall. Khenko drooled over ancient, soaring columns and the sheer grandeur of everything.

Realizing the group had left him behind, he hurried to catch up and found himself open-mouthed again. Not since the last ComicCon, or maybe that last episode he had watched of *Men in Black*, had Khenko seen so many non-human beings in one place. Or so many species of them.

Most continued working, but two broke away from their stations to greet them. Khenko skidded in beside Randy, and Agent Johnson scrunched her nose at him. Then, speaking in exacting English, she introduced herself and presented Khenko, Randy, and Freya.

The beings nodded vigorously, obviously pleased. Then, the tallest stepped forward. She bowed, long and lean with a thin face and wispy white hair, and her flowing white robe gathered around her. Then her pale lips, narrow as slashes, parted to speak in lilting English.

"I am Lahda, from the Pleiadian system." She nodded toward similar beings. "My brethren and I have come to aid Earth in her time of need." An icy chill ran through Khenko when her eyes lingered on him. "Please allow me to introduce my colleague."

The other being stepped up beside Lahda. He was almost as tall but meatier and looked like a human.

He bowed slightly, gestured toward several comrades nearby, and boomed in a deep voice, "I and my sages have been summoned from Shambhala to help save our planet. Our names, unfortunately, are difficult for human tongues to pronounce. Most call me Basketball." He grinned mischievously and added with a flourish, "Or Jones."

A hearty laugh burst from Randy, and Khenko snorted. The Marine clapped a hand over his mouth, gaze flying to Elise, but she was laughing, too.

"Yes, Randy," Lahda smiled, "Basketball here is quite the comedian. As you have discerned, he has chosen his handle from an old American film."

In a screech reminiscent of the song by pot pioneers Cheech and Chong, the being threw back his head and shrilled,

"Basketball Jones, I've got a Basketball Jones, I've got a Basketball Jones, oh baby, ooo ooo ooo…"

Then, he fake-dribbled an imaginary basketball, made a pretend layup, and strutted around the hall in a mock victory dance.

Everyone in the room laughed—all but Lahda. She smiled graciously, but when Jones was done, and the laughter died away, she clapped and regarded them solemnly.

"Please follow Jonesy. He will show you to your quarters and introduce you to your teams."

☼☼☼

"Can you believe we're in Atlantis?" Hamilton crooned inside Elise's head. They followed Jones through a crystal-lined cave. "Aren't you glad I talked you into coming?"

"Oh, yeah," Elise snarked silently. She stopped and flapped her hands to release the adrenaline surging through her system. "I'm sure it'll be an adventure to remember."

Her last visit had changed Elise forever. And not necessarily in a good way.

"Weren't you stationed here during the war?" Kowalski asked.

Elise shuddered, then decided he was making conversation, not listening to her and Ham's silent discourse. She nodded over her shoulder, grateful when they entered a garden, and the towering plants claimed everyone's attention.

The sky was visible through the soaring dome, relieving some of the tension Elise always felt when underground. A group of tall, humanoid gardeners acknowledged their presence with nods and grudging waves. Most Atlanteans distrusted outsiders and would prefer not to have them roam their queendom, but this had not always been the case.

Hamilton ooo'd and ahh'd inside her head, prompting Elise to pay attention to the crystals of every shape and color that lined the wide walkway. Her hitchhiker explained how each crystal emitted

336

different bursts of energy when sparked by the sun. She had not known that.

Birds sang in shade trees and pecked in the grass framing the central garden. Butterflies flitted from one brightly colored blossom to another. The path curved, and there, in the center of the grounds, a massive tree soared, its umbrella canopy reaching for the dome.

Jones paused to speak to a gardener. Kowalski's gaze roved side to side. Freya bent to inspect boulder-sized crystals. But Khenko made for the umbrella tree. Her breath hitched when Elise realized he looked a lot like the Atlanteans. That would explain a lot.

Something niggled at her attention, biting around the edges. Something that wasn't Hamilton. Words formed, but Elise didn't understand.

"There will be an opportunity to explore later," Jones called to Khenko. "After we get you settled and introduced to your team. Earth's time grows short."

Chilled by the reminder, Elise dismissed the intrusion and groaned to Hamilton, "Why did I let you get me into this?"

"Let me? HA! You orchestrated the whole thing!"

"Did not."

"Did, too."

"No. I did not. Now hush, Ham!"

Khenko returned to the group reluctantly. Like the plants outside the city, the ones here were familiar but many times larger than those on the surface. The gigantic tree reminded him of the Kapok on Zephyr Cay, and for a moment, he was seized by homesickness. He missed the Atlantean Center and his island boyfriend.

Several tall gardeners ceased working and watched them pass through their sacred domain. One pointed at Khenko and mumbled something that prompted odd stares from the others. Shaking off the prickles, Khenko sped up to follow his group into a humid grotto where the spring burbled over crystalline boulders, pebbles, and scree.

The ceiling soared overhead, and stalactites and stalagmites lined both sides of the narrow path. Some grew together to form gigantic columns that glittered in the artificial light.

"I have never seen anything this beautiful," Khenko murmured reverently.

"Me neither," Freya said. He could tell from her rapt expression that she, too, was boggled by it all.

Randy, on the other hand, sagged as if ill.

"You okay, Rowdy?"

"Not even." Misery oozed from Randy's pores. Khenko stepped closer.

"What's wrong, dude?"

Tears filled his friend's eyes, then he blinked them away and wagged his head. "I'll tell you later."

"You sure?" In Khenko's memory, not much had ever bothered Randy. But his friend nodded vigorously.

"Gentlemen," Elise called from the far side of the chamber. Khenko had lagged once again.

She started to say something but instead shrilled, "holy shit!" and sprang to the side of the path. Then she went up on her tiptoes and shrugged away from something Khenko could not see.

"Agent Johnson?" Randy said as he reached her. "Elise?" He touched her shoulder, and she screamed like a teen.

Then the AD recovered, tucking her emotions away, and turned to join Basketball Jones and Freya, who had come back to find them.

But Jones had witnessed Elise's odd behavior. He took her hand and said quietly, "It's okay, dear. They are fierce but harmless."

That left Khenko, Randy, and Freya staring at one another, wondering what had transpired.

"What was it?" Khenko asked, but Elise ignored him to follow Basketball Jones into a larger cave.

Inside, Jones regarded them with a knowing smile, and everyone gasped. Long, thick columns of milky gypsum and selenite crisscrossed the cavern from floor to ceiling. It was so rare that only a few such formations had been discovered worldwide.

Khenko was reluctant to leave the gargantuan crystals, but the heat was oppressive and the air foul. He followed the group as they hurried out.

Soon, they came to the Crystal Room. The domed chamber was open to Inner Earth's lofty sky, and a colossal six-sided rod of quartz stood in the center. Easily as thick as the umbrella tree's trunk, it stood upright and pointed to the heavens. A soft light emanated from its depths, and several of the tall beings they had encountered in the garden stood around it.

Freya squealed and dashed across the clearing, making a beeline for one strangely familiar being. When the diminutive Fomorian launched herself and threw her arms around him, shouting, "Dr. B! It's you!" Khenko's jaw dropped. And when the being's booming laugh bounced off the walls of the caverns, Khenko couldn't believe his ears.

He knew that laugh. But it couldn't be.

Khenko inspected the man Freya had called Dr. B.

Randy poked him with an elbow. "Dude. Isn't that your father? How'd he get so… huge?" The abnormally tall man chatted with Freya, but his gaze kept darting to Khenko.

"Pa?" It couldn't be. He was too tall, and the skin that had looked so sallow in Princeton two days ago didn't sag around his jowls. But the eyes pierced like his Pa's. They focused on Khenko with laser precision.

"Big Bird."

The pet name skewered Khenko's heart, and the ever-present tone of disappointment was missing. But when Khenko remained motionless and slack-jawed, it crept into hazel eyes that were no longer tired or run down.

Elise Johnson stepped between them and introduced herself. The giant took Elise's hand and pumped it gently. "Assistant Director Johnson."

She pinked and cooed uncharacteristically. "Please, call me Elise. I am here as an interpreter for these three."

Eyes on Khenko, the man rumbled, "Elise, I am Dr. John Blitherstone. Thank you for enlisting my son."

He reached out and drew Khenko into an awkward embrace and spoke to Elise over his head. "I don't know if you know this, but my son is the most gifted medical intuitive in the world."

Khenko's stomach did a loop-de-loop. His Pa's compliments were rare.

"I'm certain he'll be an asset to Lord Thoth and Lady Druantia."

Recognizing the names, Khenko slipped from his father's grasp and, at almost seven feet tall, had to crane his neck to look into his sparkling eyes.

"How did you get here, Pa? Was it Ma's vision about Druantia and the Azores?"

A clear, crystalline laugh rang behind him, and Khenko's heart thumped. He wheeled as his mother, still normal-sized, broke away from the others to embrace him. She beamed with pride.

"I knew you would come," she whispered to Khenko, then patted her husband's elbow and gazed up at him adoringly. "See. I told you our son would be here."

"You did," he admitted with a benevolent smile.

"Pa! You must be nine feet tall. How did *that* happen?"

But his mother interrupted, extending her hand to Elise.

"Assistant Director Johnson, I'm Valerie Blitherstone. You probably don't remember, but I worked with you briefly at the agency." She glanced up at her husband. "That was how I first ended up in the Azores. And where I met John."

Khenko listened, his curiosity piqued. He had not known that, nor did he know why they were here. But it appeared he would have to wait for answers.

MUTINY

Nergal slammed his empty mug on the bar and motioned to the bartender, a cross-dressing Jacquadian who teetered on ridiculously high heels.

"Another furroot?

"Aye," Nergal growled.

His mood was foul after so much destruction. He became more reluctant to lead his Dracs against AboveEarth with every attack. Every sortie ended with mutilated corpses of humans and Reptilians, followed by dragon attacks against their bases.

Xibalba IX had been a precautionary strike, a taste of what to expect if the Reptilians proceeded against the Humans. Yet neither Shibboleth nor Nergal had taken heed. Now, many Reptilian cities were stinking wastelands of scorched and gutted buildings, homes, and businesses. All because of the lies and deceit that had been perpetuated for millennia.

Nergal had forgotten how uncomfortable and depressing Earth's surface could be. Why would anyone trade thousands of years to live in a world without a canopy? Yes, there was beauty. But the sun blazed down with little protection, and the howling winds stripped all moisture from the living.

Worse, Nergal had lost another brilliant scientist. Now, none like Azi or Ishkur were left—a death knell for Reptilian technology and a travesty in Nergal's reckoning.

He threw back his second glass of furroot and belched loudly, sending an Octedron scurrying. Nergal's penchant for rage was legendary. The other patrons had already moved away.

"Well, well, General Nergal. Drunk again?"

He spun on the barstool. "No, Commander Inanna. Just getting started. Care to join me?" He signaled to the barkeep, whose fake lashes fluttered as they hurried to take Inanna's order.

The Draca straddled the nearest stool and nodded at Nergal's drink. "What he's having."

The Jacquad fished a chilled mug from the cooler. They filled it to the brim and slid it on the bar, red lips parting in a leer that revealed small, razor-sharp teeth.

"Ten quisha."

"He's paying," Inanna snarled.

Nergal nodded assent and ordered another. The bartender peered at him intently as if deciding whether they should cut him off.

"Now!" Nergal barked.

Lip protruding in a sulky pout, they drew the furroot and retreated to the other end of the bar.

"What's eating you, General?" Inanna took a long draught of the strong, fermented beverage, then burped somewhat daintily for a Drac.

Nergal swirled his potent brown liquid and stared into the glass. "Did Shibboleth send you here to reprimand me?"

She snorted, drained her glass, and signaled the barkeep. "Is that really what's bothering you? You know how much I despise my litter father."

That he did. Nergal hesitated, then said flatly. "You don't want to know."

"I asked, didn't I?"

He stared at Inanna a long while, then sighed and sagged against the stool. Maybe misery did love company.

"It's this war, Inanna," he finally said. "I am the last you would expect to hear this from, but I cannot stomach the senseless killing of our Dracs or the humans. For millennia, I've been hearing how awful they are and how Humans were allowed to keep the glorious AboveEarth while we Reptilians were relegated to the pits of UnderEarth.

"But in all my long years, the humans have never done anything to hurt us. And I don't know about you, but I like it down here much better than up there on the surface."

She stared off into space, then at Nergal. "I agree."

His jaw fell open. "You do? Which part?"

"All of it, Nergal. And I have a plan. Want to hear?"

He gawked at Inanna, then slid from the stool. "Yes. But gimme a minute."

Nergal strode through the crowded bar to the loo. One of two remaining gin joints not razed by the dragon, the Empty Spike was anything but. Every species imaginable had crammed into the dim space. But only a few were Dracs, either wet behind the ears or aged and feeble.

As Nergal shouldered his way back through the sea of bodies, he spied an Azi lookalike at the front door and nearly choked on regret. If he had obeyed Shibboleth's order and kept Azi in the lab, the brilliant scientist would still be alive.

Hailing Inanna, Nergal sat down heavily and waved for another drink. But when razor-sharp claws dug into his shoulder, Nergal shirked and countered with a fist to the owner's jaw.

"Oww, Nergal! What was that for?" a husky voice grumbled from the floor.

Yelping loud enough to be heard outside, Nergal helped the cheeky scientist up from the floor and clamped his arms around Azi before shoving him away.

"We thought you were dead."

"Or captured." Inanna bent to inspect the new abrasion on Azi's face. "How did you escape?

"Long story." Azi leaned toward the Jacquadian, who was watching their exchange with much interest. "Furroot, please. The larger, the better. On his tab."

Nergal grumbled but nodded consent.

"I am not your bank. Or yours either," he snapped when Inanna snorted.

Fluffing their teased hair with one hand and delivering Azi's drink with the other, the bartender batted false eyelashes and propped bony elbows against the bar. Their dreamy golden eyes roved Azi up and down.

Ever pragmatic, the scientist seemed to be unaware that they were flirting. Azi guzzled the furroot, wiping the spillover from his chin and chest before belching long, loud, and proud.

The barkeep's narrow nasal bridge wrinkled in disgust. Then they pivoted on the ridiculous heels and pranced away.

Chuckling, Azi winked at Nergal and Inanna, then leaned close.

"We have to stop this war."

THE JOINING SPELL

Elise had not known that Khenko was the famed Dr. Blitherstone's son. Or that the lanky medicine man had such remarkable abilities. But she now understood why Kowalski's friend had been recruited to join the mission.

Dr. B, as their leader preferred to be called, had introduced each team member. Now, he was briefing them on their assignment—to find the tuning for Earth's vibrational frequency that would return it to homeostasis.

For centuries, a catastrophic pole shift had been held at bay by the light beings. But Thoth and Queen Druantia's methods were no longer working.

White Star, the Pleiadian, entered the dome and joined the conversation.

"The bottom line," the gentle being sighed, "is that Earth has lost her song. Her frequency is out of warp, and she can no longer hold any tuning we try. Our task, and now yours," she bowed to Khenko's group, "is to help Earth find her song. The council feels once we accomplish this, Earth's frequency will stabilize."

Randy groaned, but Khenko nodded approvingly, and Freya bounced on excited toes. Then, as Dr. B expounded, White Star stepped into line beside Elise.

A high-pitched tone filled Elise's skull. She jiggled her head and glanced around. No one else seemed bothered. Then, the words that had been nipping at her finally came through.

"Obedo folter, nihema inci, combe ohm."

Elise wiggled her fingers in her ears.

"Obedo folter. Nihema inci. Combe Ohm."

What in the world?

White Star leaned closer. "Are you okay?"

"Do you hear a ringing? Or odd words?"

White Star wagged her head, eyes wide.

Then Elise heard it again. "Obedo folter, nihema inci, combe ohm."

Khenko leaned forward and asked, "Is everything okay?"

"I keep hearing a ringing. And words. Do you hear it?"

Khenko wagged his head, but White Star hissed, "I did that time. It is an ancient invocation. I believe it is called the joining spell."

"The joining spell?" Elise pulled at her chin. "I don't believe I've ever heard of that. Why would I be hearing it now?"

"Maybe someone is calling you," Khenko muttered. "Do you know the meaning, White Star?"

"The literal translation is 'united in womb, separated at birth, joined in life.'"

Dr. B called them to attention, but the spell kept careening through Elise's mind. She mumbled it quietly and, when nothing happened, sighed in frustration.

"Maybe it's meant to be a command," Hamilton suggested silently.

"OBEDO FOLTER, NIHEMA INCI, COMBE OHM," Elise said much louder.

Several of the team turned to eye her with alarm as a sparkling star tetrahedron appeared around Elise and began to spin.

The group gasped in unison, and she swallowed hard. Elise knew better than to perform spells she didn't understand. What in heaven's name had possessed her?

The tetrahedron's components spun faster and faster until there was a brilliant blue flash of light. The dome and its gigantic Atlantis crystal disappeared along with the workers, and Elise found herself hurtling through a tunnel of light.

A long-ago lesson came to mind. She was in a wormhole. The spell had somehow activated her light body, something Elise had forgotten she even had—and only God knew where she was headed.

ATOP YR WYDDFA

Rona changed clothes and collected her things while Alexis retrieved a stylish backpack from Honey's Porsche. Then, they gathered in the living room, faced one another, and joined hands.

Having had an inkling she might need her merkaba, Rona had been practicing over the last couple of weeks. She'd only traveled short distances, afraid to go further. But knowing Alexis was with her bolstered Rona's courage.

In the middle of Canongate's massive living room, Rona breathed deeply, grounded, and connected with the elements. Then, visualizing her light body, she watched it appear. When the whirling rings blurred, Rona drew Alexis inside the merkaba and focused her attention on Emily's location.

There was a flash, then a thick haze enveloped them. When it parted, they were in a long, stretchy tunnel of light. Letting go of Alexis's hand, as Awen had taught them long ago, Rona embraced the sensation of gliding weightlessly through the fluffy tunnel.

☼☼☼

Inside the accidental wormhole that had whisked her away from the Atlantis project, Elise emptied her mind of all but the spell.

"United in the womb, separated at birth, joined in life… united in the womb, separated at birth, joined in life…"

The light brightened, and Elise opened her eyes to find she was hurtling toward a snowy mountaintop. Below her, two women exchanged curses. Then, the redhead went down, and two others appeared from nowhere.

It suddenly occurred to Elise that she would die on impact if she didn't slow down. Then she "saw" herself drifting gently to the ground. As her heels made contact, an invisible force struck Elise, slamming her backward into a snowbank. What the heck?

The sounds of battle rose around her, curses sizzling and women grunting. She kept her head down, assessing the situation as a spell zinged past. Emily lay crumpled in the snow, red hair stark against the white expanse. Elise knew one of the other women. Two were strangers.

Her old druid friend, Rona Wainwright, slung curses at a witch with long black hair. Elise winced as the witch sent Rona flying, then faced the blonde, lips twisted in a sneer.

The witch might be beautiful, but wickedness oozed from her, dark, stinking, vile evil. Insults spewed from her sensuous lips.

The blonde laughed and tossed her thick, luscious hair over one shoulder. "Seriously? All you have are insults?"

Incensed, the witch sent lightning from her fingertips.

The sassy blonde sidestepped and slung curses of her own. One struck the witch's shoulder, spinning her in a circle. Then, wobbling precariously, the witch planted her wand and sent the blonde cartwheeling backward.

Ice spewed from the wand's tip to race across the frigid landscape. A brittle wind shrieked, wielding tiny frozen crystals that bit into Elise's skin. She wracked her brain, trying to remember her rusty magical skills. Coming up with nothing, she threw her body between the ice and the downed women.

Inside her head, Hamilton growled, "Let go, I've got this."

He halted the ice with a complicated spell and battled the witch curse for curse.

Elise paid close attention to each of his spells, several of which she should have known and advanced ones she had never learned. But her feet were nimble, and they eluded the witch's curses until the snow fell so hard that it obscured their vision.

From the corner of one eye, Elise saw Rona stagger to her feet and charge. The witch wheeled to counter, but none of Rona's spells landed.

"Ham, help Rona." Elise leapt in front of her to block a sizzling hex.

Then, Hamilton and the blonde slung curses simultaneously.

The witch screamed and crumpled to the ground. She writhed in the snow, glaring up at them. Then she stilled, and the light of awareness dawned.

"Well, if it's not my bastard daughters. And all this time, I thought you were dead."

Elise's jaw fell open. For most of her life, she had ached to know the identity of her birth parents. Now, her heart pounded, and she felt sick to her stomach.

"*You* are my mother?" Never in a million years would Elise have imagined… THIS.

The witch cackled and sat up.

"Why, yes, I am, deary."

Then, as the druid women stared in disbelief, she leapt to her feet, whirled her wand above her head, and planted it in the accumulating snow. Wind-driven ice whistled down the mountain, and the temperature plummeted.

Ham flicked Elise's wrist to bind the witch's arms behind her. Then, he quickly wove a protection spell around Elise and the women.

Rona stood over the witch, hands on her hips. "You're claiming the three of us are *your* daughters? And we're sisters? First off, I highly doubt it. And second, I'll be the first to say you are a lousy mother." Elise had never seen the typically gentle woman so angry.

The witch laughed and struggled to escape Ham's restraint.

"You are hardly the first, deary. And not only are you sisters, you shared my womb."

"Then why don't I remember you?" Rona wailed.

"Why?" the witch shrilled. "Because you are all supposed to be dead. I left you where I squatted to shit you out."

They gasped at the sheer insensitivity. But the blonde crouched and thrust her nose in the wicked witch's face.

"Who are you?"

The proud chin went up, and the witch stared haughtily.

"My name is Bé Chuille, Witch Goddess of Marduk and the Tuatha de Danaan. Some call me Cailleach, and I am that. But I am so much more. Ancient of ancient, I have lived over twenty thousand years, half on this planet. Over the millennia, I produced many bastards and raised none. I never wanted a baby, much less three humans."

Horrified by her revolting confession, a shudder gripped Elise. But, the joining spell suddenly made sense. Hot molten lead coursed through her veins. She pointed to the blonde.

"We are not the same age."

"This one's hiding inside a younger body," the witch pointed at the blonde. "But you look like your fathers."

The blonde gasped. "Fathers? There is more than one?"

"It was the 80s, deary. Who the hell knows? But you're definitely half human."

☼☼☼

While the women debated the authenticity of Bé's claim, she escaped the binding curse, snatched up her wand, and hugged it to her chest. Beams of electricity shot from her body, and the three women flew backward to sprawl unconscious in the snow.

She laughed and glared down at them with contempt. "You, I'll deal with later."

Then, wondering why she was surprised her offspring had survived, Bé stalked to Awen. Her redheaded nemesis was buried beneath a blanket of snow, spellbound. Bé poked her hard with the wand.

"It was you, wasn't it? *You* rescued my whelps, you insolent cur. You'll be sorry for that."

She reared back to strike the killing blow, and was shocked when a thin sheet of plastic wrapped around her arms and lashed them to her sides. It encircled her head and body several times, then jerked tight, sealing Bé inside a painful, airless prison.

Eyes bulging, she gasped for breath and labored to escape. But the light grew dim and the consciousness slowly eked from her body.

The belligerent blonde prodded Bé's shoulder with a toe.

That was enough. Bé left her dying body and slipped into the woman.

☼☼☼

Elise watched aghast as the witch struggled to breathe. The throes of dying was never pretty, but soon, the shapely body stopped thrashing and went slack.

The blonde prodded it, then leaned down to feel the neck for a pulse. "She's dead," she announced with a vacant expression. "Ding-dong."

"What the hell *was* that, anyway?" Rona groaned. She stared down at the plastic-wrapped corpse gathering snow.

"Our mother, apparently." Elise shuddered and crossed her arms over her chest. "Makes me feel stupid for all the pining I did over the years. How about you?"

Rona's snow-covered head bobbled up and down, and her wide eyes brimmed with tears. Then, a sob escaped, and Rona fell to her knees.

"Don't cry. She's not worth it." The hard voice sounded vaguely familiar.

"Who *are* you?" Elise demanded.

"Your sister, according to this freaking witch." She kicked the corpse for good measure.

"But you're way too young. And… well, hell, too pretty."

"Like she said," the blonde gestured to the witch, "I'm hitchhiking in someone else's body." She grabbed Elise by the shoulders and stared into her eyes.

"I'm Alexis, you old bat. Don't you recognize me?" Then, spying something, she let go and bent to slit the plastic with a manicured nail and retrieved the witch's wand.

Elise thrust out her hand. "I'll take that." It was not a request. "And no, I do not recognize you. Alexis Mayhall is dead, ergo, you cannot possibly be her. So, who the fuck are you?"

The blonde laughed, a tinkling cascade that was utterly enchanting. Then she plopped the wand in Elise's waiting palm.

"Ergo, huh? I *was* dead, 'Leesy. A dragon brought me back. You know, you always were bossy. I like that about you."

Elise snorted and flipped her head upside down to shake the snow from her hair. "Yeah, right. A dragon brought you back." But what about the nickname?

She studied the blonde claiming to be Alexis, then Rona Wainwright. At the moment, they looked like angels hovering over a dead witch. Then, the absurdity of their situation struck Elise, and she busted out laughing. As it bubbled out, Rona started laughing, too.

The blonde stomped her foot. "Stop it, y'all. I *am* Alexis."

But they kept on laughing, and she planted her fists on the curvy hips.

"It's true. I borrowed Honey's body. Didn't I, Honey? Tell these idiots so they'll stop laughing at me. Or rather, at us."

The lovely face morphed to a younger, more radiant version, and a sweet molasses voice left the plump lips.

"Hi, y'all. I am Honey Dewars, Alexis's willing hostess." She looked down at the witch. "That 'bout scared the dickens outta me, but I'm having the time of my life. And, I'm pleased as punch to meet y'all."

Chills roamed every inch of Elise's body. Taking the hand the blonde offered, she yanked the woman to her. She knew having a hitchhiker was possible—she had one of her own—but people didn't just come back to life. She searched the blue eyes for a hint Alexis might be in there.

The voice changed again, and the eyes hardened.

"Remember how much we hated the Katy Kats?"

Elise recoiled. Then, satisfied, she nodded and let the blonde go.

"I still do. But damn it, Alexis. How can this be?"

There was a sudden thwap, and Rona wheeled. Standing in the blinding snow behind a tall dog was her son and Lugh MacBrayer.

"Mitch!" Rona ran to wrap him in a bear hug.

But when Lugh yelped and rushed to the redhead crumpled in the snow, shame washed over Rona.

They had come to rescue her long-lost daughter. But after battling the witch, they had left Emily lying in the snow while they argued. She dragged Mitch with her to watch with bated breath as Lugh gathered her in his lap

"Wake up, Emily," Lugh breathed softly against her frigid ear.

Cu whined beside him. They worked to bring her back while the others tried every spell they knew to stop the snowstorm. Instead of ceasing, it blew stronger.

Mitch's mom and the blonde squatted on the other side of Emily. "Honey, this is Lugh MacBrayer, our priest. Lugh, meet Honey Dewars."

He nodded but kept his eyes on Emily.

"May we try?" Rona asked gently.

Grateful, Lugh relented. He carefully transferred Emily's head to Rona's lap. Honey placed her palms on either side of Emily's face, leaned close, and spoke an unfamiliar incantation.

Emily's eyelids fluttered, but she didn't wake.

"Try the druid kiss," he urged.

"You do it, Lugh." Mitchell loomed above them. "She loves you."

Honey nodded to Lugh and moved aside. He kneeled and lovingly laid his palms where hers had been. Then, leaning closer, he kissed Emily's forehead, nose, chin, closed eyes, cheeks, and mouth.

This time, her eyes opened but remained vague. They traced the faces, beginning and ending with Lugh's. Then Emily shivered hard and mumbled, "Br-rrr."

Lugh lifted her upright and held her against him until her violent trembling eased.

"Thank you," she whispered in a voice that wasn't Emily's. Then, she escaped his embrace and brushed snow from her robe.

Lugh stared. Had Awen spoken?

She reached for Elise, then Rona, then Honey, lightly running her fingertips over their cold-reddened cheeks.

"My angels," she crooned in a deeper, older timbre.

What was going on? The women had been here before Lugh and Mitch. But how had they arrived? And what did Awen, if it *was* Awen, mean by 'her angels?'

A deep rumble of thunder sounded nearby, and Emily's eyes went vague.

"We must get off the mountain," the deeper voice decreed.

Lugh wholeheartedly agreed. But what was going on? Was this Awen or Emily?

"It's Awen." Rona placed a reassuring hand on his shoulder. "You're not going crazy. She's speaking through Emily."

Cu yipped and jumped, front paws landing on Emily's shoulders. She threw her arms around the snowy hound's neck, blinked the flakes from her lashes, and decreed in Awen's voice, "It's time to go."

The wind intensified, and there was another rumble of thunder.

"Where to?" Lugh and Mitch yelled.

"And how?" Elise yelled, hands cupped.

"Cu could take us," Mitch offered. "That's how we got here."

"Indeed? Good job, Cu. Stay by me." Awen patted Emily's thigh, and the wolfhound snugged close. "Everyone else, join hands."

Lugh took her and Mitch's hands. The earth trembled beneath their feet as Honey, Elise, and Rona completed the circle.

"What about Bé Chuille?" Honey yelled.

The earth groaned and shuddered. Then Awen/Emily waved her hand at the plastic-wrapped corpse, and it disappeared.

Lugh stared in amazement. Moments later, his breath left his body as they were sucked into a massive wormhole.

The group entered as one, then let go at Awen's instruction and flew solo through the billowing light trails.

SHARHEA

ShaRhea gently massaged Shibboleth's aging hips and feet. He had won her several thousand years ago from a human despot, and the Reylian had been with Shibboleth ever since. In the beginning, he had taken her as a lover. But over time, Shibboleth had come to crave her companionship more than her fleshly gifts.

Few knew about ShaRhea. She stayed because he made sure she wanted for nothing. That and their fondness for one another. She was Shibboleth's confidante and confessor. His refuge in every storm.

An ultra-intelligent and strong-willed creature, she liked to boss Shibboleth around. He took it in stride because she was also brutally honest, a trait difficult for rulers to find. ShaRhea never sugarcoated anything. Plus, the Reylian human was psychic, a rarity in UnderEarth.

"What do you see, ShaRhea?" It was his second time asking. The first had been met with moody silence.

"The news is not good today. We shall let this one pass unheeded, Sir."

Shibboleth swung a leg off the table and stood, appendage bulging beneath his cloaca. It was a rarity for him these days. ShaRhea's human hand reached out to caress it, and Shibboleth moaned.

"It's been so long, She-Ra." And even longer since he had used the affectionate nickname.

"How long?" Her other hand reached inside his flap, gently releasing Shibboleth's throbbing schlong. No longer was it old and withered as it had been since the witch sucked him dry and then betrayed him.

"A long, long, looong, time." His cock lengthened and enlarged as if on command.

ShaRhea fondled it gently, feathering her gifted fingers up and down its sensitive underside and around its tip until Shibboleth moaned with desire.

He knew she was distracting him from what she had seen, but he leaned into her, happy to have his wood back. ShaRhea worked his schlong, smiling mysteriously until he ejaculated, then she wiped him clean and stood to go.

Shibboleth grabbed her arm.

"Tell me. That's an order."

ShaRhea's smile vanished. She drew up a chair and regarded him briefly. When she spoke, he wished she hadn't.

"This will not end well. Especially for you."

A tightness squeezed Shibboleth's chest. "This, what? What do you mean?" A touch from ShaRhea released the band, and he could breathe again.

"This war you have started. It will not end well."

"Your point?" Shibboleth stared at the Reylian. Wars never ended well. But he had to get off this forsaken planet, and for that, he needed to get to the surface.

"You tell me."

Shibboleth's stomach roiled. He stared into her violet eyes.

"What do you see, ShaRhea?"

"I see an old lizard tilting at windmills."

He stared at the woman. She had lived among the humans and often used phrases Shibboleth didn't understand.

"What does that mean?"

Her penetrating gaze chilled his blood.

"That you are running around in circles. You are like a tempest in a teapot, making a lot of noise and commotion but going nowhere." She touched his claw. "What is it you want, Warlord Shibboleth?"

"To take AboveEarth from the Humans."

"And then what? You don't need the land. Your race inhabits only a fraction of UnderEarth, so it can't be that. What is it you want, Mighty Shibboleth?"

Temper spiking at her interrogation, Shibboleth snapped.

"I want off this forsaken rock."

"Ahhh," ShaRhea purred. "So you believe you can finally leave Earth if you gain control of the surface?"

Shibboleth had asked himself the same question over the millennia. He glared at the Reylian.

"Aye. I hate it here."

ShaRhea closed her eyes and seemed to drift away. Then they snapped open and locked on him.

"Have you always hated it here?"

"Aye. I never meant to stay. Not indefinitely."

Her pert nose scrunched. "So what happened?"

Shibboleth's thoughts raced back to his arrival on Earth.

"Marduk. Our planetship came too close to its orbit, destroying the planets and exiling both races to Earth. Without their queen, Druantia, we would have died in space. All of us." Shibboleth sighed. Long had it been since he had thought of the druid goddess from Marduk.

ShaRhea stiffened, and her features morphed, becoming sharper, more angular, and less pliable.

From previous instances, Shibboleth recognized the Reylian leaving her body and another taking her place. She even spoke in a lower, huskier tone.

"Lord Shibboleth, thank you for making contact. It is I, Queen Druantia."

Shock coursed through him. How did the goddess find him?

"You must cease this ill-conceived war. You cannot win. Earth faces the same fate today as our homeworlds, Lord Shibboleth Enki's Son. I petition you to send us your best scientists. Once again, we need your help to correct Earth's imbalance. Before it is too late." Queen Druantia was silent for a long moment, then touched his claw. "If it is not already."

Shibboleth recoiled. Shaking off her hand and the memory, he stood to pace. "Why should I? Inner Earth shall not be affected."

"Would you prefer the alternative? Billions of refugees from the surface world crowding into your precious UnderEarth?" ShaRhea/Druantia stood too, violet eyes narrowed.

"Is *that* to your liking? I tell you now, Shibboleth Enki's Son, there is no guarantee Earth will not implode. Then all will die—including you, your Dracs, *and* our planet."

"I could care less about this planet. And my *liking* would be not to have this conversation. Go away, Druantia. It's what you do best." Druantia had scorned the Reptilian race before.

Her face flushed. "I am afraid that is no longer an option, Warlord. You should not have called if you wished not to get involved."

Shibboleth shuddered. He plopped in the chair, instinctively tracing the keloid that transected his cheek, a wound sustained while enslaved in Inner Earth's gold mines.

Druantia had eventually freed Shibboleth and his Reptilians from the Anunnaki. But she had then turned her back, taking her Druid gods and the precious humans to live on a surface newly terraformed with the help of *his* Dracs.

She had a lot of nerve asking them for help again. Fuming, Shibboleth stalked from the room.

Mot limped through the tunnels, fighting the urge to lie down and go to sleep. Every step was a supreme effort, a battle of will. His limbs felt like columns of ice, and his usually sharp mind struggled to make sense of the horrific scene he had just witnessed—his entire regiment flash-frozen before his eyes.

Usually, Mot would have been in the lead. But as they exited the cave, he paused inside to answer a communique from Shibboleth. Otherwise, he, too, would have been caught in the vortex of frigid air that had ended his warrior's lives and turned them into ice statues.

For the thousands of years Mot had lived beneath Earth's surface, he had never encountered anything like the brutality of AboveEarth's extreme climate.

Tripping on loose scree, Mot nearly went down. He sagged against the rough wall to catch his breath. Then he forged on, dragging the foot he could no longer feel. Soon, the cave grew warmer, and the feeling began returning to Mot's limbs. But the numbness gave way to exquisite pain.

He stopped to rest and retrieved the dense black stone the witch had given him. Clutching it in one claw as he had earlier, he rubbed it the way Bé Chuille had instructed. But she did not come. Again.

Restraining the urge to toss the infernal thing into the darkness, Mot slid the charm back into the slot in his waist belt. Then he forged ahead, trying to ignore the pain.

Bé Chuille had said all Mot had to do was rub the stone and say her name. What good was a talisman if it didn't work?

Shibboleth hurried to the medical wing. Mot had returned— alone and injured, possibly mortally. Anger and frustration ate at him. Would he never make it off this forsaken rock?

QUEEN DRUANTIA & THOTH

❝Shit, shit, shit, shit, SHIT!" Khenko yelped, then ducked to avoid a backhand from his Pa.

"You think cussing will help tune that crystal, Bird?"

Khenko sucked his scraped knuckles and glared up at the oversized man. They'd been working in close proximity all day, and both were well beyond their limits. When AIA Director Elise Johnson had blackmailed Khenko into joining the project, she had failed to mention he would be working with his father—no, not with his father—for his father. It was exasperating.

The new John Blitherstone was everywhere at once. The mysterious ailment he had suffered in Princeton had vanished as inexplicably as it began. He ran circles around the rest of the team. And while Khenko was supposed to work with Lord Thoth and Lady Druantia, he was stuck with his Pa.

Needing to cool off before he did or said something he knew he would regret, Khenko carefully placed the tool in its proper place. Then, drawing a calming breath, he said politely, "Excuse me, Sir. I need air."

He fumed inside, but hoping to hide it, Khenko strolled casually from the crystal cathedral. Wasn't it his luck that Lord Thoth and Lady Druantia had business away from Atlantis? Surely, they would be back soon. Then, he could escape the torture his father seemed to delight in delivering.

Retracing their path from yesterday, Khenko passed through the caverns, then the crystal cave. His heart swelled as his feet carried him to the garden. There, Yggdrasil, the Tree of Life, towered. Or so Khenko had decided to dub her.

He had spent hours in Zephyr Cay lounging on the roots of a Kapok. The umbrella tree had nourished Khenko's spirit. And if it was true that all trees originated from the first, then Yggdrasil must be the kapok's ancestor.

The evenly placed stones lining the path were smooth and warm from the afternoon sun. Khenko kicked off his shoes to feel the grass beneath his bare feet. Then the path curved, and Khenko gazed up at the mother of all trees.

This tree was easily five times the size of the kapok. Curling beneath its welcoming branches, Khenko nestled in a crevice between two exposed roots.

It was quiet except for the drone of bees savoring the nectar of nearby flowers and birds warbling in the tree's crown. A conversation between gardeners rose, then quieted again. Khenko's anger and frustration melted as the garden's fragrant peace washed over him.

He must have dozed because he woke gasping for breath with two gigantic beings kneeling before him. The male's kinky hair was bright red, shot through with gold. But it was the woman's striking beauty that caused Khenko to sigh. Luxurious blond hair outlined a narrow waist and ample assets, and when her lips parted in a radiant smile, his heart melted.

"Khenko Rainman Blitherstone, Descendant of Thoth and Favored of Corr the Crane, I am Queen Druantia, and this is Lord Thoth, your grandfather many generations removed." She bent to extend a hand to Khenko.

Taking it without hesitation, he let her draw him upright. The two radiant beings towered above him heads nearly reaching Yggdrasil's canopy.

"Come," Thoth commanded. "Time draws short."

After conversing with John Blitherstone and meeting Khenko's team, Queen Druantia and Lord Thoth led Khenko and Freya to a nearby cavern. A computer screen took up half of one wall. The rest were covered in interactive maps and charts.

Khenko stopped to eye one that looked familiar, then realized it was a layout of the underwater Mid-Atlantic Ridge, the longest mountain chain in the world. Unlike other charts Khenko had seen, this one showed the ridge extending from the Arctic Ocean between Greenland and Siberia all the way down to the South Atlantic Ocean.

The Gakkel Ridge Caldera, a supervolcano that showed signs of awakening after a million year sleep, marked the northernmost terminus of the Mid-Atlantic Ridge. The active Bouvet Triple Junction where the South American Tectonic Plate met the African and Antarctic Plates, marked the southern boundary. Odd things had been happening there for decades.

In the North Atlantic, the Mid-Atlantic Ridge curved like a backbone from the British Isles to the Guatemala Basin of South America. Then, its coccyx ventured eastward toward Sierra Leone in Africa before it crossed the equator into the South Atlantic. East of New York City and west of Lisbon, Portugal, the underwater chain jutted skyward to form the Azores Islands.

Here, a marker had been placed on the map and the area enlarged. Khenko studied it closely, jumping when something brushed his shoulder. Freya stood beside him. Her pointed ears poked from her ponytail, and her big eyes were glowing. She sighed ecstatically.

"Khenko, come see."

He followed her to the computer screen where Earth rotated slowly, revealing easily discernable patterns that checkered the surface. Freya touched the Adam's Calendar formation in Southern Africa, and it zoomed in to reveal what looked like a gigantic motherboard. Then she showed him another and another and another.

All over the globe were tens of thousands of these near-perfect grids. Some were natural formations, but many were manmade. Stonehenge, the Giza complex, Gobekli Tepe, and other circles and pyramidal structures were among the latter. Modern megacities also looked like motherboards from overhead.

Fascinated, Khenko touched the Azores, gulping when the computer zeroed in to showcase the tiny islands and their massive mountain roots. Spotting a grid along the eastern edge of the island chain between Terceira and Sao Miguel, Khenko tapped it to reveal an underwater pyramid and its related complex.

"Would you join us over here?" Thoth's tone was deep and sonorous.

They hurried to the other side of the cave, where Druantia and Thoth rested in a sitting area with tables and chairs large enough to accommodate the Atlanteans. Settling in a human-sized chair next to Freya, Khenko leaned forward, fingertips together in an unconscious Hakini mudra.

"Now that you've had time to acclimate, what do you think of our home in Atlantis?" Druantia asked, eyes resting on Khenko.

"Seriously? I am ecstatic," he gushed. "I have searched for Atlantis all my life but never imagined it to be at the top of the Bermuda Triangle rather than down by its feet."

Thoth's laugh boomed across the cave. "Did it never occur to you that Atlantis encompasses the whole globe, not just one tiny patch?"

Khenko's guts knotted. "Yes. I have heard that but never believed it to be true. The earliest account was by Plato, who describes Atlantis as an island."

That booming laugh echoed again. "Long ago, it was. The Earth's surface was home to one large land mass, the Kingdom of Atlantis, surrounded by a mighty ocean. Then, the land split to form continents that slowly drifted apart. After that, Atlantis became an island nation comprised of ten realms, each with a ruler and government. But all answered to me, the one king." Thoth stood, placed his hand over his heart, and bowed. "I have ruled Atlantis since that time."

"And you, Freya?" Druantia asked. "Are you finding comfort in Atlantis?"

"Yes, ma'am," she said demurely. Then she grinned, eyes sparkling. "I have studied crystals my whole life, but never have I seen crystals like the ones here. I believe the Atlantean Crystal must be the largest intact rod of quartz in existence."

"Ahh, yes," Druantia said. "It is larger than any on Earth's surface. But the Atlantean Crystal was mined in Jehu, here in Inner Earth."

"Inner Earth?" Khenko interrupted. "Is that real?" Then Talav's cave came to mind, and he knew the answer before Thoth spoke.

"You are in Inner Earth. Or UnderEarth, as some races call it. But let's save that discussion for later. Earth's end draws near."

A shudder passed through Khenko. "But why? Can you tell us more?"

"Aye, son. Earth is a living entity with a north and a south pole, the same as all beings. The openings allow Earth to breathe. But more importantly, they provide the conduit for Earth's power source, her magnetic torus."

Druantia cut in. "Can you explain about the torus, dear? You know hard science is my least favorite subject."

"Of course, my queen. Earth's torus runs through the planet's center and creates our atmosphere. But everything, down to the tiniest speck, is surrounded by an energy field. This "torus," as it is called, is a self-sustaining balanced energy flow. Each torus consists of a single axis and two vortices. In Earth's case, think of a line bisecting both poles. The energy passes through one pole, along the center of the line, out the other pole, then it wraps back around the circumference to pass through the original pole again.

"Tornadoes and whirlpools are visible examples of tori, whereas magnetic fields and the energy fields surrounding living organisms like people, plants, planets, and the stars are not detectable by the naked eye."

"Crystals have tori," Freya interjected. "I find this aspect captivating. Thank you, Thoth. You explained it way better than my professor at Berkeley."

Khenko yawned. Like Druantia, he was more interested in esoteric subjects.

"My pleasure, dear. But the point is that Earth's magnetic torus is out of balance. If not corrected soon, the planet will undergo a pole shift. These reversals are not unusual for Earth. She will experience monstrous disasters, but she will survive.

"That is not true for the untold species calling Earth's surface home. Most shall perish, including humans. We have avoided this pole flip for centuries, but our past methods no longer work."

"And that," Druantia said, "is where you, Khenko, and the rest come in. We hope you will help us develop a new tuning mechanism. Something that will reset Earth's energy field before it's too late."

"How about down here in Inner Earth?" Khenko asked.

"Inner Earth shall be mostly unaffected," Thoth said. "It is a planetship designed to withstand any calamity."

"Anything short of planet death, that is," Druantia added. "But Earth's guardians must see that she survives. We in Atlantis are but a few of her caretakers. But we are mighty. Especially Thoth." She laid a hand on the giant's elaborately decorated sleeve, and Thoth beamed.

Freya pulled thoughtfully at the lobe of her ear. "Have you tried networking other stones with the Atlantean Crystal to increase power output?"

Thoth wagged his prodigious head. "We thought of that but ruled it out. Maybe we should try it anyway."

"Are you familiar with crystal harmonics?" Khenko asked the Fomorian.

"Yes, but I haven't worked with them. Or not extensively. I helped one of my professors set up a research project a few years back, but I graduated and didn't see it through."

"Ahh, harmonics," Druantia purred. "You have entered my territory."

Khenko's fingers thrummed his thigh, excitement rising.

"As you know," the Atlantean queen continued, "every iota of matter vibrates at a unique frequency or resonance. And every frequency exhibits a distinctive sound. Earth's resonance is difficult to calculate because it comprises many different substances, each vibrating at its own frequency. But historically, it approximates 8 hertz. Now, that frequency fluctuates."

Druantia stood then and stretched, prompting Thoth, Khenko, and Freya to do the same. Then they followed her to the computer screen.

"This is one of the tools Thoth created. You glimpsed what it can do when you first came in." Druantia beamed at Thoth, and it was apparent the two were madly in love. "The Harmonizer, as he calls it, seeks and maps formations of sacred sites and worldwide locations that exhibit a grid pattern when viewed from overhead."

"That's brilliant!" Khenko exclaimed.

"It was Druantia's idea." Thoth's cheeks mirrored his red hair. "I merely created the program."

Freya eyed the screen thoughtfully. "Viewing these sites as grids is genius. But what does that tell us?"

"It gives us an idea of what we must work with, harmonics-wise."

Khenko frowned. "I'm not sure I follow."

"Then let me explain. We have talked about Earth's magnetic torus and how it behaves to create Earth's power engine and atmosphere. But the harmonics produced by the wind rushing along the same course—through the mantle, then across Earth's surface—is another part of the equation. Together, they keep Earth properly tuned and spinning on her axis through space." She paused a moment. "Does that make sense?"

"More so, yes. Earth's tuning has to do with both magnetics and harmonics," Khenko said. "Is that where the grids come in? Do they help shape the acoustics, er, the harmonics of the planet?"

"Yes! Very good, Khenko." Druantia shot Thoth a satisfied smile. "Earth's pyramids and pillar complexes, like the one called Stonehenge, serve as antennae and conductors. They shape and propel the sound and light energy around the globe and through Earth's navel tube. We expect Thoth's mapping program to identify grids that may be interfering with this transmission and blank spots that need fortification."

Khenko's mind raced. "How would you mitigate these problems?"

"Excellent question, one to which Thoth and I have given much thought. We've tried everything. But it may take placing powerful beings—druids, dragons, and animal Elders—at these critical global points to help amp up or tone down the frequency."

Druantia pulled up a screen that showed a colorful rendition of the globe. Much of it was swathed in bright reds, yellows, blues, and greens. Khenko pointed to a large black area over the east coast of the United States.

"What is that?"

Thoth snorted angrily. "One of the many disruptions created by man's artificial tuning of the world's electronics. In the century since your governments adopted the universal frequency of 440 Hz, it has driven Humanity past war to the brink of insanity. Now, that dissonance has disrupted Earth's natural resonance. The Atlantean Crystal acted as a filter. But it too has failed."

AIA DORMITORY

Brian scanned the huge dormitory and smiled at his mother. Never in his wildest imagination would he have thought she was an agent for an organization like the Alien Intelligence Agency, much less the Agent in Charge. Aunt Elise had appointed her to it, then taken administrative leave and promptly disappeared. Brian bet Hamilton Hester had a hand in that.

Beside him, Ethnui stiffened. Then, she squealed and ran to the far side of the room, where a group of young adults surrounded a television.

Brian relaxed a little. It was the first joy Ethnui had displayed in a while, and it worried him that she was adapting more slowly to his world than he had to hers.

"Who's that?" he asked as the group greeted Ethnui.

"The latest Fomorian refugees. We rescued them near the Underground. They said they escaped when the Reptilians attacked last night. It looks like Ethnui knows them."

"I'm glad." Brian grinned. "She couldn't find her people in UnderEarth and thought they might be dead or in a Reptilian dungeon. But if those guys escaped, maybe her relatives did too."

His mom looked down at him, eyes glowing.

"We shall hope so. Want to see the rest of the dorms?" She took his hand.

"There's more?" he crowed. "Can Ethnui go with us?"

"Of course, dear. If she wants."

Brian hurried to ask, but shyness struck as he approached. Ethnui was the center of attention. Maybe he shouldn't interrupt. But she waved him over and introduced him as Brian, the Human who had saved her from UnderEarth.

Blushing, he greeted them, amazed at how different yet alike they seemed. Most were Ethnui's age or younger, except for one male who was a bit older and interested in Ethnui. A tad jealous, he pulled her to the side.

"Want to come with us? Mom's giving me a tour."

Ethnui didn't hesitate. "Absolutely. Will we come back here after?"

Brian glanced at his mom, who nodded in affirmation.

As it turned out, the first level below the ground was ginormous. Room after room, as large as the first, housed different species of beings. They lounged in partially hidden nooks and spoke languages Brian had never heard. Ethnui, on the other hand, was familiar with each. She spoke or understood most of the dialects.

Brian was impressed, and so was his mother. She quizzed Ethnui, becoming more excited with each of her answers.

They wound their way back toward the front and stopped at a vast dining hall. With another happy squeal, Ethnui chose fare Brian recognized from UnderEarth. He opted for a ham and cheese sandwich with a large pile of salty potato chips, a dill pickle spear, and a fizzy root beer. They carried their trays to a long table and dug in.

After a while, his mom cleared her throat. "Ethnui, would you consider coming to work for us at the AIA? We need beings like you and would pay a healthy starting salary. Plus, there will be ample opportunity for income growth and advancement within the agency."

Hand halfway to her mouth, Ethnui gaped at his mom. "Are you serious? You would pay me to work here?" She surveyed the gigantic room of chattering beings of different colors, shapes, sizes, and races.

"Do they work here?" she asked with awe.

His mom slurped something that reminded Brian of the eyeball soup Ethnui had brought when she rescued him from the dungeons of Agartha.

"Some. But most of the beings here are in transition." She laid her spoon aside, lifted the bowl to her lips, and slurped.

"What do you mean by 'in transition?'" Brian asked, mouth full of food.

His mom wrinkled her nose but refrained from commenting on his table manners. Instead, she explained.

"This is only one center that houses alien species. The main one is back home in Utah. But as they, or you, arrive in AboveEarth," she said to Ethnui, "we offer sanctuary. Sometimes, that means a rescue, like last night. Other times, they find us. We supply each with medical care, food, and a safe place to stay. Then we teach them about our world and how to survive and thrive here."

"Wow." Brian sat taller, intrigued. "Now, that sounds like something I could get into."

His mother smiled warmly. "You could, if you want. We mainly provide support. We help each race adapt their appearance and actions to blend in with human society." She took a deep breath, then let it out in a long sigh.

"I haven't been to your UnderEarth, Ethnui, but I understand it is not that different from up here. Without adjusting to our ways, other races are open to harassment, persecution, assault, and even enslavement and death."

Ethnui gasped and reached for Brian's hand. He squeezed it and chewed his last bite of lunch. His mom's eyes misted.

"I'm afraid there is as much evil here as was present in your world, dear."

"Ethnui knows about being different," Brian interjected. "When she was little, she and her mother had to live on an island near Ireland, away from the rest of the Fomore. Then, after being kidnapped and taken to UnderEarth, her people were mean and spiteful to her. They even tried to kill her."

Ethnui laid down her fork and hung her head. "I forgot I told you about that."

He squeezed her hand. "From what mom's saying, they can teach you to blend in so you don't have to suffer through that again. Right, Mom?"

"Right, son." She laid a hand over Brian and Ethnui's.

"With your technical genius, Ethnui, you could help us establish communication with UnderEarth. Then our residents could let their loved ones know they are alive and okay."

Ethnui leapt from her chair. "Yes, yes! I can do that! I know I can."

"She can," Brian seconded. "To rescue me, she uploaded a computer virus to the Drac's mainframe—a virus she created. It blinded their system to the comings and goings of all but the Reptilians. That was how we were able to escape."

Ethnui waved her handheld in the air. "That virus also planted a subroutine that sent their data to our processor in UnderEarth— and to this device." She sat down with a discouraged thud. "Only I can't get it to work up here."

Holding out her hand, Brian's mom said, "I have a feeling it will soon." She turned the device from side to side, studying the design. "Will it power up?"

"Yes." Ethnui showed her the on-switch, then pushed her plate away. "If I had the tools and the time, I could get it to work."

"This is advanced technology." Brian's mom regarded Ethnui with a new, speculative gleam in her eyes. "Very advanced." Sitting back in the lunchroom chair, Cybele MacBrayer returned the device to Ethnui.

"I can give you that time. How about I introduce you to our resident computer genius? She'll get you the tools you need, plus brief you on our technology."

"You would do that?" Ethnui gulped and looked at Brian, then back at his mom. Tears leaked from the corners of her eyes. It was the first time Brian had seen her cry.

He poked her with an elbow. "You're not gonna get all squishy, are ya? Please don't. My mom has ulterior motives. Don't you, Mom?"

His mother blushed and gave him the stink eye. "Ulterior implies underhanded. If Ethnui's device can help us communicate with UnderEarth, as she believes, not only could the beings living here have a way to talk with their families and loved ones, but we could also negotiate with the Reptilian leaders. Maybe we could work out a peaceful resolution."

Brian's ears burned. He was sure his face had turned cherry red, but neither noticed Brian's embarrassment. They were in a breathless conversation about the possibilities such technology presented.

The dining hall was half empty by the time his mother stood to leave.

"Ethnui, let's get you settled in the dorm." She handed the girl a cell phone. "My number is programmed in here. Use it to call me when you're ready to get started. I'll introduce you to Sepi. She can take it from there."

She turned to Brian. "I'm going to run you to my house. I know you rested in the infirmary, but you look exhausted. I don't want you getting sick." She traced the dark circle under one of his eyes.

But Ethnui looked stricken.

"I want to stay here with Ethnui," he said gently, watching her.

"No, honey. Ethnui probably wants to get settled. And you need sleep."

The Fomorian wagged her head almost imperceptibly, and Brian insisted, dropping his volume so that only his mother could hear.

"Mom, look at her. She's freaked out. I'm the only one Ethnui knows. Just let me stay. I'll be okay. And, in case you forgot, I'm pretty good with computers, too."

She almost resisted but gave in. "I'll see if they have an extra bed. But promise you'll get some sleep before you start futzing around with that thing." She nodded toward Ethnui's handheld.

"Yes, ma'am. I promise."

As they reached the Fomorian dorm, Brian remembered his father. "Hey, where is Dad staying tonight?"

"At the house."

Instant regret took Brian's breath. How could he have forgotten his dad?

"You should go be with him," Ethnui said quietly. But her eyes begged him not to. Then her Fomorian friends appeared, and her hesitation vanished.

"It is your dad, Bri. You have waited a long time to be with him."

"But, are you sure?"

"I am. Go on, I'll be fine. I promise. And when you get back, we'll figure out how to communicate with UnderEarth."

GLASTONBURY

The snow was so thick Awen could see nothing beyond her nose. They had reached their destination in less than a minute. But had they left Yr Wyddfa? She relaxed when she sensed Glastonbury's rolling hills had replaced the high mountains of Wales.

"Gather to me." Awen amplified her words so the others could hear above the wind's roar. "Come to my voice, to my voice, to my voice," she repeated until they had all found her.

"Now, hold tight to each other while I locate the abbey and the Lady Chapel."

Raising her arms to the heavens in supplication, Awen grounded, then spoke the calming spell. The wind quieted, and the sideways snow fell straight to the ground. In the brief respite, Awen spied what she sought. The remnants of the ancient abbey nestled among the snow-shrouded, freestanding walls. Behind it loomed the town of Glastonbury.

Awen pointed. "That is our destination. Hold on to one another, stay close, and follow me. Do not lose your grip. If you do, call out, and we shall retrieve you, lest you face an icy death."

The wind whistled through the courtyard, and visibility worsened again. Awen's spell had not lasted. That did not bode well. She forged through the accumulating snow, threading the standing walls where snow drifted high. Soon, they reached the solid outline of Glastonbury Abbey.

As her charges milled behind her, Awen rapped on the soaring door to the Lady Chapel—three taps, silence, and three more. Presently, the door inched open, and a spectacled nose peeked out.

"Is that you, Lady Awen?" an aged voice called.

"Aye, Father. It is I."

"Awen. It has been—" catching sight of her companions, the aged priest hesitated. "It's been a very long time. Come inside, mi' lady."

"Quickly," he urged, and Awen crowded through the door, stomping snow from her boots onto the mat. "Neither man nor beast should be out in this blizzard. It feels… unnatural."

"You are right, Father." Awen shivered in the foyer as the others passed. She was sure her old nemesis had conjured the malevolent storm, but she wasn't ready to share her suspicions. "Thank you for receiving us. Your shelter is most welcome."

The wind shrieked through the Lady Chapel as the last of them entered. Then the priest slammed the door and fastened the lock.

"Follow me."

☼☼☼

Emily shivered as they clomped down the long staircase. After their harrowing journey, the warmth and energy of the abbey's Lady Chapel had been most welcome. But this might be the end of her. She had thought she was done with her fear of the dark and tight spaces. But if Lugh wasn't in front of her and Mitchell and the three ladies behind her, Emily would turn and bolt back up the stairs.

Swallowing shame, she tried to focus on the positives. She was no longer stuck in the eleventh century or frozen in that icy hell. Bé Chuille didn't kill them, they were safe from the storm, and she could finally get some much-needed rest. Besides that, the stairwell and the space below was well lit. Plus, Lugh was here.

She rested a hand on his shoulder, and he reached up to give it a squeeze. Then, he threw her a reassuring grin.

That worked. Emily's fears scattered as butterflies took flight in her belly. Then Mitchell Wainwright said something and the fluttery insects landed with a thud.

Why in the world had Lugh brought the asshole with him? The three ladies were an even bigger surprise. Emily had met Elise, a distant cousin, the day they'd brought Da home from the hospital. But Rona Wainwright and the blonde were strangers.

When they reached the bottom of the stairs, Emily heaved a sigh of relief. They gathered in a rectangular room beneath the Lady Chapel, with doors lining its length.

"Follow me," the priest instructed. "I'll show you the community washroom and the common area. Then you can each choose a bedroom while I rummage up some food. Simple fare will be the best I can do until this storm passes."

"Thank you, Father," Awen said through Emily's lips. "Anything will be greatly appreciated. I am hungry. Is anyone else?"

370

"We ate a big meal a while ago," Lugh said, nodding at Mitchell.

"Us too," the blonde said.

"Well, I'm hungry." Mitchell plopped into a chair.

"You know, I'm kinda peckish too." Lugh scratched his head. "Maybe it was longer ago than I thought."

"The priest started back up the staircase. "Feel free to get settled. I'll be back soon."

"Father, wait." Lugh held up his cell phone. "Do you have access to the internet? Or the news? I'm worried about this storm system."

The aged priest blinked, then produced his own cell from a pocket in his robe. "Not down here, and the service is spotty in the chapel. But you're welcome to come upstairs and try if you'd like."

"Yessir, I would." Lugh followed the priest while Emily and the others wandered into the side rooms.

The one Emily entered was reminiscent of a cell. Its narrow cot, simple wooden table, and ladder-backed chair filled the space. Hanging Awen's robe on a hook, she hurried through the common area to the community bathroom, where she did her business and washed her face in water that was more tepid than cold.

Back in the common area, the priest had returned. Rona poured what appeared to be a hearty red wine from a well-used flask into mismatched glasses. A basket of fragrant bread and a platter with cheeses, grapes, and cut cantaloupe had been laid on the large round table. The priest passed the plates around then retreated upstairs while Cu wolfed scraps from a large bowl and started in on a meaty bone.

The group settled around the wooden table, and for a while, silence reigned. Then a lighthearted conversation about Glastonbury Abbey and the town sprang up as they sipped wine and wolfed the tasty fare.

Elise leaned close. "Emily." The familiar voice was not Elise's.

"Da?" Emily whispered, staring into the hazel eyes.

"Shhh." Elise cast a cautious glance at the occupants of the table. "Not here."

And that was definitely her Da's shush. Jubilation lifted Emily's spirits. She reached for Elise's hand beneath the table and squeezed it hard.

"I thought you were with Brian."

"I was, a ghrá. But a lot has happened since we last spoke. I spent several weeks as the guest of our young friend." Lugh clomped down the steps, and her Da hissed, "I'll tell you the rest later."

Mitchell met Lugh at the bottom. "How bad is it?"

"Bad, bad. I took screenshots of the weather map." Lugh handed his phone to Mitchell. "The system is enormous. It stretches around the globe, covering most of the Northern Hemisphere."

Brows knit, Mitchell scrolled through the screenshots and passed the phone on to his mother.

"Holy crap." Rona did the same, then handed the cell to Honey.

Eventually, the phone made its way to Emily, who looked at the images and swallowed hard. Her insides had gone to liquid, and for a moment, she thought she might be sick. Then Awen spoke.

"This looks dire. What is the forecast, young raven?"

Lugh's dark brows arched at the pet druid name.

"NOAA says the system is growing stronger and wider as it moves south. That, by itself, is not a bad thing. Earth's midsection suffers under extreme heat, so this will help cool it down. But they're concerned about what will happen when the two fronts collide."

Lugh rubbed a hand over the stubble on his chin and cheeks, and the butterflies stirred in Emily's tummy. Like a pirate, he always seemed in need of a shave. It was one of the many things she adored about him.

"Air traffic is suspended in the Northern Hemisphere, and all travel has ground to a halt. The U.S. declared a State of Emergency and urged everyone in the affected areas to stay inside. The U.K. has done the same, so it looks like we're stuck here for a while."

Solemn looks passed around the group.

"Not me," Mitchell snorted, crossing his arms. "This is your problem. I have no skin in this game." He thrust something at Emily. "Here. Take this."

Electricity shot up Emily's arm. Her fingers closed around a vintage brooch and the sight of it sent heat through her. She thrust out her chin.

"How did you get this? I saw one just like it on Zephyr Cay."

Mitchell's blue eyes widened. He sat down hard, and stared into space, then turned to the woman named Honey.

"That's why you look so familiar. You were there. On Zephyr Cay." His lip curled. "I saw you with your sugar daddy."

The buxom blonde recoiled and her face pinked.

"Who are you, anyway?" Emily asked.

Honey regarded Rona and then Elise. "Should we tell them?"

Elise shook her head almost imperceptibly, and an odd feeling ravaged Emily's gut.

"Tell us what?"

"I DON'T CARE!" Mitchell yelled, face as red and apoplectic as the day Emily had fired him as the Order's attorney. "I gave you the damn brooch, now send me home." He wheeled to Lugh, who seemed unsurprised. "Send me home. NOW!"

"Mitchell Albom Wainwright the Third, what did you say?" his mother demanded. She planted her fists on her hips, and hissed through clenched teeth, "You're telling me you would run out on a fight?"

The color drained from Mitchell's face, and Rona's expression softened. She caressed his cheek with her fingertips.

"Emily needs you, son. We all need you. You might not be trained in druidry, but you are a smart man. I know you can help us somehow." Then she hardened, all business again. "Now sit your ass down. You're not going anywhere."

Speechless, Mitchell did.

Emily eyed his mother with admiration. She'd put Mitchell in his place, and done it with love. What a concept. It would be nice to have a mother like that.

On the other side of the table, Honey flushed.

☼☼☼

"Your mama is fierce," Lugh told Mitchell after the women retired. "I don't remember her being like that."

Staring moodily at the inlaid druid symbols above the doors, Mitchell sighed. "Oh, she has her moments." He sipped his wine.

"The sapphire is one of the wandstones. Now, only the diamond is unaccounted for." Lugh caressed the back of Emily's hand. "Why were you so upset?"

"Because it was on the table beside the pendant the shopkeeper gave me." She reached inside her gown and held up the ruby. "Why didn't she give it to me then? Why did he have it?"

"Oh, get over yourself," Mitchell sniffed. "That old hag shoved it at me and demanded I bring it to you."

The tension between them was so strong Lugh wondered if Emily would coldcock Mitch like she had at Wren's Roost. Instead, she inspected the filigreed pin.

"But why did she give it to you and not me?"

The attorney groaned and rubbed his face in his hands.

Laying the brooch in her palm beside the pendant, Emily curled her fingers. The air crackled with electricity, startling them all. Then, it shot from the blue stone to light up the ruby, then sparked Aóme on Emily's finger, connecting the three gems.

Something stranger happened then—a bolt of electricity shot from the ring to the brooch to the pendant and back, creating a looping circuit. They stared agog at the play of energy dancing in the palm of Emily's hand.

Then she looked up at Lugh, eyes sparkling, and the zinging quieted.

Lugh couldn't help but grin like a loon.

"What?" she demanded.

"You're glowing." He said it reverently, but Emily hiccupped and brushed his remark aside.

"A temporary side effect, I'm sure."

Then she shocked both men. Rising from the chair, she drew Mitch from his and hugged him, then let go abruptly, strawberry brows raised.

"Did you feel that?"

Mitch nodded, startled. "The electricity passed from you to me.

"And back again. It happened the day we met. Do you remember?"

He nodded, eyes wide.

"I appreciate you bringing this to me. You must have gone through a lot. I know it couldn't have been easy." Emily peered into eyes the same cornflower blue as their father's.

"Seriously?" Mitch shoved his bangs back, and Emily removed the question mark.

"Seriously."

Then, the two plopped into their seats and stared at one another. Finally, Mitch relaxed, stretched his feet before him, and stared at his shoes.

"You're right. It wasn't easy. I basically refused." He looked up, defiant. "No way was I going to help you."

Lugh watched, fascinated. For twins, they couldn't look or act more differently.

"The feeling was mutual, believe me," Emily smirked.

"Oh, I know," Mitch leered.

Lugh grinned. Their smiles might be different, but their smirks were not. "When Mitch is not being an arrogant ass, he kinda grows on you, doesn't he?"

Emily snorted. "I guess."

Then she drained her wine and set the tumbler on the table. "But don't think I like you just because you helped, Mitchell Wainwright. I don't." She pushed back her chair.

Lugh emptied his glass and stood, too.

Mitchell belched and continued contemplating his ruined tennis shoes.

☼☼☼

When the kids finally retired, Rona and Honey tiptoed to Elise's room. Honey settled on the bed beside Elise, leaving the lone chair to Rona. Then Alexis leaned forward and rested her elbows on Honey's ample chest.

"Are y'all as freaked out as I am?"

Rona and Elise nodded.

"Do you think we're really triplets? Is that witch our mother? *Could* we be sisters? If so, that would've been nice to know."

"More likely, Bé Chuille was yanking our chains, Alexis," Elise snorted. "We looked nothing alike. Even before you switched bodies." She turned to Rona. "And you and me? No resemblance at all. Nothing, nada, zilcho."

"She's right, you know," Honey chimed in. "Alexis, I've seen your photograph. The three of you bear no resemblance."

"Then what the hell?" Rona grumbled. "Why would she say such a thing if it weren't true?"

"Well, she did mention the possibility of more than one father."

"But wouldn't at least one of us resemble Bé Chuille?" Rona asked.

"Maybe we do. She could have altered her looks. Hell, if she's as old as she says, she must have. Otherwise, she would be dust." They eyed one another, pondering the possibilities.

Then, Alexis asked the question that had been needling them all. "Where do you think Awen sent Bé Chuille?"

"We could ask her, you know. Do you think Emily's asleep already?"

"Uh, no, she's awake," Honey snickered. "Sleep ain't what's going on in that room."

375

"Then we shouldn't disturb her." Rona scrunched her nose.

"I'll do it," Honey said. "I need to know."

Giggling like teenagers, the women padded down the hall and knocked lightly. Furtive voices whispered on the other side before a blushing Emily cracked the door.

"Yes? Is something wrong?"

"No," Elise said. "We're sorry to bother you this late, but could you tell us where Awen sent Bé Chuille?

"Pardon?" Emily widened the crack. "What do you mean?"

"The witch," Honey hissed. "Where did Awen send her?"

"Ohh, hold on." But Awen was already answering.

"If my full powers have been restored, Bé Chuille is in her final resting place." Then she shrugged, sighing. "If not, she's wandering the Otherworld. Or, knowing Bé Chuille, the Underworld." Awen zeroed in on Alexis. She held her gaze for a long moment, then murmured gently, "You're familiar with the Underworld, aren't you, little one?"

Alexis glared. "So you don't know where you sent the witch."

"Not specifically, no. I'm sorry." Awen hesitated. "Of course, there is one other possibility, but we won't worry about that tonight." Then Awen morphed into Emily again.

"Anything else, ladies?"

The three exchanged looks, then wagged their heads.

"Nope, that's it," Rona said. "We'll see you in the morning,"

The women returned to Elise's room long enough to make a pact. They would not tell a soul about Bé Chuille's audacious claim until they had time to investigate. Then, yawning, they retired to their individual rooms.

As Honey climbed into the tiny bed, something shifted inside her. Alarmed, she sat up and turned the lamp on. Then, attributing it to Alexis, she rolled to her side and went to sleep.

DRAGON LIAISON

Hopeful once Nergal and Azi were on board, Inanna had returned to Irkalla to approach Shibboleth. But as they had all suspected, the warlord flatly refused to cease the attack, citing a long list of grievances against the human race.

Inanna boarded the chute, prepared to put Plan B into action.

Ooschu ignored the buzz in her ear, but the low, breathy pleas continued, so she paused to identify the sender. Shocked, Ooschu dipped her attention into the Otherworld after first making sure none of the Dracs posed an immediate threat.

The source was distant, somewhere in Inner Earth. Or Terra Prima, as the dragons had called it in olden times. The sender was Inanna, daughter of the warlord, Shibboleth. Centuries ago, the Draca had saved Ooschu's life. They had had no contact since.

"Ooschu, Queen of the Water Dragons," the distant voice beseeched, "I need your help."

"Inanna," Ooschu acknowledged, dodging a laser beam that barely missed her chest. Her tail sent the offender cartwheeling from the ship into the sea.

Telepathically, she called to the earth Keeper battling the Reptilians from the wharf. "Talav, Inanna Shibboleth's Spawn needs our help." Ooschu mind-connected the two beings, then sent another Drac into the choppy water. "I need you to go to UnderEarth in my stead. Find out what Inanna needs, then hurry back. I'll deal with the rest of these lizards."

Rumbling displeasure, Talav disappeared from the shore with a thwap.

The wormhole dumped Talav in a clearing surrounded by wooded hills. Shocked, she recognized the quiet oasis, though she had no memory of when she had been here. The feathery fronds of an enormous willow fluttered in a light breeze, half concealing a Reptilian female.

"Inanna Shibboleth's Spawn?"

The creature slowly emerged to stand before Talav, red eyes narrowed. Then planting sharp claws on slim, belted hips, the Reptilian cocked her scaled head.

"Who are you? And where is Queen Ooschu?"

"Ooschu is otherwise occupied. I am Talav. She sent me in her stead. Are you Inanna?"

"That I am."

"How is it that you know Ooschu?"

A faraway look softened the red eyes. Then, they hardened to focus on Talav. "Long ago, before they sealed the borders between our worlds, I came upon Queen Ooschu on a mountaintop. She was weak and dehydrated, unable to make it back to the sea. I helped her return."

Talav studied the battle-scarred female. "There is an ocean down here?"

Inanna stared. "Well, of course. It is not that different from AboveEarth. But you should know that. Your kind lived here for millennia before migrating to the surface."

Shockwaves rocked Draig Talav. She sat down hard, crushing vegetation and shaking the ground, as forgotten memories skated across her mind—her wormholing Marduk's populace to Earth when their homeworld exploded, then rescuing the Reptilians, whose planetship caused the devastation, and standing high upon a tor to address a meadow full of displaced dragons.

Stunned, Talav wagged her head sorrowfully. "Someone or something has tampered with my memories. I remembered nothing but life on Earth's surface and not all of that. But your revelation jarred some memories loose." She lowered her head to level a grateful gaze at the wiry Reptilian. "Thank you for that."

"My pleasure, Talav."

"That is Queen Talav."

Inanna bent forward at the waist and struck her chest with a fisted claw as she raised back up. "My pleasure, Queen Talav."

Bowing her head in return, Talav stood to survey her surroundings. A narrow path led in two directions, one toward a sheer mountain and the other toward the pine-covered hills.

"Where are we?"

"Not far from Agartha."

"And where would that be in relation to the surface world?"

"I believe your nearest city is Atlanta in North America. But I'm no expert on geography, so that is a guess."

"Your life doesn't seem to be in danger. Why did you call Ooschu?"

"At the moment, it is not." Inanna fidgeted with the firearm that dangled from her belt.

"That won't hurt me, you know," Talav smirked. "My scales are impenetrable."

"And beautiful. You might be the most majestic creature I have ever seen." Reverence lent sincerity to the Draca's words. "The dragons I have encountered would not compare. Not even Queen Ooschu." She dropped her claws to hang by her sides. "I have no intention of firing on you, Queen Talav. I need your help. We must stop this war."

Relief coursed through Talav. The Reptilian was no match for a dragon like her, but violence was never Talav's first choice. She dipped her head, then shook it proudly so that her new face horns sliced through the pine-scented air.

"What is it you require? Time is short. I must return to Ooschu."

"Is she in danger?" Inanna seemed genuinely concerned.

Talav studied the Draca, gauging how much to reveal. "Not particularly. But your forces have overrun the humans' defense installations. It is our task to clear them away."

Inanna sucked in a sharp breath. "By clear, you mean kill?"

Surprised at her distress, Talav studied the Draca. It was said the reptoids possessed no soul. If that were the case, why would she care?

"Our duty is to protect Earth and her life forms, including the humans. Your attacks have left us little choice."

Talav felt a sudden tug from Ooschu and muttered urgently, "Have you a request?"

"I do." Inanna folded her claws over her heart. Then, glancing wistfully toward the pine-laden hills, she addressed Talav.

"My litter father started this war because the witch Bé Chuille assured him she had secured the portals. But that was a lie. Now, Shibboleth refuses to concede. Our ranks were thin before the war. Now, each time we leave UnderEarth, more Dracs die. But worse, a nasty fire drake roams our lands. Many of our cities and bases have been burned to the ground." She stopped to inhale.

"Do you smell that? Agartha was the first to go up in flames. And though we are rebuilding the city and the base, the stench of death and char remains. Nothing of my race or our homeland will be left if your dragons do not stop."

Talav sighed. "Why would a Reptilian care about such things? You have no souls, no morals, and no couth. Your race exists only to maim and destroy."

The Reptilian remained quiet, claws over her heart and head bowed. But when she finally looked up, a fierce gleam shone in her red eyes.

"You speak the truth. Our ancestors did not have souls. But as with humans, that is no longer the case. My race is dying out, Queen Talav. Few Dracs are left, and the youngest are mostly clones. If our species is to survive, we must focus on its renewal rather than seeking to add more territory to our holdings. I do not condone this war and gladly risk my life to stop it to save my species."

Talav nodded, satisfied. It was what she had needed to hear.

"Rest easy, Lady Inanna. I will recall the dragons while I present your case to the Master Druid Awen. But you must agree to cease incursions against the humans and surface world."

The Reptilian relaxed, obviously relieved. Then, consulting a chirping wrist device, she rolled her eyes. "Now, the fire drake is laying waste to Araf."

The news troubled Talav. "That must be Draig Tienu, King of the fire dragons. I will start with him. Then, I must return to help Ooschu before meeting with Awen."

"Can you fly?" Inanna wondered. "If so, I will take you to the drake. But I will need to ride."

Pondering the request, Talav felt a firm yank from Ooschu.

"Stay here," she instructed. I will be back in a few minutes, assuming I can. Either way, I shall take your concerns to Awen."

Then, engaging her merkaba, Talav created a wormhole to return to the overrun ship.

MORNING SICKNESS

Emily woke in the abbey cot wrapped in Lugh's arms. She burrowed closer, savoring his warmth, but the movement caused the world to spin. Then nausea struck. She held very still, breathing and trying to will it away, unable to respond when Lugh nuzzled her cheek and nestled against her.

Saliva pooled at the back of her tongue as the nauseated feeling grew more insistent. Untangling arms and legs, Emily slipped on Awen's robe, then held her head in her hand to stumble through the main and common rooms. She barely reached the bathroom before last night's supper spewed forth. And maybe, judging by the way it felt, some of her guts.

She retched again and again, lamenting the bit of wine she had before bed. When the urgency passed, she settled on her shins and waited. When a minute had gone by without heaving, Emily pulled herself up from the surprisingly warm floor and rinsed her mouth at one of the sinks.

Then, peering at her puffy, sleep-deprived eyes in the leaded mirror, Emily felt someone or something behind her. She wheeled, expecting one of the women, but only shadows thrown by the antique light fixture shared the bathroom with her. Chill bumps roved Emily's body.

She hurried to her room and snuggled in next to Lugh, but a few minutes later, she was in the bathroom again. Very little came up this time, but the heaves were strong, and each wave sapped her strength further.

Resting her cheek on the warm stone lavatory, Emily closed her eyes and fell into a waking dream in which the underground structure and its fixtures came to life. Not frightened in the least, Emily basked in comfort as they heaped blessing upon blessing upon their Awen. Then, a leg cramp jarred Emily awake.

She straightened, massaging her aching calf, then breathed in and out when the nausea reared its ugly head.

Luckily, it passed, and Emily thought about the dream. It had seemed so real, and Emily had read about such things in Hope's druid books. Feeling foolish, she asked the commode, "Is this building alive?"

There was no answer.

"Are *you* alive?" she asked and jumped when the toilet answered in a slight brogue.

"I am, mi' lady. This structure and all that is in it are as well. It is our duty and pleasure to attend to the Druids, especially our Awen."

Then, it asked something strange, and Emily nearly fainted.

"How is the morning sickness?"

"The what?" She scrambled to her feet. It might be time to get her head examined.

"The morning sickness. It seems to have passed."

She *was* going mad. Emily gaped at the toilet.

"No, Awen. You are not going mad. Your confusion is understandable, but you are sane. As an untested Awen, you have likely never heard your privy speak."

"Um, no." Emily gulped and hurried to the sink to splash cold water on her face, hoping it would wake her from the odd dream. But then the sink spoke.

"It's an honor to serve you, Awen. Welcome back."

"Um, likewise."

Thoroughly spooked now, Emily hightailed it to her room. But she couldn't get comfortable in the tiny bed. Lugh snored loudly and would not budge. She thought about going to his room—until the toilet's words returned to her.

"How's the morning sickness?"

Terrified, Emily counted backward. It had been a week since she and Lugh first slept together. Without protection. She shucked off the blanket and sat, heart pounding, on the edge of the bed. Surely, to God and all that was holy, Emily wasn't pregnant. She couldn't be. It was way too soon.

EARTH SPEAKS

Despite her foreboding, Emily finally drifted off. She slept fitfully for the rest of the night until prodded awake by Lugh's morning boner. She slid from the bed, senses cranked to high alert. Kissing the pirate priest's scruffy cheek, she donned Awen's robe and boots and hurried to the bathroom.

"Good morning," she purred to the sentient fixtures.

Silence answered. Maybe they only spoke at night.

Emily peed, then took a sink bath, closing her eyes to dream of luxuriating in a long, hot shower. Combing her fingers through hair that had reached below her shoulder blades in a few short weeks, Emily gathered it in a bun and fixed it in place with the bobby pins Khenko bought her in Zephyr Cay.

She paused to think of her rescuer, the tall, lanky Iroquois medicine man, and their hours lazing in the sand. Her respite on the beach seemed so long ago. Wetting her hands, Emily slicked them over the loose strands, willing them to stay in place. Knowing they wouldn't, she eyed her handiwork.

Snatches of conversation broke the silence, and Emily hurried to the common room. The three druid women huddled at the table, sipping a hot beverage from earthenware mugs. A spicy aroma perfumed the air.

Rona Wainwright chirped, "Good morning, dear. Doesn't your hair look lovely? I like it like that."

Emily self-consciously tucked in a curl that had escaped.

"Why, thank you."

Feeling awkward, she settled in the chair beside Rona to study her from the corner of her eye. Mitchell's mom looked nothing like her son. Rona glanced over, and Emily quickly hid her musing.

"What is that fabulous smell?"

"It's hot mulled cider. Would you like a spot?"

The priest appeared from the corner to hand Emily a steaming mug.

When the zesty aroma tickled her nose, Emily set the mug on the table and scrubbed her face in her hands. Three pairs of eyes were fixed on her when she looked back up.

"What?" she mumbled defensively. "What'd I do?"

Elise guffawed and slapped the table while Rona stared, open-mouthed.

Then, a high-pitched tone sliced through Emily. She tried to resist, but a trance-like state overtook her senses.

The spirit of the Abbey took Emily's arm and flew her high above Glastonbury Tor. The night was clear and warm, and the inky sky was thick with stars and no sign of the blizzard anywhere. Beside her, the agender earth spirit named Afsel waxed eloquent.

"As you know, Awen, Earth is a living, breathing entity. Like in many sacred places, these rolling acres of Glastonbury mirror the constellations of the sky." Afsel pointed out several on the landscape below—Sagittarius the Archer, the boat representing Cancer, the Gemini twins, three fishes of Pisces, Sirius the dog, and even King Arthur were depicted upon the terrain.

Then, they quickly passed over Avebury, Stonehenge, Adam's Calendar, and other stone circles around the world as Afsel pointed out the megalithic spires, natural and manufactured, pyramids, and ancient shrines, tall, squat, round, and square.

"When ancient enemies felled Earth's native trees, it disrupted her natural frequency. These structures were set in place to help Earth recover and thrive again."

They passed above the North Pole, and Afsel drifted lower. Emily was shocked to see a black, sharp-spired mountain guarding the entrance to Inner Earth. Surrounding it was a giant whirlpool clogged with the plastic and waste of modern civilization.

Earth's agony hit her full force, and tears sprang to Emily's eyes.

"This is one of two main outlets that allow Earth to breathe. You can see the entrance is beyond congested. She gasps for air."

Emily wept as Afsel whisked her to the Southern Pole. This entrance, too, was blocked, and the circumference of the opening and surrounding area was jammed with military bases.

The flags of many countries flew above them—the United States, England, China, Russia, Japan, India, and Germany, along with others Emily couldn't place. Radio and cell towers competed with buildings, and the drone of heavy equipment filled her ears.

Then, the keening assaulted Emily again as Earth cried out in desperation, "Awen, please. I cannot breathe or find my song. Please help me."

A pain traveled up Emily's forearm, bringing her back abruptly to find Elise's hand clamped around it.

"Where'd you go?" her Da whispered through Elise's lips. "What did you see?"

"Hamilton?" Honey shrieked in that odd voice. "Hamilton Hester? Is that you?"

"Alexis?" Ham growled. "What the hell? I thought you were dead."

Emily stared. Her Da was going mad, too.

But Honey batted her eyes and cooed, "I was dead, Ham." Then she leaned forward to touch Emily's cheek.

"I'm sorry I didn't take better care of you. After I died, I ended up in the Underworld, reliving all the awful things I had done. Then, a few weeks ago, a dragon named Talav offered me a second chance. In exchange for helping you, she brought me back from the Underworld."

"And now you're a disembodied spirit, like me?" her Da gurgled, obviously pleased.

Honey nodded, and Emily finally understood. She rounded on the blonde.

"You mean to tell me my mother is in there with you?"

"Yes," Honey said in her normal voice. "Most people would be happy about that, sweetie."

"Yeah, well." Emily sniffed. "Most people weren't raised by a mother who despised them."

"Oh, boo hoo," Elise cut in. "We have bigger problems to deal with now. Did I hear correctly? Did Earth say she can't find her song?"

Emily's jaw dropped as anger surged. "You were listening to my vision? My thoughts?"

"Oh, sue me," Elise said, though not unkindly. "Did Earth tell you she lost her song or not?"

Remembering Earth's plaintive cry for help, Emily nodded. "Yes, but she didn't use the word 'lost.'"

Elise stood to pace the perimeter of the common room, then stopped in front of a simple carving depicting Goddess Brigid.

"That's what White Star said in Atlantis."

Everyone stared at Elise's back.

"Who's White Star? And Atlantis, Elise? Really?" The words dripped with sarcasm.

Elise wheeled. "Yes, Alexis, really. Before I was so rudely yanked to Snowdonia and struck by a witch's curse, I was in Atlantis, below the Azores. John Blitherstone is there leading a team of scientists working to avoid an imminent pole shift."

"Blitherstone?" Shock reverberated through Emily. "A healer named Khenko Blitherstone helped Talav rescue me from the Otherworld. It's an odd name. I bet they're related."

Her revelation brought a sparkle to Elise's eyes.

"Absolutely. John asked us to recruit his son to help tune the Atlantean Crystal. Khenko is an expert in harmonics. But White Star, one of the other beings, told us that Earth had lost her song." Elise's chin jutted then, and she rounded on Alexis. "So, why is my story less believable than yours?"

Freaked out by these new events, Emily gulped lukewarm cider, hoping the sugar would jolt her back to reality.

Mitchell padded barefoot into the common room and flopped in a chair. "What's going on out here? Can't a man sleep?" He lifted his mother's cup to drink, and his face twisted in disgust. "Yech, what is this? Where's the coffee?"

Rona huffed loudly. "Mitch, for God's sake, grow up. Not everything is about you. Have a cup of spiced cider."

Hurt pinched the handsome face, and Mitch shuffled toward the bathroom.

☼☼☼

Jake MacBrayer grinned at the nurse. He felt like death warmed over, but the agency doctor had given him the okay to leave. Ducking into the bathroom to dress, he ran into Cybele and Brian on his way out.

"Dad!" Brian yelled, running to throw his arms around Jake.

Jake hugged him tight and started to lift Brian to twirl him, but his lanky son had put on some meat since Jake had last seen him. So, he rocked Brian back and forth instead.

"Me and you are staying at Mom's tonight."

Shocked, Jake peeked at Cybele. "We are?"

"Yep. Mom said so."

Cybele nodded. "I will be on duty for eleven hours, longer if they need me. But I'll find someone to drive you. Grab your stuff, and let's go."

Jake looked around. "What stuff?" He held his arms out and turned a circle. "This is all I have to my name." Then something struck him. "Do you think my landlord kept my flat open?"

Cybele snorted. "Fat chance. Unless you paid your rent far in advance. You've been gone over a year."

"Yeah. Well. So much for that. Hey, do you think my landlord kept my stuff?"

"More likely, they tossed it on the street. But someone is using it. Road-kill furniture is a big deal these days."

"Road-kill furniture?" Brian laughed. "That's funny. I never heard of that."

Jake hugged his son and chuckled as they followed Cybele to her office to get her keys. But when they reached the bullpen, she gasped and ran to the bank of windows. Thick, wet globs of snow slanted sideways, sticking to the windows and blanketing the corners.

"Didn't you say it was May? What in Brigid's name is going on out there?"

"It's snow, Dad," Brian said matter-of-factly.

"No. Not just snow." Cybele's eyes grew large and rolled back in her head.

Brian reached to touch her, and Jake stopped him.

"Wait," he whispered. "She's seeing something."

"Huh?" Brian's brow creased. "Like, things that aren't there?"

"Uh-huh."

His son's face lit up. "I didn't know Mom could do that."

"It doesn't happen often. But when it does, watch out."

The next Jake knew, Cybele grabbed him and Brian, and they glided through a long, fluffy tunnel of light.

Jake MacBrayer grinned at the nurse. He felt like death warmed over, but the agency doctor had given him the okay to leave. Ducking into the bathroom to dress, he ran into Cybele and Brian on his way out.

"Dad!" Brian yelled, running to throw his arms around Jake.

Jake hugged him tight and started to lift Brian to twirl him, but his lanky son had put on some meat since Jake had last seen him. So, he rocked Brian back and forth instead.

"Me and you are staying at Mom's tonight."

Shocked, Jake peeked at Cybele. "We are?"

"Yep. Mom said so."

Cybele nodded. "I will be on duty for eleven hours, longer if they need me. But I'll find someone to drive you. Grab your stuff, and let's go."

Jake looked around. "What stuff?" He held his arms out and turned a circle. "This is all I have to my name." Then something struck him. "Do you think my landlord kept my flat open?"

Cybele snorted. "Fat chance. Unless you paid your rent far in advance. You've been gone over a year."

"Yeah. Well. So much for that. Hey, do you think my landlord kept my stuff?"

"More likely, they tossed it on the street. But someone is using it. Road-kill furniture is a big deal these days."

"Road-kill furniture?" Brian laughed. "That's funny. I never heard of that."

Jake hugged his son and chuckled as they followed Cybele to her office to get her keys. But when they reached the bullpen, she gasped and ran to the bank of windows. Thick, wet globs of snow slanted sideways, sticking to the windows and blanketing the corners.

"Didn't you say it was May? What in Brigid's name is going on out there?"

"It's snow, Dad," Brian said matter-of-factly.

"No. Not just snow." Cybele's eyes grew large and rolled back in her head.

Brian reached to touch her, and Jake stopped him.

"Wait," he whispered. "She's seeing something."

"Huh?" Brian's brow creased. "Like, things that aren't there?"

"Uh-huh."

His son's face lit up. "I didn't know Mom could do that."

"It doesn't happen often. But when it does, watch out."

The next Jake knew, Cybele grabbed him and Brian, and they glided through a long, fluffy tunnel of light. Emily nearly jumped from her skin when Elise touched her hand.

"This could be the answer the Atlanteans seek. In your vision, you saw Earth's clogged poles. If we could clear them somehow…" Elise's voice trailed off, eyes fixed on something in the corner.

"What the hell are you doing here? You're supposed to be in Cheltenham running AIA."

Emily twisted in her chair to see Brian MacBrayer running toward her. "Emily!"

She sprang up, and he threw his arms around her. "I can't believe it. I thought I might never see you again."

He seemed to have grown another foot. Emily hugged him close, but her eyes were on his mother—the woman who had abandoned him on Lugh's doorstep. Then Brian let go and gave her an excited grin.

"I want you to meet my mom and dad."

Emily shook both hands, trying not to let her disapproval show as Brian introduced Cybele and then Jake, who thanked her for rescuing him from the witch's curse.

"Yes, thank you for that," Cybele chirped, pulling Brian close. "And thank you for befriending our son."

"What's all the commotion?" Lugh said, emerging from the bedroom. Butterflies overtook Emily's stomach at the sight of the tousled pirate priest.

His eyes lit. "Hey! What are you all doing here?"

"Ask her." Brian scrutinized his mother. "How *did* you do that, anyway?"

Jake laid a hand on Brian's shoulder, and Emily marveled. The exuberant teen bore a strong resemblance to his Uncle Lugh, but side-by-side, he was the spitting image of his father.

Cybele blushed modestly. "I will explain it to you later," she promised Brian, then answered Lugh as Mitchell strolled from the bathroom.

"After you and Mitch left with Cu, I decided to take these two to my flat and get them settled. But on the way out, we saw the blizzard, and I sensed something unnatural was going on. I followed the storm to its source. It brought me here."

Elise broke the shocked silence that descended. "Bé Chuille created the storm, but she fell to a curse."

"No," Lugh said quietly. "Cybele is right. The storm should have ended when the witch died. Right?" He looked around for confirmation.

No one moved or spoke. Exasperated, Emily plopped into the chair.

"Spellcasting 101. We should have known. But if Bé Chuille is still alive, where is she?"

"Who touched her last?" Lugh asked.

A hot wind blew across the room, and Draig Talav's head materialized at the bottom of the stairs.

"Awen, I need a word."

Everyone's face registered shock for a split second, then returned to normal. All except Jake's.

"Y'all figure this out." Emily hurried to Talav.

"Master," the glittering earth dragon rumbled, "one of the Reptilians has requested an audience. They wish to strike a truce and reach a settlement."

Emily glanced behind her. The druids were deep in conversation—all but Jake, whose eyes remained on Emily and the dragon head.

"Can Jake see you?"

The golden eyes flicked to Jake and back.

"Aye, Master. That is the one we call Dragon Seeker."

"I thought only the Awen was immune to the forgetfulness curse."

"That is true. But over the millennium, there have been others of Awen's line who have the sight, too. He is one."

The priest clomped down the stairs carrying a loaded tray. His eyes grew wide on spying Talav's head, and he promptly turned and retreated.

"And him?"

"He is another."

Emily wondered just how many *others* there were. "Tell me about this Reptilian. How did they make contact?"

"Inanna, daughter of the Warlord Shibboleth, called Ooschu."

"How?"

"They have a connection. But as a result, we have halted our attacks on the Reptilians, except for Draig Tienu. You must speak to him, Master. He will listen to you. If we don't stop this war, the Reptilian race will be no more."

"Isn't that what we want?"

Talav's head recoiled. "Master, no! All life is precious. Even that of the Dracs."

Shame humbled Emily. "Of course. You are right. I will speak to Tienu. Where can I find him?"

"On some rampage, I'm sure. Just call. He will answer."

"Emily," Lugh called. The druids were gathered around Honey, who stood defiant and teary-eyed, shaking her head.

"One minute," she told them and turned to Talav. "Find Tienu. Tell him we spoke, and the destruction must stop. At least until we meet with the Reptilians."

Talav wavered. "The fire drake will not listen to me."

"Then tell him it is an order from his Master," she snapped. "I cannot go now. Bé Chuille's storm is wreaking havoc on our world. I must deal with this first."

"And Inanna?"

Emily glanced at the druids. They stared at her. Jake grinned, but the others were likely wondering why their leader was in the corner talking to herself.

"Stop Tienu, then tell Inanna you have halted the dragon attacks. I must confer with—" Who *did* Emily need to confer with?

According to Elise, law enforcement worldwide had been notified and were battling the Reptilians. Who would have the authority to speak for all of them?

"Just make sure the Reptilians stand down. I will confer with Inanna later."

But before Talav could disappear, Emily sought her advice.

"Any words of wisdom on how to locate and deal with Bé Chuille? We think she hid in one of us when her body expired." Emily shuddered and glanced at the group. They now argued amongst themselves.

Talav's golden eyes narrowed. She drew a bead on each of the druids, then snorted, producing a tiny puff of smoke. They both stared as the tendril curled and disappeared.

"What was that?" Emily chuckled. Talav's long lashes batted self-consciously.

"Heartburn, mi' lady."

"I didn't know you could produce fire."

"Me either." The Keeper pondered it a long moment, then wagged her head.

"I sense the witch is inside the blonde. But I do not know how to end her without harming the vessel or your late mother. Now, I must find Tienu, stop his destruction, and rendezvous with Inanna. Maybe you could ask Cu or Hope for help with the witch."

OFF TO ATLANTIS

Inanna paced the clearing and silenced her communicator. It had tweeted regularly since Talav left—Shibboleth, likely demanding her presence in the command center. If the dragon did not return soon, Inanna would be forced to answer and comply. She jumped at a loud thwap.

It was Talav with two dragons—Ooschu and a large male whose scales reflected the sky. Not sure whether to run or hide from the massive creature, Inanna stared open-mouthed, thrust out her chin, and struck her chest in welcome.

"Greetings, Draigs Ooschu and Talav. Who is your companion?"

The drake's head dipped, and his mighty wings fluttered, creating a whirlwind of loose leaves. "I am a-Ur, King of the Air Dragons."

Inanna returned the bow, fist to her chest. "And I am Inanna, daughter of Warlord Shibboleth, the leader of the Reptilian Nation."

a-Ur's bugle rustled the willows and pines and challenged Inanna's resolve.

"What does that scum, Shibboleth, want now?" the air dragon growled.

Talav snorted and stamped the ground with her front feet. "Inanna is requesting our aid, a-Ur. Lord Shibboleth does not know."

The air drake crouched, but his anger smoldered, making Inanna wary.

"I consulted Awen, our Druid leader," Talav said. "She cannot meet in person, but she, too, wishes to end this war. We have ceased the dragon attacks on your people and lands and have come to ask that you do the same until we can reach a peaceful accord." She crouched beside the other dragons. "What say you, Inanna, Shibboleth's Spawn?"

"I have agreement from my peers. Now that you have ceased your attacks, I will approach Shibboleth. Can you stay for a minute while I contact him?"

The dragons nodded cautious assent, and Inanna stepped behind the willow to place the call.

"Inanna, report!" Shibboleth sounded unusually anxious.

She hurriedly conveyed her news.

"You parlayed with the dragons? Without my permission?"

"Aye." She kept her tone neutral. "Three of their leaders are here with me now. Shall I put them on, Sir?"

A loud moan rose behind Shibboleth, and he turned away. Then his ancient scarred face filled the camera.

"Report to Irkalla. Immediately."

Gulping, Inanna stared at the blank screen. Now that she had met with the dragons behind his back, would her litter father execute Inanna as a traitor on her return?

☼☼☼

ShaRhea appeared at the door to the medical unit. Shibboleth waved her in and ordered Inanna to report to Irkalla. He would deal with the subject of the dragons then, plus have his spawn near if Mot's health declined further.

"What is it, my Lord?" ShaRhea peered through Mot's sheer tent. "What happened to Mot?"

"The medics say his Dracs were flash-frozen in AboveEarth. Had he not stayed in the cave talking to me, Mot, too, would be dead." Emotion threatened to consume him, and Shibboleth glanced away. "I fear Queen Druantia might be correct. The surface conditions have deteriorated."

"Air dragons are capable of such freezing."

"Yes. They are. So is Bé Chuille. But Inanna says the dragons have ceased their attacks. And Mot believed it to be a freak weather event."

"Then, Queen Druantia was right. Earth has lost her balance." ShaRhea stilled, and a pained expression twisted her features. "I am too young to remember the surface when it was uninhabitable. But I heard tales." She paused, then pressed on.

"You must help them, Shibboleth. You must do as the queen requested. Stop fighting and send your scientists to help them restore Earth's balance."

He slumped into a chair facing Mot's tent and pondered the news. Then, making up his mind, he herded ShaRhea back to his chambers.

"Can you bring Queen Druantia back?" He latched the door, and ShaRhea squirmed. She rarely allowed other spirits to possess her.

"I do not know. Druantia came through unbidden. Did she not say that it was you who called her?"

"I did?" Shibboleth scratched his chin, tucked his wings, and settled in the chair. Then, retrieving the black stone, he turned it over and over in his claws. "This stone calls Bé Chuille, the witch goddess. She no longer answers, so I suspect something may have happened to her." He considered it a moment, then shrugged.

"But, I have no idea how I called Queen Druantia." He shoved the stone back in its slit, and ShaRhea settled opposite him.

"I had asked you why you stayed on Earth when you hated it so much."

Shibboleth thrummed his thigh with his claws. "And?"

"You said your planetship exploded, and Druantia saved you. She manifested immediately after that." ShaRhea closed her eyes. When she opened them, they gleamed. "Return to that day. Remember what it felt like. Then think of Druantia and say her name."

Shibboleth snorted but did as ShaRhea bade. He traveled back in memory to the depths of outer space and the knowledge that he and his race were about to die. Then, Druantia and her dragons appeared to transport them to the safety of firm soil.

He jumped when Druantia's hologram appeared next to them.

Shibboleth had forgotten how beautiful the druid queen was with her luxuriant blonde tresses, intelligent blue eyes, and voluptuous bosom.

Hands folded, she said solemnly. "Thank you, Lord Shibboleth. Without the ingenuity of your race, the surface world would not have been habitable these last millennia. Your expertise was invaluable back then, and I pray, despite any past disagreements, you will help bring our planet into balance again."

Shibboleth did not hesitate as he had before. It was past time for that.

"Send me the location, your queenship. I will travel by chute when I put things in order here."

"You won't regret it, Sir," Druantia said, bowing.

Shibboleth stuck his chest and dipped his head. "I already do."

A few hours later, Azi arrived in Irkalla, and after a hasty meal, Shibboleth and the scientist departed for Atlantis.

Azi could not believe his good fortune. He had studied Atlantis for millennia and was fascinated by it. The famed civilization had once dominated Earth's surface, springing from the Druid gods and goddesses after migrating there from UnderEarth. Then, the infighting began, and disaster struck. The surrounding seas consumed the capital city and sank to the ocean floor. Over time, the other cities fell, too—or so the legends said.

When Azi and Shibboleth arrived in the mystical city, they were shuttled to a reception area where a tall, pale being welcomed them to the Queendom of Atlantis.

"Few are allowed entrance," White Star confided. "You are the first Dracs to set foot in this fair city."

She led them through a garden where curious Atlanteans watched them pass. Most expressions were reserved or blank, but a few registered mild interest or amazement. One or two seemed outraged.

Azi's gut tightened with a sense of foreboding. He moved closer to his commander, who took the scrutiny in stride. His calm demeanor was a stark contrast to the tension in the air.

They passed through a maze of crystal caverns, and then the path opened to a large grotto. Its soaring ceiling was open in the middle, and the longest, thickest crystal rod Azi had ever seen jutted toward the sky.

A GATHERING OF SCIENTISTS

Queen Druantia and Thoth introduced Shibboleth, the Reptilian Warlord, and his scientist, Azi, to the assembled team. Then, Thoth recapped their mission.

"Earth has lost her balance. As a result, the surface is reverting to chaos, and if we do not intervene, it will no longer be habitable. Billions of creatures will die if not relocated. Including humankind." Thoth paused to let the gravity of the situation sink in. "We have called you here because you are the best in your fields.

"As I mentioned earlier, Warlord Shibboleth is the leader of the Reptilians of UnderEarth. After they and the Druids lost their homeworlds, Shibboleth and his Dracs helped terraform Earth's surface to sustain life."

Khenko gasped loudly. "I didn't know that."

"Me either," chimed Randy and Freya.

"Oh, yes," Thoth explained. "Earth was originally a planetship. And though both the interior and exterior were designed to be livable, its outer atmosphere was too harsh for that. The Druids had lived on Marduk's surface and wished to do the same here. So, with Reptilian technology, which far exceeded any on Earth then, Lord Shibboleth and his Dracs molded the surface to harness and direct Earth's energy.

"As you know, the ionosphere forms a boundary between Earth's lower atmosphere and the vacuum of space. In it, lightning strikes produce standing waves of electricity that race around Earth. These waves combine and amplify each other, producing an electromagnetic effect. You probably know it as the Schumann resonance. Earth's average resonance is a frequency of 7.83 hertz— meaning the electrical waves make nearly eight trips around the planet *per second.*"

Freya raised her hand. Thoth paused to let her speak

"I read recently that Earth's Schumann resonance has been spiking as high as 36 hertz, causing mass anxiety and even hysteria and psychosis."

Shibboleth rolled his eyes at the Fomorian but did not comment.

"That is correct," Thoth said. "Would you like to address this, Druantia?"

The queen stood. "The fluctuations you speak of indicate the chaos we are trying to correct. But, yes, any changes to Earth's frequencies can cause issues for her residents, especially the more sensitive ones. But this is only one component of Earth's harmonics—and it works as designed, even with the fluctuations.

"We are focusing on a different mechanism. Like the electrical waves, wind and light energy rush across the planet's surface and through its mantle to keep Earth's merkaba properly tuned. That allows her to spin smoothly on her axis through space." Druantia nodded to Khenko, who wished to speak.

"Could you please explain what a merkaba is?"

"Merkaba is what we call the light body. Most beings have a Merkaba, or Lightbody, that can propel them through time and space. It is this lightbody that is out of balance." Druantia motioned to the crystal rod behind her.

"When Earth's merkaba began faltering about a century ago, we utilized the Atlantis crystal to hold it together. But over time, that tuning also deteriorated. It is now off-kilter, and nothing we have tried seems to work. At least not long-term. So, we are now looking at Earth's terraforming.

"Tall structures like Stonehenge and the pyramids act as antennae and conductors. They shape and propel the wind and light energy around the globe and through Earth's navel tube. Many of these sacred configurations were used to terraform Marduk. They were transported to Earth before Marduk exploded." Druantia turned to the Reptilians.

"This is where Shibboleth and his Dracs come in. To stabilize Earth's surface conditions, they helped relocate our monuments, placing them in strategic locations around the globe. They also helped build many new ones, like the complex at Angkor Wat, Gobekli Tepe, the Adams Calendar magnetrons in Africa and worldwide, Bagan, Borobudur, the Egyptian obelisks, and Sacsayhuamán, to name a few you might be familiar with. But there are many, many, *many* more."

"Shibboleth," Druantia said. "Thank you for traveling to Atlantis to help us get Earth back in sync."

Shibboleth's wings fluttered and then tucked again. "To determine if terraforming is the problem, I must get above the surface and assess the terrain."

"Of course," Druantia said. "But I don't know how much information that will yield. A storm system covers Earth's northern half. Clouds fill the sky, and snow blankets the land."

"Then it would be hard to tell. If you could clear the skies, we could at least make a pass to assess what is visible."

"Then, let me see what I can do." Druantia swept from the room.

SHOWDOWN

Talav disappeared, and Emily sucked in a breath. The urge to run away had grown so strong, it nearly consumed her. And though the Druids waited, she couldn't face them right now. She needed to be alone.

She pondered the last time she had been able to jog and realized it had been weeks—since before the earthquake. She had tried on Zephyr Cay while recovering. After fifty yards, exhaustion set in, forcing her to stop.

Now, longing to run free with the wind in her face and the earth beneath her feet, she hurried to the staircase, propelled by the overwhelming need to escape, to be alone doing something routine and therapeutic, something that didn't require Emily to think or be someone or something she wasn't.

Behind her, the voices called out in surprise.

"Emily, can you help?"

"Where are you going?"

"What's wrong, Em?"

She climbed faster, slipping through the door into the sanctuary.

The wind howled, and rattled the shutters as the priest appeared. Recognizing the resolve in Emily's eyes, he stepped to an alcove to retrieve an ancient fur wrap, and held it out. She thanked him, slipping it on and tugging the hood over her tied-back curls. Then, hearing footsteps on the stairs, Emily shot through the outer door the priest had shoved open.

"I shall delay them, Mi' lady. But take care. The weather is most foul."

Pulling Awen's robe closer in the thick snow, Emily heaved a sigh of relief and wove a spell of protection around her and the occupants of the Lady Chapel. Then, with a ghost of a smile, she plodded through the snow past the white-shrouded trees and eerie sentinel walls.

If Emily couldn't jog, she could at least work up a sweat.

She wiped the accumulating flakes from her lashes and slogged on. In the distance she spied St. Michael's Tower atop Glastonbury Tor. Its ghostly outline beckoned mockingly through a wall of snow—too far on a day like today. Still, she persisted.

When the terrain began climbing, she glanced up and gasped. The tower loomed directly ahead. She looked back, confused. The Lady Chapel was no longer in sight. No way had Emily walked that far. What sort of magic had propelled her here?

She had been about to turn back. Instead, she kept going.

With no cover from the wind and snow, Emily lowered her head and tackled the hill, one halting step at a time. Slipping and sliding in the sometimes waist-deep powder, she ranted at herself.

What was she thinking?

She wasn't. She'd given in to whim. Now she was climbing a stupid hill in the middle of a blizzard with god-knows-how-many-miles-an-hour winds. The higher she climbed, the steeper the slope and the louder the harangue became.

Emily was about to turn back when she tripped and fell spread-eagled in the snow. She lay there with her face buried, wondering what the hell she was trying to prove. Then, dragging herself up, she plodded the last steps to the roofless tower and bent forward to gulp air. Her strength was spent, and Awen's boots were swamped. But Emily had made it.

When she could breathe again, she shook the snow from her hood and cloak and faced the wind. Contrary to common sense, the squall seemed calmer at this elevation, the snow less dense. From Afsel's aerial tour, she knew that the entire zodiac lay at her feet, carved into and teased from the landscape.

A sensation in her midsection drew Emily's attention, and goosebumps spread across her scalp. Had Bé Chuille transferred to Emily without her knowledge? Then she remembered Afsel's question—"How's the morning sickness?"—and her hands flew to her womb. A shudder went through her as knowing dawned.

Bé Chuille was coming. And everything, *everything* hung in the balance.

"Cu," she whispered, reaching out with her senses. "Bring Hope and the Elders. Prepare to fight Bé Chuille in a blizzard. And, hurry!"

With Aóme on her forefinger, she laid her hand between the brooch and the pendant on her chest. Power flowed into Emily as the three gems connected. Then, planting her feet wide, she prepared mentally for the approaching threat.

Thunder boomed in the distance. Then, another echoed, closer this time. Emily's insides quaked as a whirlwind of snow shrieked through the tower.

It was Bé Chuille. The witch was taunting Emily.

For a moment, the storm lessened, and the outline of the Lady Chapel appeared in the distance. The lights of the city glowed beyond. Emily leaned against the stone archway, relieved when its energy calmed and grounded her.

Then, Afsel's disembodied voice whispered in her ear. "The winter hag approaches. She has seized your friend's body and rendered her helpless to interfere."

"And my mother?"

After a silence, the ethereal voice countered, "The mother who bore you or the one who raised you?"

Anguish tore at Emily's heart.

"Are they not the same? The one known as Alexis."

"That spirit has gone silent, though I sense she is there."

Emily yearned to ask about the other mother, but a haunting hoot and a raven caw sounded through the snow veil.

Cailleach-Oidche and Bran lit on the tower. Then an enormous hawk swooped with a long, shrill screech. It attacked the shrouded figure coming into view, then circled and dove again. The owl and raven joined Shevug, and the three birds drove Bé Chuille to her knees.

There was a snuffle behind Emily. She wheeled and squealed when an exuberant Cu nearly bowled her over.

Hope meowed and wove through Emily's ankles. "What is the plan?" Her tail switched as she watched the fierce birds battle the witch.

"Force Bé Chuille to stop this storm." If she refused, the only other way would be to end the witch's life. Praying that wouldn't fall to her, Emily shivered. The idea of taking a life cut to her core. Even one as evil as Bé Chuille.

"But do you have a plan?" Hope peered intently at Emily.

"Not really, no. But can we tell the Elders not to hurt Honey? The witch has taken over her body, and my mother is in there with them."

Cu proceeded to do just that. But a dying shriek interrupted his howls.

Where the bird Elders battled the witch, Shevug writhed in the snow. Her mighty wings flapped, then went still as the other two swooped and attacked Bé Chuille. Then, suddenly, the witch disappeared.

"Where'd she go?" Emily gasped.

A deep, threatening growl came from behind them, and Emily whirled.

Artis and the other ferocious animal Elders had surrounded the hilltop. A curse sizzled through the snow, slicing through their circle. Emily blocked it and crouched between Cu and Hope.

"Where is she? I don't see her."

"There!" Hope snarled when the shrouded figure materialized. Hair on end, the wildcat yowled and pounced.

For the second time in as many days, Emily watched Bé Chuille, this time in Honey's body, spin in a tight circle, trying to dislodge the forty-pound wildcat. Then the witch shot backward, slamming Hope against the tower, and all hell broke loose.

The animal Elders attacked all at once, and Emily found herself on her hands and knees in a snarling, spitting, howling pile of animal flesh. Then, a clap of thunder shook the tor, tossing them to the ground, and Bé Chuille reared back to hurl a curse.

Instead, she flew in the opposite direction, dragged backward, kicking and screaming, into a dark, swirling wormhole.

A momentary silence descended as the wind dropped and the snowflakes thinned and drifted aimlessly. Emily levered herself upright and dusted her wrap as the stunned animals emerged from the snow.

"What happened?" she wondered aloud, then realized the snow had stopped. "Is Bé Chuille dead?"

A woman appeared then, blonde, beautiful—and giant-sized. A goddess in the flesh? She spoke, and Emily recognized her voice.

"Bé Chuille is not dead." It was Druantia, her ancestor.

"But the snow stopped."

"Only temporarily. Wormholes block any active spells. But the storm will continue once she reaches the other end."

The animal Elders bowed before Druantia in apparent awe.

"Hail, Druantia. Goddess Queen of Marduk and Mother of Awen."

"Hail, dear Elders," Druantia crooned with a beatific smile. "You've been busy of late."

"That we have, my queen," Artis chuffed and shuffled closer. "It is an honor to see you. But, where did you send the winter hag? It is time to end her, once and for all."

"Artis!" Druantia seemed stunned. "You finally agree?"

"Aye," he shrilled. "Any good that once dwelt in Bé Chuille is no longer there. Or it is buried so deep, only death can pry it loose."

"We must be careful," Emily said. "Bé Chuille's spirit now dwells in another's body—an innocent named Honey. My mother's spirit is in there too."

"Your mother?" Druantia stared, brows knit.

Anguish tore at Emily one more and she hung her head. Then anger flared, and she glared at Druantia.

"The woman who raised me."

"Ahh, yes."

Emily squirmed beneath the penetrating gaze, then pulled her cloak tight as the wind shrieked through St. Michael's Tower.

"That is our cue. Bé Chuille has reached our destination." The snow began falling.

Druantia took Emily's hand, and bent to kiss her palm. Kindness and compassion flowed to Emily.

"You are not like the others," the goddess said. "My daughter is lucky you came along."

"Awen?" Emily asked, gobsmacked.

"Yes, my dear Emily. Awen is lucky to have you."

A warmth, sweeter than anything Emily had known, enveloped her. She could feel a grin stretching across her face until it split the corners of her chapped lips.

"Not as lucky as I am to have her. And now you."

The animal Elders cheered as a reanimated Shevug flew overhead and landed nearby, wings flapping.

"Hail, Awen and Queen Druantia," the hawk shrilled.

Druantia bowed, then clapped her hands. "We must go now. Bé Chuille is bound, but given enough time, she will escape and cause more havoc."

"How do we defeat her without hurting Honey?" Emily asked.

"We shall extract the witch." Druantia peered at her closely. "But you will need your wand."

"My wand?" Guilt punched Emily in the gut. Lugh had brought it from Atlanta, along with Awen's journal. But it lay on the table in the abbey next to her cot.

"Yes, your wand."

"Umm…" She peered down the hill through the thickening snow and started the long journey to fetch it.

"Where are you going?"

"To get the wand."

A melodic laugh wafted across the picturesque Tor.

"There is so much to learn, isn't there? Come hither, dear."

Not sure whether she should obey or run, Emily turned back in a huff as the goddess opened a new wormhole. Then, sending the Elder host to guard Bé Chuille, Druantia eyed Emily.

"Hold out your hand." Emily did. "Now think of the wand and imagine it lying in your palm."

Rolling her eyes, Emily sighed heavily. But she drew a deep breath, brushed an escaped curl away for the umpteenth time, and anchored in the snow. Then connecting with the elements, she out held her hand and did as Druantia instructed.

When she peeked, nothing was there. But it jarred loose a memory of the salt shaker in Khenko's kitchen. Calling on the triumph she had felt that day, Emily closed her eyes and tried again.

This time, a thrill of satisfaction swirled in her gut. She wrapped her fingers around the slender shaft and hugged it to her chest.

"Well done, dear. Well done." Druantia beamed. Then, opening another wormhole, she waved to it. "You first, Emily. I will follow."

✹✹✹

At the end of the wormhole was Stonehenge. Chills rippled up and down Emily's spine as her eyes swept the tops of the standing stones. She had no recall of being in this place, but a sense of déjà vu sat heavy upon her, as gray as the snow-filled sky beyond the henge. Druantia touched down beside her in the outer circle.

The Elders milled in the inner circle, forming a loose ring around Bé Chuille. Some stood on the fallen stones while the raptors peered down from the lintels.

The witch sat hunched on a fallen bluestone in the center of the famous monument, conversing with herself. Or, more likely, with Honey. Or Alexis. Or both.

Snow pelted everything, driven by the wind.

Emily's stomach roiled, and nausea threatened. Oh, God. Not now.

She sucked in a ragged breath and felt that hint of a flutter in her abdomen again. The truth registered, and a cold sweat broke across her brow. Afsel was right. Emily was pregnant whether she liked it or not. Fear clutched at her throat, making it hard to breathe.

Then, her resolve hardened. She would not let Bé Chuille, nor anyone else, harm the baby growing inside of her. Ready to do battle to the end if she must, Emily clutched Awen's wand in her right hand and cradled her womb with her left.

The Elders turned toward her, and Druantia peered down at the wand with obvious concern.

"Where are the wandstones?"

"They weren't... they aren't..." That awful feeling of having mucked up royally plundered Emily's gut and traveled all the way to her toes.

She gulped and presented Aóme, the ruby pendant, and the sapphire brooch to the goddess.

Worry marred Druantia's features. She drew Emily behind a bluestone trilithon, and the wind shrilled through its opening.

"And the diamond? Where is that?"

Despair formed a lump in Emily's throat. She swallowed hard. "We never found it. So, what now?"

Leaning her forehead against a snowy bluestone, Druantia drew a deep breath and expelled it forcefully.

"Now, we call the Keepers. Or rather, you do."

"Me?" Emily froze.

"You."

"But how?" Her brain had frozen, too.

Druantia sighed but spoke gently. "Let Awen out. She knows what to do."

Of course. She would. Emily closed her eyes. "Awen, are you there?"

"Always," Awen reassured. "You've got this, dear one. Anchor, center, and call their names. Just like you did with Losgann."

That helped. Emily had successfully called the frog Elder more than once. She returned to the center ring and followed Awen's instructions. Then she spoke the Keepers' names, starting with Tienu.

A ferocious, metallic shriek filled the henge, and fire streaked overhead as Tienu landed on the northernmost stone in the outer circle.

A series of roars announced the others as they settled opposite the fire dragon in the remaining cardinal directions according to their element—a-Ur in the west, Talav in the east, and Ooschu in the south.

When they were all in place, the dragons joined in one long, ululating trumpet. Goosebumps roved Emily's body as their combined voices set up a vibration in the stones of the henge and teased out an otherworldly hum that filled the circle and rose into the heavens.

"Show them your wand, Emily," Druantia instructed over the reverberating tone.

She held it up to the Keepers.

"The stones, too," her ancestor prompted.

Emily held up the ruby pendant, the sapphire brooch, and Aóme's emerald while Druantia explained about the missing diamond. The standing stones sang, sending chills up the back of Emily's scalp.

Talav soared to the ground. "Take one of mine."

The earth dragon bared her sparkling chest. Next to a dull black stone glittered a smaller, clear one.

"Can you break off a chip?" Emily asked.

Talav sliced off a shard with a sharp claw and dropped it into Emily's palm beside the others. The vibrating stones began to glow and throw off sparks.

"That will work," Druantia murmured. "Now, unite the stones with your wand."

"Huh?" Panic seized Emily. Performing on demand was not her forte.

"Ask Awen," Druantia sighed, and Emily could tell the goddess's patience was wearing thin.

She closed her eyes and ignored the rising panic to focus on her breath. As her body relaxed, words formed in her head. But when Emily spoke them aloud, nothing happened.

Ashamed to fail in front of her ancestor, she repeated the spell. Again, nothing happened. Only this time, the witch cackled gleefully and stood to watch.

The wind shrieked, and the snow-covered animal Elders tightened their circle around Bé Chuille. She cackled louder. It echoed around the singing stones and chilled Emily's blood.

Even if she could unite the gems with the wand, would she be able to banish the witch from Honey and protect her mother?

Desperate now, Emily cast about frantically, trying to decide what to do. Her legs trembled as everything Emily had ever learned trickled from her brain. Panic rushed in, and her breathing shallowed.

She was near hyperventilating when Hope's voice rang inside her head. "You can do this, Emily. You were born for this. You have trained for this. Hell, you have suffered for this. You *are* the Awen. Concentrate."

As Hope's words buoyed her spirits, Emily let everything slip away until she was alone with the wand. Then, instructing it and the gemstones to unite, she peeked through one eye.

The stones abandoned their settings and flew to the wand. A resounding boom shook the henge when they were all in place, and a pulse vibrated through Emily, Druantia, and the Elder host.

Honey fell to the ground, thrashing wildly.

Then Bé Chuille's form separated, and Honey went limp as the witch's apparition shimmered beside her.

Without thought, Emily flicked her wand, and Honey flew backward to land between the bluestones. Cu sniffed her limp body and barked an okay.

The spirit's eyes grew large with fear. Bé Chuille was parted and exposed. She climbed to her feet, wobbling as if weakened in the transition.

The Elders crowded closer, growling, bawling, hissing, and spitting at the evil witch. Each had been a victim of her over the millennia.

"Kill her, Master," Artis shrieked as Bé Chuille darted away, trying to escape. "Put an end to the wicked witch once and for all."

Emily lifted her wand and tilted it toward Bé Chuille. But she could not strike the killing blow.

Artis could.

The enormous bear pointed his mighty claw, and a thin stream of electricity shot through the snow and struck Bé Chuille's chest.

As the specter screeched in impotent rage, it caved in on itself in slow motion. Then, it imploded dramatically into a swirling vortex. The last vestige of spirit tried to escape, but the vortex devoured Bé Chuille and then disappeared.

A stunned silence fell upon Stonehenge. The wind calmed, and the snow ceased. Then, the animals raised their voices in jubilation.

Emily crumpled to the snow, spent in every sense of the word.

AWEN SKY

I t was well past midday when they left Stonehenge. Emily rode Draig a-Ur, and Druantia was atop Draig Tienu with Honey in front of her, clinging to the horns. They would return to the Lady Chapel, then go on to the Azores.

The black clouds were breaking up in places, and the brightening sky was a welcome relief after the massive snowstorm. But Emily sighed heavily nonetheless. She had not been able to finish Bé Chuille. Luckily, Artis had had no qualms. Now, the witch was gone, hopefully for good.

The other two Keepers flew abreast, and Emily clung tighter when a-Ur zigged to open up room.

"People are pointing," Talav trumpeted. "Something is wrong."

Their flight path was over snow-clad pastures and land separated by walls and fences. Few humans were about.

They soon approached a farmer whose head jerked up. He dropped the armful of hay flakes he was carrying and hightailed it to the barn, horrified. Then, he peeked out as they passed overhead and held up a phone camera.

Druantia reacted quickly with a distortion charm. "Your spell must've ended the forgetfulness curse. I will reinstate it." She raised her wand and swished while Emily clung to a-Ur. She was thankful her ancestor hadn't asked her to do something else she had no idea how to do.

It must have worked because the next humans they encountered went about their business as if the dragons were not there. Druantia pointed ahead.

"Look, Emily!"

Black clouds still dominated the western sky, and the horizon below them was clearing. Sunrays had broken through a jagged hole near the southern terminus, forming a long-armed, sideways starburst.

Emily grinned, and Druantia flashed a warm smile.

"Did you know we call that phenomenon an awen?"

"Really? No. Is that where Awen got her name?"

"That and more."

Sunrays soon pierced the bottom of the cloud, forming a full lower awen. Glowing light fingers reached for Earth in the shape of a fan.

As they flew toward Glastonbury, more rays penetrated the bottom of the clouds. And soon, a whole series of iridescent awens danced beneath the gray wall.

Emily's heart swelled with wonder.

Within minutes, the line of awens had expanded until it stretched from south to north. Tears trickled from the corners of Emily's eyes as profound gratitude welled up inside her.

She glanced back and broke into a watery grin.

Behind them, in the east, cornflower blue peeked through torn, patchy clouds. The storm was receding.

But in the west, above the largest awen, rays shot skyward to create a full starburst. Then, the clouds parted, and a welcome sunbeam shone on their entourage. It struck Emily, and the sweetest love she had ever felt washed gently over and through her.

Then, Awen was there, and they lifted ecstatic arms to the numinous light. If the tri-moon formation they had witnessed on Beltane was a once-in-a-lifetime phenomenon, how rare must this spectacle be?

The cloud closed, and for a moment, Emily felt utterly alone. Then a-Ur spoke inside her head.

"See what you did, Master? The elements are showing out for you." The other Keepers raucously agreed.

Druantia beamed, and something inside Emily shifted.

Whether as Margret, Dee, Ebby, or the other personas she had been forced to live, Emily had tried so hard, for so long, to be what she thought she wasn't.

When all along that was who and what she had always been.

She chuckled. It had only taken dead ancestors, four dragon Keepers, an entire Elder host, a Grand Druid, a Druid priest, his teenage nephew, and many others to get Emily here.

Approval enveloped her like a warm hug, and she knew Druantia and the Keepers were listening and were proud of her.

For the rest of the short flight, Emily's gaze remained on the western sky where scores of awens stretched from south to north.

There, the sky remained ominous, and lightning danced inside the black clouds.

Was a different storm brewing up Yr Wyddfa way?

After a hero's welcome for Emily, ooo's and ahhh's over Queen Druantia, and an early dinner at the Lady Chapel, the druids were departing. Cybele, Jake, and Brian left first for AIA Headquarters in London. Emily, Druantia, and Elise would travel to the Azores. The rest were returning to Atlanta to take care of matters at home.

As Rona prepared to shuttle Mitchell and Honey, Alexis grabbed Emily and held on tight.

"Thank you, Emily. Talav told me I can stay. I don't have to go back to the Otherworld." Tears gathered in Honey's baby-blue eyes. "I don't deserve a second chance. But—" her voice broke. She swallowed hard and started again. "Thank you for giving me one."

Emily had dreamed of this moment and was shocked when she said, "You know, Mother, I want to thank you, too. I wouldn't be here if not for you."

Alexis's gaze flew to a wistful Rona, and she started to say something, but Rona cut her off. "It was great to finally meet you, Emily. Thank you for everything. It has been an honor."

Alexis regarded Rona curiously.

Glimpsing a yearning in Mitchell's eyes, Emily grabbed his hand and squeezed.

"If, or when, we all make it out of this alive, I wouldn't mind too much if you joined my adult druid classes."

Mitch's mouth fell open. "Seriously?" He glanced at his mom, then back at Emily, shuttering his excitement. "I stay pretty busy. But I might take you up on that."

"Hey, I'd like to get in on that action." Honey grinned.

Emily smiled at the irrepressible woman graciously hosting her mother. Being possessed by Bé Chuille had not dampened her spirit.

"Absolutely. I look forward to having you there."

Then Rona engaged her merkaba, and they disappeared.

Turning to Lugh, Emily gave him a long, lingering kiss. Then, she hugged Hope and Cu before they, too, vanished with a thwap.

That left Druantia, Emily, and Elise.

Each thanked the priest for his hospitality and shelter. Then, joining hands, Druantia spirited them to Atlantis.

REPTILIAN TECHNOLOGY

Khenko shoved his plate back and belched. It was a long, satisfying burp that had his mother scowling and Randy snickering like they were back in high school.

"Bird!" his mother scolded.

He grinned at her, and punched Randy's shoulder. The burly Marine was in better spirits after talking to his fiancé via what Khenko had dubbed the bat phone. But it had yet to be explained how today they could get a signal this deep inside Earth, when yesterday, it wasn't an option.

They had worked nonstop since arriving in Atlantis, only stopping to take short breaks to eat and nap. But after the Reptilians' shocking appearance, Queen Druantia had given them the afternoon off, then left for the surface to neutralize the blizzard. Khenko had spent most of the interim meditating beneath Yggdrasil. Now, it was dinnertime, and they were the last ones in the dining hall.

A petite woman with hair like Thoth's peeked through the door and squealed. "Khenko!" Then, she dashed across the room.

He barely had time to stand before the compact woman slammed into him and wrapped her arms around his waist.

"I can't believe it! I had to see for myself."

Khenko stared, struggling to place the quixotic face.

"Ahh, you don't remember." She let go and shoved kinky hair from her eyes. "Talav must have jiggered with your memory."

"Talav?" The vision of a brilliantly-gemmed dragon tearing through palmetto palms flashed before Khenko, then was gone, replaced by the growing sense of frustration he had known since "coming to" in his boat near the Bermuda Triangle Vortex. Those laughing green eyes were recognizable. So, why could he not recall their owner?

She stretched up to touch the angle of his jaw, and Khenko flinched. But her gentle touch released a flood of memories—diving the blue hole behind the dragon queen to rescue her druid master, nursing the small but formidable woman back to health, and the two other dragons who had arrived on Zephyr Cay to finish her training.

"Emily!" he crowed, lifting the redhead and spinning her around in circles. "Thank you so much. That hole in my memory was driving me crazy."

He set her down gently to introduce Emily to the others, but his mother stared open-mouthed.

"It's you!" she whispered incredulously.

"HUH?" they exclaimed.

"You're the woman in my dreams." Excitement pinked Val Blitherstone's cheeks. "Remember, Khenko? I told you about her."

"I remember the dream. But I thought it was about Druantia and Thoth."

"The first one, yes." His Ma's face scrunched. "But since then, I've dreamed about the prophecy often. Each time I do, you appear," she said to Emily, who stared in amazement.

In a singsong voice, his mother recited the prophecy.

When Armageddon threatens,
The sleeping one will wake.
Along the same meridian
The fallen steps in place.
One coast will gather light and kind
The other dark, despair,
But each will yield its suffering
To a world laid waste with fear.
The call will soon be answered
Old wounds doth fester e'er,
The battle begun before Earth was wrought
Must be won in the helm of the sufferer's heart
And from thence, She leaps forth
Once again.

As she spoke the last lines, Queen Druantia hurtled into the dining hall and made a beeline for Val.

"How do you know the prophecy?" She took Val's hand.

"It came across my desk years ago when I was head of Ancient Studies at Princeton," Val explained. "But lately, I keep dreaming about it. And Emily."

Druantia's eyes rolled back a moment, then refocused on his mother. "I believe this is a critical piece of our puzzle." She let go of her hand and turned to Emily. "What do you think, Awen?"

Emily's face blanched. She clung to Khenko's arm, eyes wide in that "deer in the headlamps" look she often got when placed on the spot.

"It's okay, Emily. Take your time. You can answer when you're ready." To Druantia, he murmured, "She suffers from performance anxiety."

But Emily recovered quickly and reached out her hand.

"Hello, Mrs. Blitherstone. I'm Emily Hester of the Awen Order of Druids. I'm thrilled to meet the mother of the man who saved my life. And, yes," she offered to Queen Druantia, "I believe you are right about the prophecy." Her eyes took on a faraway look.

"Soon after arriving in Atlanta, I dreamed about Artis and the animal Elders. In the dream, Artis chased me down, insisting I memorize this prophecy. At the time, I knew no magic and wasn't even sure I wanted to be a druid. I didn't understand the prophecy or its significance—or how it could possibly relate to me. But now…" Her voice trailed off. "Do you have some paper?"

"Paper?" Druantia asked, brow crinkling.

"I would like to write down the prophecy. It helps me think."

Val removed her phone from an inside pocket. "I have it saved here. Will that work?"

Thoth strode through the door.

"I am taking Lord Shibboleth and his scientist up in the hovercraft to assess the terraforms." The god glided toward Druantia, but on seeing Emily, his face lit in wonder. "Awen?" He went down on one knee and held out his arms. Emily moved as if drawn magnetically but stopped short of his reach.

"I am Emily. Your great, great, great-something granddaughter."

Then her expression softened, and she leapt into Thoth's waiting arms.

Delight filled Khenko as Thoth engulfed Emily in a bear hug and held on tight. A tear even trickled from the corner of the god's eye.

"My dear, dear Awen," the god murmured. "It has been so long."

"Too long, Father." The words came from Emily, but the voice was not hers.

Khenko watched, mesmerized, as the two cried and laughed in happy reunion.

Then, the Reptilian leader marched through the door. "I thought time was of the essence. Are we leaving, or what?"

Thoth straightened but kept a hand on Emily's shoulder.

The creepy red eyes locked on her, and the Reptilian froze. Then, Shibboleth struck his chest with a fist, thin lips parting in a besotted smile.

It was clear to Khenko the warlord was smitten.

"Lady Awen," he all but purred, wings fluttering. "I did not know you were here. When did you arrive?"

Emily fidgeted but curtsied, lifting the skirt of the soiled fur robe.

"I am Emily, Awen's descendent," she squeaked. Then, clearing her throat, she continued in a shaky voice. "I arrived with Queen Druantia. You must be the Reptilian leader. I am pleased to meet you, Sir." She bobbed and dipped her head in respect.

Taken aback, the leader hesitated, then reached out a claw.

"I am Shibboleth, leader of the Reptilians of UnderEarth. You look identical to your ancestor."

Emily laughed, a tinkling melody that rose and fell and echoed around the hall.

"So I have been told. Awen is here with me and has a word for you." Her expression and voice shifted again.

"Lord Shibboleth, I am happy to see you. Have you come to help us save the world again?"

Khenko gawked. The transformation from humble human to mighty druid priestess was remarkable.

"Aye, mi' lady," the ancient warrior rumbled, gentle as a puppy.

"From what I have seen, the bulk of your terraforming is still in place. You will assess it from the Atlantean hovercraft?"

"Aye," Thoth interjected. "And if we are to save the planet, we must be off."

Khenko watched in amazement as the Reptilian took Awen's hand tenderly, pressed his lips to it, and backed away with a reverent fist to his scaled chest.

"We should not be long," Thoth promised Druantia.

Khenko cleared his throat and asked the question burning within him.

"Sir, may I go up in the craft with you? Seeing the lay of the land from above might jog something loose that will help me be more useful."

Shibboleth hissed, but Thoth stroked his chin thoughtfully.

"I believe we have enough room. Come, young crane. You may accompany us."

Stifling the urge to whoop and holler, Khenko thanked Thoth, said goodbye to the others, and followed the tall beings from the hall.

☼☼☼

The sleek craft zipped from UnderEarth to AboveEarth in a matter of moments. It happened so fast that Khenko didn't realize they were transitioning until they skimmed the snow-covered Azores Islands.

The shiny airship Thoth piloted looked nothing like Earth's aircraft. Nor was it similar to those utilized by the Space Force to travel to the moon or Mars. This one was iridescent and mirrored the environment, making it next to impossible for observers to see.

It was also supersonic, and it made no noise. Within minutes, they were flying over a snow-ravaged Europe, and in a little over an hour, they had circled the globe and returned to Atlantis, where they rushed to the main hall. With an air of anticipation, Thoth uploaded the information, then sat back to let Shibboleth and Azi comb through the resulting data.

The Reptilians fascinated Khenko. After the initial shock had worn off, he realized they were not all that scary. They were bipedal and walked upright like humans but had reptile faces and scales. Shibboleth's scales were a creamy white, while Azi's were olive green. Shibboleth towered above his scientist, who was a hair shorter than Khenko.

Azi's head was much larger than the warlord's, and his eyes were dark instead of red. Both had nose and ear slits, knobby horns, and fearsome claws on their hands and feet. Neither wore clothes, though both had a belt riding low across their hips.

However, the main difference was that Shibboleth sported a complete set of wings similar to angels, or at least to the depictions Khenko had seen. Azi's shoulder blades protruded but ended in nubs.

The warlord grunted and gestured to Thoth, who joined them at the monitor. Khenko crowded beside them to peer at the screen.

"Earth's surface is not the problem," the warlord announced. "You can see from this column of data that the most significant stoneworks still stand. And the tall buildings and monuments erected by Humans have since replaced those lost to the ravages of time."

Thoth slumped back into his chair.

"Then we are back where we started." He looked around at each of them. "We are out of time. Earth is almost off-kilter. Any other ideas?"

NOW OR NEVER

After taking a much-needed shower and changing into soft, flowy clothes provided by Druantia, Emily settled into a human-sized chaise. She folded her legs underneath her and sucked in a shocked breath when her curls fell in her lap.

A couple of weeks ago, her hair had barely reached her shoulders. The rapid growth defied reason. Too bad her magical abilities hadn't kept pace. Or maybe they had and Emily was being hard on herself.

She read through the prophecy on Val's phone again. Then, using the pen and paper Freya had scrounged up, Emily began writing the verses in longhand.

By the time she made it halfway through, she no longer needed to consult Val's phone. The words flowed from memory. On the second go-round, Emily wrote the entire prophecy without looking, but no clues jumped out on either pass.

Yawning wide, she left the common room in search of Val to return her phone. She found her in the crystal room visiting quietly with Elise Johnson. Thanking them both, she returned Val's phone as Thoth, Shibboleth, Azi, and Khenko entered the room.

"That was fast," she said.

"You won't believe their aircraft," Khenko crowed, either pumped or highly caffeinated. "We circled the globe and made it back in just over an hour!"

Pumped it was. And little wonder. Unable to resist egging him on, Emily grinned. "Seriously? That's some next-level aviation."

"It is! And I thought the X-5900 was fast."

Curious about the craft, Emily was about to ask when Thoth interrupted. His words chilled her to the bone.

"Lord Shibboleth and Major Azi have finished analyzing the data. Earth's terraforming is not our problem. I'm afraid it is back to the drawing board."

"But we've tried everything else," Val groaned. An edge of desperation had crept into her tone. All of the scientists were running on fumes.

"I suggest we take a time-out," Thoth said. "Take a walk. A nap. Eat. Do whatever it takes to get your brains in top working condition. I don't need to remind you that time is running short. If we don't soon find a solution..." his voice petered out, and Druantia took his hand.

"How do I get to that beautiful park we saw on our way in?" Emily could use a dose of nature that didn't include snow

Khenko's eyes gleamed. "I'll show you, Em."

They walked through the crystal caverns in companionable silence, then Khenko asked, "Remember the kapok tree on Zephyr Cay?"

"Yes. I loved that tree." Beneath it was where Emily had first felt Awen's presence in a non-threatening way.

"Then you're going to love the one here. I believe it might be Yggdrasil herself."

"The Tree of Life?"

"The Tree of Life. I've been meaning to ask Queen Druantia or Thoth. It matches the depictions I have seen."

And so it did. Emily nested in a cradle of thick twisted roots. Khenko coiled in a larger one on the opposite side. The only sounds were those of a burbling stream and the buzzing of very large bumblebees.

Emily's mind swirled as she tried to make sense of the prophecy, but soon her thoughts slowed and quieted. In that state of emptiness, she must've dozed off, because Artis appeared.

"You are close, Master," he said in the nasal tone she had grown to love. "You know the answer. Search your heart."

Then, Losgann appeared in the guise of an old crone. Her nose was bulbous, her chin warty, and her watery eyes bulged. But her voice was all Losgann as he ribbited and croaked, "Master, the answer is before you. Below you. All around you. Open your eyes. You will see."

Then, Emily woke.

The last rays of UnderEarth's smoky sun shone on her face, and a verse from the prophecy popped into her head.

"...the battle begun before Earth was wrought,
Must be won in the helm of the sufferer's heart..."

What if the sufferer was not Emily as she had been led to believe? What if the sufferer was not a person but Earth herself?

She scrambled up, leaned her belly against Yggdrasil, and extended her arms in an embrace that covered only a fraction of the tree's formidable girth.

"Thank you, thank you," she sang aloud, then jumped down to tell Khenko.

He, too, had fallen asleep. When she called his name, Khenko startled awake, fighting for breath.

"Are you okay?"

He gulped air, then brushed off her question. "I'm not sure why that keeps happening, but I'm fine."

"I think I have a clue." She shared her aha, and he nodded thoughtfully as they headed to the main hall to tell the others.

"But what about the helm of the heart?" he wondered aloud. "What part of Earth would that be?"

"Hmm. Could it be a translation error? Maybe it's supposed to be something else." They exited the first cave. "What is a helm, anyway? A ship has a helm. Isn't that the steering?"

"Yes, but helm could also mean a helmet. At the helmet of Earth's heart?" He laughed heartily.

"Nah," Emily grinned, wagging her head. "That makes no sense, but neither does steering." They entered the cavern of stalactites and stalagmites, and halfway through, she stopped and smacked her forehead with her palm.

"It's the North and South Poles! Elise was on the right track. They are the main entrances to Earth's inner realms—her heart, Khenko. The prophecy refers to Earth's heart, and the poles are the helms of her heart, her access points."

She juked and jived in a happy dance. Khenko laughed and boogied beside her on the narrow trail.

Then, recalling Earth's heart-wrenching pleas for help, Emily came to a halt.

"That's why Afsel showed me the clogged poles. She wanted us to know. Earth even told me she couldn't breathe. Elise was right, and this confirms it."

Khenko's eyes had grown enormous, and he grinned. "That also must be why I wake up out of breath when I nap beneath Yggdrasil. Earth's trying to communicate her condition."

"See! More confirmation. We have to tell the others."

Beyond sure now, Emily broke into a run.

It was now or never. Emily gulped. She had stretched her goodbyes out as long as she could.

Over the last hour, the Atlantean team had hashed out the details and conversed with the Keepers. Emily with Awen would ride a-Ur to tackle the waste at the North Pole. Druantia and Thoth would team with Tienu to demolish the structures blocking the entrance to the South Pole. The other Keepers would fly ahead to scout and provide backup, Ooschu down south and Talav in the north.

The remaining dragons would station themselves atop strategic megaliths and waterways across the globe. Once the poles were freed, they would facilitate the flow of energy to minimize injuries.

But, none could predict how that would manifest. Whether in the form of a worldwide tsunami or a blast of energy unheard of in remembered history, it would likely shake the foundations of Earth.

Whether from Azi's tinkering or the spells Emily had woven at Stonehenge, they could now communicate directly with AboveEarth. Elise had already notified the Alien Intelligence Agency so that Cybele and her agents could notify the authorities worldwide. Shibboleth had contacted Inanna at his command center to do the same for Earth's interior. It was short notice, but hopefully, both the surface and inner worlds would be prepared for any possible disaster.

"Are you ready, Little Wren?" Thoth asked gently.

Awen nodded, but Emily swallowed hard. *She* was nowhere near ready—for any of this. Inside her, a cry sounded.

"Daaa."

Anguish clutched at Emily's throat. Was she hallucinating? Or had the spirit in her womb just spoken?

Spurred by a deep sense of urgency, she turned to Elise and whispered, "Da, I love you. Thank you for everything."

"What's got you talking like that," Hamilton Hester growled, gruff voice making heads snap up. "I love you, a ghrá. Now, call Lughnasadh. Then go give those poles hell. You can do this. You're stronger than you know."

"You can do this," Elise seconded.

"Yes, you can." Khenko added his own reassurance.

"You can use my phone to make that call." Val's knowing smile quieted Emily's fear.

Thoth, the Reptilians, and Freya eyed her oddly as she excused herself to step from the hall. But they didn't argue or intervene. Grateful Lugh had made her memorize his cell number, she punched it into Val's phone, then rehearsed what to say while inhaling a fortifying breath.

But as soon as Emily identified herself, Lugh started asking questions, and she had to cut him short.

"Lugh, I have something shocking to tell you, but you can't freak out because I only have a minute." She sucked in a breath. "I'm pregnant with a baby girl and she wants her Da to know."

Lugh gasped, then let it out slowly and deliberately.

"Really? Are you sure? Are you okay?"

Emily laughed out loud. "Better than okay."

"Did you say 'the Order's next Awen'?" he asked in disbelief. "We're having a baby girl?" Then he paused, and Emily knew he was counting. "Has it even been long enough to tell?"

She laughed harder, and the rest of her nervousness faded away.

"Normally, no. But the Order's next Awen is in my womb nonetheless. She wanted her Da to know before we set out on what I pray is our last dangerous mission." Something occurred to her then, and she gulped.

"What?" Lugh sputtered. "Are you alright?"

"Yes, but Lugh, my body now holds three Awens. Three in one!" Buoyed by the knowledge, Emily smiled as Khenko stuck his head around the corner.

"Pacey, pacey, time's a wasty."

"They're calling me, Lugh. I have to go. I love you," she nearly sobbed, wiping tears of happiness from her face.

"G'bye, Beautiful." The druid priest's voice had gone husky, as if tears clogged his throat, too. "You take care of yourself, Emmy. Bring both my babies home safely to me."

"I will, Love. I promise."

SHARHEA AND MAGDA

Inanna exited the chute and strode through Agartha. Repairs to the base and city progressed nicely. The doctora's office and several other buildings had been completed since her last visit. More were in the final stages of construction.

Ducking through the entrance, Inanna remained in the empty waiting room while the assistant fetched the doctora.

"Inanna." Magdalena emerged and struck her chest in greeting.

"Magda." Inanna reciprocated. "Are you ready?"

The doctora gave last-minute instructions to her pert aide, then walked with Inanna to the chute depot.

"So, *was* that an earthquake we felt?"

Magda had asked her on the communicator, but Inanna had not answered at the time.

"It was something like that. From what I understand, the druids and dragons averted some catastrophe. The explosion caused a shockwave, which created a tsunami that passed through our oceans. The dragons managed to minimize the damage. Down here and up there."

They boarded the express chute, and several beings greeted the doctora.

"And why am I going to Irkalla with you?" she asked after acknowledging their helloes.

Inanna smiled. "I told you, it is a surprise."

Magda's expression soured, and Inanna added, "But Nergal is there," and the doctora brightened considerably.

The trip to Irkalla passed quickly. Inanna led Magda to the command center, where Nergal leapt from his chair.

"Magdalena, what a pleasure. What brings you here?"

The doctora stiffened and eyed Inanna with suspicion, then took Nergal's claw.

"General, it is good to see you." She gave him a quick once-over. "I am pleased to see your wounds have all healed."

"Excuse us, please." Nergal drew Inanna to the side.

"What is going on? Why is Magda here?"

"To meet ShaRhea, though neither of them know."

"ShaRhea?" Puzzlement knit the Draco's brow.

"Shibboleth's aide. And consort."

He gazed at the doctora, who had settled in a chair and spoke into her wrist communicator. Then, a gleam sprang to Nergal's eyes.

"The one with the lavender irises?"

"The one with the lavender irises."

"So you think—" He stared at Magdalena. "No. I don't see it."

"I do."

"You are taking her to Shibboleth's quarters then?"

"Yes. Has my litter father indicated when he will return?"

"Later today."

"Then we had best get going." She returned to Magda. "Come with me. There is someone I would like you to meet."

The doctora recoiled. "Not Warlord Shibboleth!"

Inanna chuckled. "No, I promise it is not him." She sauntered through the capitol with the reluctant Magda in tow.

"Can you tell me what to expect?"

Inanna smiled and rapped on Shibboleth's door.

ShaRhea answered. "Inanna, what a pleasant surprise." Then, she did a double take. "Why, who is this?"

"This is Doctora Magdalena from Agartha. She is the one who saved General Nergal's life. Magda, this is ShaRhea, Warlord Shibboleth's longtime aide and consort."

Magda stared a long moment before striking her chest. "Pardon me. I have not seen a human since I was young. It is very nice to meet you."

ShaRhea invited them in and offered them chairs. "Can I get you a drink?"

"Nothing for me," Magda squeaked, peering around at the grandeur of Shibboleth's quarters.

"Or me," Inanna said. "But may I ask, does Magda remind you of anyone?"

The human hesitated a long while. Then she heaved a resigned sigh and sat down next to Magda.

"Doctora Magdalena, I might know your mother and father. Could you tell me their names?"

"Oh, please call me Magda." She hung her head and twisted her claws in her lap. "My adoptive mother is Wymar. I do not remember my birth mother, and I never met my father."

ShaRhea smiled. "Which one is human?"

Magda's head snapped up. "How did you know that?"

"Your lavender eyes." ShaRhea grinned, showing blunt teeth. "It is a rare color for humans and nonexistent in Dracs."

Magda burst into tears. "But our eyes are the same. Does that mean you are my mother?"

ShaRhea took Magda's claws in her hands. "I know you are of mixed descent. I believe half Reylian-Humanoid and half Reptilian. And yes, dear, I could very well be your birth mother."

Tears coursed down Magda's cheeks.

"Long ago, I lived on Earth's surface. I birthed a baby like you. To keep her safe, I placed her with a kind Reptilian woman migrating to UnderEarth. I believe you could be that daughter." She glanced at Inanna. "And Inanna does, too. That's why she brought you to meet me. Isn't it, dear?"

Inanna nodded, and Magda threw her arms around ShaRhea. "I cannot believe I am finally meeting you."

ShaRhea beamed and mouthed "thank you" over Magdalena's shoulder.

But Inanna needed to know the rest. "Is Shibboleth her father?"

"What?" Magda jerked away from ShaRhea. "Please say he is not."

"I am afraid I cannot, though Shibboleth does not know about you. If you wish, we could keep that to ourselves. But his bloodline would offer privileges you do not currently have."

Inanna interrupted, "Is it true that my litter father plans to attend the summit in AboveEarth and then leave the planet, possibly for good?"

A shadow passed over ShaRhea's eyes. "Yes, he told me the same. Lord Shibboleth has yearned for the stars since first landing on Earth. I would not ask him to stay. Nor do I believe he would, anyway. His itch to leave is too great." She gazed at Magda. "How about we keep you a secret for now, then announce it after he leaves?"

The doctora nodded, eyes wide and unbelieving.

"You know what that means, right?" Inanna grinned.

Magda shook her head, dazed.

"You have royal blood. You and I are sister spawn. General Nergal is not out of your reach."

AT LOOSE ENDS

It was lunchtime in Atlanta when Cu delivered Lugh to Jocko's Pizza before going on to Wren's Roost with Hope. The snow was melting, and the scorching temperatures of the week earlier were pleasant post blizzard.

It did Lugh's heart good to see the stores nearing completion along Oxford and North Decatur Roads. Last month's tornadoes had mostly spared Jocko's, leaving it the only business on the block still standing. Across the roundabout loomed Emory University's vast, walled campus, looking much as it had when Lugh left for Wales.

Jocko's parking lot was packed. Despite his grimy appearance, Lugh shoved through the front door and kept his head down as he made a beeline for the bar. His assistant manager, Alfie, poured drinks for servers and patrons alike. On seeing Lugh, he grinned and signaled the bartender, then ducked beneath the gate to drag Lugh into the kitchen.

When they burst through the swinging doors, the cooks and wait staff turned and cheered.

"Thank God, you're back," Genevieve said, wrinkling her nose. "But, I hope you plan to run home for a shower and clean clothes. I'm surprised they let you on the plane like that."

Lugh sniffed his stained button-down shirt and laughed. If they only knew.

"You've got *that* right. And, yes, I'm heading home in a few."

"We were worried about you." Alfie's brow scrunched. "You heard about the creepy lizard men, right? We had no sign of them here, thank the Lord. The nearest reported were at the zoo. And Underground Atlanta."

Lugh breathed easier. He stayed a few more minutes, chatting with the servers that came and went, then readied to leave.

"Looks like everything is under control. Unless you need me, I'm going home. I'm exhausted and looking forward to my own bed. Even if it is the middle of the day." His back ached from the tiny cots he had shared with Emily.

"We're good, boss man." Alfie followed him to the bar. "And don't worry about coming in tomorrow unless you want. The schedule is covered for the week, so sleep as long as you need. We've got Jocko's covered."

Relieved, Lugh said his goodbyes and left.

He started to walk home but decided he was too tired. Hailing a passing cab, he checked his messages for the umpteenth time, wondering where Emily was and what she was doing right now.

But more importantly, was she okay? He prayed to Brigid, then punched Arthur Creeley's number, leaving a message when it went to voicemail.

☼☼☼

Happy to be home, Mitchell peeled off his clothes, turned the shower on hot, and stood beneath the spray for several minutes before lathering and rinsing. Then, toweling dry, he tugged on an old Braves teeshirt and a well-worn pair of sweatpants.

He was still hungry after the light meal in Glastonbury, so he padded to the kitchen, opened the refrigerator, and gagged. The maid hadn't touched it. He decided to order pizza and rang Jocko's, then flopped into his recliner with the remote.

A clip of the lizard people aired on WNN. Mitch tensed, waiting for the panic to suffocate him. When it didn't, he was shocked. Huh. No shakes, nausea, or flashbacks.

Relieved, he ran through the stations and found the Braves and Mets early game.

☼☼☼

After a long, hot shower, Lugh read and answered emails, went through snail mail mostly consisting of flyers, and dressed to pick up Cu. He had notified Mary Cobb earlier to expect them. After expressing her delight and asking about Emily, the caretaker had promised to feed and water the Elders.

He climbed in his Land Rover, grateful he hadn't left it at the airport. Luckily, the company in Caen had sent a driver to Falaise to pick up the rental car. Lugh had gasped at the cost, but he figured he'd gotten off easy considering he'd abandoned their car. *And* they'd had a tough time finding it. He chuckled, remembering the washboard side road.

427

He was nearly to Wren's Roost when something made him detour. Next thing Lugh knew, he was standing in front of Mitchell Wainwright's house, looking up at the widow's walk. Swallowing hard, he rang the bell.

☼☼☼

Mitch must've dozed because the doorbell catapulted him from the chair on high alert. He squinted through the peephole, shocked to see Lugh MacBrayer.

"Is everything okay?" he asked, opening the door.

Lugh shrugged and pushed past him to stroll through the living and dining rooms to the kitchen.

"Got any beer?"

"Always." Reaching around him for two longnecks, Mitch started when the doorbell rang. "That will be pizza. You hungry?"

He twisted the top off one bottle and handed it to Lugh, then hurried to the door with the other.

"If it's Jocko's, yes."

"Seriously? Is there anything else?"

Neither talked as they tore into the pizza, but Mitch side-eyed Lugh, wondering why he had shown up at his door. They watched in silence except for an occasional cheer or comment on the game.

Two beers in and pizza half gone, Lugh's cell phone rang.

"Want me to pause it?"

Lugh wagged his head and took his phone in the dining room. Half a minute later, he was back with a dazed expression on his olive brow.

"Everything okay?"

"I, um, yeah, I guess."

Then, a silly grin lit Lugh's face. He flopped on the couch, shaking his head in disbelief. "Emily says I'm going to be a father."

Mitch's jaw dropped. "Duuude. You? A father?"

"I know, right?" Lugh smirked. Then he sagged into the sofa and stared at Mitch.

"What if something happens? They were breaking up the blockage at the North Pole, and you know how off-limits the Arctic Circle is. What if a military defense drone kills her on sight? What if she never comes back?"

Lugh's face twisted in agony, and he stood to pace. Then, lifting a curtain, he let it drop again and turned to Mitch, wailing, "What if they die up there?"

Terror seized Mitch. Until that moment, he had been fine. Being back home had given him the semblance of normalcy he desperately needed. Now, the horror came rushing back. Swallowing around the lump in his throat, he tried to dismiss Lugh's fears and ease his own.

"Stop it. Emily is with a real-life goddess. The dragons will take care of her. Just focus on that."

"Yeah, you're probably right." Lugh sat back down, and his features lit again. "She said it's a girl. The next Awen."

Mitch's breath caught. Another Awen?

The secret hope he had harbored for so long rushed to the surface. He had dreamed of one day leading the druids. He thought of all that Emily had endured since becoming the Grand Druid and realized he wanted no part of that fate. Then, something else occurred to him, and he grinned.

"Hey, if you marry Emily, we'll be related."

"Well, hell. Who'd a thunk?" Lugh pulled at his chin, sipped his beer, and smiled.

THE NORTH POLE

The wormhole collapsed, dumping a-Ur and Emily in the air somewhere above the North Pole. She reached for his horns, but a-Ur disappeared in the dense fog, and Emily plunged toward an Earth she could not see.

"a-Ur, where are you?" she called psychically, the mode of communication they had all agreed upon for the mission.

When he didn't answer, Emily broke her momentum with a simple spell. She glided slowly through the heavy mist and prayed fervently that there was land beneath her. The thought of ending up in the ocean or the whirlpool terrified Emily.

Then a-Ur was beneath her, and she slid gratefully into his natural saddle.

"Thank God," she breathed.

a-Ur snorted. "That's me you should be thanking." Then, he dove, and Emily wrapped her arms around his horns.

"Thank you, a-Ur. Are we at the pole? I can't tell in this mist."

"We are, mi' lady," the old dragon grunted, then landed effortlessly on solid ground.

The fog was even denser down here, but the air was balmy rather than frigid, as Emily had expected.

"I can't see anything."

The dragon sighed. "One cannot always see with one's eyes. Have you learned zilch? Close them and look again."

Emily did.

"Still nothing." But chill bumps waltzed up her back.

"No, Awen. Don't use your eyes. Be still and feel out with your other senses."

The technique was the same one Talav had used to get Emily out of her cave in UnderEarth. Playing along, she closed her eyes, took a vivifying breath, and was shocked to see a massive, lazy whirlpool surrounding a tall, jagged black mountain. She opened her eyes and saw nothing but mist.

A familiar hiss came from their left. "Psst, over here."

The air dragon plodded in that direction, and relief washed over Emily as they broke through the fog to join the earth Keeper.

"Talav," she hailed, climbing from a-Ur's saddle. "Have you discovered any useful information?"

"Aye, Master." The earth dragon took a cautious step toward the sluggish maelstrom and cast a wary eye at the swirling mist. "There is a defense system inside the fog that guards the area. Like you, I came in under the radar, but as I investigated, I triggered a strike and was nearly annihilated by a volley of missiles. Lucky for me, my scales are impenetrable." She wagged her head woefully. "But my ears are still ringing."

"I'm glad you're okay. Did you disable the system?"

"Aye. But the government it serves will have been alerted, so time is short." Talav contemplated the black mountain. "Plus, there is something weird going on here. I have not been able to discern what. But hurry and perform the spell and get us out of here. This place gives me the creeps."

The hairs on Emily's body had been standing on end since exiting the wormhole. She peered up at the peak. Its tip hid high up in the clouds.

A shudder passed through her. "Me, too."

She studied the gigantic whirlpool at the base of the mountain. It rotated slowly and contained every sort of trash imaginable. Much was plastic—bottles, containers, toys, and the like. Emily could also see scrap metal, appliances, wood planks and other building materials, glass, logs, and even animal carcasses. Every form of waste seemed to be stuck in the morass, and the outgassing was atrocious.

All would be well if she performed the spell and the debris disintegrated. But if it exploded, Emily and the Keepers would not be spared. And if the energy release was as enormous as Druantia and Thoth suspected, they would likely be blown to smithereens.

They needed to get further away or be shredded in the blast.

"Or we could shield ourselves," a-Ur suggested, reading her mind.

"Oh. Huh. I didn't think of that." She eyed the whirlpool, then studied their eerily quiet surroundings. They would have to move out to sea or high in the air to get far enough away. Or, as Talav said, they could shield themselves. But that would have to be one helluva spell.

"Would the barrier be stronger if we conjure it together?"

"Aye," the dragons said in unison.

"But even then," Talav added, "It may not fully protect us."

Emily's legs trembled, and her stomach gurgled, reminders that she was way out of her league. Her hands unconsciously cradled her womb, and she jumped when Awen's voice sounded in her head.

"Pull it together, Emily."

Gulping air, she glanced at the clouds floating high overhead and shoved everything from her mind except the task at hand.

"So, what's the verdict? Should we go up there?" She pointed skyward. "Or try the shielding spell?"

"We should stay close," a-Ur said, "for the spell to be most effective."

Still not sure they were doing the right thing, Emily paid attention as Awen wove the unfamiliar spell. Talav and a-Ur reinforced it with those of their own. Then, pointing Awen's wand at the whirlpool, Emily summoned the enchantment and swished and flicked.

The nearest debris disappeared, but it barely put a dent in the jam. Emily grounded, centered, and tried again with similar results.

"Dammit," she huffed and closed her eyes to call Druantia.

"Yes?" Druantia grunted breathlessly.

"My spell is not working. Is yours?"

"Not yet," the goddess shouted. "We have a full-scale war going on down here. The dragons are taking the brunt of it, but—"

Then Druantia was gone.

a-Ur and Talav gaped at Emily. "What now?"

"I'm back." Druantia's voice rang in their heads. "The dragons immobilized the artillery, but none of my spells are breaking the blockage."

"Shit," Emily grumbled.

The sun broke through, forming an awen overhead and reminding Emily of their earlier flight.

"Hmm, I wonder… What if the dragons sing? Like they did at Stonehenge? It seemed to help then."

"You mean that eerie chorus?" Druantia asked, then huffed loudly. "For the love of Brigid, they are shooting aga—"

"Druantia! Are you there?"

"Yes," the goddess answered breathily. "a-Ur, can you coordinate the Hum? We are a little busy here."

"Of course." The air dragon swelled with pride.

"Can you get all the dragons to join in? Make the chorus worldwide?" Emily asked.

"Aye, Master. That might work."

The air dragon closed his eyes for a long moment to communicate. Then he lifted his snout to the sky, and Talav joined in. Their voices grew in pitch and intensity, vibrating the North Pole with dragon song.

A faraway hum soon became audible as dragons around the world lent their voices to the chorus. Like at Stonehenge, their combined intonations created a vibrating, otherworldly hum. It rose into the heavens in one long trumpet that went on and on and on and on. Goosebumps roved Emily's body until lost in the moment, she lifted her chin and howled with the dragons.

"Now!" shouted Druantia.

Startled from the reverie induced by the hum, Emily raised her wand and spoke the incantation.

Bubbles appeared in the whirlpool. It began to boil, swirling faster and faster until it inverted in the center, where it circled the mountain. While Talav and a-Ur continued singing, Emily waited with bated breath, willing the blockage to ease.

To her dismay, it got worse.

The garbage from the bottom gushed to the surface, making the clogged whirlpool roil and expand. Emily and the dragons were shuffling backward into the mist when the vortex made a great slurping noise. Then, every trace of rubbish disappeared, exposing the broad base of the mysterious mountain.

"Yeeehaaa!" She moved away from the fog, and the humming dragons moved with her.

The sea remained calm, and Emily was beginning to relax when an ominous roar came from the belly of the Earth. They watched in horror as the garbage resurfaced in a mighty rush and shot a geyser of trash high in the air. The shield held as tons of projectiles battered the invisible barrier.

"Emily, my spell is working," Druantia shouted. "But it is dragging us—" The sinister sentence ended abruptly.

Clear water exploded from the vortex then, and Emily gasped, heart pounding, as it collided with the garbage falling from the sky.

This, she had not expected.

She hastily spoke the calming spell to no effect. The deluge continued in both directions, and their spit of land quickly submerged under the water and debris.

a-Ur signaled Emily to climb aboard, then stopped singing. They took to the sky with Talav beside them, wings beating furiously to escape the massive spout. The air still vibrated with dragon hum.

Without warning, the water column gushed and slammed into Emily.

She tumbled from a-Ur's saddle and was caught in the undertow of an unfathomable wave. She kicked and struggled, desperate to find a pocket of air.

But there was no up nor down and no way out, only the crushing tsunami of befouled water.

☼☼☼

Agents crowded the busy AIA communications center, notifying worldwide governments of a probable energy surge. With luck, they were acting in time to prevent any major disasters. Elise hung up the phone and thrummed her fingers on the desk then decided to call Kate at the FBI.

She retrieved her cell phone and punched Kate's private number.

"Elise." Kate answered on the first ring. "What in the hell have you druids done this time? We just received word of an eminent energy surge that could cause worldwide disasters."

"Might, not will. I was just making sure you got the heads up. Y'all be on alert."

☼☼☼

Morgan's cell phone dinged—a text from Kate Hobbs.
"Hold onto your britches. Something bad about to happen."
"Tks!" she texted back, then shared the message with Arthur.

"Nice to get confirmation from the government," he said. "But our druids are already in position."

☼☼☼

The crowd went wild when John Riggins hit his third grand slam of the season. Mitch and Lugh hooted and cheered as the Braves shortstop circled the bases behind Gerald Finney, Rodrigo Sanchez, and Ned Talbot.

"It's the top of the seventh, with the score tied at six," the announcer declared, then cut to a news brief that had Mitch's heart racing.

434

"In a startling move, Reverend Shalane Carpenter's Evangelical Tour of America has been canceled. Last week, Reverend Carpenter collapsed in Las Vegas during a live performance and remained in a coma for two days. After resuming her tour online, Carpenter reportedly urged followers to side with the Reptilians. The show was immediately preempted. Details after the game."

What the fuck? Shalane had sided with the lizard men?

Lugh jumped up indignantly. "Hey, isn't that the witch that was stalking Emily?"

The civil defense sirens blared, and Lugh's eyes widened.

Mitch's heart pounded, on high alert after the last few days. He grabbed his cell phone and nearly dropped it when it whooped. Then, Lugh's phone joined in, followed by the TV's high-pitched warning.

"This is not a test," the solemn computerized voice intoned. "The Federal Emergency Management Agency has issued an alert for the entire U.S., including both coastlines and the interior. Shockwaves originating at the North Pole could trigger earthquakes, volcanic eruptions, massive ocean surges, and worldwide tsunamis—"

"Holy shit! Emily's up there!" Lugh yelled over the clamor, eyes wild now.

Mitch waved his phone. "This says the same thing."

The house began shaking, and the windows rattled. Were they having an earthquake? Mitch ran to the door and wrenched it open. The trees swayed ominously, and pictures and ornaments began crashing to the floor.

"Get out of here." Lugh shoved him out the door.

The ground trembled as they hurried down the steps to the manicured lawn. Mitch fell to his knees, then onto his belly to ride out the jerky waves.

Beside him, on all fours, Lugh mumbled something Mitch couldn't understand. Then, the ground calmed momentarily, and he realized the druid priest was muttering spells.

A disturbing thought chilled Mitch. Emily's mission had failed. Now, the world was falling down around them.

He closed his eyes and whispered a real prayer for the first time in many years. It was the only brand of magic Mitch knew. Over and over, he repeated the prayer, vowing that if the world survived and him with it, he would devote his life to helping others.

His mother would be proud—if they lived.

AWEN TIDE

Patty stared at the television. The news brief made it official. Shalane's formal reprimand had been swiftly followed by backers swooping in to pull their support. The press would be jumping all over it now, spreading word of the tour's cancellation.

Oddly, Shalane seemed fine with the whole thing. She had not been herself since waking from the coma, but Patty had been sure she would have a conniption when the news broke.

She switched off the bigscreen. "How about we get out of the house? Maybe go to Rodeo Drive, do some shopping, and have lunch. You mentioned a haircut. We could see your stylist. You know he would be happy to fit you in."

Shalane stared at the black screen, expressionless.

Patty tried again. "Latoya and I ate at the new sushi restaurant. It was fabulous. Want to try that? We could catch a movie or just come home after. Whatever you'd like."

Still no reaction.

Cecil strode into the posh living room. "Hey, doll, let's go out for a bite. I'm bored and hungry."

Shalane reacted. She regarded her husband with that awful blank stare, then levered up from her chair to shuffle to the wet bar. It was barely lunchtime, but she poured a drink and left the room without a word.

Cecil plopped into the chair she had vacated, worry etched into the lines of his face. "I don't know what to do. She won't take the pills the doctor prescribed. And she won't talk. She won't even respond sexually. I've never known Shalane to be like this. It's like she came home as someone else."

Blushing at his mention of sex, Patty nodded self-consciously.

"I know. She pushed me into the talk show tour but gets mad when I mention it or the Reptilians. I'm worried, too."

"Should we go check on her?"

Patty pondered before answering.

"Yes, you go. At least she still responds to you."

Shalane dragged herself up the stairs to the terrace, shielding her eyes from the bright sunlight. The snow was gone, but everything was wet. She propped her elbows on the rail and peered at the traffic threading the San Fernando Valley. Then, making her way to the opposite side, she sipped her drink and sighed.

In the near distance, the ocean churned, relentlessly eating away at the cliffs of the south slope of the Santa Monica Mountains. A few years ago, the ritzy city of Malibu had thrived there. Now it was gone, completely underwater, as was Pacific Palisades, Bel-Air, and parts of Santa Monica.

A balmy breeze blew in from the Pacific, ruffling her hair and carrying a high-pitched hum and a familiar scent. Shalane leaned over the railing and breathed in the aroma of the trees lining the driveway. But not even the Jacarandas' purple blossoms lifted her spirits. She was dead inside and had been since the day they left Las Vegas.

She wondered, not for the first time if part of her had stayed behind that day. She didn't even care about the tour ending early. In fact, Shalane was glad. With her God connection gone, the online appearances had been difficult. Then, the Reptilian remark had slipped from her mouth. Shalane had been horrified and recanted on the spot. But there were no backsies on this one.

Like a freight train rumbling over an endless intersection, a vibration came into her awareness. It grew stronger and louder, drowning out the hum, and seemed to be coming from the north. Facing in that direction, Shalane felt out with her senses.

An enormous rush of water approached Point Conception. Her heart beat faster when it reached the tip, then hugged the coastline east and south.

The mournful wail of the tsunami warning shrieked as the wave swept along the Santa Barbara coast. Shalane covered her ears as the siren cycled, wondering why it didn't sound earlier. Then, Cecil came up from behind and spooked her.

"Come inside, Shalane!" He spied the wave, still miles away, and stood transfixed, arms snaking protectively around her. "It won't come this far inland, but if it does, we're high enough to be safe," he said over the siren. Then, he glanced south and groaned. "But, I think we can say goodbye to what's left of L.A. and our makeshift airport." Cecil had helped build that airport.

Patty appeared and tugged at Shalane's elbow. "Come inside, Shalane."

But like Cecil, Shalane was mesmerized.

She watched as the water drew back from the mountains and drained the shoreline, exposing what was left of the drowned city of Malibu.

"Oh. My. God." Patty was horrified. "What is happening?"

Shalane pointed toward the approaching wave. Miraculously, it skirted the Channel Islands and swept past Point Mugu. Patty's eyes grew big.

"What about Los Angeles? You have to stop it, Shalane."

Shalane created weather. She had no idea how to stop a tsunami.

"The seawall will hold like it has in the past. If not," she added, only half joking, "L.A. could use a good bath."

"Shalane!" Cecil cautioned above the wail of the sirens. "Don't talk like that."

The whoop of local alarms joined the tsunami sirens, and Patty's cell phone squawked. She held it up and read the message out loud.

"The Federal Emergency Management Agency has issued an alert for the entire U.S., including coastlines and the interior. Shockwaves from the North Pole could trigger earthquakes, volcanic eruptions, massive ocean surges, and worldwide tsunamis."

"Ya think?!" Cecil growled.

They all sucked in a startled breath when the water flowed inland to reclaim Malibu then sweep south to L.A.

Something miraculous happened, then. Something Shalane wasn't expecting and could not explain. The wave's landward edges folded upward. But rather than swamping the shoreline, it arced and moved south past the seawall, threading the channel between the mainland and Catalina Island.

The alarms continued wailing as the intense rumble slowly subsided. Shalane and the others stayed on the terrace for a long while. But when nothing else happened, and the sirens quieted, they returned inside.

BIRTHRIGHTS AND BEGINNINGS

Nergal's new wrist unit vibrated and he nearly shat himself. He hated wearing the damn thing. It startled him every single time. But Inanna had insisted he upgrade his equipment.

A glance told him the communique was from Shibboleth and was addressed to him, Mot, and Inanna.

Druids breaking up pole blockages. Get immediate word to bases. Upheaval of oceans and land masses imminent. Then report to Irkalla Command Center in three hours.

UnderEarth still trembled but had largely calmed when Nergal stepped from the crowded chute in Irkalla. He strode to the Command Center, where Inanna paced, and Mot's claws clattered across the console. The overhead screens projected scenes unfolding from cameras stationed around UnderEarth. If upheaval had occurred, none was apparent. And from the messages flooding in, the damage had been minor.

"Hail, Shibboleth," Inanna intoned, striking her chest.

Nergal wheeled, and Mot did the same as Shibboleth strode in, followed by the diminutive scientist, Azi.

Returning the salute, the warlord announced, "The planet has stabilized, and I prepare to leave." An emotion that may or may not have been wonder softened Shibboleth's grizzled features. "Lord Thoth flew us above the surface to assess Earth's terraforming. Now, he and Queen Druantia have granted me permission to take one of their craft to outer space. I leave today, but before I go, I have several announcements.

"First, I will be away for an indeterminate length of time. I place our subjects' joint care and rule with Mot and Nergal. Together, you shall rule the Reptilian Nation."

A gasp escaped the two Dracs. Nergal was shocked, but Mot looked angry.

Shibboleth ignored them both.

"I leave it to you to determine who is responsible for what." The warlord glanced at his litter son. "I'm sorry, Mot. But you can thank Queen Druantia. The payment she demanded for use of their spacecraft is that I reveal and honor Nergal's parentage."

He heaved a great sigh, squared his body to Nergal's, and blurted as if spitting out something nasty, "You are a direct descendant of Lord Enlil, Enki's brother. This heritage gives you a claim to the Reptilian throne."

Nergal sagged against the console, legs gone weak. The last thing he needed was to collapse in front of Shibboleth and the others. He had suspected he was meant for more. But Shibboleth's revelation was shocking.

"That cannot be," Mot snarled. Then understanding dawned, and he plopped into a chair. "This is how the witch convinced you not to execute Nergal, the secret she threatened to reveal."

"Aye," Shibboleth admitted. "But that is just the first of my announcements."

He eyed Inanna, the daughter-spawn he had spurned, tried to execute on several occasions, and, only recently, brought back into the fold.

"In recognition of your resourceful negotiation with the dragons, and despite your lack of leadership training, I name you, Inanna Shibboleth's Spawn, as our First Ambassador to AboveEarth."

The back-handed praise was late in coming but much deserved. Nergal approved.

Inanna's chest swelled, and she beamed with pride. "I won't let you down, Sir."

"Good. With experience, I believe you will be a wise leader. Mot and Nergal, you will make training Inanna a priority. Meanwhile, her ambassadorship, as the humans call it, shall not be easy. The veil between our races has been lifted, and their entire population now knows about the Reptilian Nation. Inanna will be responsible for creating and maintaining a treaty with them."

The warlord gestured to the scientist, who had been absentmindedly picking at his peeling scales. "You must be vigilant and safeguard our technology. While we were in Atlantis, Azi networked our devices with those of the humans. This groundbreaking development allows for direct communication with AboveEarth, but our data may become vulnerable to prying eyes.

"Also, Azi has requested that the borders remain open, allowing free passage for all races between our worlds. We have received tentative agreement from the humans on that matter."

Azi grinned, obviously pleased. Nergal didn't like it on the surface, but the scientist did, and others would too.

"Lastly, I hereby decree that my Royal Confidante, ShaRhea, shall remain in my palace with the same rights and privileges she now enjoys." His laser beam gaze pinned each, daring them to argue. "ShaRhea has advised me for centuries and will continue to provide guidance for each of you." He paused to summon his confidante via wrist unit. Then, they waited quietly.

Within minutes, a feminine figure of slight stature hurried into the Command Center. Nergal stared at Shibboleth's human advisor with lavender eyes.

"ShaRhea is a Reylian humanoid and wise beyond your ken. Treat her well. Make use of her wisdom. I shall check in periodically to make sure that you do."

ShaRhea greeted Inanna, whom she had already met, then held her hand out to Azi and the still-fuming Mot. When she came to Nergal, the woman paused. After regarding him at length, she took his claw.

"There is a question in your mind. You are free to ask."

Nergal let go of her hand and decided to speak. Shibboleth was leaving, so it would matter little.

"The doctora known as Magdalena. The one Inanna brought to meet you recently. Is she your spawn?"

Shibboleth sucked in a breath.

ShaRhea glanced at him fondly, took his claw, and smiled. "Yes, Magdalena is our daughter."

The warlord's features darkened. "You never told me this."

"No. I did not." She touched his face tenderly. "And I am sorry. Warlord Shibboleth, you have a second daughter spawn. One you sired long ago when I lived on the surface. A Reptilian couple raised her in UnderEarth, and I lost track of Magdalena until the other day. She resides in Agartha, is a doctor, and looks like you." ShaRhea smiled, proud but wistful.

Shibboleth's voice softened. "What is done is done. I regret there is no time to meet this spawn, but I must return to Atlantis before the jump window closes." Then, he spoke to Inanna and

Mot. "This Magdalena has my blessings. Invite her to the throne. It is her birthright as it is yours."

Then, giving ShaRhea's hand a long, lingering squeeze, Shibboleth strode to the door.

"I leave now, litter spawn. Take care of each other and the Reptilian Nation. I hope to see you in the future when I return."

To Nergal, he nodded grudgingly and struck his chest. Then, the ancient Warlord of Gamma Reux turned and was gone.

For hours after the freak tsunami, Shalane watched clips of it on every news station she could find. Then, she queued up the footage from the villa's security cameras. Fast-forwarding through most of it, she finally hit gold. One of the cameras on the villa's back roof had captured the event.

Shalane watched over and over, trying to figure out what had kept the tsunami from obliterating the coastline. Each time the footage rolled, she thought she saw something appear and disappear as the water rolled up at the edges and folded back upon itself. Then, it happened again and again as the tsunami swept southward.

Finally, exhausted and none-the-wiser, Shalane poured a deep glass of Glenlivet and took it up to the terrace to smoke a doobie.

DRAIG TALAV

Emily woke, gasping for breath and arms flailing.

"Shh, shh, shh, you're okay, Emily. I've got you."

The voice was Lugh's. What was he doing here? And where was she?

She tried to look around but found she couldn't. Her head was restrained and throbbed like holy hell. Something covered her eyes, but she couldn't lift her arms to find out what.

"W-where am I?" Her voice grated like a sick bullfrog, and it hurt to talk. Her throat was raw, and her chest burned like fire. "What h-happened? Is Earth safe? Where are the dragons? "

"You are in Atlantis under the care of Lord Thoth." Lugh's voice soothed. He told her not to move, and Emily realized she had been struggling.

"Rest, Emmy. I'm going to get Queen Druantia. I'll be right back." His warmth seeped from the room, and Emily knew he'd gone.

She shivered and cast about her memory, trying to piece things together. The last she remembered, she was separated from a-Ur and fought to escape an ocean gone airborne.

"Awen." Her condition must be bad if Druantia's tone was indicative.

"What happened?" she croaked, dreading the answer.

"You almost died." The catch in Druantia's throat barely covered a sob. She wrapped large, warm fingers around Emily's cold ones.

"But you are safe now. Go to sleep, little wren. You will be better soon. You just need time to heal. Go to sleep."

a-Ur, Ooschu, and Tienu surrounded Emily's bed when she awoke again. Or, their heads did.

"You're awake," a-Ur crooned. "Welcome back, Master. We've been worried about you."

Emily stretched and yawned. "Did we succeed? Will Earth survive?"

"Yes, Earth is safe for now," Ooschu assured. "But you have slept forever."

"Three days," Tienu muttered. "Not forever. How do you feel, little wren?"

Emily sat up, then squeaked and slumped back when her head swam. She coughed, chest aching, but the fire was no longer there.

"Better. But not great. Where's Talav?"

The dragons ogled one another, but none spoke.

Lugh hurried in and rushed to her side.

"Emily, you're awake!"

She smiled when he planted a kiss on her cheek. Then, needing to know, she asked again, "Lugh, where's Talav?"

The color drained from the druid priest's face. He looked away.

"What? What happened?"

She sat up, ignoring the dizzy to implore the dragons, "Tell me. I need to know."

Ooschu crowded close. "You know Talav was not a strong swimmer. She didn't make it."

"She… WHAT?"

Ooschu hung her head, and looked at a-Ur. "Will you tell her?"

a-Ur's great head wagged solemnly, and a tear rolled down his cheek.

Ooschu tried again. "Talav didn't make it. When the water swept you from a-Ur's back, they kept diving, trying to find you. Talav reached you first and trod water until a-Ur arrived. But once he settled you on land and came back for Talav, it was too late."

Still not fully comprehending, Emily stared at Ooschu and the other dragons. a-Ur's head hung low, tears streaming. The other two regarded her with deep sorrow.

"Talav drowned?" For a moment, the room disappeared, and Emily was alone in Talav's cave with the sweet, clumsy dragon. Then, the full realization sank in, and grief wrapped cold fingers around her heart and squeezed without mercy.

"Nooooo!" she keened. "No, no, no, no, no! Not Talaa-aav!" Her heart hurt so badly, Emily thought it might burst. She rocked back and forth, wailing, "No, not Talav. No, no, not Talav. Please, God, not Talav."

Lugh tried to console her, but she shrank away, retreating into herself as the grief washed over her, threatening to drown Emily like the water had Talav.

She should have known better. She should never have let the earth dragon accompany her on such a watery mission. She sobbed uncontrollably as Lugh held her hand and the dragons looked on.

"It is not your fault, Master. It is mine," a-Ur wailed through his tears.

"No, it is mine," Ooschu bleated, tears coursing down her aqua scales. "I knew she wasn't a strong swimmer. I should have said something to begin with and gone myself. Or sent another water dragon."

"Nonsense." Druantia bustled into the room with Thoth on her heels. "It is no one's fault. Not yours, Ooschu. Nor yours, a-Ur. And certainly not yours, Emily Brigette. Talav knew what she was getting into. And besides, as one of our druid Elders, Talav will be back. See," Druantia crooned, and Thoth held out what looked like an egg covered in tiny gemstones.

"What is it?" Emily sobbed.

"A dragon egg." Thoth smiled. "And inside is Talav."

Emily fumbled for a tissue. Lugh gave her a handful.

"What do you mean?" She sniffed, and blew her nose.

"I mean that Talav, the earth Keeper, is inside this egg. When she is ready, she will come back as good as new with her memories intact."

"But how?" Emily whispered.

Thoth rolled the egg into her waiting palms. It was heavier than it looked, and the gems glittered in the light.

"This is how Talav reincarnates. As long as Awen lives, so do the animal and dragon Elders. Their fate is tied to hers. And now, to yours."

Wonder smoothed the jagged edges of Emily's grief as she cradled the large egg and the dragons ooo'd and ahh'd over it.

An urgency seized Emily. "I want to see Talav."

Lugh's head snapped up. A fire ignited in Druantia's eyes, and Thoth nodded in approval.

"And, so you shall."

The red-haired god lifted Emily from the bed, set her upright, and held onto her until her legs steadied. Then, he supported her as they made their way through several lit caves before coming upon one that was dark inside.

Thoth reached in, and light blazed, throwing multicolored sparkles upon the rough walls, reminding Emily of the cave where she had first met Talav. The earth dragon's gem-scaled outer shell rested in the middle, but not Talav. Tears streamed down Emily's face.

"When we laid her to rest, she was still intact," Thoth explained. "But this morning, Talav was gone, leaving only her shell and her egg."

Emily hugged the bumpy egg to her chest. Then, obeying an inner urge, she handed it gingerly to Lugh and walked around Talav's shell. When she reached her chest, Emily knelt beside the earth dragon and felt along until she came to a smooth, dull stone, unlike the rest.

"What are you doing?" Tienu gasped when Emily tried to pry the stone away.

She sat back on her heels and blew hair from her face. But it was Awen who answered reverently.

"This is the royal mandar of Marduk. Talav was keeping it safe."

Druantia's breath hitched, and Thoth's face glowed.

"We thought that was lost forever," a-Ur cried.

"No," Druantia laughed. "Talav had it the whole time.

LEAVING ATLANTIS

Khenko folded his clothes into the duffel bag and slid the precious crystals Thoth had gifted him between the soft material. He added his toiletries and other effects, then made sure the sprig from the tree he called Yggdrasil was damp enough to survive the journey. Carefully tucking its sealed packet into the side pouch, Khenko zipped the bag.

His mother and father had left a few days earlier, along with Randy, Freya, and the rest of the team. They had jobs to get back to—Khenko, not so much. He'd stayed behind with Emily until she was well enough to travel. Now, that day had come.

His throat tightened as emotions welled up. Khenko slumped to the bed.

They had restored Earth's harmonics, so he and the other Earthlings had a few more years. Then, why did he feel like crying?

"Because I don't want to leave."

The prickles on his neck confirmed his revelation.

"Well, of course," he said aloud. "After searching for Atlantis my whole life, it would be odd if I wanted to go."

Sniffing back tears, Khenko slung the duffel over one shoulder and surveyed the small room that already felt like home. Then, he trudged to the crystal cave to meet Emily.

☼☼☼

Tears streamed down Emily's cheeks as she said goodbye to Ooschu, a-Ur, and Tienu. She'd told herself she wouldn't cry, but between her natural sensitivity and the pregnancy hormones, she didn't stand a chance.

Talav's egg was tucked safely in her shoulder bag. According to the Keepers, Emily needed to do nothing special. Just keep the egg with her at all times, and Talav would hatch when she is ready—whether that be days, months, or years. But Emily hoped the dragon didn't wait that long.

447

Pressing her lips to the snout of each dragon, she wiped away tears and hurried to the crystal cave before she broke down completely. Druantia and Thoth strode in before her, but Khenko was already there.

Thoth bowed to the healer. "Thank you, Khenko, for coming to Earth's aid. You are a true son of Atlantis." He paused with a sparkle in his green eyes. "Now, Queen Druantia has a proposition for you."

Khenko's heart pounded as the queen leaned down and laid a hand on his shoulder.

"Khenko Rainman Blitherstone, long have you yearned for the land of your ancestors. Now, your task is complete, and the time comes to leave. But I have a favor to ask."

"Anything, my queen." He bowed, waiting. But she turned to Emily first.

"Has my daughter spoken with you?"

Puzzled, Emily started to answer, but Awen did instead.

"No, Mother. I decided not to."

"Talk to me about what?" Emily asked.

"My daughter is exhausted. Like me." Druantia sighed heavily and folded into a chair. "For millennia, we have stood at high alert, defending Earth against the Reptilians and other catastrophes. Now, for the first time since Awen's death, one of our descendants has shown remarkable strength and resilience. Plus, you are young in Earth years." Druantia paused and glanced at Thoth. He nodded encouragement.

"My point is—Awen needs to rest. She craves time in the Otherworld with her William, unhindered by the need to keep a watchful eye on Earth. Would you do her the honor of being vigilant in her stead?"

A vague sense of uncertainty tugged at Emily, but she ignored it and laid a hand over her heart.

"Dearest Awen, I would be honored to provide a break for you. I can contact you if anything threatens or I cannot fulfill my end. In the meantime, rest well. And thank you for believing in me until I could believe in myself."

"Thank you, dear Emily," Awen said. "I cannot tell you how happy this makes me."

"You don't have to. I can feel your joy." It filled her so full that Emily nearly wept again.

☼☼☼

Queen Druantia turned to Khenko. "I, too, am beyond exhausted." She hesitated, and Thoth wrapped an arm around her waist with an indulgent smile. Bolstered, she continued.

"Atlantis generally runs itself and requires little guidance from me or Thoth. But we have labored long trying to stabilize Earth. Now our mission is complete, at least for the moment, and we, too, could use a break." She drew a long breath and held up her hand when Khenko would speak.

"You, Khenko, have one of the most brilliant minds we have encountered. You are also a direct descendant of Lord Thoth. As such, we ask that you do us the honor of leading Atlantis for a while so that we may roam Earth freely."

Shocked, Khenko's thoughts went to his center in the Bahamas and his family in Princeton.

"You want me to stay here? *And lead?*"

"For a while, yes," Druantia laughed. "Not indefinitely. We shall give you instructions. And be available for advice any time you need."

He hesitated, daunted by such an enormous responsibility.

"Khenko," Emily said, excited. "This is a fabulous opportunity. Didn't you tell me, more than once, that you had searched for Atlantis your whole life?"

He nodded. "I did."

"Then, what are you waiting for? Say yes!"

Euphoria rushed in then, evaporating the heaviness.

Khenko grinned. "Okay, yes. I'll do it."

AN EYE TO TOMORROW

Nergal strolled through the streets of Agartha, head high. Thanks to Shibboleth's departure and Mot's agreeable nature, Nergal had returned to Agartha as Commander of the Northern Territories.

His reception was a far cry from the day he had slunk into Magda's office, dying. No posters declared him a wanted Drac. And, no longer did he have to hide. He was free to come and go as he pleased, and the Dracs and other beings saluted as he passed.

He walked past the dive where they had joined forces with Inanna and Iskur to escape Shibboleth's wrath. The Cerulean bouncer struck her chest, and Nergal returned the salute. Indeed, it was a far cry from being hunted and near death.

Spying the doctora's sign, he straightened his hip belt. Then, limping inside, Nergal nodded to her assistant and made his way to the back.

"Doctora Magdalena."

"Commander Nergal!" she cried with delight, one claw resting on her emerging baby bump. "Is it time to go home?"

"When you are finished, yes. I am in no hurry."

She beamed and went back to debriding a Pharechi's wound, and Nergal settled in a chair to wait.

Inanna left the meeting feeling vaguely disappointed. It had been less than auspicious. She had imagined something grand like the ceremony Shibboleth had orchestrated for her and Nergal's pardons.

Instead, they had met in a small, sterile office in a human base between Irkalla and Washington, D.C. The only attendees had been Inanna; the Druid leader, Awen, whom everyone called Emily; Katarina Hobbs, head of an organization called the FBI; and Elise

Johnson, representing another human agency known as the AIA, short for Alien Intelligence Agency.

At least none of the representatives had treated her like a monster. Inanna had learned that was how most humans viewed her kind. Shibboleth was right. Assimilating into human society would not be easy.

Still, Inanna was grateful for the opportunity. After a lifetime mainly spent alone, she was eager to prove she could be a valuable asset to the Reptilian Nation.

Thinking back over the events that had landed him in this Kern River paradise, Azi smiled, grateful. An owl hooted, and he squeezed Hannah's hand when another answered in the distance. The two wise birds had called back and forth since dusk, moving occasionally but staying near the river.

The water burbled happily over the rocky bottom as the waning moon wove in and out of high clouds. Azi was pleasantly full from Hannah's tasty meal of fish and green salad. Now, he lay beside her on the riverbank.

His heart swelled, as full as his stomach, as they gazed at the stars and made plans for their future.

Backstage at Infinity Castro's show, Patty sucked in several deep breaths. The make-up man had yet to show. She was near hyperventilating when he finally stumbled in with an offhand excuse about the director. Then he stopped to stare.

"What the hell?" His whine had a distinctive New York accent. "Why is your hair up already? It is in my way."

"Deal with it," Patty snapped, ready to tear him a new asshole. "You're the one who's late."

"Well, aren't we bitchy?"

But Anton went to work, carefully avoiding her coifed hairdo. A few minutes later, he twirled her around to face the mirror.

"See. You are a masterpiece. Now get out there on the stage."

Minutes later, Patty lurked in the wings while Infinity introduced her.

"Today's guest, Patrika Tolbert, is familiar to us all. When the Reptilians chose her to be their human representative, Patrika was dismissed by the FBI and ridiculed by the world. Now, she is here to tell us why we should not be frightened of this technologically advanced race of beings. Ladies and gentlemen, please welcome Patrika Tolbert."

Patty pranced across the stage to a swell of applause mixed with a few rude boos. All she had ever wanted was to be accepted—and to be *somebody*. Now, she was appearing on the most popular talk show in the country, fueling her rise to fame.

Beaming with pride, Patty gazed out at the audience, and gasped when she spied Shalane and Cecil on the front row next to Latoya.

The craft was on the verge of outer space when Shibboleth felt a tickle against his thigh. It became unbearable, and he scratched, then jumped, when a shimmering light appeared in the seat beside him.

The light grew in intensity and began to take on a form. Shibboleth sucked in a shocked breath, and a sense of foreboding washed over him. For a moment, he seriously considered turning the craft around.

"Well, well, you finally did it."

The familiar voice was gleeful and wicked.

"You found a way off that accursed rock. And you brought me with you. How sweet."

The craft lurched into space as Bé Chuille's form solidified.

Shibboleth groaned.

Why did he not discard the witch stone when he had had the chance?

HOME AGAIN

It felt good to be home. The carriage house was exactly as Emily had left it, only the gardens were thick with flowers that had bloomed in the heat. The cursed snow had melted, and to Emily's delight, the blossoms had survived.

She'd lit a small fire in the solarium to knock off the morning chill. Now, she snuggled in the overstuffed armchair with Ralph purring in her lap. They contemplated the flickering flames, content to sit quietly.

Her fluffy white companion had been ecstatic to see Emily. He had thrown himself at her, winding through her legs and meowing like crazy. Then, later, he'd landed a few well-placed swipes to express his displeasure at her long absence. She inspected the scratches on her arms and hand. None were deep and would heal quickly.

Talav had not been so lucky.

Sadness washed over her, and Emily bent to kiss the egg swaddled next to her, then sipped her favorite white tea. The earthy flavor mixed with local honey tickled her taste buds, drawing an involuntary "Mmm."

It was the little things that made home a home. Ralph was one. Her tea with honey was another.

She stretched, and Ralph slid from her lap to pad to the storm door. Cu and Hope lounged on the other side of the Plexiglas, waiting for Emily to muster the oomph to let them in.

"Good morning, Sunshine," Lugh crooned, startling Emily. She had left him sleeping soundly in the four-poster bed.

"Good morning, Luc-Mac." She had adopted the nickname given long ago by his friends. "How'd you sleep?"

"Honestly? Best sleep ever." He shoved tousled bangs from his eyes and kissed the top of Emily's head. Then he sniffed her tea and rolled his eyes.

"Any coffee in the house?"

"You know there is. Want me to make it for you?" She started to rise, but he pushed her back in the chair.

"Nope. I can do it. Want out, boy?"

He opened the door for Ralph, and Hope and Cu rushed in.

Ralph hissed and took a jab at them both. He had forgiven Emily. And Lugh, too, since he had brought her home. But Ralph still nursed a grudge against the Elders.

Joining Lugh in the kitchen, Emily reheated her tea. He snapped a pod in the coffee maker and leaned against the counter as the machine popped and spit a stream of black liquid into the thick mug.

"Any plans for today? Other than resting?"

"No. That's all I have energy for. You heading to Jocko's?"

"Yeah, I have to. I've missed the old girl." He took Emily's tea and set it on the counter to gather her in his arms. "It's amazing how attractive routine can be after a lengthy absence." He gazed down at her with an adoration that took Emily's breath.

The doorbell warbled.

Cu barked and nearly knocked them over in his haste to reach the door. Lugh's eyebrows arched.

"Expecting someone?"

"Uh-uh." Emily hurried to the peephole. "It's Elise and Honey. And Rona," she added with trepidation as Mitchell's mother peeked around the vivacious blond who hosted Emily's mother's spirit.

"I'm gonna grab a quick shower." Lugh hightailed it to the red room, coffee in hand.

Emily opened the door, and Cu sniffed each visitor before sticking his nose in Elise's face.

Elise laughed and ruffled the hound's head. "Yes, Cu. Your bestie is with me."

Lamenting the do-nothing day she had planned, Emily retied the belt of the fuzzy pink robe.

"Ladies, can I get you something to drink?"

"No," Elise said. "Can we sit?"

"Of course." Emily led them to the cheery sun porch. "Are you sure I can't get you anything?"

Honey planted herself in front of the fire. "No thanks, Emily. But, were you serious about that druid school for adults? It was so crowded I didn't get to ask you at the meeting yesterday. But I very much want to learn the druid way. Mitch does, too."

The meeting at Wren's Roost had sapped what little energy Emily had mustered since waking in Atlantis. It was great to be back and see everyone. But she had left the tale-telling to Lugh and the others, only speaking when asked a direct question.

The Awen Order had survived the attacks and the tremors that had shaken Atlanta. A few of their druids were in Emory Hospital with injuries, but all were on the mend.

"I don't know about formal classes. I understand the Order's standard is to train us as children. But I imagine my classes will resume soon, and I would love some company. What do you think, Mom?"

Alexis gasped. "Me?" She glanced at Rona and Elise, then back at Emily. "You want to know what I think?"

"Well, yeah." Emily rubbed her face in her hands. "How do you feel about being in a beginners' class when you could teach Honey yourself? Assuming you plan on staying with her?"

A mischievous grin lit Honey's face.

"Why not?" Alexis said. "I have nothing better to do. Plus, Honey has the hots for Mitchell."

Emily smirked. "I'm still confused about who is what, but isn't Mitch your nephew? If so, you'd better find another vessel."

"Emily!" Rona and Elise scolded.

"Well, you all need to sort this shit out. It's a bit creepy."

Her Da answered. "We have a plan, little wren. Your mother and I want more time together. These two will help us figure that out."

"And, since Elise has chosen to retire rather than be canned," Rona added, "we're talking about going into business together."

"Doing what?"

"A detective agency for humans, ghosts, and intraterrestrials. But that's not why we're here. We have something to tell you. But can we talk to Awen first?"

"Maybe. She's off with William in the Otherworld. Hold on." Emily called silently for her ancestor, then sighed.

"Awen isn't answering. Maybe I can help. What would you like to know?"

"Damn." Alexis groaned, and Honey plopped into a chair.

"When we were on that mountain, Bé Chuille told us that we," she gestured to Rona and Elise, "are sisters. Triplets, actually. She also said that *she* was our mother. Is this true?"

Emily knew it was, but she wanted to make sure.

"Hold on." She closed her eyes and grounded, then searched through Awen's memories, recoiling when she witnessed the birth and abandonment of three baby girls. She came out of the trance with the women watching.

"Well?" Alexis pounced. "Is it true?"

Emily sighed. "Yes. I'm afraid so. Awen watched you being born from afar, then rescued and brought you to Wren's Roost, where she raised you until you were four. Then, she placed you in good druid homes with a warning to the parents to never reveal the adoption."

"I knew it," Rona said.

"So did I." Alexis brushed Honey's hair from her face. "I had memories of Wren's Roost long before I came here as a teen."

"What now?" Elise wondered.

"Now we know." Rona stood to pace, then stopped to face them. "This doesn't change anything. That was long ago and far away. We all survived without the wicked witch. But after being raised as an only child, it's good to know y'all are *both* my sisters."

"I'm still unclear," Emily said. "Is Mitchell my twin? Or my half-brother?"

Honey's face drooped. She looked at Rona, who nodded gently. "It's okay, Alexis. Go ahead. Tell her."

"Half," Alexis murmured. "And this is what we wanted you to know. Mitchell is *my* birth son, and you are *Rona's* daughter."

A hole opened in the pit of Emily's stomach, and a chill wind blew through.

"Wait, what? You are not my mother?"

"No, dear, I'm not. I'm sorry. But the Order needed an Awen, so Rona and I had to switch. God knows we didn't want to, but it's the druid way."

"Is that why you hated me so much?" Emily asked.

"I didn't hate you, hon." Alexis pulled Emily into a firm embrace and held on tight. "Not deep down. But I missed Mitchell. And your Aunt Morgan fed my insecurities, telling me horrible lies about your father. And about you."

Longing, regret, and a deep sense of betrayal tore at Emily's heart. She tried to pull away, but Rona, the one who had let her go, wrapped her arms around them both.

"It's true, Emily. Morgan tormented us relentlessly. But especially Alexis. We were young and did what we were told—what was best for the Order. I hope you can find it in your heart to forgive us."

"Me, too," Emily said, backing from the embrace.

She peered at Alexis in Honey's body. "In the end, you did come through for me." Then, she looked at the others. "All of you. I would have died many times if not for you. So," she paused and took a deep breath, "regardless of the past, I owe you for that."

She sat then, and they did, too.

"As for what is best for the Order, we should revisit what constitutes the druid way. For one, studding a man out to father an appropriate girl-child is barbaric and disgusting. Two, any child born from these trysts should be brought into the fold. Poor Mitchell is permanently scarred because Da never claimed him. How many others out there feel the same?"

"Ham, do you have anything to say on the matter?"

Elise waited a few beats, then said, "I guess not. I'm sorry, Emily. Your Da keeps trotting off to the Otherworld to look for clues about Morgan's whereabouts."

The Hester matriarch had disappeared soon after the catastrophe had been averted. The Order was searching, but not even her husband or kids had heard from Morgan. Or so they said.

Elise huffed and rose to stare out at the garden. Then she wheeled, hands on her hips.

"I'm so angry at Morgan. Did y'all know she is why Brian grew up without a father? She told Cybele that Jake was her brother. Poor thing didn't know it was a lie. She left Jake immediately."

Emily gasped. The others did, too.

"Cybele never said a word. Morgan made her swear not to. But she finally told me earlier this year." Elise scratched her head. "So, add this to the long list of awful things Morgan Foster has done. The Order voted to suspend her privileges until after a hearing. The evidence is mounting, so I doubt she'll get back in. Assuming we can find her."

"I still think we should notify the cops," Emily snorted. "She killed Da, for Godsakes."

Alexis tsked. "We don't know that for sure."

"Well, he thinks so. Plus, she sent Mitchell to the frozen fields. We can't let her get away with this."

"We won't. Olga Phagan is old school," Elise said. "She'll catch Morgan. And make a good Security Chief without the lies and politics. Oh, and by the way, Ham never boinked anyone except

Alexis. That I know of, anyway. In this day and age, it's all very clinical. All he had to do was donate sperm."

"Well, that's a relief." Emily meant it. Thinking of her heritage made her nauseous.

Rona sighed heavily. "Then, I guess that's that. Earth's balance is restored, our mother, the witch, is dead, Ham and the druids are searching for Morgan, and we can return to living relatively sane lives."

Something occurred to Emily, and she leapt from her chair, startling the women.

"Except…" She sucked in several deep breaths, trying to regain her center as the women stared. "That awful witch is my grandmother?"

Lugh poked his head out of the kitchen just then.

"Hi, y'all! Bye, y'all! See you later, Em." Then the pirate-priest was gone. Cu ran to catch him, but Lugh was already out the front door.

"At least she didn't shit you in a field and leave you to die," Honey snorted. "What kind of mother would do that?"

"It's a wonder any of us had a clue about mothering." Rona stood and hugged Emily to her. "But you, my dear, will be a fabulous mother. And the three, well, five of us will be here to help."

A FEW YEARS LATER

After the pomp and circumstance of the dedication ended, a very pregnant Emily emerged from the bathroom at Zoo Atlanta. She waddled to the new Hester Pavilion overlooking the gorilla compound's bachelor pad. Then, spotting Lugh by himself, she looked around frantically, heart in her throat.

"Where's Dru and Talav?"

"With Mitch, Brian, and Ethnui. They wanted to see Uma and Willie D.'s baby."

Relieved, Emily chuckled. "And Druantia just couldn't wait." Their headstrong daughter never stood still for long.

"Exactly." Lugh took her hand. "You ready?"

"Ready for these two to hurry up and drop." Emily wrapped her free hand around her bulging womb and lumbered toward the path with Lugh. "Did the others go with them?"

"Jake and Cybele did. The ladies will stop by Wren's Roost later. They had a lead on a case."

True to their word, Elise, Rona, and Honey had formed a private investigative firm. With the help of Hamilton and Alexis, who had access to the Other and Underworlds, their services were in high demand—especially when it came to ghosts and other beings.

They rounded a bamboo-lined curve, and Talav shrieked.

Dru's head snapped up, and she ran toward them. As she wove through the crowd, the tot's silky blond hair ruffled in the breeze.

Her name was supposed to have been Awen—at least, that was the plan. But she was the spitting image of Druantia, Awen's mother, blue eyes and all. The precocious toddler was always into something and got around too well for one so young. Luckily, Talav kept a close eye on her. The two were inseparable.

"Co' see, co' see," she babbled excitedly, dragging them to the enclosure.

Uma sat cross-legged near the wall, cradling Willie B. III. When she saw Emily, she stood and transferred her baby to her hip, then moved closer, striking her chest with her fist.

"Hail, Awen," Uma grunted inside Emily's head.

Hearing Uma's salute, Dru did the same.

"Hay-awn," she said, hand on heart, and then grinned proudly at everyone.

Flabbergasted, Emily scooped her precious daughter up against her enormous belly.

"That's you, baby."

"No, *you*, mama."

Emily kissed the top of her sun-warmed head. "But it will be you someday."

Dru grinned and reached her arms out for Brian. At seventeen, he towered over Emily and had even surpassed his Uncle Lugh. After graduating recently from druid school in Gloucestershire, he'd accepted a full-time position at AIA Cheltenham where he'd been interning as Ethnui's assistant.

The young Fomorian tweaked Dru's cheek. Working at the AIA had opened new horizons for Ethnui. The haunted angles of her face had disappeared, and she was happier and more self-assured. Once the travel restrictions between worlds had been lifted, she helped institute a relocation program, starting with her people. Most of the Fomori had migrated to an island in the North Sea.

Talav left the low rock wall with an endearing squeak and landed beside Emily. She had hatched a few hours before Dru's birth and had made it her mission to shepherd the precocious child. Now, the earth dragon had grown too large for the city. She would soon make her way to her queendom.

Sadness threaded through Emily as she stroked the dragon's gemmed head. She would miss the silly, clumsy, sometimes cantankerous Talav. But the city was no place for a grown dragon. Still, she was glad Talav refused to leave until she met the two boys, due any day.

"It was a beautiful ceremony." Mitchell came up behind them with Jake and Cybele.

Dru transferred from Brian to her uncle's arms.

"The new pavilion is nice." Cybele mopped her brow and kissed Dru's cheek. "But, sheesh, could it be any hotter?"

"Aw, baby," Jake teased, pulling her close. "It's no worse here than across the pond." He looked out over the compound. "They did a great job with the renovations. The gorillas have a lot more room, and you can barely tell an earthquake ripped it apart."

Zoo Atlanta had incorporated the rift into the design of the gorilla compound with jute and bamboo swings that the adults enjoyed as much as the youngsters.

To help the zoo recover from the quake, the families of the Awen Order had banded together and donated several acres of adjacent land. Then, the Hester Foundation funded most of the rest. Hence, today's dedication of the Hester Pavilion.

"Look," Mitchell pointed. Dru pointed too, bouncing on his hip in delight.

Mama gorillas and juveniles of various ages were leaving the swings and hillside to wander down the incline. Joy filled Emily. The animals never failed to gather when she visited the zoo, and it was always a sight to see.

A sudden, intense cramp nearly took her breath.

Emily crumpled a little and tried to shake it off. But the pain deepened, piercing and twisting like a dull knife carved through her organs. She grabbed Mitchell's arm, and he yelped and almost went to his knees, balancing Dru on the other side.

Then his eyes grew wide, and a lopsided grin split his face.

"The twins are coming! Hey, Lugh! The twins are coming!" He motioned wildly, barely wincing this time when Emily's fingers bit into his arm.

"Waz wong, Unca Mits?" A solitary tear hung on Druantia's cheek. Like her mother, it hurt her to see people in pain.

Then, Cybele scooped her into her arms. "Is it time?"

The spasm passed, and Lugh was there beside Emily. She let go of Mitchell and thanked Cybele. Brian grabbed Ethnui's hand and spun her around.

"It's time, it's time!" They laughed and danced around Emily in a circle, making her grin.

Then, Lugh shouted, "Go find security! Emmy's having the babies!" And her extended family scrambled to find a security guard.

She watched their Keystone Cop antics and remembered how alone she had felt that day in Venice Beach. All Emily had ever wanted was to be loved—and to have a family. Since arriving at Wren's Roost, her tribe had grown exponentially. And now, it was about to get bigger by two.

Agony ripped through her, and she clamped down hard on Lugh's hand. He hopped like a grasshopper and howled in pain.

"Tell 'em to hurry," she squealed through gritted teeth. "And bring a car, or our babies will be born with Willie B."

Then, everything happened at once.

Security arrived.

An ambulance approached with its siren on low.

Talav took wing, bawling, "See you at home."

And, Uncles Jake and Mitch took Druantia, Aunt CeBe, Brian, and Ethnui to meet them at Emory with the rest of the Order.

As the EMTs helped Emily into the ambulance, she waved to the people who had gathered to cheer them on. Then, Lugh climbed into the back of the van, eyes brimming with love.

THE END

EPILOGUE

A GHOST OF A DIFFERENT STORY

Elise shivered so hard she had to flap her hands to release the pent up energy. They had finally made it past the oldest section of Oakland Cemetery, where the collective grief and enmity of its residents was overwhelming. Elise couldn't see them because of her blocking spell, but their silent suffering pierced her heart.

"Come on, Rona. I told y'all I can't stay here long." They had only been in Atlanta a few days, but Elise's Southern accent had resurfaced.

Rona glanced up from the flowers she'd been admiring. A genius, she was great at many things, but sensing energy wasn't one of them. In her defense, the profuse tangle of blooms covering centuries-old graves was captivating. Reds, yellows, and other happy colors spilled over low walls that lined the lanes.

"Sorry. I couldn't help it." Elise's "new" sister wore a bemused grin. "I had forgotten how beautiful it is here." Rona was a Master Gardener and could rattle off the name of every plant in the nearly 50-acre park. If they weren't in a cemetery, Elise might be tempted to ask.

Instead, she peered nervously over Rona's shoulder at a stubborn wraith. It had followed them since they'd walked through the gate, and Elise had thought she had exorcised the damn thing. But there it was, ogling her.

Oddly, his clothing suggested a more recent era than most buried here. She grabbed Rona's hand and dragged her away from the fragrant lavender to catch up with Honey. By the time they reached her in the Druid section, Elise was grateful for the abundance of shade trees.

The heat and humidity were palpable. She fanned the front of her shirt. Of course, summer in Gloucestershire could be just as steamy. But why hadn't they thought to bring water?

"I didn't know there were famous people in here."

Honey had gone ahead at Alexis' urging.

"Besides Margaret Mitchell, I saw Kenny Rodgers and the man Austell was named for." She squinted at a faded marker worn by time and weather.

"Hope said to look for the plot with a white marble Celtic cross." Elise peered down the lane. "It should be planted with flowering quince."

"More like overgrown with it." Alexis swiveled Honey to the right.

A black hip-high wrought iron fence barely contained the woody quince shrubs. Their salmon-red blooms had passed their prime but gave a festive air to the deadly tangle. A pair of pink Georgia marble vaults peeked from beneath the bramble.

A mama Killdeer zoomed past Honey's head, calling to her babies.

"Oh, shit!" the blonde squealed, diving to the pavement. She straightened with a sheepish grin, then dipped again when the fledglings flit past, followed by a tentative sibling.

When they finally stopped laughing at Honey's antics, Elise wiped her brow and eyed the quince thorns. Her arms were bare. So were the others.

"It looks impenetrable."

The three stared at the impassable thicket. The imposing statue rose above it at the back of the plot.

"Now what?" Alexis wondered.

"Hope said the gems were secreted in the false bottom of a decorative urn beneath that cross."

"Shit," Rona moaned. "How are we supposed to get to that? I know from experience that quince thorns are gnarly. I don't fancy being ripped to shreds."

Honey edged away and circled to the plot behind the cross.

"Maybe we could reach it from here. This one doesn't have any thorns."

Elise and Rona joined her to tiptoe around a family of Nelsons whose descendants had kept the grass mown and flowers trimmed.

The ghost watched from atop the Celtic cross, one knee over the other, eerie eyes on Elise. She looked away.

"This feels very wrong," Rona said.

"It does, doesn't it?" Elise agreed, pointedly ignoring the spirit. "But I don't think we can reach it from here either."

"Well, hell," Alexis grumbled. "There has to be a way." She walked Honey along the boundary, peering into the dense thicket. "I can just make out the back of the cross. At least, I think that's what it is."

She squatted, then went down on her knees to poke an arm through the greenery. "I think I feel the base. Or something hard." Backing out, she brushed smut from her clothes and eyed the bramble. "We need lopping shears."

"Let me see." Rona shouldered her aside. Then, carefully peeling the thorny branches apart, she inched inside the thicket on hands and knees.

"Oh, ow, ow-y!" she yelped, then, "ooo, OWW, it *bit* me!"

"Something bit you?" Elise hunched, ready to rescue her "new" sister.

"Yeah. The quince."

"Oh. Do you see the urn?"

"No, but the cross is here. Hold on." Twigs snapped and swear words poured from the bushes, then a loud, "OUCH!"

"What is it?" Elise called. "Are you okay?"

"Yeah. I found the urn. Hang on." More twigs crackled and popped.

A welcome breeze lifted the hair from Elise's neck and rustled the trees. She had learned all the species in druid school but didn't remember most of them.

Honey hissed, "Someone's coming."

They stood still, and the couple passed without noticing them.

"Okay, they're gone. You alright in there, Rona?"

When no answer came, Elise hissed, "Rona?" and was greeted by the sight of her dark crown emerging from the thick greenery.

"I found the urn and the fake bottom, but there's nothing in it. Assuming that was the right urn."

"Was there more than one?"

"Nope. Not that I could feel." She extended arms covered in angry scratches. Drops of blood oozed from the deeper ones.

"Elise, you should try," Alexis urged. "Maybe you can sense something."

"Yeah, no." Elise had forgotten how bossy Alexis was. "I see dead people. Not missing gems."

"Won't you at least try?" She was also persuasive. And Honey was so disarming, it was hard to say no.

Eyeing the welts on Rona's arms, Elise sighed heavily. Then, glaring at Alexis, she crouched to enter the bushes. Rona squeezed her shoulder, grinning like she was having the time of her life.

"It's to your left. I made a path for you."

Smiling back, Elise wrinkled her nose at Alexis and gingerly pulled the tangle apart to stick her shoulders inside. Then, clenching her teeth, she tried to remain stoic as the thorns tore at her arms and cheeks.

"Fuck!" she growled when she could take it no longer. "Why didn't I wear pants and long sleeves?"

"'Cause it's hotter'n Hades, goofy," Honey snickered.

Spying the urn, Elise bit back a snide retort.

The trampled brush where Rona had rested was at the base of the cross. She inched to it and carefully rearranged her body, wincing when the nerves in her hip protested.

"Ow!" Ham bawled, and Elise nearly jumped from her skin.

"You should get this hip fixed now that you're retiring."

"Where the hell have you been? I've been calling and calling."

"In the Otherworld scouting for news about Morgan. What are you doing?" He turned her head to look around. "And in a cemetery, of all places?"

Elise's body shivered.

"Why, Ham, are you afraid of ghosts?"

"You know I am. Are you being spiteful because I ghosted you?"

She could feel his mirth at making a funny and her own unsettled chills. "Don't say that here."

She peered up at the top of the cross. The wraith was still there, watching intently. Hamilton shivered again.

"You can see him, can't you?"

"Yes, and I think he can see me too. I don't like this, Elise. Get me out of here."

"Can't yet. Hold on, wuss." She ran her fingers along the bottom of the urn.

"I don't see or feel anything," she called to Rona. "Where is the opening?"

"On the back of the urn. Against the cross."

Elise scooted closer, and a thorn jammed into her knee, shooting pain up and down her leg. She bit her lip, wiggled the thorn out, and pressed her fist against it to stop the bleeding.

Then, taking a centering breath, she used her other hand to run her fingers around the urn. One edge wobbled. Pushing against it, she felt the bottom spring open.

"Bingo," she muttered.

"What?" It was Rona.

"I found it. And you're right, there's nothing in here."

"Do you sense anything?" That was Alexis.

Doing her best to avoid thorns, Elise hushed Ham's attempt to say something, settled on her good hip, and peered into the opening. Then, closing her eyes, she felt out with her senses.

"Well, I'll be a monkey's auntie."

"What? What is it?" Alexis asked. "Did you find something?"

"Shhh."

In her mind's eye, Elise could see the gems. But when she felt inside, they weren't there. She followed the magical thread as she had taught Cybele, and, surprise, surprise, it led to Morgan. Pushing the hinged door shut, she turned around carefully and crawled out, emerging with her own scratches.

Honey helped her stand.

"What did you find?" Alexis asked through Honey's lips.

"Nothing. Or, no gems, anyway. Morgan took them."

Alexis stroked her host's chin. "That makes sense. The emerald was in Aóme. Or, was. Then, Emily and Mitch found the ruby and sapphire in a pendant and brooch. The diamond must be set in a piece of jewelry, too."

"I bet Morgan has it," Rona said.

"I bet so, too. She had a fit when Mitch pulled that brooch from his pocket and got even madder when he wouldn't give it to her. That's why she sent him to the frozen fields."

A chill ran down Elise's back. She looked around for ghosts. The same one hovered nearby, half-hidden between the limbs of a tree.

"Let's get out of here."

Elsie hopped from the low concrete wall and bolted toward the east gate. When they made it to Memorial Drive, they were huffing and shvitzing.

"I need a drink." Honey nodded to a pub across the street. "Anybody else?"

"Hell, yeah." Maybe it would dispel the ick that clung to Elise. And get rid of the haint.

The light changed, and they crossed to enter the boisterous establishment. While Elise held the door for the others, she searched for the ghost. It had not followed, but hovered at the edge of the Jewish section watching them.

Relieved, Elise hurried after her sisters, smiling when she spied a prominent sign—No Ghosts Allowed.

"Hey, 'Leesy!" Honey leered and hiked her thumb to it, then mimed wiping her brow in relief.

"Phew, indeed!" Elise laughed out loud, surprising herself.

When was the last time she had done that?

Then, Honey snapped her fingers in front of her nose in that annoying way Alexis had had when they were kids.

"Earth to 'Lees—whoa!" Lex jumped backward, hands high in surrender.

Elise had instinctively drawn her sidearm. Lucky for Alexis and Honey, she'd come up empty. Her handgun was locked in a safe at Wren's Roost, where she was staying.

"How about here?" the server asked.

Rona grinned and slid into a booth near the corner, and Elise marveled. The woman had just found out her wealthy husband was screwing an intern and wanted a divorce, but there she sat, literally glowing.

"Bring us three margaritas, frosted glasses, salted rims. We're celebrating." It was a command, not a request. But a very respectful, well-mannered one.

"Works for me," Elise grinned.

Regarding Rona with new appreciation, she slid in beside her and took the menu the server offered. Honey smirked and claimed the bench across from them, bouncing expressive eyebrows up and down.

While the server recited the day's specials, Honey made silly faces, and they struggled not to explode. Then, the girl left to get their drinks, and the three grown-ass women dissolved into snickers and giggles and snorts.

※ ※ ※

The spirit wrung his ethereal hands. The ladies had disappeared inside the bar. After years of investigating, he had no time to waste on another clue leading nowhere. But, he recognized a couple of the women and had a strong feeling they could bring the entire shit show crashing down.

Steeling his nerves, he glided through the open restaurant door. Then, balking at the noise and gaggle of flesh, he kept his focus on the food and frosted beers and threaded through the dining rooms until he located the druids.

Then, taking up a post near the hallway, the ghost settled in to wait.

Finally. No more cliffhangers. But I'm a little sad that the story has ended.

Thank you for taking this wild and fantastical ride with me. I hope you have loved Emily, Lugh, Brian, their friends, allies, and enemies, as much as I have loved writing their story.

The bad news is their quest has ended.

The good news is you will see them again.

As you could probably tell from the epilogue, a spin-off series is in the works. The title is not yet firm, but the stories will take place in the Awen Universe. The main characters will be the bad-ass babes who lend a big assist in *Awen Tide*—Elise, Rona, and Honey (with Ham and Alexis along for the ride).

If that sounds like something you would enjoy, please stick around. I will be starting a serial soon, likely on Ream or Patreon, where you can read the chapters as I write them before they get bound into a book.

I WILL SEE YOU SOON! Olivia/O. J. Barré

OTHER BOOKS BY O.J. BARRÉ

Awen Rising, Book One of the Awen Trilogy
Awen Storm: Book Two of the Awen Trilogy
The Druids of Marduk, Part I: An Awen Prequel
The Druids of Marduk, Part II: UnderEarth
The Druids of Marduk, Part III: AboveEarth (available soon)

REVIEWS

Honest reviews help grab readers' attention when deciding whether to read an author's work. If you enjoyed *Awen Tide*, please take a few minutes to leave a review on the site where you purchased the book. It can be as short or as long as you like—even a star rating without comment helps.

MAILING LIST

Guess what, y'all! I send out newsletters a few times a year, sharing details about the goings-on in the Awen Universe. The emails are infrequent and usually short and sweet, sharing new releases, freebies and special offers, and stuff like that.

Bookseller Terms of Service prohibit me from including the link to my mailing list, but if you would like to stay in touch, I'd love for you to join me via social media (@ojbarreauthor) or my website. And, pssst, you'll get a free book.

ABOUT THE AUTHOR

O. J. Barré resides in beautiful, windswept Cheyenne, Wyoming, U.S., with her writing partner, a twenty-four-pound mixed Maine Coon cat named Rambo. But she grew up in the lushly forested, red-clay hills near Atlanta, Georgia where much of this story takes place.

From birth, O. J. was a force of nature. Barefoot and freckled, headstrong and gifted, she was, and is, sensitive to a fault. Books became her refuge as a young child, allowing O. J. to escape the confines of a turbulent alcoholic home for adventures to untold places and times.

Her daddy's mother was a Willoughby, making O. J. a direct descendant of William the Conqueror. Her Awen series is a love letter to that distant past.